Blue Graffiti

a novel

Calahan Skogman

un

THE UNNAMED PRESS
LOS ANGELES, CA

AN UNNAMED PRESS BOOK

Copyright © 2024 by Calahan Skogman

All rights reserved, including the right to reproduce this book or portions thereof in any form whatsoever. Permissions inquiries may be directed to info@unnamedpress.com

Published in North America by the Unnamed Press.

www.unnamedpress.com

Unnamed Press, and the colophon, are registered trademarks of Unnamed Media LLC.

Hardcover ISBN: 978-1-951213-95-4
EBook ISBN: 978-1-951213-96-1
LCCN: 9781951213954

This book is a work of fiction. Names, characters, places and incidents are wholly fictional or are used fictitiously. Any resemblance to actual events or persons, living or dead, is entirely coincidental.

Cover Design and Typeset by Jaya Nicely

Manufactured in the United States of America

Distributed by Publishers Group West

First Edition

For mom and dad

Blue Graffiti

Part One

1

You see it, or you don't, and from the back of the bar, I see her drinking alone.

Bathed in bar light: dirty blonde hair spun in a loose ponytail, a green Ninja Turtles T-shirt, blue jeans shaped tightly around her legs and brown leather sandals. She turns her glass slowly, like the universe in orbit. Her mind appears to wander, alone in her world. In the buzz of the Budweiser, I admit she could be a mirage. Truth is, I've seen every kind of girl come and go outta Jimmy's Place over the years, but they're never, ever, like her.

I reach for my pack of Marlboros and the stick is almost lit when my buddy Prince goes, "What the hell are you staring at?"

Prince has slicked back black hair, a clean face, and a big toothy smile with teeth that are way too white if you ask me. He owns an assembly line of black shirts doing for a living what he'd call business shit. If you ask for details on that he'll say he's an entrepreneur, but really he's just soaked in cash from his father who passed away when we were in eighth grade.

His old man fell from a giant maple tree in their backyard while Prince held the ladder below. He broke his neck on the ground and died right there on the spot. Sometimes, when he gets real blazed, Prince talks about how he tried to catch his dad as he was falling but didn't get there fast enough. Imagine. He refuses to let himself pass through the world guiltless and clean because of it, but that's Prince.

We've called him Prince ever since he became obsessed with the Purple One as a child in the early 80s. He had deemed him the musical icon of our time, surpassing, he said, even the great Michael Jackson. I wasn't sure about all that, but I didn't care much one way or the other. It's just nice when somebody has a hero.

I can't take my eyes off this girl across the bar.

"Who the hell is that?" I whisper to myself. My other buddy Leon arrives with a couple more pints. I'd asked for Budweiser because it's the most nostalgic beer there is. Leon is on the burlier, gorilla side of our species with a hairy chest and beefy arms— a big football player back in the day. He's also a genius, though perpetually misplaced and misaligned. He does well, heading up the only construction company in Johnston but he hates it most days. In response to my questions regarding his general lack of ambition, he always comes up pretty empty. I still have faith that one day he'll find it in him to go out to college somewhere and learn astrophysics or something profound. He's the only friend we've ever had that could pull that kind of thing off, but in the end, it doesn't matter.

Leon sets the Budweisers down and says, "Who we talkin 'bout?" I nod my head across the room.

"That blonde over there," Prince grunts. Leon takes a look and goes, "Ah. I dunno."

A woman bumps into her gently as she passes by, breaking her reverie. She flashes the stranger a smile, sincere, beautiful, and forgiving.

"It's okay," I see her say. It's okay. The stranger believes her and carries on, then she falls back, deep into her daydream, her careful, steady hands spinning that glass. She's the eye of the storm, the pure burning light of a lamp in the dark and I'm drawn.

"I bet she's drinking Budweiser," I say. And Prince, a tad more interested than before, takes a quick look over but just grunts again and says, "maybe."

Prince is going through a slow burn break up. One of those real bummer in-and-outers where it takes weeks to finally die. Just torture. Shelby didn't love him anymore but lacked the courage to cut the thing off swift and bloody. She was probably scared of being alone, just like all the rest of us, terrified of shoving chips into her mouth, solo on her carpet couch which was so old it rained cotton and almost swallowed you whole when you sat on it. The last time I was in her mossy apartment with the two of them I couldn't stop staring at it, high and anti-social, transfixed by its age, and convinced Prince should never have gotten together with a woman who owned a couch like that in the first place.

If you asked me, Prince was lucky to be rid of her and was getting over it a bit too slowly for my liking. He's annoyingly uninterested in everything at the moment. I forgive him for his apathy, but only because I'm so damn distracted. There's no doubt that I've fallen in deep. I take the biggest drink of beer you could imagine and think, *she is havin a Budweiser*. I just know it.

2

I'm at Prince's watching a Bob Dylan special with my feet crossed on his stolen coffee table. By stolen, I mean one day Prince and I were walking to his place after work and saw the thing on the side of a driveway, abandoned and patiently waiting to be picked up by the garbage man, Joey, this obese, mean grinder with a perpetual dip in. Joey was your classic younger-year playground bully who grew up to be constantly annoyed and furious about the little things. We don't appreciate Joey much because we still remember those elementary years when he scratched his belly button with uncut nails and pointed sausage fingers at our haircuts, laughing. Well, we couldn't let Joey get his grimy paws on such a table, so we picked it up and hauled the thing three miles, all heavy as hell. Now it's in Prince's living room and we probably tell that story too much. We're just so damn proud of our accomplishment.

Prince allegedly bought his couch off some junkie right outside Johnston for cheap. Though I've always known he made that story up, I never once bothered him about it. I haven't seen a junkie outside Johnston in my entire life, but I dug the story enough to go along with it and even nod my head when he tells it to people for the first time. We do that for each other with all our best stories. Prince stares at his portable black home phone on the table, waiting for a call from his long-ago woman, who is far gone and probably off chasing a new love already. I try to help and say, "Put the phone away man and quit starin at it," but he doesn't appreciate the suggestion and says, "what's it to ya?" God, I love that. *What's it to ya?* He stole that line from me.

I shake my head a little.

"Not much," and I consider going back to the television since the conversation ain't captivating a soul, not anywhere, but I can't help myself. "It just ain't doing any good is all I'm sayin." He ignores me. He's depressed and wants to embrace it.

Thick pomade glistens on the top of his head so I say, "Hell of a lot of glue up top today, pal," to which he responds, "Fuck off, Cash," and now at last I'm back to Bob Dylan. I don't know why I'm antagonizing him. Guess I just can't stand the funk.

I love Bob Dylan, but I've never forgotten what Prince said to me once.

"He's faking it."

"What do you mean?"

"This whole schtick. It's a scheme. He's a salesman, can't ya tell? He's just another American hustler with beautiful words."

"Nah you've got that all wrong. He's a genius."

"I heard he sold his soul."

"Where the fuck did you hear that?"

"I heard it. I hear things."

Now, almost every time I hear his music I think about that conversation and how some artists are so desperate to be great that they'd shake hands with the devil. Well, if Dylan had done that, I couldn't tell, and I've always liked to think of myself as someone who could see through the lies.

I used to say to Ma, "Nothing gets passed me and don't you forget it" and Ma, in her blue overalls, cutting an onion, would say, "Hope you're as wise as you think you are." I smile at the memory, but miss her badly.

"Ever think Dylan is just a bit of a con man?" I joke.

"Cash, I've been saying that for years."

"I know you have, man, I know."

We smoke and my mind wanders back to that girl from the other night. God, she really seemed like some sort of magnetic beacon of all things Midwestern. Rugged, patient, and kind. The sort of girl you want to hear from through letters when you miss her and she's away. The kind you can't help but admire as she speaks all the fine, elusive, and mysterious truths that have evaded you for a lifetime. I can't believe I didn't even talk to her. Before I gathered up the courage to cross the bar and say something, she had paid her small debt and left. I let the moment pass and that's as bad as it gets, trust me. I've been around long enough to know that you can't feel something like that and do nothing about it. I don't think she even saw me and on top of it all, she isn't from around here. She's just passing through and trains keep moving. She'll be back on the road, heading to whatever blessed land she came from, never knowing that I've missed her and messed it all up. She'll haunt me forever and that's that. She was wearing a Ninja Turtles shirt and drinking a Budweiser, for fuck's sake.

"Hey Prince—" he doesn't look up from the phone and goes, "What's that?" And as I watch Dylan say something to Joan Baez about sex, cracked out of his mind on some kind of witchcraft upper, I go, "I can't believe I didn't fuckin say anything to her." Prince grunts.

"Yeah man. Love is dead."

3

Post workday, pants speckled with paint, I'm sitting at the table with Prince eating peanuts and Leon comes running into Jimmy's Place. He's sweating like a dying hog, and breathing gusts of wind out everywhere.

He's so worked up I almost laugh. "What the—" but that's all I get out. Leon holds up one giant paw and the other goes to his knee. He stays like this for a minute, catching his breath with his hand up to command silence. So dramatic. Beads of sweat run down his bare head and face. I try again. "Did you sprint here—" but he stops me again as it appears, at last, he is ready.

"Just, shut up for a second. Christ. Yeah, I ran. Just a few blocks from the factory corner, the property there, Matchbox is fucked."

Matchbox is one of those guys who isn't so much a buddy, per se, but more a buddy of a buddy who just so happened to be around sometimes. He's this scrawny little skeleton man who does way too much coke and loves Zeppelin more than most, which is saying a lot because we fucking all love Zeppelin. Matchbox works for Leon's construction company, and Leon has a soft spot for him, though he kind of has that for everybody.

"He was talking all this shit to Deangelo at break, somethin 'bout Lyla or some shit, like he fuckin, yeah, fucked Lyla or some shit, I don't know. Anyway, Deangelo said when the day was done he was gonna fuckin kill him, so Matchbox is, I kid you not, locked in a Porta Potti right on the site. He's locked himself in there, and Deangelo and a few of his crew are just waiting him out man, right outside the thing."

I start laughing now, and Prince chuckles too. I can't help but nearly lose it thinking of this poor bastard Matchbox in a Porta Potti scared shitless as this group of Johnston woodworkers wait furiously outside, ready to, quoting Leon, *kill him*. Of course, Leon didn't find any of this funny.

"What are you laughing about?"

Let it be known that Leon is unbelievably, ridiculously sincere in not only his telling of the story, but in his genuine love for us humans as a whole. He cares, man. He really cares.

"Oh come on, it's fuckin funny—"

"I don't see what's funny about it—"

"Leon, he's trapped in a Porta—"

"Yeah, yeah alright, ha ha ha, he's in a Porta Potti. You think it's all one big circus, huh? Some backward ass harmless entertainment, nothing on the line, whatever. *You* didn't see Deangelo, Cash. He wants to kill the guy, I'm serious, kill—"

"Really? Kill him? Relax."

"Would you stop? Fuckin—we need to head back over there and sort this out—"

"Why do *we* gotta go?"

"You're the only one here that really even knows Deangelo—"

"You work with him!"

"I rarely speak to him."

"Besides, I don't *know* Deangelo. We had the same babysitter in grade school—"

"Don't matter. Let's go." I look at Prince and he shrugs.

"Oh, for fuck's sake—fine."

"Thank you."

Leon heads back out the same way he came. As I stand to follow, I say something to Prince about him not backing me up and generally being lame as fuck lately to which he just shrugs and doesn't pay much mind. As we're heading out, I pop one last peanut into my mouth and feel a bit of adrenaline. The door to the bar opens and without warning, the world spins. There she is, walking in, silhouetted by the late afternoon behind her. She passes and her deep green eyes meet mine, nearly stopping my lonesome heart. There's a constellation of freckles on her cheeks. We have only a second and she's on, determined and moving to the bar. Head turned to her, transfixed, I follow Prince through the door even though everything tells me to stay. I can't believe it.

She's back in Jimmy's Place and I'm coerced to deal-making with Deangelo.

Out in the sun, Leon jogs away and Prince goes, "Hey, wasn't that your girl?"

4

I haven't had a single real conversation with Deangelo in years, but back in the day we managed to have a really solid tune between us. We used to spend afternoons together on this old ranch owned by a couple of ancient creepy folks who were the grandparents of an incredibly regrettable pair of identical twins in our grade named Casey and Dalton. These two were the type that despite their uniquely symmetrical lives, had little interest in doing one another any favors. They never quite got on, and didn't desire to. Their only purpose, as far as I saw it, was to make each other and those around them, as miserable as humanly possible.

The first time I met them, we were in Ms. Walter's kindergarten class together. They were particularly grimy and juiced up that day on what I imagined were three or four bowls of cereal and Pop-Tarts. They were feral beasts. That day, I saw Dalton rip all the sugar packets out of Ms. Walter's coffee drawer and pour them into his mouth as fast as he could manage. His sticky gremlin lips were already lined with some sort of grayish green, vomitous gook and after that, he sat there shaking and hyperventilating for an hour. He had a fucking armful of sugar packets, rocking in the corner of the classroom during nap time and nobody did a thing about it. He kept tearing more and more tiny pink packages at the tops and plummeting the sugar straight to his gullet. It was repugnant, but I couldn't look away. I almost hated him for it. His brother Casey was no Casanova either. That same year I saw him pick Dalton's nose and then place it on the tip of his tongue like a tab of acid and eat it. He had this long monkey grin, spread wide and thin across his face as he giggled low-like and did it proudly. He was a psychopath, and I knew it. They were both twisted forms of mountain children stripped of any intricacies of human behavior. They bit people too.

Deangelo and I had to spend time with this lovely pair and the pair that had raised them every day after school. It was hellish. Five minutes with their grandparents and you'd know Casey and Dalton never stood a chance. Their gramps and grams were skeleton thin, white-haired monsters and their ranch just so happened to be where the bus would drop Deangelo and me off in the country. For three unsteady hours each afternoon we were subjected to their sinister property until one of our moms came through post shift and took us home, some five miles down VV and Woodland.

One day, shortly after arriving, Deangelo and I were ordered to join the grandpa out back in the barn, a towering, decrepit structure that was always shedding red paint as if it were bleeding. Casey and Dalton sniggered behind us as they followed, rolling around in the grass together and yelping like hyenas. Deangelo and I didn't speak a whole lot on that ranch and that day was no different. We were always on the brink of some sort of terror, and what was there to say about that? Unfortunately, there were no midday snacks, no milk and honey.

On that particularly hot sun-setter, this grotesquely aging, some 100-pound grandfather led us to his chicken coop and handed Deangelo a small, rusted hatchet. In the thick Midwestern barn-hay heat, the old crook picked out a poor chicken from behind the wire and stretched its neck over a sanded tree stump. The chicken screeched and moaned hideous, heartbreaking sounds as it flailed all around. It knew what was coming.

Wide-eyed Deangelo held the hatchet, shaking, as the grandpa loomed over him, spitting his tobacco and commanding him to split the thing's neck clean in two. When Deangelo began to tear up from dread and compassion, the old man growled the order over and over again, "Do it, boy, do it. Do it now boy!"

Though the old man would be no threat to us now, so diminutive in his sickly nature, he sure was vicious and threatening back then. Deangelo didn't have a choice. He swung the hatchet through the neck of the chicken and screamed out to God while he did it. The blood erupted, squirting all over his shirt and his face and a bit of my shoe lace.

Later, on the upper deck of the haystacks Deangelo wept as I patted his back and swore to never tell a soul about any of it.

*

Now, I'm smiling at Deangelo next to a tipped over blue Porta Potti that's muffling Matchbox's whimpering.

"He won't come out, huh?"

Deangelo, a medium build with solid shoulders and a tightly carved face, has a toothpick hanging loosely from his large mouth, dark lips. He has a thin mustache and thick black ultra-curled afro type wonderful hair. He's flanked on either side by a couple guys, Jermaine and Sosa, quiet types that I'd never had any quarrels with. Their jaws clench but we nod our greetings in respect. They're both mammoth-sized and pretty mean if pushed, but simple souled. Not evil or anything. Leon and Prince hang back some five feet behind me. I smirk. They're always weirdly confident I can sweet talk our way out of a good old-fashioned scrum, and most times, I can, though I've failed in my efforts plenty. Over the years, we've found ourselves in many battles. Johnston is a bit of a pressure cooker that way, a place where boys and men often struggled with words and preferred to use their fists to settle things. All to say, we're not afraid. It's not our first rodeo. Still, we'd all prefer it doesn't go down that way. We know what it will cost us. It's just that, around here, sometimes there's no other way.

Deangelo grins and takes the tooth pick out of his mouth with his right forefinger and thumb.

He scratches the middle of his forehead with it, wet with sweat and says, "Nah, he won't."

I find myself thinking about the chicken, wondering if Deangelo remembers that afternoon, but somewhere deep in his eyes, trying to hide, I can tell that he does. It's wild how far we've come in all these years. His dark brown eyes are the same, deep and serious and fixed. The whites are streaked bloody with fatigue and the grind. Matchbox whimpers desperately from inside the Porta Potti.

"Cash? Cash is that you? Man, please, you gotta get me out of here. Please man." It's the sorriest sound. I look at Deangelo and say, "You didn't have to tip the thing over on him man."

"Did."

"What do you want with that lump anyway?"

"Don't matter none to me if he's a bitch."

"He's covered with shit in there. *And* piss."

"Don't matter."

"He's probably going blind with the smell and whatever that, uh, chemical is they pour in there, what is it, uh, that fuckin blue shit," and from behind me Leon mutters, "Biocides," and I repeat, "Yeah, biocides—"

"I don't give a fuck."

"This all over a girl?"

"Not just any girl."

"What'd he say?"

"He was running his mouth."

"'Bout Lyla?"

"Mhm."

"Come on, man, what's he got on Lyla?"

"Not a damn thing."

"He ain't fuckin 'round with Lyla—"

"I know he ain't."

"Look, he didn't fuck her, I promise—"

"I ain't said he fucked her—"

"He didn't—"

"I ain't say that."

"Well, what'd he say?"

"He say he fucked her."

"But he didn't—"

"Man *fuck*, that ain't what I'm sayin—"

"Alright, alright—"

"I'm sayin he *said* he did. And, man, you know."

"I know?"

"You know that's enough."

"He really said that?"

"He did."

"Why?"

"I don't fuckin know. Ask him."

I look at the Porta Potti as it rumbles a bit more and say, "Matchbox."

"Cash. You gotta get me outta here Cash. Please." He begs.

"Why'd you say that about Lyla?"

"Cash. I'm dying in here man, please."

"Why'd you say something like that?"

"I dunno, I dunno. I'm sorry. I can't breathe—"

"You're fine." Deangelo cuts him off.

I rub my mouth with my hand, scoffing at the sheer absurdity of the situation. I feel terrible for Matchbox but what did he expect?

"You're not gonna let me get him out of there, are you?" I ask.

"No." He shakes his head. "Sorry Cash. Can't let you do that."

"Well." I look back at the guys. Prince just purses his lips and shrugs his shoulders. Leon's upset but what can we do? We aren't about to fight to the death over this, not when Matchbox brought the whole thing on himself. So, I relent.

"Fine."

"Fine?"

"Fine. Yeah."

"Yeah?"

"I didn't know he was saying all that about Lyla. Matchbox?"

"Yeah? Cash, c'mon, please—"

"I'm sorry, man. You can't go around talking like that, you know better. Just hang tight for a while, yeah? We'll get you out when we can."

"No, no, no—"

"Shut your fuckin mouth," Sosa growls and kicks the thing.

"Alright. What are we talking about, then?" Deangelo asks.

"I don't know. Just don't kill the guy."

"Aight."

"And we'll come back later."

"Not before midnight."

"Okay."

"I mean it, not one minute before."

"Deal."

"Deal."

And I believe him, more or less. I know he finds it all justified. It's brutal, but things like this are sometimes settled this way here in Johnston. We brokered deals for justice when we could. Matchbox has always been prone to running his mouth, and Deangelo just simply wasn't the guy you ran your mouth to, anyone could tell you that. I know some sort of punishment is deserved but I also know Deangelo. If he cried over killing a chicken, he wouldn't kill Matchbox. We stop talking for a second and I feel myself becoming pretty sentimental for a beat.

"How's your mom?" I ask.

"Mom's aight."

"Good. Good man." He takes a fine long look at me and wipes a bit of sweat off his forehead which moves from side to side. He says softly, "She still sorry 'bout yours."

"Yeah, well."

"As am I, man. As am I."

"Appreciate that. Long time ago."

"In a way."

5

Turns out Deangelo had a lot more sentimentality about our younger days than I would have imagined and was true to his word. He let us release Matchbox at midnight and the thing was finished. Still, gruesome stuff. We got there when the moon was high in the sky, and I couldn't help but feel like it was judging us all. Matchbox stumbled out of the Porta Potti like a newborn, soaked straight through with all the biocides and smelling like the most rotten skunk of your life. We got him to his car, and I think he drove to the hospital. He survived and everything, but I hadn't remembered feeling so damn bad for somebody in all my life. The poor bastard probably wanted to die in that thing, all for running his mouth when he shouldn't have.

I knew that I would see Deangelo again after that. Sometimes you just get a feeling that a person ain't done passing through after they pop up again from the past and show face.

I'm sitting on my couch and listening to Tom Waits's album *Bone Machine* while tossing a few Miller Lites back. Truth is, I hate Miller Lite, but Leon loves it and always leaves the extras here at my place after an evening spent hangin around. He's just gone and now I'm left to sipping these beers alone.

On some evenings, Leon's a lunatic and comes over so messed up and high out of his mind that he really begins to forget all the tiny particulars about his own life, insisting that memory is an illusion and that he is always near the brink of a phenomenal new frontier of thought and experience and existence or something. I don't *not* believe him. He's insanely compelling when he wants to be, but sooner or later he'll really be off to the races and start talking about string theory and all of his other research. He always loses me a bit there. It's not so much what he's saying but how he's saying it that really locks me in. His eyes light up, his cheeks get flushed, and the passion basically explodes from inside him. He'll go on for hours sometimes and all I have to do is give him a simple, sincere, no way or man, *really*, and he'll be so blacked out of his mind high and revved up on his own miracle genius that he won't remember hardly any of it the next day. I can't tell you how many times I've said, "Leon you gotta write this shit *down* man," but he never does.

He was over this evening and Tom Waits was playing. Leon started tripping out about murderers and death and other horrors. He went really deep into the psychology behind it all.

"Cash, do you even KNOW about Charles Manson?"

Then he went spinning off into this huge thing about cause-effect weblines and his eyes were bloodshot while unfolding and refolding up the million layers of his own complicated past. "And if that woulda happened, Cash, *Cash*, are you listening?" He always repeated my name like that to make sure I was still following.

"Always pal," I responded.

"Okay, good, good, Cash, Cash, you see, we were that close," and he puts his forefinger and thumb a millimeter apart, "that fuckin close to not being here, you and me."

Leon's dad was an alcoholic who died when we were sophomores in high school. He was a mean motherfucker who used to belt Leon over the kitchen table for no real reason at all other than a rip-roaring jealousy in his heart that drove him to bouts of madness. He was green thinking that Leon's mom loved Leon more than him. He was a fucking crazy loser is what he was. When he finally did pass out drunk at the wheel, and sent his semi-truck tumbling through the median on an off abandoned Wisconsin highway, not one of us cried. Leon still claims he *can't* cry. Not for his father and not for anybody or anything, but I was there the night Leon found out about his dad, and the truth is he cried for hours.

After that, both Prince and Leon had lost their fathers, and I hardly ever spoke to mine. I figured we all became brothers, in part, because of the symmetry of our lives.

Anyway, Leon started talking about his father and the psychological impact the leather belt had on him as a kid, and it was so terribly sad that my eyes almost started to water. I'm not a huge crier or anything but I've known Leon my whole life, ya know? What he was saying about his dad was true in his heart, and to see that it still caused him so much pain was a tough pill to swallow. I also knew that Leon not being able to cry anymore definitely had to do with the fact that his father belted the flesh off him as a five-year-old kid while his mother sobbed hysterically in the corner and watched, helplessly.

But, in true Leon form, just when he really had me on the ropes, he executed the cleanest transition you'd ever witness. All of a sudden, he starts talking about all the different kinds of flora and animals and algae in the Fox, the small river that runs through the outskirts of Johnston. I had no idea how he made the connection, but all of a sudden his smile was giant on his brimming face, just like that. This led him to bringing up the time where he jumped off the Fox Bridge on Carson nude as hell and holding the hand of his now wife Mo, short for Morene, while they both screamed silly like kids in the night. I tell ya, you really have to be on your toes when Leon goes leaping from one thought to the next. God, he could make me laugh. What eccentric joy he had in his heart.

I don't think he stopped talking for the whole three hours he was over, not even for five seconds. That was fine by me. When one of us hit a wave, it was their time, *roll roll roll* we'd say, and sometimes chant. We kept the thing rolling as good as any, all high and alive, on the brink of our own great something.

Well, Leon loves Miller Lites and he brought an entire case over tonight but only finished half. In the end, beer is beer, so I drink them out of respect to Leon and because they won't drink themselves, as my father used to say.

I'm on the last of the bunch, decently tossed and listening to Tom Waits in solitude and doing some of my own thinking. Tomorrow, I have to go do some painting at the Millers's house. The family won't be home, which is always nice. I like painting most when I have the place to myself. Still, I might see what Prince is up to and if he wants to drink some and keep me company. Maybe play a little Springsteen.

God, every five seconds I'm back to thinking about that girl, her green eyes and the mission she seemed to be on. What are the chances she comes into Jimmy's Place yesterday just as I was leaving to help Leon save Matchbox? Two nights in a row. What miserable luck. My knee bounces, electrified by the memory. I lean my head back against the couch, let out a breath, and whisper softly to myself, "Fuck." I know now for sure, I'll never see her again.

Waits is singing about a pistol, a Bible, sleeping pills and falling in love with a sailor's mouth, about a wounded-eyes-type girl and lust. He's such a dark bastard. It ain't all war, Tom. It ain't all war, you gravel stoned cold throated crazed poet.

Fuckin Matchbox and his blue stained skin. He cost me my chance.

6

The Millers had a son named Tommy who was the same age as me. We were the best of friends growing up, always laughing, exploring the woods, getting our hands muddy and our hearts open and imaginative. He was a really sweet kid. Everyone thought so.

When we were in the third grade, Tommy went missing and nobody ever found him.

It was the most fucked up week. Search parties, the entire town on alert, complete chaos. Worst part, by far, was that Tommy was so damn kind. We really could have used him out here in the world.

I like to pretend that Tommy made it out somehow and just never found a way to make it home, being so young and blond and hopeful. I imagine Tommy still out there being beautiful to everything, visiting nursing homes and playing the guitar for the less fortunate and things like that. I imagine him like this otherwise I can't sleep nights. Tommy ran through my nightmares for a decade, and sometimes, still. I'll wake in a burning sweat and his eyes will blink on my ceiling like blue mournful stars above.

The Millers never really got over Tommy being taken and who could blame them? They only lived a mile or so from my place, and I still remember them somber, eyes swollen and faces beet red at our kitchen table the night after it happened. Mr. Miller had his hands crossed gently in front of him and he rubbed away layer after layer of the nail on his right thumb while Mrs. Miller bit her left cheek, wanting to cry but being all out of tears. My father didn't have anything to say, so he sat quiet. Ma was some ten feet away preparing a small basket of bread and butter, vegetables and fruit, trying to say something healing and kind. She put the gifts in the center of the table, and nobody moved. I was eight years old. I didn't know anything about kids being taken away from their families and atrocities like that yet. We all sat in silence for a good long time, and nobody ate the vegetables in the basket.

I would find out later, that was the same night the police pronounced Tommy was dead, or gone, or whatever. More than missing or however they said it. What I remember is, at the time, I still believed with all my heart that I would wake up one day and Tommy would be ringing the doorbell, candy-faced and asking my mom if I could play a round of imaginary something or another with him out in the woods as long as we were home for dinner. But that day never came.

Twenty-one years later, listening to Springsteen with Prince and cracking a cold Budweiser, I'm standing in the Millers's kitchen wondering where to start the paint job.

"You remember Tommy?" I ask. Prince takes a gulp and nods.

"Yeah man. Of course." I look around the place almost hoping they'd have a picture of him hanging somewhere still, but they don't. Suppose that's healthier, though I guess I'm not sure.

The Millers are solid people, but in the years following Tommy's abduction, I would describe them as stifled. It's fucked up, man. People go through unbelievable horror and sometimes I wonder if everyone else really understands that those horrors are real. They aren't fake or imaginary even though sometimes it feels that way when you read about them in the news, or you hear about them from a stranger. They're real lives out there and the stories are real. These tragedies were happening all the time, and a guy needn't look any further than the Millers to know that was true.

I'm painting the whole interior of their kitchen a calm, off-beige color Mrs. Miller picked out a week back when I stopped by with some options. I have a book filled with these choices. It ain't much, but it works. Anyway, she picked out the beige, and so beige it would be.

"You know, I think Tommy might have been the nicest kid in the entire town."

Prince grunts, nods, slicks his hair back and says, "Yeah man." And he looks up at me more thoughtful. His eyebrows raise.

"I had a dream about Tommy like, last month, man."

"Really?"

"Yeah man, it was kind of fucked up."

"Yeah?"

"I was like, driving past this field man, this tall green field of corn. And I pull off to the side where there's this big old opening, ya know? Bunch of it cleared. And I get out of my truck, and I start walking toward it, and sure as shit, there in the middle, standing there looking at me, is Tommy. His hands were all muddy, man and he was wearing this old battered tank top. He was just staring at me."

"No shit?"

"No shit."

That was the funny thing about Prince. He had *that* fuckin dream. You just don't have dreams like that unless something is really entrenched in your thoughts. He had been thinking of Tommy, but he wouldn't admit nothing like that to anyone. He's not the most vulnerable sort, my friend, but that's fine by me. We don't all have to be open wounds. I scratch an itch on the back of my neck—I need a shave—and I say, "Fuckin crazy man."

Prince scoffs, runs his hair back again.

"Yeah man. It is."

Sitting on the Millers's kitchen counter in procrastination I find myself thinking of Tommy and all the terrible things we people went through in Johnston.

7

By the time I finished painting, Prince and I were riding a heavy magnetic buzz. We locked their place up, and I pocketed the key.

"You know, when the Millers get back, I'm going to take them out to dinner or something man."

Prince laughed. That was a thing about me, whenever I drank, I started making plans, big, magnificent plans. They very rarely played out, but how exciting and pure an experience it was to cook them up in the moment. They'd float perfect and definitive from my mouth, all clear and romantic in their drumming up, that was me drunk.

"I mean it."

"I know you do, Cash."

We're in my Saturn and driving slowly, in no rush to be anywhere. Best thing about the buzz is it finally puts Prince in a place where he wants to talk. He hadn't said a damn thing in a week or two about much of anything, so I don't even care that when he finally opens up, it's about Shelby again.

"Cash, I'm telling you, when I'm lying there, I'll be sweating man, sweating in the middle of the night. And I can't ever get it back. I can't sleep. My mind is going loopy, ya know? You ever get into that circular kind of thought, man? Ya know what I mean? It never ends."

It's funny, Prince never got an "A" in his whole educational life, but if the spirit moved him, he could talk philosophy like Aristotle himself. He claims he got his quiet and brooding nature from all that time he spent alone as a kid helping his father haul wood while never saying a word.

We all had silent fathers, and in that ongoing quiet, like many of us whose only real company was ourselves, Prince was imaginative.

"If I could find a way to break the cycle then I'd be fine, but I'm telling you, I'm sweating man, and almost, man, I'm like hyperventilating and going crazy as hell. It's never ending. I'm obsessed. Next thing you know I'm sitting out back on the porch with the mosquitoes, in that bloodsuck, and feeling fine, not giving a fuck cuz it's cool at least and calm and, I don't know man, more peaceful out of the house, out my mind, know what I mean?"

I just nod. Time to let Prince roll it on through. He shakes his head in dissatisfaction.

"Cash, where you wanna go?"

I pause.

"What do you mean? We're going to Jimmy's, yeah?"

I'm still driving and a bit light-headed, non-focused and daydreaming as our quiet town passes by. All the lamps in the windows, all the familiar crooked gutters that line the tops of the small, warm homes. All the flowers in the sidewalks, emerging like fireworks in the pavement.

"I mean, say you left for a while man, say you went off somewhere—you ever think about where you'd wanna go?"

"I don't know. West. Arizona maybe. The desert somewhere. Out by the canyon or something."

"Arizona? Yeah man. The canyon. Yeah. Wow. Fuckin Arizona. You know I know a few cats out there. Pops used to tell me stories about those settlers out there from way back in the day. Like his great gramps. If he ever heard me complain he'd remind me there were people in the world with real issues, ya know? Like those people. They crossed the *frontier*, man, the frontier. They forged forward to the *West* and didn't have shit at all. It's crazy. How can any of us complain about anything that happens today? Those people were starving and going mad and fending off thieves and dust storms and shitting themselves to death. Pops loved those Old West traveling stories, man."

"Yeah."

"Yeah, man. I don't know, I've been thinkin maybe 'bout heading West myself."

"Heading West, huh?"

"Yeah, man. Heading West and figuring it out."

"Yeah."

"I'm serious."

"Didn't say you weren't."

He takes a big breath as if to reset things a bit. I haven't heard him talk this much in a month. He's rubbing at his chin with his thumb and goes "If I see her out tonight man, I'm gonna fuckin kill myself."

"Man—"

"I'm not kiddin, Cash. I can't see her out. I can't. If I see her out with some guy, I'm gonna be prisoned."

"She ain't gonna go anywhere you are."

"Yeah, well, I'm just sayin. What a fuckin nightmare man. What fuckin bullshit it is."

Prince could be such a serious romantic sometimes though, again, he'd never confess to that. His black eyes kind of twitch in the night every time he starts talking in circles around love and his feelings. This whole Shelby thing has really sent him spinning. Sadly, I'm not sure Prince ever gave it all much thought before she went off and made him feel so inadequate in the first place. Her leaving was something of a shock, and now that she'd left, he was philosophizing and agonizing about it constantly. Tell me it ain't ironic how it goes. My friend was feeling like he was all alone again. Like he was a boy or something small. Only weeks ago, he was a hero, smooth with a crown. How fast it can all turn to hell.

Prince, man. He was a real midwestern hot shot, the sculpted sort. Didn't work out or nothing, not ever, but he was just one of those bastards born with the veiny biceps and the washboard gut. The girls always loved him, and I assume that will never change. So fuckin quiet and charming all the time. He'd talk in this hushed tone to make a girl work to hear him. That's another reason why this whole recent circumstance had him so messed up, I think. I couldn't name a single woman in his young life that had dropped him quite like this before, and so casually at that. Shit, it was good, man. It was good for him. I maintain that. It'd all be best for him in the end, he'd see that someday, but God, I don't want the whole thing to send him out West, least not now, so I say, "don't mean you gotta run off though."

"Yeah, I don't know."

Johnston is situated right in the middle of a couple larger cities some forty miles to the east and west, but there's nothing much in between. We're driving through the neighborhoods of Main Street, the only road that cuts straight through the entire town. Johnston has a variety of small eclectic homes scattered across this static avenue. Some are painted white with near flat stacked rooftops only fifteen feet high, and others were built and housed long ago by the *Addams Family* types, gothic and sharp, tall and black and abandoned. I love the differences. I've always felt the polarity lends itself to mystery.

Johnston is nothing like the urbanized neighborhoods you'd catch wind of in papers these days. To think there are jokers still selling the suburbs as these sorts of utopias where all your dreams come true. I just found them boring, a straight and narrow path towards a lifeless, cookie-cutter human future. I prefer Johnston's slanted houses and the honest families inside them who are mostly oblivious to the larger, far less desirable and convoluted picture. Truth is, none of that big city, big money way had anything to do with the lives of the people here. They're universes apart.

I'm going twenty-five miles per hour through the crisp Johnston air, hopeful. Prince and I are making our way towards Jimmy's Place, like we do on many nights, each just desperate enough to be inspired and drunk for adventure, filled with our visions.

8

We drink our beer from our corner table and from here, we can see the whole bar and all its movements. I can't keep my eyes from the entrance. Each time it opens, I keep hope alive for a perfect world, where she comes walking in and I think of something to say. The Budweiser helps my nerves as Prince talks about the idea of buying the bar from Saul, Jimmy's son. Prince first had this idea years ago, but like his newfound dreams of going out west, his breakup seems to be spurring his plans ahead more urgently.

Emphatic, he goes, "Saul don't *love* the place man, not like us, not like us. We're the lifeblood of this bar, let's be straight. We're the caretakers, really. Sure, he runs it and gets his money but he's tired, Cash, don't you think?"

He has a point. It's true Saul is tired and lifeless.

Saul is a bald, big-bellied Italian we grew up with. He can often be a bummer of a man in his thirties going on seventies. Saul's a decent enough guy if you get to know him, but the problem is nobody really gets to know him. He keeps everyone at a grand distance, and though he's a loyal worker, he can be, as Prince suggests, a bit listless, beaten, and exhausted.

"Cash I might just make him a proposal once and for all."

I know Prince is serious, and that he has the money to be so, but this is the first time that his plan doesn't seem so out of reach to me. We're getting older. I take a sip and eye Saul over there, black Bon Jovi shirt tucked in and moving behind the bar. I can see it, the exhaustion. I look back at Prince as he sits smirking. I raise my eyebrows and shrug as we begin to legitimately consider a future that finds Jimmy's Place as ours and I gotta say, it feels kind of sweet.

We keep drinking. There's a few regulars around, but it's Wednesday and midnight. On the floor there's scattered and crushed peanut shells.

"First thing I'd do is get rid of the fuckin peanut pails."

Prince nods. "Yeah, man."

I laugh. I'm starting to feel drunk now. My body is a bit numb and relaxed, and I'm not thinking particularly profoundly about anything but feel inspired nonetheless. It's in this near floating feeling where I do some of my best dreaming. Prince leans his head back against the top of the booth pushing out his Adam's apple and closes his eyes. I stare at that front door, begging for it to open. I imagine all the thousands of people walking in and walking out of this place over the years. This is the heart of our town and there are a million stories to be told. God, I get romantic about this bar.

I remember all the times Ma would send me into this place from the car to get my father as a kid. My old man would be sitting at the bar, curved and broken, with a pint, trading barbs with old Jimmy himself. Pops had a workman's body, sort of caved in but strong from long continuous labor and too much roofing. He came to Jimmy's for a pint or two—or three—or more—every day after work. On some of those days he'd be late for dinner, and that's when Ma would drive me over and make me skip on over the gravel outside and into the establishment, my father's bit of heaven, little hands pushing forward through the rusted metal doors.

I'd make my way in, and take a big breath of second-hand smoke which always got my heart pounding. I'd peek my head around the entrance and spot my father. He was always sitting in the same seat, jacketed and low. I'd sneak on over, real shy like, and press my skinny finger into the low of his back where I could reach. I'd feel the tar on my skin, the smell of it still fresh enough on his coat to make my nose scrunch. That scent of tar and smoke and dirt was something I longed for, it made me feel close to him. His neck was a darkened red tan from the burning sun and growing more wrinkled and leathered by the day. His form was giant and tough and unshakable. I'd hear his low voice rumble over his beer and see a small chuckle shake his jacket. That shape of his spine, bent but not broken like the wood of the bar where he rested his stained black hands, made me wonder. I wondered if he was in pain. I wondered what it was really like out there, working on the roofs of strangers' homes all day. What did it feel like under that harsh and unforgiving sun, working your life away forever? When the day was done, he was here, smoking and drinking his heart and brain to decay, looking for an answer. I just never knew what it was. God, how blindly I loved him back then. My hero. He'd stoically feel my soft nervous touch on his back, and I'd wonder if he was hoping for something or someone other than his six-year-old son. He'd turn around slowly and look at me red-eyed and exhausted and he wouldn't say a thing. He'd just as slowly turn himself back around to Jimmy and say,

"Go on home to your mom, boy."

I didn't know anything about being drunk, but I knew there were different versions of my father and that there were some that loved me a little, and some that didn't seem to love me at all. Embarrassed and defeated, I'd tell Ma that Dad wasn't coming home yet, and I always felt like a failure when I said it.

Those were the worst days and nights. I never really knew when my dad would get back on those late evenings because Ma wouldn't let me stay up and find out. I would cry sometimes and bury my face in my blanket and pray. I'd pray to God that my dad would make it home safely. Somehow, he always did.

I think Prince might be asleep against the booth top. I don't know what comes over me but for the first time in years I entertain a nearly forgotten longing. I almost whisper out to the universe, asking it to deliver my father before me, but I don't. Instead, I watch Saul clean a few pint glasses and find myself wondering if he really would decide to give the whole thing over. He sure did look like his father drying those glasses.

Prince is right. Saul is strung out. Even from across the bar I can notice the purple half-moons under his eyes. I pick up my pint and walk over to him. I take a seat where my father once did.

"Another?" Saul asks.

"Yeah, man." And he gets to pouring.

When he sets the pint back down, I say, "Saul, you know, my dad used to come in here every day."

"Mhm."

"Every fuckin day Saul."

"Like father, like son."

"Come on. I'm not in here that much."

"Pretty damn close."

"No, not like *that* man, my pops would come in here like it was his religion, Saul And your pops was the pastor. And man, here's the thing, I've been thinking. I'm really wondering right about now what in the fuck it was they'd even talk about? Your pops would be standing right there, kinda like you are now, as a matter of fact, towel slung over his shoulder and smoking up a storm, and he'd be listening to my pops go on about whatever the hell it was, and I'm wondering now, if you have any idea what they were talking about?"

"I don't know, Cash. Life."

"Life? Yeah. But what about it?"

"'Bout whatever it was."

"Yeah. But what was it?"

9

The sun wakes me at eleven, and I remember I have to take my Saturn in for a much-needed oil change. With no shave, shower, or anything in my stomach, I'm hungover as hell and step straight into Wisconsin's scolding peak. The air hits me thick. It's the type of suffocating heat where you're sweating immediately, blanketed by humidity. I walk to the car and open the door. I turn the key of my old and loyal silver bullet. A million miles and counting.

My house isn't enormous in the rearview but it's plenty big enough for me. It's my parents' old place, an old wooden make with the furnished stained maple through and through. It's a beautiful brown, sure fire country home. A cabin or lost-artist-in-the-woods type, which suits me just fine. I pull out of the driveway and start heading to town.

Tubbs Road is lined with miles and miles of farmland—crops and live-stock. I know every single home out here, and every family that lives inside them. I drive past a particularly familiar property filled with cows in the pasture and smile. Growing up, I had a buddy named Trevor who lived on that farm. His family had what seemed like thousands of cows back then, all penned up together, some twenty times our size. From time to time, during long days of boredom, Trevor was liable to start poking them with sticks. He wasn't ill meaning or anything, but he'd poke hard enough to get a solid stir out of them. It was relatively harmless I suppose, but something about the whole thing always made me uneasy. I don't care how bored I was, I would never go around poking cows with sticks. Not only did I find the whole impulse sort of odd, I also didn't fully trust the look some of those cows had in their eyes. Trevor never seemed to notice, and if he did, he just didn't give a shit. He would boss them around and get them where he wanted them to go, but the way he'd mess with them and play around I never found wise. They're far more intimidating than you'd think up close, cows, and the way I see it, they're just as liable to have bad days as the rest of us.

Well, all that joking around damn near caught up with him one day when he almost got trampled to death. He revved them all up just a bit too much and they tried to stampede him like you see those bulls do in the streets of Spain. I nearly had a heart attack watching it as he barely escaped, laughing his maniac head off. Later that night, I helped him steal a road sign he'd always wanted and we carried that thing two miles through the dark country back-roads like morons. Trevor was always dragging me into these schemes of his. It took me a while to understand that he had more dangerous and question-able desires than I did, but I cut bait with him eventually. As I drive past the farm today, I laugh at my young stupidity and wonder if I'll be laughing in another twenty years at all the things I'm doing now.

I gotta say, the cows look more and more lifeless these days, almost as if they're catching wind of the agenda, little by little, one blade of grass and one nipple tug at a time. They're probably one irritating stick poke away from revolution. Poor bastards. What a war that'll be when it happens.

I've made it to town and I'm only a mile from Sal's Auto. God, I feel like hell. Signs of life on Main Street: a couple kids sell husked corn out of their truck bed on the corner of Ash Street. Miss Morris, a silver-haired angel and town librarian, walks hand in hand with her grandson back toward the doors of Johnston Public Library. A group of teens ride their bikes and take a turn down Marshall, no doubt heading to Lion's Park where their friends will all gather and invent ways to pass another hot summer afternoon. Sprinklers are scattered about in a few yards, and I find myself jealous of the grass bathed in water. I'm sweating like mad and feeling delusional. My air conditioning is long since broken and the small droplets forming on my forearms are begin-ning to run down my skin like rain on windows.

It's moments like these where I consider swearing off drinking forever. I really should have eaten something. My stomach turns a bit. My head pounds a light drum, and I rub at my eyes. It's insane, but right when I blink awake, I swear to God I see her, appearing like a blazing Johnston desert mirage, walking away down the sidewalk. She's holding a guitar case in her right hand with a duffle bag slung over her left shoulder. A banging crescendo like orchestra under my skull jolts me from my malaise and my hands grab tight to the steering wheel. I flash my eyes through my mirrors and like a lunatic I swerve off and squeal to a stop on the side of the road. The sound doesn't make her turn around though. In the rearview I see her white shirt reflecting the sun and her ponytail swaying between her shoulders, even her shadow on the sidewalk draws something out of me as she journeys out of town.

Before a logical thought appeals to any reason I might have, I rip my car door open in a sudden burst and bound jackrabbit-like out of my vehicle to the sidewalk. I'm fuckin light-headed, and I know I look ridiculous but what does it matter? I'll never be able to live with myself if I miss one more chance. I'm heading toward her and gaining some ground but now I'm seriously pouring sweat. Salt stings my eyes. Head spinning, sick, hungover and driven crazy with irrational impulse and no plan whatsoever, I make my way.

What does one say at a time such as this? Suddenly my state repulses me but I've come this far, and I have to try. I have to. I continue on, one ragged step at a time and as she sways slightly there back and forth, effortlessly and beautifully aligned, I'm mesmerized. My heart in my chest pounds. Everything is electric. She hauls that guitar in the 95-degree humidity as the bright white Wisconsin sun beats down on us both. Now or never, man. These are the moments you remember.

Some thirty yards away I let out a primitive "Hey," and she turns around. She's squinting and I know I must look clownish—neglected and crazed. I push some wet hair off my forehead and try to breathe. My God is the air thick. This is ridiculous. I'm still closing the distance but the world all of a sudden begins to darken around the edges. In a pulsing orb of washed feeling that comes reverberating through my shoulders and spine, my focus blurs and becomes unstable. My breathing is labored and you've gotta be fuckin kidding, I know this feeling. I'm twenty yards out and my consciousness is fading, escaping down the burning sidewalks of Main Street and abandoning me. God, not now. How pathetic. I stop and try to stand my ground, but my knees are growing weak. Oh for fuck's sake.

10

I'm propped up against the orange brick wall of Mario's pizza parlor. The harsh grains of the building dig into my shoulders as I start slowly coming back to life. Mario is wiping a cold wet cloth against my steaming forehead and muttering to himself. My sight is blurry but starting to come around as I make out Mario's trademark black mustache quivering while he quickly speaks Italian to his son, Cole, concerned in the parlor doorway. I don't understand a word they're saying but Cole rushes back inside the restaurant while Mario turns to me and repeats.

"You're alright Cash, you're alright, you're alright."

Finally, my vision begins to settle around me. Dazed and confused, miserably on fire, I put my hands to the ground and try to stand. My legs wobble as I scan the area. Where the hell did she go?

"Cash, easy easy easy now," and Mario is up and putting his hand on my back. His calm spirit helps me a bit. He can tell my adrenaline is all out of whack and says, "Don't panic. You're alright."

I've known Mario for decades. He's been with me for years, looking over and caring about all the bizarre details of my life. When I was fourteen, I worked at this very shop and learned all there was to know about pizza, pasta, and Italy. His bald head, his mustache, and big belly laughs are staples in this town.

"You took one heck of a fall, Cash. Scared me, you really did. I was just cleaning the window here and I saw you, lucky I caught the whole thing. You looked like you saw a ghost, my friend. God, you're drenched, what's going on?"

"It's a long story, man."

"You don't look so good my friend, you should sit down, come on, come inside and sit down."

Cole comes back through the doorway and hands me a big red cup of water.

"Thank you, man."

"You okay?"

"I'm fine, man, thank you."

"Alright." Cole nods, sincere and kind like his father.

"Are you sure, Cash? Come on inside, cool down for a minute. You are very pale." I can hear the worry in his voice. I take a few gulps of the ice water and try to sort through my confusion, "I'm fine, Mario, really. Thank you." I close my eyes and rub the water from my face best I can.

"Did you happen to see a girl?"

"A girl?"

"A girl yeah, a girl, did you—uh—happen to—" God. What am I saying? Why is it so fucking *hot* today? I look back down the long stretch of sidewalk where she had turned and saw me just moments ago. She was right there, less than a block away. I passed out, and she just—left?

"A girl, Mario, there was a girl here too. Tell me you saw her."

I'm pushing my hands through my wet hair, resting them behind my head and catching my breath. It's extremely difficult to not become furious with myself for how deranged I must have just looked.

"I didn't see a girl Cash, no, no. I didn't look around much though. Are you sure you're okay?"

I scan far up and down Main Street as far as my eyes can take me and, well, she's nowhere in sight. What a mess. Maybe she was never there in the first place and I'm losing my mind here at last. This is it then, the start of a long and painful, incomprehensible journey to madness. I want to scream into the earth, but the energy isn't with me. The adrenaline has passed and now I'm nothing but a tired wet scrap. I saw her though, I swear it, and she left me passed out on the sidewalk. My head starts pounding that relentless drum of monotonous ache again. I'm hungover, rattled and still in need of an oil change. The sun bounces off the old asphalt street and the cars continue to pass. On it all goes.

11

Sal's Auto is one of two car repair joints in Johnston. The cement building with enormous maroon garage doors housed many of the town's lifelong mechanics. Most days if you came by, there'd be a group of greased up smoking car junkies cracking beers and running their mouths about their cars, wives, and hardships; spouting their general observations on the all too complex changing world around them. The shop is run by Sal and his two twin boys Lenny and Steve and they're all here today. Sal has wispy black and white hair that runs thin off the top giving way to a wide bald patch on his crown, but the rest of it runs thick as ever down his sides and back giving him a sage-like appearance. With a cigarette in his mouth, he takes off his Sal's Auto baseball cap and scratches at his bare scalp. He's got a long black beard and I think he aims to keep growing it all the way past his plump stomach and down to his feet, which, given his stature, aren't so far away. With oil-stained hands and disappearing finger nails he hikes his belt up and gets to talking to me about all things political.

He's saying something about Reagan but I'm still sweating and growing more uncomfortable by the second, distracted and watching his boys fucking around in the back of the shop with what looks like a rusted old nail gun. Lenny and Steve. A couple of low rolling balloons without much air. They were town bullies growing up, real mean and stunted. Look at them now. They stumble around and mess with one another like toddlers and they're a couple years older than me. All at once I feel a wave of empathy for Sal here, poor guy could never wax political with his sons if he wanted to. From cradle to the grave they'd gape at the world, not intellectual enough to be curious about a single damn thing. Not one clear direction in their helium heads, not one. God, I'm in a foul mood. Watching them threaten to pierce one another with nails gets me real sour about this place all of a sudden, and I start thinking about Prince's longing to travel west, far away from auto shops like these.

"When you last see your old man?" Sal snaps me out of it.

"Forever. You know that."

"Well, I don't know. Just hopin."

Sal curls the outer right edge of his lip and cheek in a wistful, sad sort of expression. Sal and my dad used to make a nice go of it together back in the day, and I can tell Sal still has a lot of love for him. If I had more information, I'd give it, but I don't, so instead I just sit here and shrug and feel even more irritated than before. Any mention of my father will do that to me even on the good days. Right now, he's about the last thing I want to think about. The fact that Sal, or anyone else for that matter, spent any time at all missing him makes the skin on my neck crawl.

"They're still fuckin around, huh?" Sal turns and looks at his pair of playful idiots. He pulls on his beard like he's wringing it out for water. He grunts some sort of disappointed admittance before bringing up a story about a lady who came by earlier in the day wearing the shortest summer shorts you ever saw. I close my eyes and nearly walk out of the shop just to burn on the sidewalk again.

Johnston men, especially the older ones, get one thought of sex and they turn into slobbering animals. Most of them were just lonesome and incapable of expressing the longing in their chests. Instead of being honest about it all, they choose to dress up their vulnerability in busty clothes and chuckle and get gross.

Sometimes they remind me of this dog I saw at a picnic lunch as a kid. My parents had taken me camping, and a group of their friends and their kids were eating with us right near a wide serene lake in the middle of the woods. Someone had brought their big old boxer along. It had a blue collar and a hungry salivating mouth just watching us eat our hotdogs and chips. Its tongue ran wild with thirst as it watched my father drink his beer. In the middle of a mouthful, I remember one of the girls there shrieking and turning away from the dog. My eyes went down to the boxer and I saw his small red erection protruding from his lower half as he just dumb open-mouth gaped at the girl and all of her food. Drooling all over with absolutely no honor.

"Ain't nothing but a red rocket," my father said.

Anyway, some men in Johnston remind me of that boxer from way back at that one ruined summer picnic. I mean, you should see the look in Sal's eye as he tells me about a short-shorted broad who stopped by looking for a spare part.

"Showstopper, I'm tellin ya, the rack on her."

Yeah, yeah, yeah. Her husband was probably out in the field somewhere killing himself hauling feed or tilling while Sal's little red erection was pulsing all over the place telling me the story and making me feel nauseated and a bit fraudulent for not telling him how he should speak about women. None of it matters that much to me right now though because my fuckin head hurts so bad. Sal sits down on the bench next to me.

"Anyway, other than that, nothing new." He lets out one of these elongated sighs of relief, the kind you earn through finished labor. Only a real middle of nowhere workman can sigh quite like that. I take out a Marlboro, "You mind?"

"Course not," and he takes one as well. My father and his friends smoked Marlboros, all my life.

We light the cigarettes and in beautiful silence, finally my soul starts to rest. From time to time, we look out to our world through the open garage-shop door as nobody passes and nothing happens anywhere. Stillness in the summer streets of Johnston. There are a few elm trees in the distance, dancing slowly in the wind and a couple of American Robins flutter around looking for worms, but other than that, things are still. Perfect in serenity. Sal eventually softly breaks the reverie.

"Ain't seen your pops in damn near"—he wrings down his beard again as he thinks deeply—"shit, five? Has it been five years? Shit well, yeah five or so."

And the way he says it, imbued with the heavy heartbreak of an old man, nearly kills me. That kind of thing could really make me weep if I wasn't careful. I never feel more depressed than when a grown old man looks back on his life with such sadness, nostalgic about a time long passed and aware that it all went by too fast, with not enough boom. Sal talks about my father like a lost lover.

"Last time I saw him, he was ridin up with that maroon, busted Ford, remember that piece of shit? Course you do. Boy he came 'round all wound up and red, ha ha ha. He says, 'Sal, I'm in a world-a-hurt, need her fixed by sundown.' Sundown, he says. Ha ha ha. And we did it for him. We sure did."

God, I tell ya, I really can't stand anybody talking about my father with such fondness. The cracks in my heart threaten to break open through the mortar of years gone by. Out of respect for Sal and his own weary tarred soul, I just nod and stay silent. I stare down at my hands and wonder about rage and revenge and if that disease will ever seep from my blood. Sal goes, "Well, if you ever hear from him tell him ole Sal's got a cold one ready."

"Alright, Sal. I will."

12

"What do you mean?" Leon asks.

He smiles, rubs at his chin, and gives me an inquisitive, highly suspicious look.

"I mean exactly what I said. What's the confusion?"

We're sitting on his porch looking over the lush front yard, dark green and shadowed in the evening. Leon and Mo have this beautiful ranch house outside of Johnston about a mile from mine. We find ourselves here often, sitting on the porch and staring up at the stars, feeling all at once infinite and small. It's one of our favorite places to try and figure out life one wandering conversation at a time.

"Just doesn't make a whole lot of sense."

"Well, it happened, just like I said it did."

"Interesting."

"Interesting?"

"What?"

"That's all you got? *Interesting?*"

I'm on my fifth straight cigarette and feeling a little revved. My fingers twitch whenever I attempt any kind of stillness. My legs bounce; my head shakes. A subtle current is spreading from my lower spine and running all the way up my shoulders, curling around the blades, and causing me to have bouts of skittish over-explaining and dramatism in my storytelling. Leon sips lemonade and smirks. He has the audacity to actually sit there and *sip* his lemonade while he *smirks* at me. I take a long drag and put the embers out in the ashtray between us.

"I don't appreciate the fuckin look you're giving me right now."

"What look?"

"You know the look."

The crickets chirp in a high frequency choir, echoing some kind of emphatic agreement. I know they're on my side. They're out there feeling all red-lined and revved themselves, trying desperately to be heard and understood.

"Mo make that?" I ask, nodding to the pitcher on the table.

"Yeah, you want some?" Leon is always so genuine in offering, utterly shameless in being pampered and recklessly adored by his woman. He pours me a glass.

"It's actually really nice."

"Really nice?"

"Yeah."

"Who are you becoming, man?"

"Still Leon, baby."

Honestly, the transformation of your friends who partake in lingering and prolonged relationships can be such a pain in the ass, but Leon and Mo really are one of those rare couples that only make each other better. I honestly don't know if it's possible for two people to be more destined for one another. Mo is a wide-set athletic woman who runs early shifts over at The Pit, the best diner in Johnston. I've always found the name of the place endearing and so does she. Mo says it either has something to do with the never-ending pit of one's hypothetical stomach or it's short for *the pit stop* since it is so highly regarded by the truckers who make their daily dawn breaks from the road there, all tired and desperate for a hot coffee and an egg or two.

Mo works her ass off at The Pit every day. She's a phenomenal cook, one of the ones who really loves it, ya know? She has an artistic sense about it all that I've always appreciated because my Ma used to be that way, a truly beautiful cook, the kind who experiences pure, limitless joy in serving others. For Mo and my mother, food was a togetherness, an act of love and grace. They lit up and felt closer to God when they were cooking and sharing that gift with others. They'd serve their wonderful meals and imbue that communion with a real spiritual significance. I didn't always understand how much that meant to my mother, but I caught on eventually. I was just a little late to the party, I suppose. I've learned many things from Mo.

She's also a waitress, and the best damn before sunrise convo an exhausted and hopeless trucker could ever dream of finding mid-work week, broke and strung out.

Mo and Leon are a large couple and as strong as they come. They have a real presence about them, immense and no doubt capable of battle, but patient, humble and kind. I have no doubt they'll eventually raise a small horde of magnanimous heroes, each more smiling and sensational than the next. The two of them have found what all the lonesome long for—of that I'm certain. On some drunken, musing nights, I think about how Mo loving Leon so much is the universe's way of evening his proverbial odds. Those two sure did deserve all the love in the world.

I'll never forget the night at Jimmy's Place when Leon first told us about Mo, all lit up and alive.

"Alright, so, I'm at the Shell 'bout to fill the Chevy and I'm grabbing the cash and there's this woman pulled over on the side street having an argument with this fuckin guy I had never seen before, but she's really giving it to him, right? They're parked to the side and from what I can tell the guy maybe pulled up and dented the back of this girl's car, and shit, so they were having it out. Anyway this fuckin guy, maybe forty or so, and wearing this torn jacket and shit, dip in, gives her the finger, man, and it's like, I'm talking, it's like to her face, like, *to* her face, inch from her face right, and when he tries to go, this woman grabs him by the back of the shirt, and then he turns and kind of shoves her off, ya know? And then she starts going buck fuckin crazy on this guy man, like crazy crazy, screaming and clawing at this guy and he's trying to defend himself and shit and they're just battling it out man right there in the street, it was fuckin *nuts,* man, insane. And by this time, I had made it over there, so I break up this fuckin crazy street battle or whatever. Man. Things lead to things, the guy gives her *cash* man, cash, and goes on his way, just like that. So, I'm left with this girl. Morene is her name, she says. And I say I'm Leon, ya know, Leon, yeah, and I'm lookin at her and she's shining man! So wet with sweat and shining from the streetlamp but she's smiling now, and she thanks me and I'm smiling too, all goofy as hell and nervous honestly, but you shoulda seen that *smile* man, and she gets in the car and just, drives off. Just like that."

He finished the tale and took the largest gulp of beer you've ever seen in your life. Prince and I sat there completely amazed in silence, admiring our pal and then Leon goes,

"What do you make of *that*?"

And we fuckin lost it laughing. It was the best damn story he'd ever told. God bless your wild heart man.

So, that was how Leon and Mo met and when he ran into her about a week later he asked her out immediately. They hit it straight the whole way, the two big old bears. Before we knew it Mo was hanging around all the time and I'd never seen Leon so happy. We all loved Morene to death from the start. She fit right in and genuinely cared about us in a capacity we weren't really used to. She was always going out of her way to make sure we were happy or healthy or having a good time or well fed. She really is, and has always been, the best of us.

Anyway, Leon and Mo found all the same things funny and all the same things fun. They'd stay up all night talking about astrophysics, I'm not kidding. All I know is that nobody in this whole world deserved that kind of love like Leon did and they were everything for one another, they'd found the good stuff. Fighters and lovers and strange intellectuals, just downright, undeniably perfect for one another. So, when Leon says the lemonade is *really nice*, I smile and shake my head because that's exactly how Mo would have described it, all sensitive and simple and sweet just like that.

Right on cue, Mo steps out through their screen door and says, "sounds like you were hallucinating pal."

I turn and can't help but laugh. She's wearing her classic Mo pajamas, this matching T-shirt and pants decorated with cows and moons. She's also sipping her lemonade and looking at me smug and amused.

"Were you listening to that whole thing?" I ask as I take a drink.

"Well shit you were practically yelling. It wasn't that hard."

"I was not yelling."

"I heard you from the bedroom."

"Alright, fine, maybe I raised my voice. Sue me. She's ruined my fuckin life."

Mo takes a seat on their porch swing next to Leon and he wraps his giant arm around her. She gives him a kiss and they sure do make it last.

"You two serious?"

They laugh.

"Relax."

"I can't relax. I feel like I'm fuckin coked out."

"Well, you've had a million cigarettes, man. What do you expect," Leon says.

"How much sugar is in this lemonade?" I ask.

"There's—enough." Mo smiles. "Anyway, I'm sure you'll see her again, Cash, this mystery girl."

"If I do see her again, I'll have something to say."

"You've seen her?" Moe asks Leon.

"Mhm. Jimmy's the other night."

"And?"

"Yeah. Seems interesting. Definitely haven't seen her around before."

"Leon, if you describe something as *interesting* one more time, I'm gonna lose it, man."

"Why didn't you talk to her?" Moe's eyes sparkle whenever she's interested.

"Long story."

"Aww Cash, were ya nervous?"

"I don't know, fuckin, yeah, maybe. I mean you should see her, Mo. She's a lot more than interesting, I'll tell ya that much."

"He's seen her twice, this girl, already in love." Leon laughs.

"Three times, man. Whatever. Mo, he tell you about Matchbox?"

She nods, solemn. "Stupid."

"Yeah. Well. Yeah, stupid."

The two of them rock slowly in that chair and all at once I see them together in a dream. They're just as they are, but eighty years old and still gloriously in love, the stars shining only for them, so close they could reach out and hold them if they wanted. Mo looks up to heaven and maybe she's dreaming the same sort of dream, "You'll see her again, Cash. I've got a feeling."

13

I'm standing outside the Millers's front door as the sun bakes the back of my neck. I pull on my white T-shirt for some circulation but it insists on sticking to my skin like plastic wrap. I've knocked and am waiting to be let in. I can't make out much through the reflective glass, just a litany of indecipherable shapes. Any second, one of those shadows will be Mrs. Miller and I begin to have the subtle sensation that I'm intruding on something serene.

I step away and admire the auburn brick of the house, squinting up at their second story watchtower window that gives view to the entire countryside. Tommy and I used to play games up there, imagining ourselves kings of the land, keeping watch over our fields, roads and animals, every inch was our endless dominion worth protecting.

"As far as the eye can Cash, as far as the eye can see," he'd whisper, wide-eyed and imagining. Everything was possible then.

I knock again but to no avail. I can't help but search through the glass one more time and sure enough, as soon as I put my face near the door, Mrs. Miller brings the thing back with enough speed to make me jump. Ignoring my embarrassment, she says, "Cash! So good to see you, come in, come in. So sorry, I was in the back bringing things in from the garden."

She's wearing a classic yellow and white sundress and bright orange gardening gloves that cover both her hands, they have leaves stitched into the fabric. On her head rests a large, opalescent straw hat.

"No worries."

She lets me in, continuing, "and John isn't home, unfortunately."

I close the door behind me and the air conditioning settles on my body like cool heaven, the interior of the home is forever spotless, nearly unlived in, perfect in its upkeep. I take my boots off and she says, "Oh don't worry about that."

"Not a problem."

I know she's just being kind. If I left my boots on, she'd be cleaning my tracks up the second I left. As we round the corner my hand drifts to the polished wood of the stairwell railing. My mind wanders to the days of my youth, sprinting up these stairs with my pal.

"Bummer though, I know John would sure have loved to see you. He went off as soon as we got back to go take care of one thing or another. It never ends."

"How was the trip?"

"It was nice, thank you. Sweet of you to ask. It was nice." And she's leading me through the kitchen where all of my work took place. "Cash, I just have to say, you did a wonderful job. Really."

"Yeah?"

"Don't you think so?"

"Yeah, I mean, yeah I like it."

"So do we. It's a completely different room now, isn't it?"

"Yeah, for sure."

"Should have done it years ago."

"I know how that goes."

"Care for a drink? Water? Lemonade? Beer?"

"Uh, well, yeah I guess, um. A beer would be great."

"Beer it is."

Her hands wrap around the dark silver doors to the fridge, and she pulls them open. The light breaks through, illuminating her face as she tilts her head slightly to the side. She bends over and looks around for a second. Little beads of sweat slip down her back between her shoulder blades. They slide down into her yellow dress. Her toes are dirty as one foot moves up the back of her other leg. She balances there for a moment, slowly tracing her calf, and humming to herself softly.

"Looks like all we have is Miller Lite."

"That works just fine."

"Great."

She takes one out and as she hands it over to me, she smiles warmly. "Thank you, Amy." I crack it open. She seems grateful for the company, and perhaps amused by life and the fact that kids become adults. If she were to close her eyes, I'm sure she could picture me young and wild like Tommy, asking for a juice box. Well, that once-little kid has grown up. He's painted her kitchen and when she hands him a beer, he calls her by name. The metallic coolness feels relieving to the touch as I stand, isolated. I am an island, myself, in Amy's newly painted home. As the beer hits my mouth it strikes me that I have never been alone with her before. She's taking some of her vegetables out of a beige woven garden bag and begins to wash them in the sink. The brisk white water runs fluid over her hands as they work, and the dirt is lost forever. There's something mesmerizing in the action.

"So, what keeps you busy these days, Cash?"

"Oh, I don't know. Little of this, little of that—" What a dumb thing to say. What does that even mean?

"John said he caught sight of you over at Jimmy's a week or two ago?"

"Oh yeah? I must have missed him."

"Think he said he just saw you and Leon going in? Maybe."

"Yeah, I mean, makes sense," and the break in conversation is gently accompanied by running water and the sipping of beer. As she washes those vegetables in the windowed sunlight, I'm reminded how undeniably beautiful she is. The light pierces through the glass in front of her face and makes her cheeks red with warmth. I suddenly desire to say stupid, sentimental and brave things to her but instead go for, "And you? John still at the plant?"

"John's still at the plant."

"Oh great."

"He's saying any day now, any day."

"Yeah, I'd imagine it's getting close to that time."

"But you know how it is. It keeps him busy more than anything."

"Right."

"Doesn't much know what else he'd do with all the time."

"Right, of course."

"But things are good. More of the same. No complaints."

"Yeah."

I take another drink. The Miller Lite tastes like nectar and gasoline. It's crisp and cold but sinister in my throat. There's so much to say but I say none of it. I wish I was drunk and courageous, but I'm not even close to either at the moment. The soft running sound of water continues, and I find it difficult not to watch it cascade over her hands. She's always had something of an effortless dance to her movements, one of those women who seemed to be gently carried along by a perfect wind. The gracious gravitational forces that surrounded her decades ago were with her even now, though a slight heaviness of spirit had gathered over the years.

Back when Tommy and I would play as kids, Amy would sit on her back porch swing and stare at the sky. I remember watching her then, always wondering just what it was she was dreaming about. She'd sit there and rock back and forth for an hour, eyes searching the clouds. She was a star of a midwestern Hollywood film, pure and perfect and free. God, she really was something.

In the kitchen today, cleaning vegetables, I convince myself she must be doing well enough, but still, if you look closely, you can see that somewhere deep inside, she's quietly, eternally mourning the loss of something precious. To this day, I doubt she gets a plain waking thought in about anything else without thinking of her son. Tommy's tragedy was to blame for the small red veins in her eyes, which are probably there to stay.

What evil there is in the world. A familiar chill runs my spine with those reverbs of hatred. Wherever he went, that devil that took Tommy all those years ago, I just hope that he died in pain and in horror. I pray he was swallowed by ants while he cried out for help or was spiked on a branch, pecked slowly to death by crows. The visions make me repulsed, and I rub at my jaw just to settle myself. In the end, I just hoped Tommy killed him and ran off to the forest, forever. I hoped he had made a life out there somewhere, and someday we'd find him at last. I finish my beer and scrunch my wet lips. What was there to say? What was there to say about *that*?

"Thank you for the beer, Amy. I think I oughta go."

"Are you sure, honey?"

"Yeah. I got some work across town." I don't, but I'm afraid if I look at her any longer, I'll either weep all over her newly painted kitchen or tell her I love her. "Well give me a second, let me dry off and get the money."

"That's okay."

"Cash, don't be silly."

"No really. It's no problem. I promise. Call it an early Christmas or somethin."

She looks at me, confused for a second, but in one more breath I can tell she understands.

God, the relentless guilt that comes to those who keep playing the game, full well knowing the far better soul got the worse hand. It's so awful I could die.

"I'll see you soon, Amy. Let me know if you need anything else."

"Thank you, Cash."

"Say hi to John for me."

"Of course."

"And I um—well, alright. I'll see you."

Conflicted and lousy, I walk away and feel sick to my stomach.

So many years, and I'm still fucked up about Tommy.

14

Quick story about Ma.

When I was ten years old, I got in a schoolyard brawl with my good buddy Scotty. We had two recesses a day back then, and the whole grade, all sixty or so of us, would flood the abandoned cement parking lot and go nuts for fifteen minutes. The grounds had a faded purple jungle gym which stood on decrepit gray wood chips and there was a pink slide which was painted in all sorts of blue permanent marker and spray paint. I remember going out to that slide every day and admiring the graffiti. All of our lives were displayed in those hieroglyphics; all of our stories. Love birds scribbled their initials into the plastic, bullies misspelled threats, and young Picassos and Pollocks did their best to adorn it in abstract works of young genius.

On the blacktop, there were a few basketball hoops with metal nets, and in the very back of the grounds, there was some trampled yellow grass perfect for games of football, but it was technically part of Mr. Samuel's property. Mr. Samuel was an older African American man that taught sixth grade English. He was a former commander of a battalion in WWII, and at six a.m. every morning, if you wandered out to the high school track, you'd see him running countless miles, all alone.

Back then, I used to tell myself that one day I'd run out and join him. He had some kind of military mile record and the lowest voice you'd ever heard.

"Cash, are *you* proud of this?" he used to ask me, staring into my hopeful soul with harrowed eyes. I'd reach over and take my paper back from his strong hands.

"I can do better sir." A small grin of pride would begin to curl his lips and he'd nod. Hard earned approval. I was a real sucker for it. All this to say, Mr. Samuel was an intimidating man and not too many of us had the sort of courage necessary to try and enjoy our breaks playing football on his lawn.

This day was ordinary other than Scotty deciding to steal my basketball and me deciding to slap him across the face for it like the thief I believed he was. He ran away into Mr. Samuel's yard where we escalated to a wrestling match of sorts, and really lost our minds. Scotty was screaming like crazy, liable to bite and claw his way to victory, but we were all like that back then, young and desperate to make a name for ourselves. He was really causing a ruckus though, and it got worse as I managed to gain the upper hand. I had him pinned to the ground and was about to land a couple of blows, but a loud bang froze me solid. Mr. Samuel, who was somehow home for lunch hour, exploded through his back doors, pissed as hell. His giant black boots stomped the yellow grass and I swear the Earth shook as he approached.

I shot up off of Scotty and tried to scram, but I slipped on the terrible dying lawn. I scrambled back to my feet but before I could flee, Mr. Samuels had me in his grasp. He yanked us both to his side by our collars. His hands were vise grips and I'm not kidding. He dragged us all the way back to the playground and sold us out to the school. We were given detention from our principal Ms. Smith, who was a sharp, black-haired, perpetually unmarried, mean old witch who wore the same pearl necklace every day. She just so happened to hate our very guts.

Scotty and I were goners that day and we knew it. Her beady bird eyes tried to melt our constitutions, slowly and steady attempting to get us to confess to our crimes or blame one another. All afternoon we wasted away in that office, cold sweating and lamenting our fate. We weren't afraid of Ms. Smith, or detention, or anything the school had to offer, we were afraid of what our fathers would say when we got back home. We were liable to get the belt for this one. In the confines of that office, Scotty and I never ratted on one another and became close pals because of it. I don't think we said more than five words that entire day. We just knew what we knew about loyalty, and we knew we were more or less the same. We shared a fate, anyway, and that was enough for us.

Ms. Smith called my mother about what happened and by the time I got home I was already guilty as charged. She sat me down in the living room and I was downcast and furious. She, on the other hand, was calm as the Fox River on a windless Tuesday morning. My father wouldn't be home for a few more hours, but I knew she wanted to sort this out before he arrived. If I was blessed, she might never tell him what I'd done.

Ma was Italian. She had this sharp long nose and the biggest brown eyes you'd ever seen. Long, curly, dark brown hair fell to her shoulders and a bright white, unblemished smile was always one second away from spreading across her face. Thing about Ma was she loved me far more than she loved herself. She loved me more than she loved my dad or anyone else. She loved me more than she loved anything apart from God himself. At ten years young, a fully ignorant kid through and through, I sat there fearing the worst, still oblivious somehow to the infinite love my mother had for me. She sat across the room, arms folded and patient like always.

"Tell me what happened."

Her brown eyes nearly absolved my rugged, unreformed soul immediately. I met her gaze, and we stayed that way until I broke. I knew she had the facts of the story, but I also knew she'd believe me no matter what, even if I played around with the truth. All I had to do was change a few details to make myself seem a bit more hero than villain, but I simply couldn't lie to Ma, never, and she knew that too. So, I let out a big disappointed and frustrated breath and told her the long stupid story about slapping the skin off Scotty and being humiliated in front of all my friends. I told her how Mr. Samuel dragged me through the entire schoolyard and how Ms. Merrill blew her fat red whistle on us and sent us inside to Ms. Smith to rot in purgatory. Ma took in every word, crossed her right leg over her other and folded her hands on that knee. Even then I think I sensed just a tad bit of amusement in her eyes. Not because of what I had done, but in how I confessed it all. Ma always thought I had a real talent for stories. Composed, she let me finish. The ridiculous tale hung in the air and then vanished when she went,

"And how do you feel about this?"

"Bad."

"Badly, okay? What else?"

"Nothin else."

"What else, Cash?"

"Mad."

"Okay."

"Mad as hell."

"Cash."

"Sad."

"Okay."

"Sorry."

"Sorry?"

"Yeah."

"Did you make up with Scotty?"

"I don't know."

"Okay. You're going to have to do that."

"Yeah."

"Have you spoken to God about it?"

"No."

"Why not?"

"I don't know. Forgot."

"I think you should."

"Right now?"

"Whenever you like."

"Before bed, maybe."

"Okay."

And she got herself off the living room couch and closed the gap to my little body. She gave me the warm hug of forgiveness, and it washed over me like a cleansing ocean wave, moved by centuries of love. Her arms were a blanket stitched together by every patient mother, everywhere. One hug comforted my restless, fearful spirit. Everything I ever learned about grace I learned from my mother. She looked me dead in the eyes and said, "Tomorrow, you're going to apologize to Scotty."

"Okay."

"And don't forget to talk to God."

"I won't."

She drew a cross on the middle of my forehead and left me alone in the living room to think about my young, oh-so-complicated life.

And that's just one little story about her.

Ma's gone, though. And I haven't talked to God in a very long time.

15

Leon's construction company is called Sureland. It was founded some fifty years ago by a former mayor of Johnston named Shawn Dunham, an old smoker with a knack for hard policy and hammering down. Dunham owned the company for a good long while and they did okay, considering they were the only real business of that sort in town. Leon's father worked there for decades and brought his son into the fold at an age when child labor laws should have gotten him arrested for it. Eventually Leon's father and Dunham retired and five or so years after that Leon took the whole thing over. He'd been there for over ten years at that point, and I think everyone involved unanimously thought the business was better off in Leon's hands. Begrudgingly, Leon took the job.

"I'll just get it running smooth and be off." He promised, reassuring himself. Well, all these years later, Sureland is stronger than ever, and my friend never went off like he promised me he would. Leon could be inventing rockets or colonizing Mars or something, but he's heading up Sureland and doing a fine job of it.

After our altercation with Deangelo weeks ago, he and Leon got to talking on their lunch breaks pretty regularly. Turns out they weren't as opposed to being good friends as they had previously thought, though I doubted either of them had really ever thought about it all that much. There was plenty of that kind of thing in Johnston. You could go years thinking you knew all there is to know about somebody just by hearing the talk that traveled around the place. I never bought into all that. You didn't know anybody you hadn't said five words to in your whole damn life.

It's a rain-soaked Thursday afternoon. I park my Saturn on the side of Mueller and watch the drops ricochet like little percussion instruments against my windshield. I love the rain. The water runs down the glass in a transient effect, each drop creating its own river and motion only to merge with another, gaining strength and speed in descent. There's a pretty easy metaphor there but I snap myself from that near hypnosis, get out of the car and let the rain run down my face instead.

At the end of the block I see the Garoppolo's Dentistry building, gilded with long trimmings of silver along its white bordered frame. A few ladders lean across its body and scaffolding surrounds an entire side. A gray tent stands in the front yard housing a variety of workers beneath. I'm just stopping by to say what's up to Leon on his break. Wouldn't you know it, but he and Deangelo are sitting together at a crusty wooden picnic table under the overhang of the tarp above. The sight makes me feel downright giddy inside, don't know why. A colliding universe, I suppose. It's a simple, outstanding image, Deangelo and Leon sharing snack time like we were kids again, traversing the great boundaries of the past.

"Well, aren't you two a damn gorgeous sight for sore eyes," I say.

I sit, lighting a cigarette. Deangelo has a Coke popped open and is chomping down on what looks to be a ham sandwich while Leon is crunching on some yellow potato chips. In a clear tiny container, Leon has what looks to be some prepared meat.

"Are those ribs, man?"

Mouth full, Leon nods and goes, "Mo made em."

Of course she did.

I raise my eyebrows and say, "Deangelo." And he nods a greeting in return, "Cash."

I realize I haven't shared a meal with him since the ranch back as kids and I remember the day we stole some turkey out of the fridge when Dalton and Casey's grandpa was too busy wandering around the yard, desperate to destroy something.

Leon says, "Mo wanted me to bring some of these over later."

"What, the ribs?"

"Yeah man."

"Really?"

"Yeah, she wanted me to."

"That's nice of her."

"Yeah."

"She doesn't have to do that so much."

"Yeah, well, that's Mo."

"It's like she's worried about me."

"She is."

"She shouldn't be."

"Like I said. That's Mo."

"Right. Yeah. You probably talk Deangelo's ear off about her huh."

Deangelo shrugs some, mouth full and mind elsewhere. He mumbles "Sometimes."

He's probably thinking about his girl and secretly wanting to mention her in conversations a little more. I assume he isn't experiencing a whole lot of trust with us yet. We all know Deangelo's girlfriend, more or less. I mean, we know she exists and hear stories about her sometimes, but we don't really *know* anything about her. All we hear is that her name is Lyla, and she cuts hair for folks over in Harris Bay, a nearby town about the same size as Johnston.

I've seen her around from time to time, wandering the streets and the shops, stopping for a slice of pizza, sharing a coffee with Deangelo out at The Pit, doing the same things we all do. She's a stunning and altogether hilarious black woman and apparently very successful in her work. Mo gets her hair done by her and always has kind things to say.

"It's hard to even get an appointment!"

Unlike most of us, Lyla isn't from Johnston, and I do wonder how she ever came to saddle up in our town in the first place.

I haven't brought anything to eat other than a bruised apple. I wouldn't have thought anything of it, but Leon goes, "That's all you got?"

I rotate the miserable lonely orb in my fingers and defend myself a bit.

"You got a problem with apples?" Leon completely ignores me, and takes a couple ribs out of his container. He places them on an off-white napkin which is fluttering slightly in the wind beneath his Tupperware, teasing an airborne departure. He slides the rest of the ribs in front of me and says, "Here."

It's funny. I've been friends with Leon my whole life but when he does this kind of thing, I still get surprised and look at him as a child would at Christ. All the graciousness of the world can, every once in a while, manifest itself in the human heart. "I'm not eating your ribs, man, come on—"

"Take 'em."

"Man—"

"Cash, I already ate and there's more where that came from. I won't be able to think straight knowing all you're eating is that purple apple all day. You need to take better care of yourself."

I would have found hearing that a little embarrassing, in any capacity, but being in front of Deangelo makes it worse somehow. It hurts because it's honest, and I have no reasonable response. I've been entrenched in a cycle of far too much drinking and smoking and sleep deprivation, it's true. I lack food and general nourishment, but is it really that bad? I couldn't have Leon and Mo actually worried about me. I feel such a deep pang of remorse that I drop my gaze. The rain pounds on the tent above and I suddenly wish to be baptized in it. I pick my head up and shake it off, now is no time to wallow.

I change the conversation and say, "So you two are real pals now, huh?"

They grunt and look down at their food while I take a great big bite of rib baked in barbeque. The meat goes down easy, and I feel better. I'm going to get it all together, I swear. I'm going to run a straight line at some point. Onward, to health and prosperity! I look up and around at the scaffolding, the once promising structure, reformed. A rebirth through wood and through iron. What an impressive operation my best friend has on his hands. I laugh to myself and think about how we really are bandits in the heart of this deep blue, rainy day, Johnston.

16

Leon, Prince, and I are at Jimmy's Place playing round after round of knockout pool. Knockout is this perfect way of a game in which three players split up the numbered balls evenly amongst themselves and, in rotation, each try to clear the table of the enemy numbers while leaving only their own as survivors. When we were younger, we used to be able to fleece out-of-towners into decent money by beating them at pool. It was never enough to break rich, but plenty enough to take care of some free pints or pitchers. That was years ago, though, and there are fewer out-of-towners than ever around here, and even fewer people from Johnston naive enough to give us a game anymore if there was money on the line. So, we played against each other. We found ourselves in deep bets on some nights and on others, no bets at all apart from pride, but what a thing pride tends to be.

We're in the trenches of our sixth straight game of the evening, drinking beers and getting more locked in by the second. Someone paid to play songs from Zeppelin's *Physical Graffiti* on the juke, and we're pocketed. It's one of my favorite albums of all time, and I gotta tell ya, when I'm playing pool in a dark bar with a Zeppelin album overhead, and the only light is that of the muted lantern hanging above the green felt, existence becomes the game and the game becomes art. These are some of my favorite nights, where everything else in our lives seems to vanish.

I grew up in the bar playing pool with anyone that would give me a chance. My dad taught me the ins and outs, in part, I think, so I could have something to do while I waited for him to finish drinking.

"It's not like life, son. It's more gentle than that."

I'd watch him lean nearly perpendicular to that green table and become so focused and peaceful.

"Come here, Cash, what do you see?"

And he'd line me up right behind the cue ball. He'd adjust my angles ever so slightly and I'd let the stick fly through my eager hands.

"Natural," he said once.

The word filled me with an unshakeable confidence. It was the closest he'd ever come to complimenting me. The look on his face when I beat the grizzled frequenters of Jimmy's was what I'd later describe as pride. I didn't know it then. All I knew was that look made me feel love in my chest, and I became the best damn pool player in town because of it. That warm magic feeling a father can instill in a son simply by smiling at him is powerful. Nowadays, Prince and Leon may not admit it, but if you pressed it and shook 'em to honesty, they'd tell you I'm the best damn pool player in the whole Midwest. The talent never really got me anywhere, but I suppose it got me little moments along the way.

Tonight, we're almost completely to ourselves. There's a wallflower couple in the far back left-hand corner, the husband being the one who pumped the Zeppelin. He pops a peanut in his mouth and her fingers tap the wood next to her glass. I've never seen them before. There's a few bikers trading war stories with a couple truckers, Jerry and Mick, who ship all sorts of dairy products throughout the country.

Those two pals were always in here, gathering the bravery to approach another journey, missing their families and not knowing where the road would end or if it ever would.

"It's long hours, but Cash, it ain't all bad. There's worse, I've seen worse. Much worse. Your pops had it worse," Jerry gruffed one night, putting his hand on my shoulder and drunkenly confessing how much he missed my dad.

It could be worse. People were always saying that around here. Any time out of town bikers found their way into Jimmy's, I always tried to be as natural as possible while keeping an ear geared towards their rumblings. As far as I saw it, all the truckers and bikers of America were winding and weaving across the sprawling continent like heroes in search of what I called *the great something*. I often found myself wondering if any of them had found it, and if so, did they ever report back? Or were they lost out there forever, stolen by promise? Perhaps I'd join up with them someday and go searching for it myself.

I'm lining up a long shot in which I have to graze the cue ball off the rail and send Prince's 9-ball into the right corner pocket to secure victory when "Kashmir" starts playing on the juke and I know everything is indeed right in the world after all. We will return, absolutely, when the dust floats high in June. The stick moves through my hands, and I follow through, just like my father taught me. White ball caresses green felt, 9-ball spins to corner pocket. I sink it. Prince and Leon don't react because they expected it. Prince leans his stick against the table.

"Are we going to fuckin buy this place or what?" he asks.

Leon turns the red chalk over the tip of his stick and he glances up, eyebrows raised. It dawns on me that Leon hadn't been there the other night when Prince and I drunkenly agreed that the whole thing was finally starting to make sense and the timing was right.

Leon goes, "Saul finally selling?"

Prince gets serious for a second and takes a glance over to Saul behind the bar, lost in a pour and out of earshot. "He hasn't said it but look at the guy." And then Prince lays the whole pitch out there for Leon, as he once did for me. He gives all those lines about Saul not enjoying it or loving it anymore. "Hell, I need a change too, ya know? Don't you two feel it?"

"I feel it." Leon says.

"We've got the money, yeah? If you and Mo aren't sure Leon, look, I can front it and we'll still split it even. You'll get me back when you can. Cash is in, tell him man."

"I'm in, yeah."

It's so entertaining watching Leon as he listens to Prince. His eyes squint a bit and the lines on his forehead coalesce into such focused thought. Every word that comes out of Prince's mouth is so *important* to Leon. I laugh to myself as Prince rants. I take a nice large gulp of Budweiser and wonder who these two would be to one another in the whole jungle of friendship if I was out of the picture. They're such a magnificent contrast. I let out a refreshed breath and feel damn near transcendent. The drunkenness clicks and I realize that I'm sensationally happy to be alive. I'm so thankful for my friends and how hilarious they are together, the beautiful odd sort of partnership they have. Prince starts laughing as Leon crosses his arms in contemplation.

"Don't just stand there man, speak!"

Leon smirks and shakes his head.

"You haven't stopped talking for one fucking second pal and ya know it."

They loved one another to no end. If I wasn't around, they'd be as straight dedicated pals as can be. They'd sure have an interesting time of it, anyway.

Leon often stares at Prince exactly how he's staring at him now, almost as if he were some kind of ethereal being. He's always claimed to have very little understanding of Prince's fine clockwork, all the knobs and levers inside his head, and so when he listens to him speak, it's with a pure, childlike fascination and willingness to learn. They've been friends for twenty years and Leon still insists there is more to understand. I remind him that he knows all there is to possibly know about Prince. He knows his soul and everything else about him, but Leon insists there's always more, and I have to admit I do find that to be a pretty inspiring way to view things.

Prince continues, "Right man? *Right?* I can see you see it man. It's time. It is. What do you think?"

Leon stands there and nods. He's listened to Prince's ideas with about as much attention as one human could ever offer another. I'm getting more drunk and need a smoke. Leon goes, "Man that's fucking great."

"It *is* fucking great, right?" Prince says.

"Fucking great."

Leon shakes his head in amazement and then gets back to racking the balls as I laugh out loud. That's all they said to each other after all of that. After a five minute eclectically crazed burst of passion and promise. An entire mono-logue was given. *Fucking great.* God it makes me laugh. They hit it right on the head. Nothing else really needed to be said, but how were they always so sure? Those two didn't need to explore the possibility that some extra banter and details were possible. My boys are straight to the point when it matters most. When they're sure, they're sure.

Leon continues racking and I say to Prince, "We should draw it up, ya know, plans wise and propose it to good Saul next week, yeah?"

Prince nods his head to the music, wheels turning, "Okay. Shit. Yeah, okay. Let's do it."

And it was really that simple. We're all high up and buzzed, but I can feel in my soul that it's real. We're gonna make a run at it. I smile wildly off the kick of potential. What a feeling, staring down the barrel and finding the frontier of some higher calling. The road is revealed, and we are confident and sure footed, forward leaning. My God.

Leon finishes racking and goes, "Hit 'em Cash."

I twirl the stick in my hands. I know that I'm going to break the fucking paint off the balls.

Ma used to take me to the theater, and if you've ever been to a play you'll know what it's like in that first moment. All the theater goes dark for a mag-netic second or two. Then, all of a sudden, the lights go up. An actor is on the stage, and you catch them in that suspended, eternal moment of time. They're right in the heart of it. This single, most important second of their lives when the real story begins. In the theater, it is always an extraordinary moment. You catch the characters in the calm of the storm, and you know that everything from that moment on is going to be essential and riveting because that's the slice of life that all those plays are about.

The polished wood of my pool stick reflects the lamp light above, Zeppe-lin is in crescendo, and I'm in the pocket with my best friends in the world. I let the stick fly, and it cracks like lightning. It's a familiar, nostalgic sound I've heard a thousand times, except this time, it's different. Everything's different because this time, well, it's the start of the show. The front door swings open and there she is, walking in. I don't even watch the balls as they break. It's the first magic moment on stage.

She's wearing tight blue jeans again and a baggy beige shirt that's a bit dirty. It has the word *hero* scribbled across it in faded white lettering. She has a few bands on her wrists, bracelets of leather and metal alike, and her hair is in that ever-sleek ponytail. She walks right past us, rerouting around Prince as he makes an *oh shit* sort of raised eyebrow face at me. She goes straight to the bar without so much as a glance my way. Captivated, I watch her make the entire slow-motion trek, her hips in slight swivel and her shoulders free. She puts her elbows on the bar, curls her hands together and waits. Everything other than her image fades into the background. She's outlined in soft bar light, head to the side, looking around, I believe, for Saul, but he's nowhere in sight.

I turn to the guys and hand my pool stick to Leon. I don't stop to explain. I down the rest of my beer and set the glass on the wooden rim of the table. I move before my mind has a say. These are the moments. There's no way in hell I let another one slip by. I'm carried on the wave of a slight drunken courage. The bravery of Budweiser and my belief in destiny. I clear my throat and run my hands through my disheveled hair. I approach on the right and I join her, standing at the bar, and though there are a million options afforded to me through language I say, "Hey."

The word comes out and hangs in the air for what feels like an eternity. So long, in fact, that I begin to question if I'd actually said it out loud. Her right thumb taps steady on the back of her other hand and at last, she turns slowly, and I mean *slowly*. Her eyes meet mine for the first time. The depth of green is striking. There's a calm knowing about her eyes. They're alluring, mysterious, and they're framed by those freckles I had only seen from afar. I realize now their divine arrangement. Hidden in their pattern is likely the truth about God and everything else. She stares at me like that for the longest second of my life before a small smile finally spreads softly across her lips.

"Glad to see you're alive."

So, it was true after all—my conclusions from that embarrassing moment in the baking sun, hungover and sick on the sidewalk. She had been there, and she'd left. It wasn't some figment of my distorted vision and longing.

"You recognize me?"

"Uh-huh."

"How?"

"How?"

"Yeah, how?"

"I've seen you before."

"Here?"

"Why? Are you in here much?"

"Sometimes."

"Hmmm. No, I don't think it's from here."

"Well, I've seen you in here."

"Is that right?"

"That's right. Twice."

"Are you following me?"

"You left me on the sidewalk?"

"Ah. The sidewalk. Yes. That's it."

"You left me on the sidewalk."

"Did I?"

"You did, yeah."

"I did not leave you on the sidewalk," and she says it with such a definitive air that I almost believe her. Obviously, she *had* left me there, for reasons unknown, but still, she denied the claim with such boldness that I have half the mind to relent and let the whole matter rest. There's an air of amusement in her defiance. Perhaps she thinks I don't notice those kinds of things, but I do. I also notice when she looks down at her hands the small golden hoop earring swaying from her ear. She has a few piercings there. The hoop, a plain subtle bar, and a tiny cross near the top, all gold. Her painfully perfect face is sculpted with precision, her jaw defined and running center to her chin, symmetrically aligned and shadowed beneath her fine lips, the bottom just a little fuller than the one above it. She scrunches her nose, the soft tip moving ever so slightly off the slope.

"Oh, you didn't?"

"I made sure you were okay."

"Ah. Thanks for that."

"I did. Mario rushed out to you right away."

"You know Mario?"

"I do."

"How?"

"Does it matter?"

"Yeah, actually—"

"Why are you passing out on sidewalks is the real question."

"It's not something I do often."

"Coulda fooled me."

"I wish you hadn't seen that."

"I'm glad I did. Don't worry, you looked good, like you'd practiced."

"No kidding? I appreciate that. Pretty bold leaving me there though. I coulda been dead."

"You're kind of dramatic, huh?"

"No, not really."

"Look, you fell and that was, I admit, a little scary, but Mario came rushing out right away and had you and I was there ya know, for a second, I saw you come back to and all. You just passed out. You were in and out man, it's not like you were on death's door. I was in a rush."

"In a rush."

"Yeah."

A thousand questions battle for a turn on my tongue, but I find her whole demeanor disarming. Not only am I completely thrown by her beauty, but she's extraordinarily certain when she speaks. She has the unique ability to make everything she says sound like the truth. In her conviction, I can tell she's seen many fights, and I wouldn't be surprised to learn she'd won every one of them. She's right. The real question is why the hell am I passing out cold on sidewalks. It's not her fault I didn't wake up with her holding my hand.

She wipes a few loose strands of hair out from her eyes and says, "Anything else?"

And no question seems to matter more than "What's your name?"

"What's my name?"

"Yeah, what is it?"

"What's it to you?"

"I'd like to know."

"What's yours?"

"I'm Cash."

"Cash."

"That's right."

"I'm Rose."

"Rose."

"That's right—"

"Rose." And I'm impossibly on fire, totally entranced. She looks around at the bar one more time and says, "Where the hell is Saul?"

"You know Saul?"

"Yeah, I know Saul."

"How the hell do you know Saul?"

"Long story. Hey, can you do me a favor?"

"Sure."

"If you see him tonight, would you tell him I stopped by? I don't have time to wait around forever."

"You have somewhere to be?"

"You're a questions man, huh, Cash?"

"Not really."

"Just tell him I was here if you see him, please."

She gives one more glance around, taps her fingers on the bar and whispers to herself a tired, "Okay." She looks at me one last time and says, "Cash."

"Rose."

She heads back the same way she came.

17

Prince is across from me picking apart shells and tossing the peanuts in his mouth like a mindless machine while Leon itches the top of his bare head in tempered interest.

"How could she know Saul?" I mutter.

Leon lets out a breath. "I dunno."

"And Mario? By name? The way she said it too. Like she knows him."

"Right," Prince nods, squinting.

"You two don't find it weird?"

"It's weird man, yeah. It's a little weird," Leon admits.

"A little weird, he says. A little weird. It doesn't make any sense at all."

The guys aren't remotely consumed by this and float some half-assed ideas about her moving here or having to work here for some reason, but none of it seems likely to me. There aren't a whole lot of folks moving to Johnston these days, and when they did, it wasn't exactly shrouded in mystery. Something just didn't add up.

"In a rush. She was in a rush."

Shit, man. I take a drink. Rose. She's seeped into my mind with such ease it's alarming.

It's been a long night of drinking, and I know I'll find zero sleep.

"Well."

Leon finishes his beer and Prince taps the table a few times with his hands and says, "'Bout that time I suppose."

The guys are tired and losing their buzz. Prince stands up and Leon follows.

"You coming?" Prince asks.

I shake my head, "nah."

"My boy's got it bad," he laughs. Leon reaches over his big, calloused hand and places it on my shoulder. "All will be well. I think it's exciting." I shrug. He pats me a few times, "Goodnight pal."

"See you guys."

Prince salutes and they're off. They know that I'll shut the place down. Prince is going up to Ironhead for a couple days to hike around and find something gorgeous to be revitalized with this weekend, and Leon just wants to go home and make love to Mo before she heads in for her early morning shift. The door closes behind them and I'm left at Jimmy's, drunk and alone.

I'm picking at the black paint on the edge of the table when it hits me that I haven't even looked up to check on Saul in an hour. I do and I remember that I'm never truly alone in this bar. I'm just the last one standing other than good Saul there, who is leaning back against the register, depressed and lost in some dark musing, shooting lifeless looks at empty pint glasses. I get to my feet and walk over to him. Without much of a glance he goes, "Another one, Cash?"

"Yeah, man."

I sit down. He holds the glass steady as the light golden liquid falls from the tap and rises to the brim. He slides it my way only to return to his curved tired lean, scraping some dirt out from underneath a fingernail. I imagine I'll get to the goods in a second, but I take a drink first and say, "Why do you do it, man?"

He crinkles his forehead and mumbles, "huh?"

"I'm just wondering why you do it, hang around here all your life, bumming around kinda bored and all."

"Fuck off, Cash."

"No man, I'm serious."

"I don't know what you're talking about. I dig it here fine."

"Nah man, you don't."

"How the hell would you know?"

"I know you, pal. I know you."

"Where's this coming from?"

"All I'm saying is I'm sitting over there most nights, and I keep eyes your way from time to time, and you look downright miserable is all."

"I'm doin just fine."

"Saul pal, I've known ya all my life."

"Maybe ya ain't so perceptive as ya think Cash."

"Yeah, maybe not."

And I knew that was the end of that road. There were only a few big talkers in Johnston, and Saul certainly wasn't one of them. It's a shame because when I'm drinking the words tend to roll out smoothly, and it's easy for me to ramble on about life. Saul is looking down at his washrag and I know the man probably hasn't had one long deep personal conversation in some twenty years.

"Saul, there was a girl that stopped by for a second here earlier."

"A girl?"

"Yeah man, some girl lookin for you while you were out back or wherever the hell you were."

"She have a name?"

"Yeah. Rose."

"Ah."

"Yeah man—"

"Thanks."

And I'm looking at him focused, thinking there's no way in hell a person could possibly let the conversation fall simple and flat like that when there was so much land left to explore. After a few more beats I see that's exactly what Saul intends to do. Poor bastard. Poor communicatively stunted bastard. All our lives.

"Saul. Who is she?"

"Rose?"

"Yeah man, Rose."

"Uhhh, I don't know."

"Bullshit man, c'mon, who the hell is she?"

"Why you so curious?"

"Pal, she came in here on a mission and was standing right next to me and told me to tell ya she was looking for you. And she left it all straight mysterious there like that. And I've never seen this girl before in my whole life, not before these past couple weeks. And now she's everywhere. Everywhere. And she knows *you*. But I know everyone you know. So, how's this possible?"

"I don't know."

"Look man, I told ya she was lookin for ya and I think I deserve to know at least who the hell she is."

"Yeah, well."

"Well?"

"Well. She's my sister."

"Your sister?"

"Yeah."

"What the fuck are you talking about?"

"My sister."

"You think that's funny?"

"No."

"You don't tell one joke your whole life and now she's your sister."

"I'm not joking."

"You don't have no fuckin sister Saul."

"Yeah, I do."

"Stop fuckin with me man, for real. Really, I gotta know, who is she?"

"Fuckin told ya Cash, she's my sister."

"That's not possible."

"Pops had her with a woman some years way back and she was raised out over wherever the hell, Ryland area roundabouts."

"What?"

"Yeah. I know."

"You're serious."

"Yeah."

"Your sister."

"Yeah. Never knew her. She's movin back this way and don't even ask me why 'cause I tell ya I really don't know."

But I did. I knew. I knew the second I saw her, and I felt it again when she walked in tonight. It was the first moment of a magnificent play. The start of the best part of the story. I nod to myself slowly, take a big old drink, and decide to give Saul the rest of the night off from any conversation. I could ask more questions later, and I would. But I know it in my soul. I know it. Everything has changed. I can't tell ya how, but it's different now, all this. I'm becoming lost in my dreams, the golden dark shades of beer in the glass are shifting. The light shines in and out like a kaleidoscope of hazel and brown as the bubbles move up to the surface. It's all one gorgeous dance, isn't it? I think of Saul's sister. Rose. I think of the beginning of theater shows, and how they're always just burning with hope.

18

The Fox River runs a few good miles north of Johnson. It's a dark, dirty, thin river that scares off plenty of visitors. On some summer days of my youth, I'd wander up and down the river for hours, checking out the boat ramps and seeing what sort of people were going to come and navigate the water. Mostly it attracted fishermen, and there were plenty that I recognized. Some I'd known for years through my parents, and they'd tip their hats to me as I journeyed. Sometimes, I was liable to run up and catch them before they set off for the day and ask them if I could join. They always found that pretty amusing.

"Alright kid, hop in, what the hell."

They thought I was a little crazy I'm sure, but I didn't mind. I was desperate to be on the water.

I once flagged down a tiny cargo boat that was moving a tractor on the river. There were only a couple guys, and from the bank, I yelled out asking if they could use any help. They definitely thought I was a maniac, but around here, nobody would say no to a helping hand. There was always plenty of work to go around. They steered the boat near the dock, and I hopped right on. I didn't end up doing all that much besides making sure nothing fell off the side while pretending to be a lookout. I tried to be useful, making sure there were no leaks or anything like that. The men running the thing were a bit crusty and cold but still rather pleased in the sun and muddy water. I asked how many times they had done something like this, and they scoffed to themselves.

"Thousands."

While we slowly drifted, I thought about what kind of life that would be, just another river, every day, every night, forever.

The thing is, I loved the river more than the next rat and for a while there, I was obsessed. I would do these long grueling hikes along the shoreline which was completely overtaken by elm and the like. I crawled up and around those massive roots and sometimes climbed out and over the water along the branches of sideways, bent trees growing at odd angles. I loved the ones that had fallen over through storms or were lightning struck. They'd hang out long over the river, suspended atop the moving water, unwilling to give it all up. Those trees didn't mind that they were different or shattered. They still had their roots, and a better view as far as I could tell. From those banks I would hear coyotes and other beasts. I felt right at home, a young Tarzan in the midst of adventure, looking out for deer, rabbits and squirrels.

A few miles along the shore there's a westward bend where a coal plant stands fat and tall. When it was first erected, I'd make the journey out there just to stand and look up at the industrial beast spewing its black smoke. The massive metal structure looked angry and loomed in contrast with the setting-sun sky but I admit I found it darkly beautiful. I loved it in a much different way than I loved nature. All these buildings came from the imagination. The insides of our minds were on display but why'd they have to be sputtering black ash everywhere? There was something insidious about it. I would just gaze at it for hours and when the sun finally set, I'd walk through the dusk and graying sky back home, ruminating all the way about coal plants with feet calloused for good. My legs were accustomed to the long journeys with no particular destination at all. I hadn't ever in my life figured out the destination of things. Not once have I ever known where I was going.

Today, I'm sitting in one of the secluded sections of the river on one of those broken, halfway uprooted maple trees that hangs off the bank some ten feet above the water. The city started an initiative a few years back to clean the Fox up, but they never did shut down that fucking plant at the westward bend. I've grown far less romantic about its design over the years, trust me, but that plant and its infection aren't going anywhere unfortunately. It will play out like this, today and the next and the next, all of us bending the knee to industry. God, I feel sick at the thought. Regardless, the water is cleaner these days. The river has become a little more popular now, though the boats and the houses on the banks are few and far between. There's still plenty of sanctuary to be found down here on the banks.

Today, clouds hang above me, the white gray kind strong enough to dim the sunlight, but not carrying the necessary amount of water for rain. A subtle shadow covers everything, giving the afternoon that old gloomy romantic feeling. The maple beneath me holds me up sturdy. I can still see my reflection as it conveys some hazy, nostalgic memory. I'm free to dream about anything.

Could Prince and I really make it all the way to Arizona? Imagine roaming across the nation and starting up fresh like a seed, reinventing yourself in anonymity and freedom. In Arizona, I could be anything. I could be a crazy cowboy out on some abandoned ranch or a slick, freewheeling western cat son of a bitch, raking in mountainous sums of cash. Perhaps it was more likely I'd become one of those street bums that went out West on a promise and couldn't swing it while Prince wandered the illuminated boulevards and found somewhere interesting to place all his wealth. I don't know. It's possible Prince would convince everyone that we were young and interesting enough to be believed in, two renegades with a dream. Time would tell.

I think about buying Jimmy's Place with Leon and Prince and wonder if it would be the grand old time we imagined. Could it really be ours? God, Saul's tired eyes gave him away. It's no secret he's ready to go. Would he white knuckle it and hold on for holding on's sake, or if we slid him a check and took care of him properly, would he be gone in a flash? Perhaps he'd ride out on the wind like a story, finding roots in another hidden corner of America. I don't think Saul's ever even left the county. An adventure of some sort is exactly what the guy needs.

I gotta say, the more I think of it, the more it seems like a damn solid proposition for everyone. All I have holding me down is my painting and odd jobs. Prince has no real obligations, and Leon could maybe pull off both pursuits. Though if we're smart, he'd be the one really running the place while Prince and I would be, whattdayacallit, associates. Yeah. That'd be the way.

Well, we'd have to pitch that to Leon and see where that line of thought took us. Who knows, maybe Jimmy's Place will be ours by year's end. Wouldn't that be something? Imagine my father stumbling back through Johnston after a ten-year journey, limping and crumpled. Bearded, drunk and cigarette-mouthed, he'd shuffle up to the bar only to look up and be served a cold one by his long-forgotten son. Chills run down my spine. If my father's alive, I don't want to see him in Jimmy's at night.

And now Amy comes to mind. Her beautiful resilience. The way she was shining in the kitchen, imbuing simple actions with quiet emotion. The wind on the river whispers changes. I remember being a child there at her counter and pouring a spoonful of sugar over cheerios and laughing as Tommy said, "Better not tell your mom!" When was it exactly that we grew up and became men in the world?

I've blinked and now I'm climbing my way to thirty, finding Amy angelic and gorgeous in a summer garden sweat. Kind and fascinating. Her love and gentleness in the face of her ongoing heartbreak filled me with adoration. We've always shared, at least a little, in our pain. We understand this about one another, our desire to be released from the past. God, I wanted her the other day. I longed to hold her close but struggled to even hold her eyes for more than a second. I can't be around her without thinking of Tommy and I'm afraid on some level I will always be some sort of distorted reflection of her son. Whenever I saw her, she seemed to genuinely love the person I've become, but was I still a kid in her eyes? Or a man? Could she find me beautiful, as I do her?

The romantic days are upon me.

What kind of mystic Midwest miracle has brought you to Johnston, Rose, and for how long? God bless you Saul, your sister!? You have a sister and you never told me? Your whole life and you ain't told nobody! What a revelation. I need to know her. I need to see her smile and make her laugh, show her all this town has. She's gone straight into the heart of my life, right where everything begins. Her eyes on mine in the bar light, what are you looking for Rose? Will you tell me? Will you let me help you find it? Have you thought about me since Jimmy's, or did seeing me weak and ridiculous on the summer sidewalk roasting with the insects repulse you? For a moment there at the bar, I thought you wanted to fight.

I laugh at the memory as the river ripples with water bugs below. That kind of strength, that *fight*, Rose, I recognized it immediately. My friends and I have it too. It's the kind that comes about only through a rough life lived. The kind that is earned through survival and bravery. Everyone I love has that look. It's in the very fabric of this town that raised me. Maybe Rose, maybe you're not so much of an outsider after all.

Rose Rose Rose. I don't know what brings you to Johnston, but I hope you will tell me. Do stay. I want to take your hand in mine. I want to kiss your red lips and see through your eyes. I want to look through your greens, and you can look through my blues. We could be the same, in the end, me and you.

I'm going to ask her what gives with the constant ponytail. I'm going to find out how she got her walk all dangerous and tailored musically like she has it. Rose. You have done it. It's obvious. You swam to the top of my soul and are floating, effortless. I will stand on this maple, and I will call out your name. Rose. The Fox will take the echo. I know this river. Up and down the banks it will travel, and you'll hear me, I know it. Just listen for it Rose, that familiar sound, whispering everything you were meant to hear from the start.

19

Some days I wake up from a drinking spree and feel downright disgusted with myself. I am nothing but green moss on the most abandoned branch in the forest, all sick and gross and non-blooming. The general gloom and sadness of my entire life rears its ugly head out, red, angered, and shouting incomprehensible nonsense through the thin bones in my skull.

On these foul mornings, I feel no love around me. I feel nothing calling in the beyond. I bemoan all the litanies of sorrys I feel. Sorry for what I've done and sorry for what I haven't. I find myself the lowest piece of flaming garbage one ever passed on the side of the road forgotten, unworthy of even the least sacrificial departure. Just trash, burning hot and ashy and useless, poisoning the sky and everything it touches. One great negativity. And I wish to paint none, talk none, be none. If fortunate, I'll put a pen to paper, drown myself in black coffee and bang my throbbing head on the table 'till the truth comes spilling out thick and painful in its viscosity. But today, I can't even bring myself to do that. Sometimes, it's this feeling or the drink, and on again. Flip a coin.

Hours have passed, and I'm with Prince chopping wood in his backyard. We smoke, have a few beers, and talk business. He has a sprawling dense green yard that lends itself to the cover of towering pines all around its borders.

Prince says, "I did some real thinking over the weekend pal."

"Yeah?"

"Yeah. There's just no way around the fact that we gotta do it."

"I've been thinking the same."

"I know this puts a pause on our migration west, man, but that don't mean it's over."

I throw my ax into an oak stump while he continues.

"When we get the thing up and running how we want, we can always make sure it's secure, in good hands or whatever and then make our way at that point, just check in from time to time taking gains, money won't be the problem. Money ain't why we'd go anyway man, so."

He had a point, and I was in no rush to leave anyway. It sure is refreshing to see Prince made alive again by something. With his ax leaning against a stump, leg bouncing and blowing smoke down to Earth, he is thoroughly enthralled.

"I agree man," I say, taking a drag of my own and wiping away the sweat on my forehead. I have no desire to slow his momentum, there was nothing worse than that.

Prince lives on his parents' old property, and what a property it is. It's a big old American house in the country, built with beige bricks and giant gorgeous windows where you can see the whole sprawling yard which leads out to a massive crop field and further, as far as the eye could see. Prince takes care of it all apart from the crop field which a farmer down the road owned.

This is his sanctuary. In the evening, the sun sets over that field, and you'd find it nearly impossible not to think pure, immense thoughts. I always marveled at the never-ending rows of tall swaying corn so far out there, rolling on forever, and how that ocean of green floods the Midwest every summer without fail. Prince and I would sit on his porch for hours and watch over this kingdom, sometimes saying nothing at all. But today, with his hair slicked back all the same, Prince holds an ember of hope, and he can't help but talk about it.

He starts going on about real business and logistics, saying things about what he learned from his father all those years just by listening.

"You fix your eyes on the point." He says it with conviction, a real aptitude for the ins and outs of how to make things possible. It's insane to me that I'm one of two people on Earth that knows he has all these opinions inside, all these bulletproof ideas of success. All I do is nod and nod some more, smoke my cigarette and chop a few logs. He just needs me to let him roll, and I'm more than happy to oblige. I find that thankful pulse beating in my chest, for my brother, for someone I can chase down mad ideas with.

So, I listen and chop as he talks longer than he has in months about all the plans he has for the place.

"Cash, it's just lost a step in some way. Don't you think? You remember, when we were young, that place was, God, it was—what? God, it had a magic to it, man. Whole world stopped when we were there."

"Still feels that way to me."

"Yeah, but something's missing."

"Well. We were kids."

"Fuck man we're still young."

"Yeah, we are."

"Most important part is on you, pal."

"What's that?"

"Saul."

"Oh. Yeah."

"You're the only one he'll listen to."

"I don't know about that."

"Guy's got one friend in the world, Cash. One."

"I don't know about that either."

"Fuck off. Saul loves you, man. Always has."

"Deep down yeah, deep fuckin down."

"All I know is he better not get strange like he gets. And scared."

"He is desperate, man, for something. I know he is."

"Right."

"Needs change."

"Just like us."

"Just like us."

"Hell. He'll listen to you, Cash. He will. Just say it how you know how. Pull the heartstrings, yeah?"

"Yeah yeah."

Prince nods to himself, assured enough for now. He has a nagging fear his plans will foil underneath the loose soil of Jimmy's lackluster son, bored and depressed and jaded. Prince has little to no faith in Saul whatsoever, the two of them have never gotten on. It's true what he said though, Saul doesn't really get on with anyone. I have much more love for Saul than the next guy, but Saul has always struggled to show me an obvious kind bone one way or the other. We grew up together in the caverns of that bar, and anyone would tell you I have a soft spot for him. Our fathers were best friends, and they always seemed more fond of one another than they were of us, and in that, I knew Saul. I knew how that one simple truth broke the poor kid's heart, and I knew how a truth like that can change the course of a life. When I see Saul, I see that part of myself, and I can't help but feel a little sorry for the guy.

Well, Prince made the appointment earlier today while he was buzzed up on coffee and fresh with morning possibilities. Saul knows we plan to see him tomorrow around noon. Just like that, it's happening, but what is it inside of me that is unsure? It's not that the plan doesn't seem plausible and all that, or that it doesn't inspire me with promise, I suppose it's just that Saul is such a variable. I've learned a few things in this life, and one thing I've learned is until it happens, it hasn't, ya know? Sometimes that's just how I navigate my mind. I'm patient in that way. I'm convinced we can sway Saul, but people are people, and Saul might get in his own way in the end.

The smoke fills me with a growing sense of alignment regardless. We're in the pocket. We're the center of some great calling, and though I'm prone to wander at length, searching for unknowns, today is not that day. Today, I'm where I'm supposed to be. The right place, at the right time. The pocket. When by luck or by vision, I find the universe conspiring for my future because I've finally taken root in something I was destined to take root in. When all creation around me puts that infinite knowing hand on my shoulder and smiles. God, talk about a feeling. Looking at Prince, squinting out to the field of green crop and sun, I know that he feels it all too.

"We're in the pocket, man."

"You better believe it."

And all of a sudden, that almighty buzz, that true high of life comes alive. It climbs up my spine, one solid branch at a time. Destiny, smoke, and the drink. Completely reborn.

I don't feel so hopeless and dark dead anymore.

20

Bang! Eyes light up and drowsiness skips me for some other man. Today's the day, illustrious plans. Prince, Leon, and I are heading to meet with Saul at noon to try and buy the bar of our dreams. I smile wide as hell just imagining the three of us sitting across from tired Saul and making demands.

Saul Saul Saul, do not be scared, ole boy. Today is your day too! I have fashioned a plan so sweet it will make your eyes water. I'm going to spin him a dream about Texas, Florida or some other alluring place of sun offering him the grand chance of new beginnings. A fresh start. I'm going to sell him on the power of ambiguity and freedom, all the potential that will come his way just by getting up and going somewhere new. I'll look him in the eyes and assure him nothing in the world matters to me like Jimmy's Place does. I'll give him the lines of it being my forever place, my destiny. I'll remind him how I've loved it there since I was just a boy, just like him, how I've been there from the start. He'll know it's in the best of caring hands. God, go in for it, Saul! Go in!

Through the window I see a few squirrels battling ground over acorns and black hawks circling above, hungry like me. All together now.

I'm looking in the mirror and realize my dark blond hair has grown long past my ears. There's some fight in my blue eyes now and the layers of ice shine off the bathroom lights. What a good ass morning I've stumbled upon here. I'm clearing out and resetting and I think I may never drink-smoke-fight-yell again. I am bound for some sort of heaven, I must be. I will trespass no longer. All these sweeping romantic fantasies of goodness are calling. I'll fly on the feeling and guzzle my black coffee. I pull my jeans on one leg at a time and my iron St. Christopher chain sways down to my lips. A kiss of potential, of all things possible. I walk to the kitchen and see the creatures playing outside. They are oblivious to it all, right in the heart of their own morning plight, each wrestling for the day. There is not a worry to be found, not here, not for miles.

Windows down in the Saturn, I make my way to The Pit to meet with Leon and Prince. We'll say hello to lovely Morene who will already be on hour six or seven of her shift. Patti Smith sails through my speakers and I'm singing and on fire. She's going on about high walls, black barns, babes in her arms and the sky splitting, planets shifting and existence stopping. And through the windows comes the smell of old Johnston. Through manure fields and tiny properties, I smell prophecy. It is the scent of settled ground, sweat and tough work. Brisk in its fresh, ongoing nature.

The streets are slow and clean as I start rolling through town. Each evening the dew settles, cleansing the streets and the homes and the gardens. The Pit is on the southwest corner of Johnston, well positioned off the highway, the only avenue that sees any real traffic in Johnston. Travelers go from bigger city to bigger city and only blink through our town on their way forward. Those dawn routers were the ones that Mo served most in the mornings. They're the reason The Pit found itself one of the more lucrative establishments in town. As for the gang and me, it's the only breakfast joint we'd ever need.

A few times a week we'd meet at the diner, drink copious amounts of coffee, and prepare for whatever awaited us. Diners like these remind me that in Johnston, we're afforded the time and the peace necessary to see the almost imperceptible details. The type of whisperings the big cities probably found monotonous or insignificant. Through the walls of The Pit, gliding over cheap black coffee and eggs, you'd catch wind of the slightest change of degree. The most carefully smuggled differences in the lives of those the world had forgotten and moved on from. Kelly and Bob, eighty, gray haired and fleeting, sharing the fresh baked outer shell of a cinnamon roll, cherishing the taste. Good Sam from Sureland's supply division, mug in hand, getting delivered his bacon. He nods a warm thank you to Mo and then stares out at the sunrise, remembering the road and facing the drive still to come. Honest and real, the people of Johnston. Quiet and together, breathing and eating and drinking in the intangible gladness of a life worth living.

When you walk into The Pit you face an oval arrangement of swiveling, typical diner stools with metal bases and faded green seats. They sit just beneath the diner bar, constructed of what always looked to me like cheap granite. To the right is the cash register, sporting bright red numbers on its submarine-like tower which is attached to its base. It shows what value is owed or not owed. Behind the oval bar is Mo, the most important fixture of the place by a mile. She takes a break from serving Kelly and Bob their coffee to say, "Hey there Cash," to which I reply, "good mornin, beautiful," and walk on by, following the worn carpet past the booths and into the backroom, a removed section of the joint just for us.

I find Leon and Prince there waiting patient and chilled, always arriving before me. For the one thousandth time, I eye the painting on the wall of our booth. It's this idyllic Christmas scene in which a whole bright community dressed in furs all go about their business. The town is situated on this frozen river surrounded by reindeer and happy playing children. The moon shines a yellow and white light down from the top right-hand corner, and the saloon is open and rowdy with cheer. The townspeople exchange gifts and smile thoroughly in joy. It's always reminded me of Johnston.

Leon's going on about the details of his current work project and how he had to let someone go late last week due to laziness.

"Gotta cut the fat, man, and it's hard, it's really hard, but you gotta cut the fat, remember that," he says.

I know how awful he feels about it. We let him get it off his chest and murmur our support. Laziness just isn't going to get it done in this town, there are always construction workers to be hired in Johnston. In fact, it's one of the more popular job outfits for young, recently graduated high schoolers wandering aimlessly in a post-graduation haze that hasn't granted them the riches and women and reputation they always hoped it would. They could usually find a safe harbor with Leon and Sureland though. Until they blew it, at least.

I actually worked with Leon at Sureland when we were right out of high school, long before he ended up taking over the company for good. It wasn't all bad, but it was some of the toughest manual labor around, so, you know, it was *work*. Straight constant sweat and all task, not for the faint of heart that's for sure. Leon and I had a good run of it there for a while. We worked our tails off and gained respect in the company because of it. In the end, I found art in that hustle and grind. I knew for a fact there were lesser, worse jobs available, but I still called it quits about a year or so in. Around that time, I more or less stumbled into the whole painting scene and never looked back.

About twenty minutes in, we've had our coffee and are diving down into the real mechanics of our noon conversation plans when Mo saunters over, takes off her apron and hangs it on the chipped gold booth hook. She sits down in a slight huff and the curls of her hair wave about on her forehead. She's exhausted but, of course, she's smiling.

"Aren't you a pip bunch this morning." I smirk at that. Nobody I know uses the word pip except for Mo. It is uniquely and solely hers. Pip, as to say, full of energy. She sure hit it on the head. This morning we're buzzing like crazy. Prince is on his third or fourth cup of coffee, as am I. We're all jittery and nervous, legs bouncing and excited and motivated and minds turning at phenomenal speed. A few cups of good coffee and I can feel truly coked-out, dangerously smooth and frenetic all at once. Prince gets the same way, but Leon is more or less impervious to any manic caffeine effects. He has to drink ten cups to notice any serious changes.

Mo starts telling us about her morning and how she's been getting real close to this red-headed driver named Stuart who has a big old family in Nebraska.

"It's all for them, all this is for them." Mo frowns a bit, feeling really sorry in the telling, "That's what he said. Broke my heart kinda. He's been a musician since he was a kid. He's a singer and a guitar player. He was telling me how he doesn't get to play much anymore because he's taking on more and more heavy-houred trips."

Despite all that, she tells us he brought his guitar with him that morning and at five a.m., with the place pretty ghosted, he played the strings for her.

"He had this gravel voice, sounded maybe sixty or older, real weathered-like. A deep soul, you know, the kind that's tired as hell, and only comes from honest work. I think Stuart might be depressed but he sure sings it well."

Mo smiles so she doesn't cry. God, you can tell Mo really feels for the guy. I think we all do. We all understood him in a way. I have the feeling we all can be small, praying at the feet of God and scrounging around for a chance, for an opportunity to play a western tune at a diner in a five a.m. dawn. We all long for a waitress like Mo in dark mornings. For just one person to listen. To be heard. To have one beautiful moment of purpose.

"That's great, man. Good for him," I say, nodding.

"I'm really rooting for him, you know. Must be a real pain trying to provide for six little ones and not having the time to do it how you wanna."

"One day the kiddos will understand where all the money came from," Prince says.

"Yeah, true. But they don't get it right now."

She frowns one more time and then goes, "anyway!"

And she switches the brightness all the way back on just like that.

"Have it all planned out straight, do ya?" Prince gives her the brief game-plan. It's impressive how accurate and coolly intelligent Prince can be when he wants to turn it on. In his black shirt and jacket, he looks unremittingly straight out of one of those greaser gangs you'd see in a film, like Elvis Presley or James Dean. He spits smooth action about our intentions, and I admit, when I listen closely, it sounds damn near foolproof.

Mo gets all worked up and giddy for us when he finishes. God, it feels swell to have her on our side. Of course, the truth is, Leon could be anything or do anything in this world and Mo'd love him all the same. Her hand reaches across the table without even looking, as Prince talks. Her fingers move up and down on Leon's calloused hand as if it were a grand piano. It really is one of the nicest damn things I've ever seen. I can't take my eyes away. I want a woman—damn, I need a woman to play the piano on me. To make me feel calm and mountainous. Prince finishes and she's lit up like fireworks. She plays the drums quickly on the table, smiling pure. She's wild in pride and anticipation for us.

"Well, God! I love it. I really, really love it. I do."

She hits the table with one final drum of the hand and says, "I should leave ya to it then, huh? Good luck out there today boys, make me proud. See you later babe," and she gives Leon the sweetest quick kiss on the lips. We watch her go and the quietness settles back in for a few seconds before I finally say, "You're the luckiest motherfucker on the planet, man, you know that?" Leon just leans back, smiles and nods.

21

Walking into a bar at midday always fills me with an anticipatory feeling. It reminds me of passing by Johnston fairgrounds in the morning as a kid. There used to be this magical county fair that would stop through town every summer and all of us went crazy for it. There were giant parties in the evenings where backwoods country and rock music blasted, the parents danced, and the kids ran wild through the rides and the grounds, cotton candy sugar-highed and falling in love, holding hands. In the morning, when I passed by those cool abandoned grounds, it got me all excited and eager thinking of all the lofty dreams that would play out in the evening. This is the same feeling I got when I was in Jimmy's Place when it was closed and empty and early.

We stride in with our chests out, inflated by purpose, ushered in by the warm day behind us. The air conditioning levels my senses but only for a moment. I'm stopped in my tracks. Saul is behind the bar talking to Rose. My mind goes all fuzzy and that damn pounding crashes in my chest again. I had no reason to expect she'd be around, especially at this hour. Only seconds ago, I was walking into this place like John Wayne, where had my stamina for heroics gone? Get it together. I swallow the adrenaline and continue forward. I lead us toward the bar.

"Hey guys, let's go round back," Saul goes, and that's that. He drops his white towel on the counter, hands Rose a set of keys and starts heading to his office. Leon and Prince stroll along after him but I can't help myself. Even though some sort of pride begs me to play it cool and ignore her gravity, I can't. I steal a glance her way, and she catches my eye. She twirls the keys in her hand and smiles. She taps that brass collection on the wood top.

"Good luck in there."

I tilt my head slightly like a dog would in thought. *What does she know?*

"Thank you."

"C'mon pal," Prince calls out as he walks away. Rose points to the back of the bar as if to say, *go on then.*

Somehow, I turn from her orbit and follow the guys into the office, all the while thinking about simple hellos and simple words, eye contact and how it can be as fine and romantic as anything.

We take a seat in Saul's office, and I quickly scan it down. He's quite the minimalist. There are a couple old photographs from the early days of Jimmy's hanging on the wall, dusted and faded, and in this collection, there is one I recognize most of all. It sinks my stomach. Yet another blow to the sublime focus I carried only moments ago. There on the wall, hanging in the center of Saul's collage, is a framed black and white picture of my father sitting at the bar, Jimmy by his side. My father holds a Budweiser and wears a flannel, his stomach pushing out through his tucked in tee shirt, and Jimmy, bar towel in hand and cigarette mouthed, stoically flanks him. The picture says everything all at once. Neither smiled. They were grounded and honest in their exhausted efforts. They were bent to the Earth but surviving, beer in hand. One drunken conversation away from figuring it out. Even after all these years, an admiration seeps into my blood. God. How do we kill our heroes?

I close my eyes and shake it off. There are pens and pencils in a black coffee mug sitting atop a pile of wilting papers. A few rays of light pour in through the near ceiling window. I have the morbid thought that there's no way in hell Saul would be able to make his way up and out of that escape if Jimmy's was ablaze, trapping him amongst this dusty barren chamber. Look no further than Saul's office to conclude the man is listless and on his way out, with or without our offer.

"Well. How can I help you guys?"

And by some miracle I keep myself from telling Saul right off about how he needn't look so morbid and stone-like indifferent. The way he said it, *how can I help you guys*, fuck's sake. I hadn't once in my life heard him use that tone. It was as if he fancied himself a bored and irritated mafia boss dealing with his lessers, mulling his legions of power. Poor bastard, Saul. You've got it all wrong.

"Saul, man, we've known each other a long time—" and I go right down to the root. "We were raised here, you and I, wouldn't you say? Remember those days, running around the parking lot back there. Remember playing those night games man, kick the can and shit, while our fathers drank the night away? Remember all those times? I do. Like they were yesterday. Forever ago but yesterday. You know I've always loved this spot, man. Nobody loves this spot like me. I'm romantic about it, Saul. I really am. My whole life has revolved around this bar in some way or another. From the beginning. But look man, and this is important, it's not all just sentimentality ya know, I also see, we also see, a lot of potential here. Real promise ya know? We believe in the place and we're hungry for something. Maybe we all need a change. All of us. God man, I know you're sick of this. I know you're tired of dealing with this place. When your pops died he gave you the bar but he never even asked you if you wanted it. You've served your time, man. Hell, I'm sure he'd be proud of ya, but aren't you ready to be off? Don't you ever think about doing something else or getting out of here or something—starting over somewhere anonymous, ya know? Could be good, could be real good."

And throughout it all, Saul just stares back at me silently, unchanging. I have to admit, it's a little unsettling how closed off he is. Still, I continue, trusting I'm in the pocket and that what I'm saying is the truth.

"Anyway man, we're giving you that chance if you want it. We'll take good care of it all, you know we will. We think it's time."

He blinks at me and scratches absently at his chin. I can't help but feel I could have said that all a bit better but my mind's running crazy now. I can't help but notice that look in Saul's eye. He's off somewhere else. I turn it over to Prince who has actually drawn up some papers and plans.

He hands them to Saul who glances back and forth between the scribbled ideas and Prince's charming proposals. Leon, meanwhile, sits arms crossed and quiet to my right, surely wondering about other things while all this is happening, his mind often working much faster than all the others in the room. I bet he's thought about the coffee mug, the window, and that fuckling looming photograph of my father on the wall. I bet he's even thought about how that's affecting me at this very second. I rub my eyes. Prince is really pushing the whole thing home while I notice a bag in the corner with some clothes hanging out. Is Saul sleeping here now?

Prince finishes his pitch and Saul lets out a giant breath.

"Well, it's something to think about." His eyes narrow and the severe lines on his forehead crunch down together as if to squeeze the life out of his face. He's just staring at the papers while we sit relatively agape at his indifference.

Prince, thrown, goes, "That's it?"

And Saul doesn't look up. He just nods to himself as he looks down at the papers, mind and heart closed off and says, "For now, think so."

I can see it happen as clearly as I can see Prince and Leon beside me, or the coat of dust on the desk which occasionally goes airborne, floating home to our lungs. Somewhere in that deep quiet heartbreak that has always defined

Saul, I know he is thinking about the past. He can't meet my eyes. What are you hiding, Saul? What aren't you saying? And all at once I remember, those many years ago, when I found him crying in the middle school bathroom. It was one of the saddest, loneliest things I'd ever seen. Saul taps the stack of papers on his desk and then sets them down. Eternally quiet. Prince stares him down, and for the first time, it dawns on me that the whole thing is a disaster and maybe we never had a chance in the first place. I'm waiting for Prince to engage, but he's by all accounts calm, though a storm rages beneath. He's a good actor. Deep down, I know that, if allowed, he would completely rip Saul to bones for such a dismissive, uninterested demeanor and lack of reason or communication. Prince is burning. My heart begins to ache for everything, but I know this is not the time to press him.

"Well, take the time you need, man," I say, to which Saul nods.

He keeps his eyes on the papers, his desk. Claustrophobia is setting in. The sweat and the dust is on us. The sunlight pierces the air, illuminating the floating dirt and debris. Five more minutes and the walls will surely cave in and crumble. We'll be buried in ruins, like the best of our glorious plans. I shake my head and let out an exasperated breath. What is easy is never easy when and where it should be. We stand up one by one, the chairs shaking against the wooden floorboards. We all shake Saul's hand and still, he meets no eye. We leave his office in need of cleaner air. We walk through the bar, and gone is that anticipatory feeling. We left it dead and bleeding in Saul's office. The place is filled with abandon now, our feet echoing as we cross the expanse in defeat. Rose is nowhere to be seen. What an empty arena of dying promise.

Outside, the sun is gaining momentum, too severe for our dispositions. The doors close behind us and to the gravel Prince goes, "What, the *fuck* was that?"

I'm looking around the deserted parking lot, clueless, stunned. I run my hands through my hair trying to think,

"I don't know man, I really don't know. Something's going on with him."

Leon sighs.

"That guy ain't sellin a damn thing."

Prince lets out a growl and curses under his breath.

"He is the fuckin worst kind of person, I'm serious."

Leon has already shifted his course, a bit more hopeful than we are.

"Gotta head to work fellas," he says. "Who knows. Talk soon." He pats Prince on the back as he stands hunched with his hands on his knees. "Who knows?"

And he's off. Prince and I stand there for a moment more, growing further frustrated and perplexed. He spits into the gravel and stands up straight again.

"Alright pal, I'm gonna go fuckin, I don't know. Swing by later if you want," and I watch him go as he mutters a couple things to himself. "Fuckin Saul."

"See you later, man."

"Yeah. See ya, Cash."

God, what a stupid disappointing drag this had turned out to be.

I stand long and strange outside Jimmy's Place, alone, blankly staring at the building. It's a relatively small place with dark brick lining and a rusted piped roof. The sign is old and turned docile in daytime. *Was it all over and done just like that?* Fuck it. I clap my hands together and move. I walk to the front doors and decide to try one more time. The place is as empty and quiet as ever as I stride the length of the room. I knock on Saul's door and when no response comes, I take a look inside, but he's gone. I walk through the kitchen, and push my head out the back to see if Saul's car is still parked in the alley but it isn't. How had he tailed off so quickly and without me noticing? I shut the heavy metal door tight and feel the rush of cold bar air back on my face and breathe it in deep. If Saul had left, he left fast. I don't know what to make of that. I head back from the kitchen and into the bar and like a spirit she has emerged. Rose is behind the counter, rearranging liquor bottles, glasses, and rags. I approach and keep the greeting short, "Any chance you know what happened to Saul?"

"Today or in general?"

"Today—just now. We just finished that meeting with him not five minutes ago—"

"Right. Yeah, he just left."

"He left?"

"Yep. Just a second ago I think."

"Why?"

"I couldn't tell ya."

"He didn't say nothin?"

"Nope, just came out from the office and walked out back."

What was spinning in Saul's mind?

"Is something wrong?" she asks.

"What? No, no I just wanted to catch him again quick. I guess I'll try and swing back later."

"Yeah, alright."

"Will you be here?"

"What's it to ya?"

"Thought maybe you'd have a beer with me?"

She puts the last of the glasses away and scoops up her car keys. She looks at me with her sharp green eyes, pupils nighttime black in the haze. She smirks a bit. "I'll see ya around I'm sure."

Without another word, she walks away. She doesn't look back, but I do hear her say, "The name's Cash right? Like Johnny?"

"Yeah, something like that."

22

I'm back on my land cutting grass while Guns N' Roses plays from my black radio on the back porch. My push mower is one hundred years old, and once belonged to my father. Though I long since had the money to replace it, I figured it'd be only fair to run it to the ground, bury it, and start over only when necessary. It was faithful to me, still cut fine, and the truth is, I'm more loyal than most. I have an affinity for things, however inanimate, and like to think that everything, even lawn mowers, can carry a certain spirit. So what if the gears and wheels require more effort than the new ones in the shops? I don't mind.

Cutting grass in the summer is something I've always enjoyed. As the lawn moves beneath the wheels and roaring blades, I take one step closer to serenity.

The smell of fresh cut grass fills my senses and makes me dream deep nostalgic dreams of summers gone by. I keep my yard trimmed and healthy and soiled, weeded out and shining like a sea of emerald swords. Something about a healthy green lawn keeps me feeling in line. Crazy, but I know all sorts of folks that don't care much for it, not like I do anyway. There are plenty that bemoan the work it requires, never understanding the process or the reward. Believe it or not, there are those that never stood out on a back porch and looked out at a freshly cut landscape and felt that sensational fresh feeling of new beginnings. I love it for its attention to detail. For me, the details were always the best.

"Take care of it, and it will take care of you." My father used to say. "A lawn says something about a man."

Today, while cutting, I'm consumed by what went down at Jimmy's Place only hours before. The whole thing didn't line up in my eyes. I tried to get ahold of Prince earlier, but he had fallen off the map. I'm sure he's somewhere smoking, staring deep and heavy, running the whole thing over and over again in his mind. He had believed it was to be. As had I, in the end. I wipe the sweat out of my eyes. How long until the fall breeze kicks in? I push the mower forward and dive into every inch of my life that played out this morning.

I can't put my finger on it, but there was something hidden in Saul. He was different and distant, but I had the feeling there were a million things on his mind. There were orchestras in his silence. All my life I've watched the quiet and the loud, and let me tell you something real that you can trust: the quiet ones are more interesting, complex, and unpredictable. What weighs heavy in their mind that stops them from speech? What do they see that the others do not? I always thought they knew some profound truth about life that all those circus folks with loose mouths, businessmen, frauds and clowns, attention junkies who never shut the fuck up for five seconds, would never understand. What a drag, that bunch. Give me the quiet, the listening folk every time.

For all his stillness, Saul showed me many things, but I have to hear him out. I need to get down to the bones of it with him, whether he wants to or not. We owe each other that much. Tonight, I'll head back to Jimmy's and when Saul's shift is over, we'll have it out. We'll get to the truth of it all. It's been enough Saul, enough sitting back for the both of us. One way or another, we're gonna shake the tree down and speak honestly. No more running around in circles, ole Saul. No more.

Sweat pours from my head and down my body, the excretion of abused things inside. Whenever I perspire like this, I can't help but think about the alcohol and the smoke and all the other badness I've done to myself rushing to escape me. What a fascinating self-preservation it is, these brief cleansing moments.

Too many bad habits. Will I ever outrun them? So many things traded in, and for what?

Sometimes, I believe it's bartering. Sometimes, I believe it's longing for romance, for dreaming, for experience, for winding and enthralling feelings. To me, to be bored and in a circular route was plain as death. To be living and scrapping for nothing, settling for checks, mediocrity, and predictable blandness. What a loss. The candle had gone out, then. A dying process, a grand submission to everything lifeless. That's how that goes. So, I fill up with drink sometimes and I smoke. That's the cost, I suppose.

I'm rounding another thick corner of lawn while the sun refuses retreat. I have always attempted to justify my behavior this way. I'm always chasing my idols, adopting their history, and getting closer to my great something, my calling, my purpose on the planet. On midnight porches I smoke long, hard, and smooth. I pour booze down my throat, all along believing it somehow brings me closer to the truth, believing I can ascend, believing I can look down over my whole life and see all the mysteries that have eluded me, revealed and naked.

In this, I've convinced myself that I care little about dying. I've convinced myself that death, at least from these origins, does not frighten me. For in these moments, high and alive, dreams become air that I breathe. The sky moves in tandem with water and wind, and everything's free, and that freedom is everything, that freedom is me. As I finish the lawn, I conclude that this is the king rumination. This is the center of the enterprise, and I am dancing on the floorboards.

I bring the red and black iron push-mower into our storage garage in a few final efforts and close the door until next time. Walking around to the front yard, I look at my lawn and I know it—this is the man I've become. Come gather round! All history, my idols, my heroes, my friends, Johnston, my dead mother, my dead others, my enemies, all! Even my father—come gaze at the grass. What does this say about myself as a man? This is mine. Take a look! Stay and peruse and make judgment. This here is my soul laid out bare. This is me. This lake of green. Judge me off this, and this alone! I smile and wipe more sweat off my brow. I am an eagle in the sky. I am free. I think about the taste of an ice-cold beer. How sweet life is, and should be.

23

Windows down, the Johnston evening air rolls in, uninhibited, effortless, and wise. The cloth seats of my Saturn are still warm from baking in the afternoon sun and the countryside is bathed in those descending hues of orange. A premonition chill sweeps my skin, a call to arms. There's something on the horizon, something coming. There's a real change brewing, I just know it. As the familiar landscape of rolling green and brown passes through my eyes, the future is illuminated through mysterious messages, hidden in shimmering leaves of maple trees just begging to change color in fall. In due time, they'll spin their way down. They'll crown the Midwest with beauty and I'll catch a few in my hands, all the while listening for the whispered plans of God. Everything is feeling alright. The farm field air holds promise. I've showered and changed. I don my grandfather Bud's old cowboy hat and my oldest pair of boots.

There's something about a cigarette in the car and not caring about the cigarette in the car. It's like Grandpa's old truck where I took so many rides as a kid. Grandma and Grandpa would light up and send the rings all along the dash. They'd float back to whomever was along for the ride.

Thumb tapping on the steering wheel, listening to The Smiths, I glide into Johnston. There are a few families on Main Street walking toward the center of town, likely to enjoy dinner at one of our restaurants, perhaps Brady's Super Club or the Junction Steakhouse. After, they'd probably take in the evening entertainment at our small-town square. Under the shelter of a humble domed pavilion, performers would float through Johnston and play a set or two. Townspeople would gather, share a few drinks, dance, or sit back and enjoy. Their children would run about all wide eyed and wonderful, playing games alongside the ancient train tracks, and peace would enter their hearts. I wonder who's playing there tonight. Performers rotated between local average bands, comedians, collections of poets, and even your rogue historian or two. You never knew what you were gonna get, but they were all sincere and wholesome around here. There weren't many places purer than the town square of Johnston on pavilion nights.

I have a buddy Pat who is a true vagabond musician. He stops by every few months or so and stands up on that stage with an acoustic guitar and plays the most heartbreaking folk ballads you've ever heard. Sometimes he'll play all night long. Bearded and large, tattoos covering his arms, he bellows a raw, broken voice out to the universe and the collection of onlookers who always wait patiently for him to come through. I never missed an opportunity to see Pat when he was in town. He gave himself fully. I drive past the square and see a few people already milling around together. A father holds his son's hand as he skips. God, I hope I'm not missing Pat. I grip the wheel. I have other plans tonight. I'm heading to Jimmy's Place convicted by changing tides.

*

From my corner booth, cowboy-hatted, I can watch all the other players spin their tops. The brim casts a perfect shadow down my face, the type you see in all those classic western films. Sometimes I dream up this vision of myself, like I'm a real Butch Cassidy on the loose, brave and smooth as can be, strapping up and picking out target after target in a long line of noble adventures.

Tonight, I have eyes on everything. The beer goes down easy, and romantic visions surround me. There's two middle-aged men, Don and Baxter, sitting at the bar having Bud Lights and chatting. They run Mick's Grocery and are often found together, an enigmatic pair. Baxter has a real entertainment bent about him, the kind who never misses a chance to tell a good story, and Don, red faced and joyful, is always willing to laugh. Everyone in Johnston loves these two. Saul serves them, when necessary, but never looks in my direction unless I go and stand before him.

"Another one, Cash?"

I nod.

"Yeah, yeah."

And that's that.

There's a family shooting a few rounds of pool, rotating around my table, and thoroughly enjoying themselves. The father is dog tired, rubbing at his eyes whenever a free second hits, but smiling all the way. I admire him. I find it remarkable how a man can work all damn day in the heat of industrial hell and still stumble out and find the necessary energy to play pool with his kids. He scratches at his five o'clock shadow with oil-stained fingernails. Perhaps he's a mechanic. He hands his wife the pool stick, and picks up his young son. The wife has puffy blonde hair, curling and reflecting the table light. She too has a smile bright as the sun and her kids, outrageous in their love for her, grab at her dress and jump around like maniacs. Watching those three kids bounce all around, adoring her, desperate for her attention, I'm reminded of the heaven-like power and grace of mothers. She must be dog tired too, raising that bunch. Instilling in them hope and joy and righteousness. Her daughter hugs her left leg as she lines up her shot. She strikes the cue and the eight spins to the pocket. She winks at her husband then rotates around the felt, her daughter clinging all the way. She's the best of them. The husband finishes his drink. Many beers down and counting. On it goes.

Other than them, there's a couple passersby I don't recognize, and a few women who work over at the town salon, Jamie and Alexa, who look hopeful, tuned up and lively. Alexa cuts my hair every once in a while, and she always treats me kindly. She likes to joke with me that her and I would figure it out together one day.

"We'll settle down, Cash, you laugh but we will."

Alexa got mixed up with this bum named Jeremy a few years back who jumped town after she became pregnant. I remember how heartsick she was then. Young and confused and abandoned. It was really something how Johnston rallied around her, though. Gifts, meals, and hugs, and anything she needed. It was like the whole town was pregnant, and that's the thing about Johnston. When it comes down to it, the whole town is a family. Anyway, she named the baby girl Autumn, and she's three now. Sometimes I see her out and about and become so full of pride I nearly burst. I love that little girl in our town. She's a lighthouse of hope and she doesn't even know it. Alexa talks about Autumn constantly, and I always listen closely. Three years old. It's true how the time goes. Alexa adjusts the strap on her bra which lies beneath her cropped tee shirt. It's subtle.

"We will Cash, I'm telling ya."

Maybe, maybe one day. For now, I'm afraid I'm looking in another direction. I have a nice long pull of Budweiser and think it tastes more and more righteous by the second.

After a couple hours and a few games of pool, the hum of the alcohol has risen. I'm nodding along to some Talking Heads, and Rose enters on cue. The world is moving, and she's right there. She heads to the bar and briefly says something to Saul before heading around back. I'm completely fascinated by the nature of their relationship. I haven't seen them say more than two words to one another but that immeasurable understanding of siblings does seem to exist between them. The Heads sing of backyards, taking off dresses, and rising above the Earth. When Rose comes in again, she has a cardboard box in her arms. She sets it down behind the bar and Saul helps her go about unpacking a variety of essentials, bottles, glasses, and stock. Rose takes the now empty box in her hands and moves to go to the kitchen. I can't help but admire her focus. She looks so serious all the time. She wears a dark pair of navy-blue jeans and a black plain belly tank which reveals a series of piercings around her belly button. Box in hand, she looks over to my corner and sees me sitting all quiet and alone. She continues to the kitchen and is gone.

An hour later, I'm back in the booth and the place is becoming further deserted. Only a handful of the committed remain. A couple out-of-towners are talking Saul's ear off, and after what seems like an eternity, Rose emerges again. A bit lighter, perhaps relieved somehow, she goes to the bar and grabs a pint glass and pours. Funny, she fills it to the brim, but for nobody in particular. A perfect pour. She gathers it and swings around the bar opening and as God would have it, heads straight toward me. At last. She nearly floats when she walks. Have I ever seen anyone so balanced and aligned? When she finally sits down across from me, I am naive to her motives. I'm only happy she's here. One conversation and a beer. It's a hell of a place to start. She wears a few rings, dirty metal bands, and that same cross necklace, tight around her neck. I love her jewelry. I love how it's weathered and worn. I'd give just about anything to feel her fingers in mine. She wraps them around her glass, takes a drink of her Budweiser and says, "I hear you can make one hell of an offer."

"Like to think so."

"He's never gonna take it, ya know."

"Yeah?"

"Yeah."

She has another drink, licks a little off her upper lip, and eyes me real inquisitive like, searching for answers. I love her eyes on me, and I return the favor. What assumptions has she made about me? And which is she making right now? We have oceans of life, don't we all, right beneath the surface, right where we're conscious and dreaming? Her green eyes flutter a bit as she drinks.

"Don't you have any other places to be?"

"Not really."

"You and your friends love it here, huh?"

"Johnston?"

"Jimmy's, Johnston, all the above."

"Yeah, yeah I'd say so."

"What do you love about it?"

"Everything."

"That's a lot."

"Grew up here."

"In Johnston?"

"Yeah. But, here. Here. Jimmy's. My father came here every day."

"Same."

"I still can't believe Jimmy's your dad."

"Well. Wasn't much of one, to be honest."

"No, suppose not."

"Your dad brought you here every day?"

"No. No, I was just trying to be around him I think."

"Right."

"Yeah."

"Is he around now?"

"No, he's not around now."

"Not around like mine's not?"

"No, not quite like yours."

"Okay."

We both take another drink as all of my life begins to rise like a tide.

"So, what's your story?"

"My story?"

"Yeah."

"Ah, I'm afraid it's boring."

"I doubt that."

"What's with the hat?"

"What's with the necklace?"

"Grandma's."

"Grandpa's."

"Can't believe Paul Newman's in our bar."

"You like Paul Newman?"

"He's okay."

"Because, I can be Paul Newman if you want me to."

"Is that right?"

"*Small price to pay for beauty.*"

"Very good."

"You've seen it?"

This gets her to smile.

"Only about a thousand times. *Who are those guys?*"

"Who are those guys?" I laugh.

Is she seriously quoting *Butch Cassidy and the Sundance Kid* with me?

"It's a cool hat."

"Thanks. It's a beautiful necklace."

"Thank you."

"So. Why won't Saul give it over?"

"It's his father's."

She shrugs.

"Yeah, well." I suppose that's the simple answer. I want more but let it rest.

"What are you doing 'round here anyway?"

"Saul's all the family I got left. We didn't really meet as kids."

"Right. I never saw you around."

"I was hardly ever here. Saul and I have different mothers, obviously. We didn't really even know about each other until we were teenagers. By that time, I don't know, I guess we didn't care much. I mean, I cared but it was hard. I didn't see Jimmy as my father, so Saul was just, I don't know. A stranger."

"Yeah."

"Yeah, but it bothered me. Not knowing him at all. Years past though. We were in Ryland. Anyway. Long story short, my mother had breast cancer and died last year."

"I'm sorry—"

"Thanks. It was slow, so, we had a while to plan things out at least. She always thought I should visit Saul here. When she died, that's what I did. Met him and all that. It went fine. I still tried to stick around Ryland, but it wasn't working. Couple months ago, he said I could come help out with the bar if I wanted and, yeah, here I am."

She finishes and nods to herself, confirming the details, then takes a long drink. The way she told it all was sharp and quick, bullet point storytelling kept close to the vest, but still, she had shared it with me even though she didn't have to.

The cold bar air created small goosebumps on her shoulders as she told the story and I don't remember blinking, moving, or breathing. Everyone has a story in Johnston. Even those who came wandering through for a day or a week or to stay. We're all wrapped up and gauzed from the battles and storms of life and have somehow found ourselves washed ashore here in the middle of nowhere. To think all around the world people have problems and that life can be brutal on most everyone. We're in the generation of scattered parents and a blooming new age of odd complexity. I know some would call Johnston simple, but some would be wrong to do that.

"Saul's had a rough one."

She's looking down as she says it. Behind everything she gives, I sense a potent hidden love. A beautiful sensitivity, guarded for survival. We're more alike than I realized. I imagine Rose as a little girl. I imagine the first time learning of her father and her brother, this whole half of her life, removed and impossible to reach. It was a choice not her own, but one she would embrace before she could comprehend what it meant. All the pain and confusion her parents had caused settled deep into her bones and had hardened there. There is so much chipping away that is needed now. For her and for me and for everyone. All these beautifully broken wanderers. My heart is theirs. Damaged and messed up and still having a go of it. We're together here, that's it, that's the thing. We're one collective, taking our shot at a wonderful life worth living. We're winding and walking through the stilled Johnston atmosphere like a family holding hands. We get our soul from the sidewalks, both the long-ago roads and the new ones ahead. We're instilled with our great something, a hope.

"I know."

She holds my eyes for a moment.

Do you believe me Rose?

"Well, I oughta go—"

"Okay."

And I feel as if I've known her all my life.

On these old wooden benches, in the far back corner of our bar, shadowed and listening, we are the night. We're sitting at a table we could have sat at as kids. Another life. She looks at me deeply, straight to my soul.

"Talk to him about that, and you'll see," she says.

She spins the cross in her hand, and then leaves.

24

Two a.m. Everyone has long since stumbled home. I'm at the bar now, closing the place down with Saul. He pours us both another beer and sits down to my left. He scratches the top of his head and lets out a pent-up breath. He wears his favorite tucked in black shirt with Zeppelin's famous Hindenburg disaster album art on the chest, stained blue jeans, and rugged dirtied cowboy boots with metal snakes wrapping 'round to the point. Poor Saul.

His spine naturally bends to the bar top, and he hangs there like that without moving, staring at his beer. Lost in the madness of life. He clearly hasn't shaved in days, and it's patchy on his face but looks fine. He's a rugged hard sort who's been worn down by many seasons, in so many ways, but this didn't make him unique. Many of us had been given a rough roll around here. What makes Saul unique, to me, is his softness. You have to look closely to see it, but it's there, I promise you. It's hidden back, way back in the depth of his eyes and in the layers of his gruff vocalities. Yes, it's in his voice. I swear, if you listen close enough, the voice will expose everything about a person. It travels up and out of the soul, from the pits of the stomach, and accidentally reveals the most intimate, buried of secrets. But you really have to *listen*.

Saul takes a drink, lets out another exaggerated breath.

"Grew up in this place, Cash."

"We did."

"Damn near thirty years."

"Yeah."

"Can't seem to shake it."

"Me either."

"You know I even sleep here some nights—"

"I know."

And he takes another extended pause where he attempts to sort through his vulnerability. I find him at the end of one very long rope, maybe the longest I've ever seen, all ratted and frayed and exhausted.

"When'd you have your first drink you think?" he asks.

"Think I was, like, nine."

"I reckon that's around the same."

"Yeah. Early."

"Early, and ever since."

"Yeah."

"Think you'll ever stop?"

"No."

"No. Don't reckon I will either."

"We never had a chance pal."

"No. Cash, let me tell you something."

"Alright."

"I hated my father."

"Yeah."

"I mean it. I have no love for him."

"Mhm."

"Nowhere in my heart."

"Yeah."

"I just don't want you thinkin I'm holdin out on this thing on his account or nothin. This ain't no gesture of love or nothin like that. I got nothin but hate where the love should be."

"Yeah. I get that."

"I know you do."

"Yeah."

"You were there."

"I was."

"Maybe I shouldn't. But I hate him."

"Well."

"I mean it."

"I believe you man."

"Jimmy's Place ain't nothin, Cash. It's the people."

"Yeah."

"It's the people. It's always been the people."

"You've got that part right, pal."

"Maybe I don't seem it, but I'd hate to leave 'em behind."

"Yeah. Me too."

"I know you feel the same."

"I do."

"I know it. I only heard you guys out today 'cause of you."

"Thanks man."

"Don't want you to think it was a waste of time."

"Wasn't it?"

"I don't know."

"It's okay, pal. It's all okay."

"Yeah. Thanks Cash."

I lift my glass and we cheers in the silence.

"You know"—Saul lets out a rare chuckle—"if my dad hadn't dragged me here all those years ago and forced me to work nights, I never woulda been a drunk by thirteen."

"Me either."

"Thirteen. And workin late shifts and smokin and takin trash out for him. Every day."

"All the time."

"He ain't never said more than two words to me, never."

"Yeah."

"And you know I'd see him 'round here, belly out and drunk himself, servin. And he'd be havin these long conversations, with your pops and some others. And I always thought, ain't that somethin. Seein him talkin like that. Really talkin. He never spoke none to me."

"Mine never had much to say to me either."

"I never got that."

"Neither did I."

"He was a big, stupid drunk, with big stupid hands and he had no business fatherin nobody. God, I got hate in my heart for him Cash, I still do—"

And just like that, tough, rugged ole Saul's poor eyes begin to water. As stoically as I'd seen a man cry, he cries. "I just say it 'cause I don't want nobody assumin nothin 'bout that when I think twice on sellin this place."

"I know, man."

"It's the people."

"I know."

"It's just that. That's all."

"Right—"

"But I don't know why you want it so bad." He wipes at his eyes.

"God, I don't know man—"

"Don't know why you're always comin in here all these damn nights and just watchin around and drinkin and playin pool."

"Yeah. I don't know either."

"Yeah, well—"

"Man, what I said earlier. You do remember playin those games in the back lot all those nights while we waited to go home right?"

"Games?"

"Man, you know like kick the can and that shit. We'd play 'em back there..."

"Yeah, I guess."

"Because there was one time, I won't ever forget it. We were sittin, you and me, back behind one of the barrels, and you looked at me all big eyed and happy and said, this was the best part of your life."

"I said that?"

"The best part of your life."

"Doesn't sound like me."

"You said it man, just like that."

"Yeah. Well. It's kinda sad I don't remember that, ain't it?"

"You do man, you do. Just a long time ago is all."

I watch as the story sinks in. It wasn't nothin crazy as far as storytellin goes, it's just one of the stories I remember most about Saul when we were younger. Out of hundreds of memories, that's one of them that stands out. He was so sweet and honest back then, so pure. His heart was still full, hanging on and hopeful.

"Was a damn long time ago," he says.

"Yeah man. It was. And it was yesterday."

"You ever gonna head out, you think?"

"Of Johnston?"

"You were talkin all about how great leavin would be."

"Meant for you."

"Didn't sound like it."

"God. I don't know, man."

"You thinkin 'bout it?"

"Nah I can't leave, man."

"Why not?"

"Place would go to shit."

"What's keepin you here?"

"You already said it, pal."

"The people."

"Mhm. It's home, yeah?"

"Yeah."

And we drink. We philosophize back and forth about a little of this and a little of that. I have half the desperate mind to ask him every question in the world about his sister, but I don't. Something tells me the time will come. I'm honestly just thankful to be in the bar with Saul while the beers poured themselves and we drank them. Alone and reminiscing and being brothers, which I always knew us to be. It's rare for Saul to feel so free, so willing for conversation. I wouldn't ruin it for the world. Let it roll, good Saul, let it roll.

About an hour later, he guzzles down the last of his Budweiser, and shakes his head. I don't know what time it is but we're only a few from the sun.

"You know she told me she loved me."

"Who?"

"Rose. She said that. After all these years. Even though she don't even know me."

"You're her brother, Saul."

"I know but. Still."

"Of course she loves you."

"Not of course. Not of course."

"Right."

"I should have went out to look for her, you know. I should have seen how she was in the world."

"Well. She's here now. Don't beat yourself up too bad."

"Yeah. Suppose she is, huh?"

"Yeah. And I think she did alright."

"She did. She did. And now we've got time."

"All the time in the world."

And with that, Saul puts his hand on my shoulder and gives me a nod of thanks. It's the first genuinely loving gesture I've seen him offer in years. He walks around the bar and picks up his empty glass. All nights eventually end, and it's too bad. Crazy, this life. I really believed Saul might jump at the chance to be freed from it all, Johnston and his roots, all of the circles and places and truth. I can see now that I read it all wrong. Saul would live and die at Jimmy's Place, here in Johnston. Just like myself and everyone else I knew. And the tired beat nature of it had nothing and everything to do with the place. Sometimes, the place holds it all, the smells and the songs and the lights and the past and the pain and the people. Everything. Truth is, Saul thinks Jimmy's Place is the most special spot in America. And I gotta tell ya, he's right, I believe he's dead right about that. I take one last pull of my beer, and I laugh because I know the bar will never be ours but it already is. It just isn't for sale, and Saul isn't so poor after all.

25

I only saw my father cry one time my whole life.

It was the night his father died.

He came home from the bar in work clothes, soaked from the rain outside. He stood by the front door, ghost-like, with heavy shoulders. My mother was in the kitchen putting some pans away and drying off her hands. I had been sent to bed some half hour prior, but I often would sneak out of my room and stay hidden in the stairwell keeping lookout, patiently waiting for him to come home. I would make sure he was okay before finally calling it a night. So, from the stairwell I sat and watched my father let his old brown work bag fall to the floor in a depressed heap, standing still as a statue and wet.

My mother didn't say a word. From what I remember, she made no sound at all. Across the kitchen, back against the sink, she watched in careful settling pain, and I tell you, she knew. The air in our house grew thick. I couldn't fathom why, but in that one image, I could see that my mother knew calamity had struck, and to think, still, she managed to stand there for a couple of minutes just watching my father as it all played out before her eyes. She gave him space. His chest rose and fell through ragged breath while he tried to gather the force necessary to speak. Finally, he wiped some water off his face and began to silently weep. And still, my mother didn't move.

Alone and soaked and broken, my father wept. He wept a slow silent crescendo that began to shake the very boards beneath his feet. In the middle of the evening kitchen like a child overwhelmed, he sucked in these huge gasps of air as he hyperventilated in a scratchy, smoked out tune. It was the saddest thing I'd ever seen. Some may think that after a lifetime of not crying, a man would somehow forget the mechanics, but that isn't true. The heart remembers how. The body remembers everything. And my father remembered how to cry just as heartbreakingly as the rest of us, if not more so. For minutes he went. His grizzled shaking hands of enormous strength gripped the kitchen counter as he suffered and shed tears into the wood. With his back rising and falling, I watched him battle to rein it all in. He tried taking quick breaths and holding them, but it was useless, and it drove him further down. Even in this dark crashing of loss, I'm sure he couldn't believe he was crying. All the while my mother stood arms crossed and tearful by the sink. I nearly ran down there to do something, but I was a rock, a silent immovable stone; heart racing and stomach turning with fear. I followed my mother's lead, but to this day I don't know how she knew to just stand there and wait. She just watched from a distance and let the levee break.

My father fell to his knees and crumbled. Quiet, head poked through the stairway railings, I began to worry he would never stop. That he was a broken clock and would be hitting midnight forever. The bell had rung and now he was helpless, weeping like a child. Like me. And I couldn't help it, all at once the memories of my childhood began to flood. My father, a hypocrite? I felt my love for him wash away, exposing a dark resentment and confusion.

What was I seeing?

Was this the same person that ruled over me in silent, brutal dominion?

Was this the same man who hit me with a belt?

What about all those times he shouted at my tears, growling at my sadness?

All my life he'd banished any weakness within me, unsatisfied until it retreated completely. All my tantrums and my turns at the wheel were silenced and scorned. Yet, here was this sculpture of my youth, broken and sobbing. What an unconscionable mess. Who was *this* man? Tears ricocheting against the floor, convulsing in despair, capable of such depth of feeling. I didn't know, but the longer he shook, the less resentment my little chest could cling to, and it left as quickly as it came. I felt my own warm tears run down my face. It was the closest I ever felt to him, and I was a million miles away.

I couldn't tell you how long this went on for. It could have been an eternity. Eventually though, he caught his breath. Hair frayed, stomach soaked, coat half haphazardly strewn and hanging off his right shoulder, cigarettes falling out of the front pocket. He wobbled a bit as he stood to his feet. Ashamed and destroyed, he croaked through a ravaged, misused throat, "Dad's gone."

That was all. That was all he could say. Those two quiet words dropped out of him and were deafening. They filled up the house, every inch of inhabitable space.

"Dad's gone." He said it again. *What did that mean? My grandfather had died?*

"Dad's gone." Yes, that must be it. My grandfather was gone, gone for good. It was the first experience I ever had with death, and all I knew was that I didn't understand it.

I felt like a stranger as I watched from above. I watched as my mother went to my father at last. She put her hand carefully and steady on his back. She moved it up and down. Up and down his spine her hand traveled to ease his despair as he tried to remain calm, reckoning with his display of humanity. I felt worse by the second. He kept softly hitting his palm against his forehead, over and over. Was he trying to forget? Did hate himself?

I think it was the first moment I ever really saw my father, not some granite figure. He was no island anymore, he was no rock, and neither was I. It was then and there that I knew the truth. We were all broken and crying. It was the same for me and for every last fragile one of us.

Soon, my mother had her arms around him, and he kept saying it

"Dad's gone. Dad's gone. Dad's gone— "

He grew quieter but he repeated it over and over and over as she held him tight and cried with him, nearly soundless. And from the stairwell in my Spider-Man pajamas, I watched. I watched until their tears stopped falling. I couldn't wander down and join them. I couldn't hold my father's hand. I couldn't weep into his jeans. He wouldn't accept my acts of love. I couldn't pet his wet hair down and tell him all the heroic thoughts I had about him. He would not listen. Instead, I slowly and quietly walked up the carpeted steps to my room and closed the door on it all.

In the pitch black, I moved to my bed and fell flat. I wept for everything. I wept for my dad and for dads dying. I wept enough for every kid that ever found something to cry for. All the lonesome souls like me. For all of the young boys who knew no love from their father, and would not miss a grand-pa in death. For all the dreams, flying themselves away into the dusk each evening. All the dead fireflies. All the misunderstanding and confusion, swallowed love and feeling. I wept for everything, and I wept for my father.

In that bed, I would not sleep. I replayed the scene from the kitchen again and again. I stared up at the ceiling, eyes bloodshot and pained, and I asked God all the young questions that enter the mind of a child. I asked on behalf of us all. What did it mean? Where would we go, and when would we get there? Would we ever leave? And even then, I knew I would always remain. I would be endless in Johnston, in that room.

I close my eyes and I still see my mother's arms around my father.

In the sky that night, I saw Jesus. And though He was an infinite and all knowing God, I knew I would never have the answers He had. I saw the stars and the moon and felt universal in anguish. I had no ability to sort it out, but it was there, in the blues, and I knew.

And I know it now, ever still.

*

I think about my grandfather dying. I think of the tragedy of fathers and sons.

As for tonight, I'm in my backyard looking up at that same infinite canvas. Those same bright stars like faraway angels; that same moon. I'm having a smoke thinking what a shame it all was and was not. I think about my father coming home from a long day's work, wet with rain.

Dad, I have a vision where you return. You're trudging through my backyard, and you fall knees first on the grass, weeping and broken once more. And I think no, I wouldn't. I would not and could not embrace you. Not then and not now. You were oceanic in distance, apart. You were a great white burning star. And I chased you and lost you and fell. And wherever you are, I hope you're crumbling, knees bent forever. I hope you're looking for Ma and for me. I hope you're hungover and desperate and crushed. I hope you see the face of God and have doubts, guilts, questions and anguish. You fool. You bastard of a man. You sufferer. In the great black void of the night, I'll hear you cry and say nothing in return. From the wooden floors, you'll crawl and you'll plead. You'll hit your forehead with your palm. You'll lie flat and defeated and wrong.

And through the fields of Johnston, I'll hear whispers: *Your Father! Your Father! He's gone!* And I'll go out to the yard. I'll drop my knees to the grass. I'll look up at the stars and weep freely at last.

I will then have it out with my God.

26

Driving home from Jimmy's in the last hours before dawn, the horizon is sweeping. The thing about Johnston at night is you can see for miles through the clear atmosphere. There's nothing out here to disturb it. Every star that ever burned throughout the ages flashes and speckles in the vast blanket of black.

Somehow in the grand infinite universe, here I am, driving my Saturn through the empty Johnston streets at three a.m.. The Mexican joint AzTeca is shut off for the night on the corner of Elm, underneath a bent streetlamp, light flickering. The reliable Shell station is still lit, though halfheartedly, open only if necessary. On nights like these, sometimes I'll tour through the whole town, visiting my old haunts and checking up on everything. Someone had to make sure it was all alive and well.

Johnston can be plotted out in a series of small squares, backroads, and blocks. It's a neat little grid with every section distinct. It's filled almost entirely with middle- to low-income homes apart from the old palace on Green Street that is held up by these heaven's gate pillars that are about a hundred feet high and nearly the width of silos. There's also the ivy laced mansion on Main Street where nobody ever lived. Everyone I knew growing up wanted to break into it for parties and such, but it was protected fiercely by the city. The ivy mansion is the one I love most, and I've always believed that one day a mustached bureaucrat would buy it for no damn reason at all and take it off the grid forever. For now at least, nobody had it. Maybe one day I'll hack some lucrative racket or write a book good enough to sell and rake in enough paper to buy it myself. *Can you imagine?*

I'd be cigar mouthed and glorious looking out the high attic window like all my midnight childhood fantasies, casting ideas down and around the street looking over everything in Johnston, my town. Maybe with a whiskey too. And a good woman who loved me. One day down the line.

Until then, I'll wind my way up Factory Street and pass by Ben Vandenheuval's old house. I'll reminisce on friends long past and distant. Ben moved away when we were fifteen, following his pops out to a military base in New Mexico. Ben was a good sort. Braced teeth and sporty and strong. A real up and comer with good discipline and a solid family. I miss him just as I miss the others who are long gone. I could tell you a story about nearly every home that lines these blocks of Johnston. Generations of families have taken root here, committed to carrying the flag, rooting down, and continuing on in the tradition of those that came before. As a kid I used to memorize the streets according to who lived there. On Factory there's Ben, Elly's house on Hillsdale, and yes, the Finchers's—if you asked—are still right on the corner, where Country Road VV meets French before carrying on to endless farmland. I dedicated myself then to knowing every crack in the sidewalk, every secret passage, every route for every place possible.

I'm past Factory now and making a right on Ivy which winds its narrow way all up and around through the back of town and to Johnston Park which has stood there all my life. Pavilioned and swing-setted, it looks over the baseball diamond of my childhood. In the distance is Johnston Hill, a looming grass mountain set proud on the very edge of the town, ancient and my favorite landmark. As kids, we would always go up there. It was one hell of a meeting spot, to plan and get away. To laugh and share hidden smokes. To make out on that tall green bit of planet while getting close to the stars was about as good as it got back then. God, I hadn't gone up there in sometime. Funny what habits you leave behind. In the winter it gets blanketed in elegant diamond snow and all the Johnston kids sled down it until their faces turn blue. I was probably around twelve when everyone became too cool for sledding. Years later, I realized that nobody was too cool for anything.

I'm driving past Johnston Park and dreaming about those days. The days of holding hands and making dares on the playground. I remember Jenna Ollie, and smile. There was one night where we slipped away from our friends and families and had the whole place to ourselves. We climbed all the way to the top of the playground and sat on the flat roof of the slide. She told me all about her parents getting divorced and her mentally challenged little brother. She had sandy hair and giant baby-blue eyes, innocent and kind.

I told her I was someone she could trust because I was sure that I loved her. That summer night, after we told one another secrets, we kissed on the roof of the slide. I thought maybe I'd found that fairytale feeling all the movies went in for. That same year though, Jenna had to pack her bags and follow her family out east to Pennsylvania and we lost touch, just like that. Our romance was just a taste, as it goes, but if she ever showed face around Johnston again, I might marry her still. *Oh, to be young.* Johnston Park.

I drive on past and take a left on French to swing by where it all happened long ago—Johnston High. It was built right on the edge of a corn field and was connected to both the middle and elementary schools. The buildings are made with deep auburn brick and thick concrete rooftops, longer than they are wide. Out back by the track is the football field where the youth were helmeted and strapped like gladiators. I never fully went in for that sort of thing, but I did go to games back when Leon played. Johnston is one of those prideful athletic communities. I still remember the smell of the field and the sound of pounding feet in the bleachers on those chilled fall Friday evenings. I remember the lights, how they were bright and shined for miles. When the city stopped everything and came together for those battles it was almost religious, like an ancient tradition. I admit it felt spiritual.

I let Johnston High fade in my rearview and continue on. A few miles through the country and I'll be home. God. My whole life in this town. An eternity, right here. I'll be thirty soon, three decades. Three decades of childhood sidewalks, parks, schools, longing, and hills.

Every hidden beautiful corner of Johnston I knew and loved so well. My heart beats and belongs to these simple times, the nostalgia and the undeniable hope of these country roads and the wind on the inside of my Saturn, swirling. My hair moves in the wind and there are no clouds or smoke in the sky. It's clear as always, running straight up to Heaven. The road feels smooth and familiar. It beckons. It begs me to drive. I smile and breathe. I bet I can ride on through morning. I know the road will take me wherever I please. It's that kind of feeling, that number on the dial. And it almost happens. I almost grip the fading leather wheel and go after it. I almost fetch me a spot somewhere in Montana or Colorado, somewhere new and promising. Somewhere waiting. Another night. I'll leave some other time. When the stars aren't burning so bright. When Johnston isn't so silent and nice.

27

At some point, Prince got it in his mind that he wanted to visit a few long-lost cousins, aunts, and uncles in Daneport, Iowa, for a weekend. I hadn't been in years, and after a long paint session at the Vances's old place, a shack-like home covered with fallen leaves from a nearby adjacent towering oak, I zoomed on over to Prince's and we packed up and hit the road.

In the passenger seat of Prince's blue Ford F-150, I hang my arm out the window and let it cut through the warm August wind. Soon the leaves will be changing and everything else will follow. That was the thing about the Midwest man, the seasons. In California I hear it's sunny all year, just one long extended summer bath. Well, what I know is that this far north, in Johnston and the whole Midwest, we have every part of summer, fall, winter, and spring, over and over again.

With each new season came change and resurrection, each year was marked in a concrete way. It's romantic how a red-hot midwestern summer simmers gently and slowly into a fresh cooling, most breathtaking fall, where the trees along the rivers shimmer vibrant yellows and reds and dying greens. Burnt orange horizons mark our part of the country before winter, and in your bones, you can sense that we are all standing at the long end of a shortening line, one last wonderful edge to look over before the harsh white winter bites and holds furious for the yearly December descent.

What is a man without these treacherous months, standing frozen and bare to the elements, humbled and struggling? Not to mention the beauty. There is no conception of man quite glorious enough to capture, paint, or imagine the year's first snowfall. There is nothing like that spiritual glide, that wonder, shining white and gorgeous, floating down from the sky. Freezing and pure, crystalloid like diamonds, it covers everything. I never missed the first snowfall. I'd stand in my yard, crisp grass beneath my bare feet and bask in it.

Winter makes the spring and the summers what they are. Just as dark defines light and pain defines joy. They need one another. To think there are places out West never freezing, places where there is no shedding of coats during the wide celebration of the revitalized sun breaking through in the springtime. For them it must be one continuous folding, day after gorgeous day. Where was the story in that? And how did they ever keep time? I imagine in California it's just one long year, where days race by in a flash. Before they knew it, they were probably on their porch in their robes, somehow sixty, smoking cigarettes, looking out at their dry grass and wondering aloud, where has it gone? Time. With us, here in the hard-earned Midwest, we bury our clocks in the snow and retrieve them in spring when everything melts, cleansed and more thankful to have them. For now, summer coats my skin. Prince drives the Ford like a pro, and most everything feels right about this.

It didn't take Prince long to get over our failed bar-owning venture. He doesn't really understand how it had played out at the core, but Prince has always had a real knack for accepting things in stride, and moving right along, perpetually assured that something else was on the horizon.

That's something most people didn't grasp, not in their whole searching lives, the idea that what is yours is yours, and what isn't, isn't. We're both pretty fantastic about the beautiful now. I never saw Prince hang onto much of anything apart from what happened with his pops, and that's a different beast altogether, that was something he would never relinquish, not ever. It dawns on me, perhaps *that* was the choice all along, that we can hold onto one single crux with both hands, but just one. There's no room for others. Regardless, Prince had it figured out. I knew he wasn't going to talk about the bar for a long time, in the same way he hadn't brought up Shelby for weeks now. I knew he was on. Moving again. Head up and wandering, curious.

We're drinking from a couple to-go cups of coffee from the Shell getting all jazzed up, and it's the energy we need on our four-and-a-half-hour journey through Wisconsin into Iowa and Dubuque.

"Alright pal," Prince goes, "well here's the deal. I ain't seen a few of these bunch in years, but I remember Kassy being all sorts of ideal and blonde and excited about you last time we saw her. I'm thinkin you play your cards right, man, and she'll be yours, all yours. Wouldn't that be somethin, Cash? You in the family? Might make me take a couple more trips to Iowa, huh? That wouldn't be so bad now, would it?"

"No, it would not," I admit. Truth is, I remember Kassy clear as day. It's been years but we'll be reunited at last. Prince's cousin in my mind all of a sudden has me thinking about how fast everything can change and how navy blue enigmatic the world really is. It's the color of hope in the heart.

God, I'm all coked up on coffee, feeling downright electric, looking out the window at the long sections of gorgeous sprawling valleys throughout the countryside. There's nothing like this Midwest landscape, these hilly swaths of land rolling and flowing all around, as far as the eye can see. Down in the valley there are corn fields and countless patches of harvestable seeds, farms, cows, and goats, winding semi-trucks and their drivers, of course, of course. But these patches of deep green oceans are the greatest. We drive all the way up through the plains and get high as possible in the land. At the top, swerving and curling, we look out both sides of the truck and see the whole country around us. Miles and miles of fields and occasional forest, always freedom. And the air is so clean it will heal you. No air comes cleaner across America and of this, I am sure. You can see herds of sheep, sometimes bison, and my favorite of all, horses, moving their way through the whole blooming universe before them— free. I tell you, driving through Wisconsin in summer can make a man think about God and angels and smile.

I say to Prince, "That's the thing about these drives, every time man, every single time, I'm lookin out at those plains and I feel like an animal myself, ya know? Like one of those birds but in cars and the air is so damn clean man! Where else could we possibly be? I can see a hundred miles east from here! All the way to fucking Maine man, I'm serious, doesn't it look unstoppable?"

And Prince laughs hard at that. I love it, whenever Prince and I are on the same page about something he'll just laugh and shake his head and say, "Yeah man, yeah man, yeah," his black hair slicked back, even in the swirling wind.

He reaches into the center dash, speeding fast as ever through the hills, and pulls out a spliff. Brown and crisp. He must have rolled it back at his place before we left. He's smiling emphatically and all at once he could be five again. Prince loves to smoke. He's one of those cats that could fool you too. It was nearly impossible to be absolutely certain whether he was high or not. It just sorta matched his personality, ya know? His sensibility. You really had to know him to tell, and unfortunately, the same cannot be said about me.

When I smoke I get red eyed and silent or too philosophical and strange. All these big, Earth-shattering thoughts fly in and out of my head and either render me mute or incomprehensible. Still, when Prince wants to smoke while driving headfirst through the valleys between Wisconsin and Iowa I say yes, and yes again. This was it, man—the life! Life on the road!

Prince goes, "take the honors, pal," and so I light the thing up and inhale. I breathe it in and hold it down, deep to the roots of my lungs. To get high is to get high, yeah? I'm never half in, not on anything. I pass the spliff back, coughing a bit out the window. The smell sails around briefly before escaping, running loose to the countryside like all of those horses. We smoke the thing down, and Prince tosses it to the pavement, flying by.

God, we're in it now. The countryside is amplified, bright and mysterious and magnificent. The sensations man, they're the whole deal. The feeling of cloth on the black old seat and the rubber beneath my forearm on the window's graying edge. The near neon red lights on the radio, the cigarettes in the cup holder, ashen. The polychromatic terrain all around, out the window, the sea! Green brown yellow gray orange and blue. The blue blue blue deep navy blue sky flying up and overhead is endless! The clean, clean air, always recycled and giving back, a gift from the countless trees of all different stature. They sideline our travels, towering over us and becoming our guides. And driving the Ford, Prince is in the pocket, I just know it. He has these square old black shades on, unshaven, smirking, and his trusty white T, black pants, and work boots, weathered.

So here we are, the heart of the journey, in matching white tees and boots. My blue jeans feel smooth, worn down, and have a couple burn marks right by the front pocket. They're black orange and singed in that spot. Prince puts some music on. U2. I coulda told you he'd play them. Prince loves these guys, often saying things like "the *Joshua Tree*, Cash, is the best, it's the best, it's one of the best albums ever made," and I'd laugh and shake my head, but I tell you what, today, moving like rockets through the valley, high, giant, and limitless, U2 might as well have been God manifested. Bono's voice sounds almighty, resounding. He's delivering the message. Prince has these great booming speakers in the truck and he blasts them throughout all the land. Bono serenades the cows in the pastures and the farmers nearing their weekend, optimistic. He's singing about running and hiding off, tearing down all the walls that hold us, reaching for the flames among the nameless streets. You see what I mean?

Today we're really on it man, rolling and rolling and rolling. We begin to sing. I'm pounding the drums on the dash, whipping my head back and forth and truly believing we have found it at last. We are U2 and U2 is us. And it dawns on me that these are the essential moments. Music, art, and life. Friendship. This communication, one and both, flying through the universe, high and alive. The sky and the valleys and the animals and the music and us. Nameless and together. One beating heart on the road.

28

The last time I saw my mother was the winter of my twenty-fourth year.

I had long since moved out of the house; and didn't stop by as often as I should have. Ma called and wanted to have dinner before she and my father left for the weekend to visit his dying uncle. I hadn't visited home in quite a while, but Ma and I had gone for a frigid walk through the winter pathways of Johnston the week before and talked about the ins and outs of everything, so it wasn't as if we weren't staying in touch. That wasn't an option for her. She never once wavered in her devotion, from my birth on up she wanted to be by my side, to help and protect me however she could. We would get together from time to time just to touch base and I'd tell her about my schemes and happenings. She knew I had no fucking clue where I was heading either, but always had faith in me somehow. I'd keep her in the loop, detailing what the gang was up to and if there was a woman or anything filling my heart. She'd always, always ask me about God and if we had spoken recently. I always told her yes though that wasn't always true.

"Good, Cash, good," she'd kind of whisper to herself, and she could breathe easy once again.

I spent a great many years growing up wanting to return the favor of her love. I wanted to defend her and shield her from things as she had always done for me. I couldn't stand anything negative happening to her, or seeing her sad or upset and I always hated the way she served my father and everyone else around her, so graciously, with nothing in return. She was always sacrificing, always taking the high road. Whenever I got angry at the injustice of it she'd look deep into my eyes and remind me, "We're called to love."

Ma talked a great deal about love and Jesus, and I mean a great, great deal. And so, she served my father and everyone in Johnston as Jesus would, and loved them all the same. I knew my father didn't deserve that love but then again, did any of us?

Anyway, Ma called me up and said it'd be nice if I stopped by for dinner. She said my father wanted to see me, and that she was going to make spaghetti. I knew the first part wasn't true, but I agreed to go all the same. Home I went, half expecting it to just be the two of us.

Utterly freezing, I knocked on the front door and remembered all the times I heard that wooden echo from the inside. Every time I came over, I still knocked as if I was a stranger or something. I suppose I was just announcing myself before walking in regardless. Muffled from behind the entrance I heard my father bellow, "come in," so I did. I took my boots off at the door and wandered around the staircase to my left, turning at the corner. My mother stood in the kitchen finishing her preparations and my father was reading the newspaper at the table. He didn't even take his eyes off it as I passed and kissed my mother on the cheek.

"Hi honey," she said.

"Smells incredible, Ma."

"You're just in time."

So, I walked over, hung my jacket on the back of the chair, and took my seat across from my father, just as I had done a thousand times before. His eyes still glued to the paper, I said, "Anything good?" And he ruffled the pages a bit and just grunted. Ma brought over a piping bowl of fresh green beans and set it down.

"Need any help Ma? Suppose I should have asked that right away, huh?"

"No honey, that's okay."

And I think what a shame. Her taking care of my newspaper grunting father and a son who doesn't call enough. My dad took a big old swig of Budweiser and set the can back down with a clink while Ma brought over the bowl of spaghetti. Her homemade marinara sauce and all the works were on the table, ready and enchanting. She finally sat down and offered a prayer.

"Heavenly Father..." and I admit my mind wandered but I knew that she thanked him for me and my safety and health. She prayed for the hungry, the sick, for the hurting families, and more. God, if everyone prayed for one another like my mother did then we'd have a much better world, that's for sure. Either God would answer, or the people would, but wasn't that more or less the same thing?

She served up the beans and we passed the food around. I buttered some bread and my dad said, "Got any work?" by which I know he meant *have you found a serious job*?

After I had given up my job working at Sureland with Leon, I had only been painting and collecting odd jobs around town. I wasn't worried about it.

"Nah, not yet. No. Here and there though."

His eyebrow twitched while he spun his fork in slow disappointment but that was all he could muster.

"So, you're visiting Dave, yeah? How bad is it?" I asked.

"Blood clot," he mumbled.

"Well, we've been meaning to visit for a while now anyway," my mother added. "We'll leave tomorrow afternoon."

"It's pretty nasty out there," I said. It was far below zero temperatures with a fierce wind.

"I've seen worse," my father retorted under his breath.

Some people in Johnston, and I'm sure other places too, had this bad habit, this way of comparing experiences saying shit like *in my day* or *seen worse* or *been better* and mostly it was harmless but mostly it annoyed me. It was just something to say. I don't know. Maybe it was just *him* saying it.

It was downright treacherously freezing fucking cold in Wisconsin come winter, especially in late January. Out there in the wilderness was the kind of air that iced the hair immediately and forced you to fits of coughing. We were in the thick of frostbite days and nights the whole of that week, and the weekend had forecasted storms. So, when my father said he'd seen worse, I knew he was full of shit. But, I kept my mouth shut.

For my mother, mind you, I said nothing apart from, "This is so great Ma, thank you."

She smiled.

"You're welcome honey, so glad you could make it."

And it was true. My mother was a sensational cook. In between bites of noodles and red sauce and bread, I watched her twist her fork clockwise in the sauce and wrap it all wonderfully clean into a bite. God, she looked so exquisitely Italian and elegant when she did it. I could never hope to make anything look that easy. She was exhausted, though. She was getting these creases in her forehead, and I really could have wept right then and there thinking about it— her being tired, yearning for love and affection and peace. Nobody with enough love and affection could get creased, I thought.

In between bouts of silence, Ma asked a few questions about Prince and Leon, and I answered best I could. That was the thing about Ma, always caring, and genuinely curious. She wasn't asking just to ask. She had real love for my friends, just as she did for everyone. God the Mother. I'll never forget, on that evening she wore her blue and red Christmas sweater that she had hand stitched. It was about as endearingly spirited as possible, growing old with a few seams running out of time. Ma, I will buy you more sweaters someday, I may even sew them myself. My father finished his meal quickly and said, "Thank you." He cleared away his plate, dropped it in the sink, and then shuffled out to the garage for a smoke.

Just Ma and me. She let out a deep troubled breath and I knew what was coming.

"It pains me to see this between you and your father."

"What do you mean, Ma?"

And my mother's eyes grew anguished. She couldn't hold her sadness back and it nearly killed me. No woman like my mother should have eyes so sad. She looked at me a bit longer, tearing up, searching for the right words to say.

"Cash, he's your father."

And that simple sentence cut right to the core. That simple sentence could have broken my young heart straight in two. There was so much to say, a lifetime of rebuttal. Poetic explanations and tragic tales of father and son, but I let none of it sail through the air. I didn't need to. She was in the room, and she knew. She was there for it all, by my side. She raised me and saw the whole story unfold. It was my time to be there for her.

So, I swallowed my pride and said, "I'll try harder Ma, okay? I will. I promise."

And she believed me, though I didn't fully believe myself. All I knew was that I owed her my life, and for her, all was possible. She smiled, wiped away a tear and said, "I'm sorry."

"Don't be sorry, Ma. Don't you ever be sorry for a thing."

"I just—I want to get on."

"I know Ma."

"I want to love one another."

"I know Ma. We will."

And with that I could tell she felt better. An emotional woman, my mother. She had oceans of love inside her. She was so damn strong she didn't cry half as much as she probably should have. I watched her closely as she took a few bites of her green beans. I reached over and took her hand like she had taken mine so many times when I needed it most. We always held there, hand and hand, for a long moment, until one of us squeezed tightly the other, and that was the signal to end it. And it was always me ending it. I looked down as I held her and thought, with these hands she has served so many. With these hands she has loved. Working, giving hands, perfect in age and grace. And for maybe the first time ever, I didn't squeeze to end it. I had tears in my eyes.

"I love you, Ma."

"I love you too, Cash, more than all of the stars in the sky."

29

I'm sitting on the fourth-floor couch in the attic of Prince's family's house positively sky'd, and talking with his cousin Kassy. She's got this cropped atomic blonde hair that goes down just past her jaw and glacier blue-gray eyes. She is covered in tattoos, and I'm transfixed by the long wrapping snake around her left forearm and wrist.

"I just got it one day," she says, and smiles, and we're on a winding tangent revolving around art. The way she speaks, animated with her hands, creates an illusion of the snake being alive. I'm doing all I can to keep my eyes open, worn out and dizzy from the day and the weed. Her arms wave and spin through the foggy smoky air as she tells me about the future of fashion and all her European influences, how if she had it her way she'd cycle through wardrobes every couple of weeks, and I dig her, I do, but she keeps asking,

"What are you thinking about?"

"What do you mean?"

"You're just sitting there staring at me." She smiles.

"I'm just listening," I say, and pleased, she continues.

Sometimes I can't get past what my eyes can see and become completely lost in aesthetics. I'm watching Kassy's lips wave and shape her language and wondering how on God's Earth she could possibly have teeth so white and perfectly shaped. I'm eyeing a couple freckles beneath her left eye, and the blondeness of her hair which reflects the lamp light from the corner behind her. What would that hair look like grown out and falling down past her shoulders, which, exposed, reveal the face of a lion, her first tattoo. Then it's her belly button and toned core. She says something about surgery.

"Surgery?"

"For my breasts."

"Oh. But they're perfect."

"Well, thank you, but—" and she's off again, talking about her sister being the tiniest, sweetest little thing ever but my eyes follow her collarbone and then down to her legs, which are painted with ripped jeans exposing her deeply tanned thighs. *You see?* So, when she speaks of London and her travels, despite honorable intentions, my mind wanders, on and on and on.

Truth is, I'm too high. Way too high. I knew this would happen. Twenty minutes ago Kassy loaded her purple pipe with her strongest stuff and giggled like a little girl packing it up.

"Just you wait, Cash. You're gonna love this stuff."

She told me some story about her weed dealer Kyle who was 300 pounds and Hawaiian.

"He's, like, gloriously lazy, but so fun. He's always just chillin and playing video games."

And she's pushing the green in, and I'm already spinning, drunk and still high from earlier. She takes a Superman lighter out of her pocket and sets the whole dramatic thing in motion. Before I know it, I'm breathing in smoke from the pipe and soaring impossibly higher and higher. With every second that passes, I'm sinking further into the couch. I hold tight to her glowing image in hopes that I don't lose my grip on reality. I listen, best I can. I still have every noble desire to be with her.

*

Prince and I show up around six or so to this grand old mix of family and friends. The house looms ancient and tall on Daneport King Street. The roads in this part of town rise and fall like valleys on uneven earth, lending themselves to breaks in concrete and deep potholes which make driving an adventure. On top of that, there are scattered patches of the street which are, for reasons unknown, composed of collections of red shaded bricks. We park near one of these patches. The house is green paneled with a weathered white roof gathering leaves from the nearby enormous maple trees. Outside, gathered on the sprawling front porch, are a collection of strangers. I don't know a single one of them.

"What the fuck have I done?"

Prince laughs. "It's gonna be great," he says.

High and hyper-aware, we walk into the fray.

Before I know what is good or bad I'm having a Budweiser and talking agriculture with a brown curly haired man I assume is Prince's uncle Eric I met once about a decade ago. Meanwhile, the sun begins to set over the rooftops of the other Daneport homes all the way down to the Mississippi River, kissing goodnight to what I assure you is a reassuringly fine city. I weave my way through conversations here and there, and an older guy in an Iowa Hawkeyes wrestling shirt is flipping brats and burgers on a red rusted grill on the far end of the porch and it smells terrific. There's something about the smell of a grill in the dying summer heat accommodated by beer and being surrounded by those of good spirit that really moves me. A Midwestern grill out, tough to beat it. Prince is off chumming with a few girls he knows in the first floor living room when I walk by to discover the bathroom. I turn the handle and enter.

A moment of silence. My first few seconds of recalibration. The bathroom, in moments like these, is a sanctuary. I close my eyes and let the muted voices beyond the door calm me as I relieve myself and check in. I'm gauging my balance, leaning a bit on each leg back and forth, mindlessly swaying in and out of delighted numb feeling and near unconsciousness. I turn to the sink and wash my hands, attempting to ground myself. I'm staring at my face in a dusty, water speckled mirror, feeling higher somehow and more drunk than I did when I first entered the bathroom.

"Get it together," I whisper. My cheeks look sweaty and my eyes are a little red surrounding the blue and black. I'm on the fringe, fretting out a bit, so I take a few deep breaths, grip the side of the sink, and try to talk myself sober. After a minute of this I feel better. I wink to my reflection like a fool and then grin. I go back out to the people, renewed.

They're a small sea of animated souls getting into bed with one another. Often at parties I'll find a way to take a seat somewhere, be still, and just watch for a while. I love to see all the different shapes coming together and moving apart. Talking and smiling widely, drinking, laughing, and of course, there are always the intense few, diving into politics or religion or something serious. It sure is a cosmic scene. It makes me think of science and the atom and the universe. How we're all just little particles moving and fluttering in and out, frenetically trying to be compatible with one another. People are really something.

So, I venture back out to the gathering and the whole ordeal seems to me a great journey. I sit on the cotton weaved beige red and yellow thing of a couch on the first floor and notice Kassy coming in through the open doorway. I hadn't seen her outside, so she must have just arrived. Years have passed but seeing her now I have the feeling that we might just be two of those compatible atoms. We're older now, and forward leaning, less hung up. Once you get into your late twenties, all bets are off. The games are direct and clear, with better odds. Kassy sits down next to me. She gives me a hug and little else matters. Her smile and pleasure in seeing me again is enough to win my heart. Two hours later, she takes my hand and leads me away from the others. She heads up the stairs and I watch her walk.

*

On the fourth story couch in the attic, I sit, gazing at the snake. Moonlight comes in through the sky window and the room is intensely warm. I'm fresh off another purple pipe hit and watching all of Kassy's movements. In between ripples of thought she stops for a moment, and we take each other in. Suits me fine, these silences. Her gray eyes are searching, smiling, and I have the sensation we're mindreading.

"Your pupils are so big," she says.

"So are yours." We both open our eyes wider, as wide as they'll go, and then we're two happy aliens laughing. When she giggles like that, so open and free, it makes me think if I had anything to my name, anything at all, she could have it.

I look down at her arm and begin tracing the snake. Little bumps, almost tinier than eyes could see, emerge from her skin.

"That one's my favorite," she whispers.

"Mine too."

I can't help but touch her, my hands want to study her figure. She rotates her arm as my fingers follow the serpent. We look into each other's eyes again but now we can't deny it. That singular vulnerability that arrives before the moment. That unknown, intoxicating current of oncoming passion. The opening. My heart beats wildly as she reaches over and takes my hand in hers. She begins to run her fingers along the fabric of my blue jeans, pulling on my belt buckle. I glide across her belly button with the back of my hand and settle it around her waist. She traces the ridges of my face, and I do the same. My thumb gently brushes her bottom lip, and she kisses it softly. Her cheek bones are round and pronounced and she moves her fingers to mine before we glide through her product laced hair. I massage her head gently, and she hums with pleasure, whispers, "That feels good."

She wraps her hand around my forearm and begins to kiss the inside of it slowly. I move to massage her back, to her lion on her shoulders. I drift down to her belt loop near her ass as she holds my iron necklace in her fingers. I take the front of her jeans and grab on. I pull her closer.

Face to face, we've arrived. Her chest rises and falls, her warm breath on mine. We stay there for a while, enjoying the sensation. Her beating eyelashes, black and long. Her smooth skin. She scratches at the scruff on my chin and she smirks, playful. Finally, I lean in, and she closes her eyes. Her lips are warm, soft, slow. Full and coated ever so slightly with the smell of marijuana. Subtly sweet, alluring, she tastes like rapture. She lets out a quiet breath as our mouths hover, and I remember that first kisses are forever. She pulls back and opens her eyes. The sounds of the party float to our attic like faraway stories. The taste of her lingers on my lips.

"I want you," I say.

The searching gaze that she had only moments before transforms. Whatever she was looking for, she's found it. A sure smile now spreads across her face. You can always tell in that first moment, that kiss. The heart and the primal part of us knows. I run my hand through her hair near her earrings and take her, thumb beneath her jaw. I draw her close to me again. Our foreheads together.

"I want you too," she whispers.

We begin again. Soft and slow and then crescendos of passion. We take turns, teasing, floating in each other's air, and in those moments our eyes open and nearly laugh. She kisses me quickly then pauses so I can wait and then press into her. We give and we take and we play. Back and forth. Her hands wander to the bottom of my shirt and start pulling at its edges. I gather it and rip the thing off. The heat emanates off my skin, my open chest. Her fingers move through the hair there as she kisses the curve of my collarbone. I see the moon reflect off my necklace. She kisses up the length of my neck and now forehead to forehead I close my eyes, all of my senses ignited.

"I'm so high," I whisper.

"Me too. Do you feel good?"

"Very. Do you?"

"I do."

And I pull her chin up just barely and we meet again, more aggressive. We sweat. Our moans of pleasure increase the temperature. Our bodies are nearly on fire. Everything else has disappeared. It's only her. We're biting and licking, hands roaming and feeling every inch. My lips and tongue are on her neck.

"God," she whispers.

And I swear she's a star. A midwestern Marilyn Monroe. The small smirk she gives, her hands running through my hair, I know that she could own the whole world.

She kisses me again and says, "It's so hot."

With her mouth on mine, I begin to pull her shirt up and over her head. She covers her breasts in a moment of innocence.

She's unbelievably beautiful, adorned in white moonlight. Hair ruffled, chest rising and falling, she sits and she covers herself, blinking, shy. And I remember her comment about surgery. I find it all moving. I'm consumed by the desire to tell her how perfect she is, every part. Any perceived flaw, any fear, any doubt. I want to help wash it away. I lean closer and I begin to kiss the arm that guards her, my hand on her side. I move my face up and brush my nose against hers, playful. She brushes me back and giggles again. I kiss her quickly and she does it back. Her face scrunches a bit and those freckles beneath her eyes move. I kiss them too and return to her arm. I brush my lips against it again, once, twice, and then slowly I pull it away. She lets out a long breath, revealed, and her fingers run through my hair as her chest now arches in sensation. Her breasts are perfect, and hers alone. I feel them with my hands and I softly kiss her nipples. She moans in release and grips the arm of the couch looking skyward. The length of my tongue traces her, and she quivers in pleasure. Her eyes return to mine and the hesitation is gone. Her hands grip my shoulders and I feel her nails dig in. I move my mouth down to her stomach and unbutton her jeans while running my tongue along her pant line. I pull the bronze zipper down slowly. I can feel her heat on my face. I'm so aroused, I need to taste her, all of her. She wears black laced underwear and I place my lips on the damp fabric. And I'm so high I do not remember anything else about my life. My soul, I'm sure, is above the house somewhere watching. I have no name or origin. I am only this. I look up to her eyes, ice gray, ignited, and she's biting her lip. I return to her pelvis as it rises and falls with her deepening breath. My hands move beneath her ass as her stomach rises up and down, up and down, up and down. I guide her black underwear off both her legs and let them fall to the floor.

In all of the world there is only her and the heat between her legs, and in the moonlight, I move my mouth down. My tongue moves along her thighs, then her lips, wet and defined, molded by some perfect design, and she pulses in the darkness. I move in and out and around her entrance, kissing the sides of her thighs and gripping them, holding them apart. I'm warming her and taking her as far as I can. There is nothing else. And when my lips kiss her again, she says, "Cash."

My tongue moves in and out.

"God."

I move the length of her opening and meet her eyes while I do. She looks down at me, cheeks reddening. We are one body of desire and I listen. I listen for it all and move in tandem with her, every sound, arch, grip of her hands, she tells me, and I bring her to the edge. By the time my fingers enter she is ready to come, and I'm with her. Her arousal drives me wild. I'm pulsing with her too and I almost feel near it myself. My fingers in rhythm, move in and out, in and out, curling and extending. I explore her, the walls and the warmth and the heartbeat, storming.

"Fuck me, Cash, I'm going to come. You have to fuck me—"

She leans up while I stand. She unbuckles my belt and unzips the bronze. She pulls my pants and underwear down my legs and now it is me who's revealed. I'm so turned on I really am pulsing. She smiles and kisses my head, licks the length of my shaft. She leans back on the couch. I kick out of my pants. I kneel down, my legs on either side of her hips. She grabs me and moves her hand up and down. And whether or not she did this often, I don't care. This is for us alone. We exist in the light between our eyes. I'm so, so high. My abs contract as she moves her hand steady. I lean forward just a bit as she comes up on her forearms and takes me in her mouth one more time. Her tongue is hot, her hand firm on the base.

"Oh my God," I breathe out. A few more seconds and I'll come. I pull away and I move down to kiss her. Tongue teeth lips hair. My hands on her face, we taste one another again. I lean her back. Her arms cross behind her head.

She whispers "Fuck me," so softly I barely hear it.

I reach down and grab myself and enter. She lets out an incredible breath of air. And there, on that fourth-floor couch, sweating, high and erect, we meet. Wet and moonlit, we move together. I'm inside and there is no other feeling in life, none. There is nothing like this. Slowly in and out, one body. I grab the back of her neck as our torsos contract. She works her hands and her nails into my chest. She doesn't cover her breasts and I kiss them. I run the landscape of her neck with my tongue and our lips meet again. She begins to accelerate as I fill her with all of me. Our breath matches. Every inch of our bodies is on fire. We'll come together in seconds. She pulses a bit and her walls come together, tight.

And the feeling arrives with enormous power. I think of the planets in the sky and our endless souls soaring a billion miles through space and time. She cries out to the same God we share as she comes. Unabashed, stripped down beneath me and bare. And the sound is so pure. It's the atom in my heart. I pull myself out. She takes me immediately in her hands, and in her passion of pleasure, I find myself coming right after. I am everywhere. We transcend this place and I only wish it could last forever. I'm breathing heavy into her neck. I'm kissing her lips, and in each other's arms, we slowly come back. I have her, and she has me. We're so Godly high and alive.

We stay there for ages, breathing in and breathing out. Floating down. And I'm so happy and lifted. I feel her heart racing before it settles into mine. She wraps her arms around me tighter, hugging me as close as she can, to keep me, to feel me beside her. She kisses my lips, and I kiss hers. I smell the scent of her atomic blonde hair. And as we breathe, we are ageless—young and older till death—we are the same. My fingers slowly move along her spine. The lion on her shoulders. Shudders of pleasure resound and they fade until next time. In an attic in the dark, warm in the arms of a woman, I know I've never been this lifted. I kiss her forehead. I can see it all now. It's clearer than ever. Love, and the meaning of life. I hold her as close as I can, it's her heart next to mine. And from this feeling alone, I could cry.

30

In the car ride home the next day Prince asks about my evening, but I tell him only the essentials.

"Are you going to be part of the family or what?"

"Ah, I don't know man, we'll see."

Of course, the chances are slim. Kassy was on her way back to Kansas and I'm back to Johnson. We were comets just passing in the sky.

Hungover as hell with sunglasses on watching the same never ending Iowa terrain fly by, I can manage no inspiring language. It's cloudy and I left my romantic reverie in the attic. My stomach is in terrible uneasiness and pain, and I'm overthinking everything. What a real out of body experience. Only hours ago I had been praying that the night would last forever, but now, through a thick hazy cloud of afterglow, I am forced forward and onward.

What had happened up there?

I've never felt like crying after sex in my life. What the hell was going on with me? Also, why do I feel so confused about everything? What kind of hungover, depressing torture have I stumbled into? There was nothing but freedom last night but today, I feel shackled. I close my eyes. This too shall pass. Goodness will return, I believe that, but for now, I am exposed. And even for this, I can't help but judge myself harshly. God. What a fight. What is alright is not right. Phenomenal highs and the lowest of lows. On it goes.

And yet, there's simply no denying it. As we drive home through the gloom of the now aching countryside, how I feel doesn't matter. It doesn't change the fact that I had one of the most spiritual nights of my life. Heart on fire, I'm certain I had seen the face of God in that attic, all soaring and plastered and making love to a woman I probably wouldn't hold again for years, if ever. It was beautiful, it was. Everything's okay. I say this to myself over and over and only once does my mind drift to Rose. I have one single thought about Rose and let it go. Fuck it. My headache pounds and I take out a cigarette. Prince drives us home in agreed upon silence.

31

A week after Iowa, I'm shaking and sweating on the stairway of a newly bought home holding what feels like a three-thousand-pound pool table and cursing under my breath.

"This thing might fucking kill me, man."

When I'm not painting, I can sometimes be found in situations like this one. I suppose I'm something of an unofficial moving company, occasionally helping folks move in and out of their homes when they're desperate. It's not my favorite work, but there's far worse, and it often pays decent enough. I'll orchestrate these big moves now and then and there's always a fresh random bunch of guys in Johnston that show up, thankful for the opportunity.

Sometimes I'd catch a note out on Main Street attached to the front door of Mick's Grocery, or calls made around town would be rerouted my way. I'd wrangle those that needed the work, and we'd jump in. You never quite knew who was gonna show up, and that was the only real fun of it.

Today, a few miles from my place on the outskirts of Johnston, I'm moving Frank and Charlene into their new home. They're a true midwestern pair, full of good-natured talk and enthusiasm. They have plans to run a hardware store in one of the abandoned storefronts on Main Street. It's pretty difficult to open a new business in Johnston, though it often has less to do with the business itself, and more to do with the general lack of pie to go around. People also love what they love here, what they're used to and loyal to. We've seen all sorts come and go. Hell, there've been at least four or five different pizza joints that have tried to make a run of it over the years. They were each more delicious than the next, but at the end of the day they'd all go broke one way or another because the people of Johnston had Mario in their hearts and there just wasn't enough heart to go around sometimes.

That didn't mean it was impossible for Frank and Charlene to make a solid enterprise. They're taking over a building that had been abandoned a half year ago when Skip and Harrow, another hardware store, went bankrupt and bounced town. God, I felt for those guys, I really did, I always made sure to visit these little places, send a smile and spend a little on shit I didn't even need. I knew how hard things got. Frank and Charlene seem to have a real solid thing between them though, I gotta say. They're certainly brimming with hope. Truth is, we need a well run hardware store around town, and sooner or later someone had to figure it out. Most of us just scrambled for goods and tools when things got hairy.

So, I'm holding this pool table dripping sweat all over its rich dark mahogany and lifting the other side is Deangelo. No shit, he showed up bright and early at the house and I was as surprised as any.

"Can use the work, Cash. Don't look so shocked. Leon gave me a heads up."

"It's good to see you, man," and that was that. We shook Frank and Charlene's hands and scratched our heads staring up into the massive trailer-truck fully loaded with their collected life.

"Wish I could have put a few more of you on, fellas, but we'll have to do," Frank said.

Yeah, we'll do, but it was gonna take us all damn day. I nodded as I began to formulate a plan, and I caught Deangelo's wide eyes as they reconciled with what awaited us. I laughed, it was fine by me. We'd take fifteen an hour and say no more or less. It was plenty. I just hoped to God Deangelo was the hard worker Leon's always raving about.

"Won't be a problem," I said. "Shall we?"

Deangelo nodded. And I felt that old swell of purpose that comes at the start of any job I began. We were workers, the whole lot of us from Johnston, and when I got myself down to it, I was one of the best around.

An hour later, Deangelo and I are holding this fucking table and I'm trying not to die. We're making it seem like one hell of a struggle.

"One at a time, man," he keeps saying, talking about the steps, "one at a time." We're descending the wooden stairway that goes down to the home through the garage, and it's a narrow sort. The table is nearly dragging the walls as we're moving down. We can hardly see a thing and are hanging on desperate to the three thousand pounds of future pool games. "One at a time, man," he goes, "one at a time." I laugh because I'm the one going down backward, liable to be crushed by the fuckin thing,

"Yeah man, I know, one at a time. One at a time. You gotta move it a little faster though, I'm just barely hanging on here."

"Shit I'm doing the same," he mutters, and like snails we inch back and forth, navigating it down carefully while Frank from the top of the stairwell goes, "There you are fellas, there you are."

Frank has a belly tucked into a plain gray shirt with *John Deere* written across it in faded green and yellow. He keeps it simple and clean this guy, old school. He'll be a fitting hardware store owner, I just know it. Deangelo and I scale down the steps slow and steady.

"There you are, fellas."

I can't help but laugh again. Get your ass down here behind me Frank if you're so sure. Finally we arrive in the furnished basement and I let out a relieved sigh.

"Nice man, fuckin, nice. Really thought I was a goner there for a second."

Deangelo shakes my hand, smiles, and wipes off his sweaty forehead.

We look around, standing on a new tan carpet. It's larger than I had imagined. Shit, if good old Frank and Charlene can afford this place then maybe they aren't hurting for cash at all and will be okay regardless. I have the same question I always have when someone new comes along. Why Johnston? I ask good Frank that and he says, "Change of scenery."

Ahhhh, yes. Simple. Frank is clean as can be.

Deangelo begins to walk back up the stairs and hasn't even caught his breath yet. I clap my hands. Hell yeah. This is what Leon meant. Deangelo knew how to work. I'm not surprised. I follow him up the steps and think briefly about how he was a solid man through and through, still, after so many years.

About three hours later, hands sore and back stiff, Deangelo and I are sitting on the back patio with Frank and Charlene as they insisted upon us joining them for lunch in the afternoon sun. God was it funny when Charlene first proposed the idea. Deangelo's face, man. The hesitation. But they insisted so here we are, and it's all classic American, too. There's lemonade, beer, and sandwiches. Charlene packed these babies with ham and turkey and spinach and mustard and mayo. She put some carrots and potato chips on the side and we're more than taken care of. And isn't it true that if God takes care of the birds, then he will take care of us? I bite down hungry through the wheat seeded bread.

"The healthy stuff," Charlene says.

Deangelo's quiet all throughout but it doesn't matter because Charlene's going on and on about the town and how cute and worn down it is all at once.

"There's a real spirit here," she says. "Really, you can feel it!"

"Yeah. For sure. It's always been that way," I say, taking a drink of lemonade.

Charlene's a school teacher and told us she'd be starting up next week when fall classes officially rolled around. She teaches fifth grade. Elementary! Ah man, I had a lot of respect for those types. It takes a special person to teach elementary school. The amount of saint-like patience that line of work required astounds me. The way Charlene talked about it though you could tell she saw it all as a wonderful opportunity and a privilege, so, there you go, to each their own.

Frank's prone to long stints of silence and staring out into the yard filled with fully grown pines.

What is it you're thinking about so thoroughly, Frank?

I know that look, I'd seen it etched on my father's face a thousand times.

I almost say "Go on, Frank! Go on! Run! Run while you can. There's a whole other free world right outside that plot of land but you gotta go and go now!"

But solid Frank here probably isn't thinking that kind of thing, and I don't want to put those ideas in his head. He's just settling down after all. So, I just sit and listen to Charlene, and she fills me with gratitude. Her eyes light up when she talks about the store and all the magical things she believes Frank will do with it. I gotta hand it to her, she sure is thankful for life. Deangelo swallows the last of his bread, nods and goes, "Should we finish up?" And I smile. He is restless but I have half a sandwich left.

"We will, man. Relax."

A few long hours after that, we stand on Frank and Charlene's new front step with tired limbs. We've been thoroughly worked to the bone. It's an enjoyable, calming sensation. We shake their hands, wish them luck, and say goodbye.

"See you around," Charlene calls out as we walk off.

I swear to God, they're two of the kindest folk I'd met in some time. They're gonna be alright, I can feel it. The slight wind throws Charlene's brown curly mop of hair around her face as they wave us so long and I wave back. She must be one hell of a teacher. We're walking down the driveway and before Deangelo gets in his truck I say, "You wanna grab a drink?" And I don't think he's gonna go in for it but he does.

"Where at?"

"Jimmy's Place, man. Where else?"

32

Like any other night in my bar-home the lamplight comes down moodily in all the right angles, blanketing us in nostalgia. The velvet on the pool table rests patient, full of potential, reminiscent of freshly cut grass. A man and woman dance together as Rush comes out of the jukebox, and they fill me with hope. It doesn't matter to them if they're being watched. They're in the world they've chosen for themselves, and that's something I admire. Imagine being so settled into one another that everything else ceased to exist. Their cowboy boots clap the floor as they spin and move from elegant to sloppy, and back again, always free, always adoring, so much larger than life. They dance on the edge. Do they know how immortal they seem, dancing in bar light?

Deangelo and I are on our second hour, buzzing and rolling along at great speed. With enthusiasm we trek back through memory lane, relishing good tales of old.

He keeps saying, "I can do *one* more, Cash. *One* more, alright?"

So, I'd buy and we'd dive further into the heart of it all. It was never one more, and we all knew that. He's talking about Lyla saying, "I know she's ready, and she ain't say nothin man, never 'bout it or nothin, but she's waitin, right, I just know it. I can see it, you know what I mean? You start to see it."

"Yeah."

"Yeah and I ain't tryin to rush nothin. I wanna take care of it all, be a man, you know what I'm sayin? I gotta be able to take care. Look, you know how our fathers were man."

"I know."

"Yeah and shit, what do we gotta do? We're talkin about family."

"Right."

"Family. We've got to be responsible."

"I agree."

"We're responsible for all that."

And this is the whole point, right? When we got down to it. We begin to talk about the sacrifice of self in this ultimate way, but what do we know? We're all just trying like hell to figure it out. Trying to do just a little bit better than our fathers did, though we still want to believe they did the best they could. I've seen hundreds of families in Johnston, all working this out just the same. As my own family deteriorated around me, I couldn't help but view the whole concept through a painful lens of longing and wonder. Fatherhood, motherhood, sons and daughters, and on. Deangelo's right. *Responsibility*. A higher calling. The desire for it all has become buried deep in my bones, and I only now feel it leak into the bloodstream. I'd almost feared it was dormant, forgotten and abandoned.

When I was younger, I remember believing that I'd find a woman early on in life and run off with her somewhere. I dreamed we'd explore our way across the nation and go from small town to small town renting out dusty old shadowed rooms above bars and staying there until we grew restless, only to find another the next day. I had romantic fantasies of buying only the bare necessities and booze, cigarettes, wrapping this love of mine in bedsheets and playing with her sleep-ridden hair and sun smile. We'd be vagabonds, adventurers, spirits of America. And on occasion we'd show our mysterious faces while walking community sidewalks but be left alone. We'd buy beers from the hefty barbacks and stumble up to our room, lamp lit and laughing, young, drunk and in love. We'd chase each other silly through the apartment canvases and discover all the secrets we were always so curious about. We'd talk endlessly for hours, exploring every hidden corner of our souls. And that would be that. I'd have the money from some long-forgotten book I'd written, or painting I'd sold. Hell, maybe I'd have robbed a bank by then, and maybe she'd have done more of the same. But money would be nothing. We would be everything. The center of the universe, migrating whenever we pleased, anonymous and growing deeper by the day. Shedding seeds and having roots all throughout this American land. God. I used to really dream about that.

But the path to fatherhood feels foreign and impossible now. I see no father in myself. Why is that? I feel no desire to sacrifice my dreams, and I can't exactly lug the kid around and keep the gig running strong now can I? No, I'd have to settle like everyone else. I'd have to sit the kid down and teach them the lessons over and over again until one day they'd finally stick. It'd take immeasurable work. I'd have to feed and clothe and bathe them as babies and forget all about myself. I'd have to abandon my freedom. I'd have to set fire to my innermost workings and reroute the machine. God. I don't know. For some people it doesn't seem so bad. There are plenty of happy families in Johnston. I see them walking around all the time, arm in arm, smiling and soaring, enjoying something I can't seem to fully grasp. A few of them have really found the good stuff, there's no denying it, and it's these few that I sincerely adore, though always in silence and from afar. And yet, the envy for what they have does not disturb me. It hasn't lingered long enough to change my ways, I suppose. Those ideas get no further into my system than the mouth. I take a drink and I wash them back out.

"But I want to be a father," Deangelo says, and I return, snapped from myself and intrigued.

"You will be, man, of course you will be," as if I have any clue what that means.

I see Deangelo's eyes move to the right a bit, surveying the scene. I sense that he's spent countless hours debating this essential leap of life. Fatherhood. He didn't have to explain all the questions and conflicts that roared inside him because I'd debated the same for myself. Seeing him now, I know Deangelo is a bit beat down. Feeling far too old while being so damn young. He's a grinder, and always will be. I saw that today, and had heard all the stories. All at once I feel proud of him, truly proud. We'd gone years and years without a night like this, never returning to the source of so much in our lives, and yet, from a distance, perhaps we did. And though he had gotten himself into runs of trouble here and there, and beaten some men nearly to death for their transgressions, I am proud. I am proud because I believe him to be a good man.

His tough, dark hands are holding the glass, and his fingers shift and move black shadows across the tabletop, blending in with the wood. His veins extend through his wrist and curl around the bones as he moves the drink. He's spinning it around and around while he thinks, and I start watching all the people that are left in the bar, writing their stories in my mind, best I can. Isn't it fascinating? Each person with a novel, a whole infinite story.

I had this girl one time, outside the River Inn, ask me a question as she watched a truck blow a stop sign in the town square.

"Do you ever think of that, Cash? Like that person has a life. A huge life of their own. And we'll never know nothin about it. And there's billions. Billions just like that Cash, *billions*"

Billions, she said, and there was nothing we could do about it. She was right. I thought about that all the time. So many people and not enough time. All of us wandering like ants through the cracks of the sidewalks and completing our business. Not stopping, not waving, not caring all that much from one insect to the next. Just on our path and the path of the few that happened to walk our same way.

I watch all these people that wander through Jimmy's, and I dream about their lives. I wonder where on Earth their souls were leading them and why, and mostly, I just pray that they'll get there. Not all of us did, in the end. We had proof. The lucky few of us were still here. Still singing and dancing around the stage before our lights got flipped off for good. But what a feeling while we have it! What a sensation it is to be alive.

And in Jimmy's Place with Deangelo, drinking and careening through time, I feel the weight of the billions of bones coming up through the Earth, knocking loudly on the door. All those that came before. They're coming for us both, and calling us home. It's me and them—them and me—we're all the same. One family. To be a father or to not be a father, to them that doesn't matter. We are called only to make the most of what we have while we have it. They must agree, the little ants and the bones and the billions of souls I feel I know but simply don't.

"You remember those days, man?" Deangelo asks.

"Which ones?"

"You know, back in those days. The ranch and shit."

"Of course."

"Fuckin crazy."

"Yeah man."

"You know you probably think I don't remember none of that, but I do."

"Nah. I figured you did."

"Yeah. This shit is crazy but, you remember that chicken?"

"Yeah man. How could I forget?"

"All the things as a kid, I remember that most."

"Like it was yesterday."

"So fucked up."

"Yeah."

"That shit wasn't right."

"No it was not."

"I still think about that all the time."

"Yeah. Me too. Honestly."

"Man, that fucker got us, huh?"

"Well, I don't know."

"Nah man, he pulled it over. Cash, if I ain't have you there, I think that guy woulda killed me."

"Really?"

"It's a feeling man, but I could tell. I just knew it, man. I'm tellin ya. I could see that look. I would dream about it, and shit, and I ain't ever told nobody 'bout those things he did. But he woulda done more if you weren't there too, I know it. Think I ought to thank you for that, Cash. I wish I'da killed that fucker myself. I always thought I'd get a chance."

"Yeah, man."

"You ever think about that? Ain't that fuckin crazy, man? After all that, he hangs himself from a tree in his backyard? Don't he think about the consequence? Whole city gon' see you hangin there dead. Purple. Birds on your head. You know I wish I woulda seen it man. I wish I woulda been there to see him hangin there all blue and shit and gone. I'da liked to see that with my own eyes."

"Yeah."

"Evil motherfucker."

"Yeah. You shoulda seen the twins at the funeral."

"What about 'em?"

"Man they were cryin."

"Were they?"

"Cryin man like sobbin like crazy. Snotting all over their faces. Ya know I never thought they could process something like that. But they were cryin, man. It was horrible."

"They were fuckin crazy, too."

"Yeah man, they were. They really were."

And I knew that we were unfortunate to have spent those afternoons on that farm, but Deangelo was right, it would have been much worse if we didn't have each other. Now here we were, all these years later, talking about our lives from the way back. As kids. And it's crazy, sometimes I forget that I am one body, one story, one self. When I look back at my life, I can forget that it was me all along. I try not to think about it too much since I get so damn sad and all. I start feeling kind of sorry for myself, ya know? It'd be nice to go back to those days, to my younger self, all kind and pure and open, just to have a conversation and share a real long hug. I think I coulda really used it back then. What a thought. I knew what Deangelo meant. We hang onto these things for so long. All our life, we refuse to let our nightmares die. The worst parts that just eat at our souls, we preserve. And I wonder now, do I wish I could have killed the creep too? Yeah. Honestly, I think that I do. Well, God got there first and stole all our vengeance. So it goes. At least we have Jimmy's tonight. Deangelo and I crossed back this whole steep divide and set things straight at last. He downs the rest of his beer, and I know I won't see him again for some time.

33

Deangelo is long gone. I nurse the last of my beer, still running backward through time. I'm one of the last remaining in Jimmy's once again. Everyone's gone. I take my glass and pour it down. I know I have to leave before I wander down into a real malaise of melancholy. I step out of the booth, give a slight nod to old Saul, and say goodnight to my bar. I'm out the door. The night is cloaked in a deep black coat and a kind rain falls down softly, the drops are so small I can barely see them tap against the sidewalk. I close my eyes and tilt my head back at the moon, the mist of the coming rain hits my face. All the spirits of my life are out here, climbing the embankments. They'll arrive soon enough. My boots grip the saturated gravel as I turn toward my Saturn. I'm lost in these dreams when I hear wheels turning stone behind me.

A car door closes, and I look back to the sound. Through the calm haze, Rose steps out of a green rusted Jeep, and strides toward the entrance. She reaches for the door, looks to her left, and sees me in all of my wonder. I assume she'll carry on and go on in, but she doesn't. Instead, she releases her hold on the door and turns to me, pausing, as if to say, *yes?*

What a moment. She's looking across the sidewalk, patient in the gentle rain. *Is she really as unphased as she appears?* I smile. I'm telling you, in the dark of the night and the falling water, painted with a few shades of neon from the bar signs above, she is the only story I'd follow.

"What?" I say, and she smirks while crossing her arms. I go for it again.

"What?"

And she shrugs.

"When are you gonna get it together?" The ambiguous question cuts me in half. *Get it together?*

"What the hell is that supposed to mean?"

She shrugs again before disappearing into the bar.

And I'm lost on an island, drifting out to space then and there. Dumb and frozen, rain falling on my head. *What the fuck was that?* The irritation creeps up my spine. She's reduced me to nothing on the growing wet sidewalk with weeds. I grab at the back of my neck and shake my head till it threatens to fall off my shoulders. Fuck it, that's it. I can't let it slide. I move forward, back to the entrance. Get it together? What the hell is that? The way she said it, above me somehow, a judgement. She doesn't even know me. How on Earth could she feel so superior? I throw the door open and stride in. She's standing in that familiar spot, propped on the edge of the bar, waiting. She makes no glance my way as I arrive by her side, hands on the bar. Saul is out of earshot. A million things crowd my mind. She meets my eyes.

"What do you want?"

And again, she's disarmed me somehow. She's gone straight to the source. *What did I want?* The simple nature of the question makes me pause.

"I want to take you out."

She raises her right hand to her mouth, pinky-ringed and graceful, surprised. She actually smiles for a second before she covers it up. She wipes it off and that beautiful, one second window is closed just as fast as it opened. She turns to me and my God it is impossibly green in her eyes.

"Okay," she says.

Okay. *Okay.* Has ever one word felt like lightning?

34

It was four a.m. and he was bandaged all over.

The lights in hospital waiting rooms burn a sinister type of horrendous white that only amplifies the fear, anxiousness, and nausea. I was floating in and out of consciousness having not slept for a day and a half and reality had long since slipped from my grasp. My father was wearing his blue and black flannel jacket over a blood-stained T-shirt, and his stomach moved up and down in slow, labored movements that I assumed caused him a considerable amount of pain. He had gauze wrapped around the upper left side of his forehead and it too was stained with blood. He had avoided any skull fracture, but he was concussed. His right arm was broken, in a sling, and how he had survived, I didn't know. He stared forward into an abyss of horror, completely lifeless and possessed by tremors, biting his lower lip over and over and over. It was raw and soon it would be bleeding too, but I didn't stop him.

There were a few exhausted, well-meaning nurses that walked by on occasion and the dark navy-blue cushions were eroding in the waiting room. I imagined the thousands that came here before me, slowly dying of their wounds or their worry, the chairs molding themselves with their bodies. I felt myself sink deeper and deeper, mind shot and numb. More afraid than ever before. My father and I were the only ones in the waiting room, and we hadn't spoken for hours, not one somber word. I could hear his haggard breath forcing its way up through abused lungs, nostrils and mouth. I'll never forget how I wanted that breath to give up, or the urge I had then to finish what God had started, to remove him from the face of the earth. To me, he was no longer a man. He was a creature, hunched, pathetic and broken.

About ten hours ago he and my mother had been driving home on a long stretch of the backroad VV and had nearly finished their journey. Johnston was in the center of a vicious snowstorm, and the roads were completely iced out, enveloped with white. We were all used to brutal winter roads, but these were particularly dangerous.

In violent wind and below zero temperature, snow fell like a torrential downpour and packed the roads with ice while my father drove cigar mouthed, sleepy and hungover. My mother watched from the passenger side because she hated driving through storms. My father, I'm sure, had insisted. Johnston's country roads are lined with long, deep, and treacherous ditches. On hot summer nights my friends and I would speed alongside them and laugh in the face of what could be a quick and easy death. Ma used to give me long warnings about this saying how scared she'd get thinking of me not paying attention and driving straight down into one of those crevices one day.

"Don't worry Ma, I won't. Don't worry about me," I'd say, but she did anyway.

Johnston had its fair share of tragic ditch stories. Cars missing a turn or sliding too far on ice, somersaulting down never to be heard from again. They were the real, backroad tragedies that you'd never hear about in your bigger city news, but those deaths would scar the hearts of all who made Johnston their home. When we caught wind there was an accident, we knew that nothing was given, and if it happened on a backroad in Johnston, far out in the belly of the country, the best thing to do was to pray. It was a long, long way down.

What happened that night was a short story, and the telling of it fell out of my father's mouth like a five year-old's' incantation of something too large to comprehend. He retched out the details to the doctors while they stood, white coated, earnest, and hurrying. He swayed, hands pocketed and kept his eyes on the floor. He mumbled about the crash in a pathetic slur of shock.

He had lost control of his truck on a brutal stretch of hidden ice and spun out and into a ditch on the right side of VV. It turned and crashed violently, tumbling down. It spiraled its way through the snow and to the bottom of the ditch. From there, my father, mangled in his own right, had to work my unconscious mother from the passenger side, head smashed and limp. And if a passerby hadn't been driving some short distance behind them, she never would have made it to the hospital alive. But through the icescape that night, a stranger who just so happened to be driving home to his family, helped get my mother into his truck and drove with my father to the nearest hospital, twenty miles away. There, she had emergency surgery.

That was the bones of it, anyway, the plain straight details of the thing. While sitting in the waiting room, across from my father, I was sure that if I lost my mother, I would no longer wish to continue. I would kill him, and I would kill myself.

Only a few years earlier a kid named Conner, who was a year older than me, had died in an auto crash. The whole town was devastated. Everyone came to his wake and wept over the unfairness of life and its dark workings. I remember Conner's mother by the casket, not crying, eerily numb and silent. That was the worst. I knew the saddest people didn't cry at all because there was no room for it, they just couldn't. There is such a thing as too sad to cry. After Conner died, I thought that we could leave the nightmares behind us. We had faced tragedy and understood. Car crashes were something that happened, could happen, and did. I was just so shocked that one happened to Ma.

The whole unending time in that waiting room I never once considered that Ma could be gone. Honestly, I sat there and *knew* she'd be fine. If it had happened to anyone else, to me or my father, I could imagine us going but the thing about my mother was she was protected by God. You never saw such a holy woman in love with Jesus in all your life. I always knew that she was favored and that she was taken care of. While I waited and waited, I was mostly just numb with the rage I felt toward my father and myself. For not protecting her. For the wicked, unforgiving winter.

All to say, at least from the outside, I looked far more serene than I think you'd imagine. In all the movies and books, you get this image of waiting room morbidity, wide-open weep sessions with the families when things look perilous. That wasn't the case, at least not for us. On the worst night of my life, it was just me and my father. Silent. Breathing. Blinking through violent white light and monotonous hospital overtones. No, the tragic sobbing hadn't begun. The sad truth was I knew all sorts of folks that didn't even blink at the thought of death and were stoic in its face. While I also knew some hysterics, my father and I were not that breed. He could barely breathe, and as for me, I'd never have the words. So, there we were, silent and waiting when the doctor finally showed his gaunt face.

Of all the moments in my life, I know I'll always remember this most. Right there and then, I stood up and I knew that everything had changed, forever. It's a strange thing, doctors having to deliver the news. Hope draining from the faces of friends and family, all gathered around, hands held and praying with water already in their eyes flowing, asking *what's the word, doc*? Begging to hear that it's all going to be okay, and that the universe protected the best of us.

But when Doctor Clark turned the corner, I knew all at once that the universe did no such thing. I couldn't help but drift up to God, and all of a sudden, I knew. I knew the simple truth. There was no confusion. It was a settling cloud of doom that I would never, ever be able to shake. The green, grinning court jester had taken the seams of the veil and torn it completely in half, showing me the face of death within life, and this image, this void, would always be with me.

Doctor Clark walked up with a gentle pained face, hollowed out from lack of sleep, and was going to have to find a way, yet again, to say what had to be said. I felt bad for him, somehow, for a flash of a second, I felt bad for *him*. He paused for a moment, and it wasn't hard to know why. I couldn't look at my father, but I was sure his face was opaque, dead and unreadable.

"I'm sorry..."

And on it went. I blacked out but I must have heard it. My face was blank as death, untethered and facing oblivion. It's insane, ya know? In all those films actors play it all skyward and faucet-like tragic. But that ain't how it goes. It isn't that dramatic. When Doctor Clark gave us the news there was nothing alive in the depths of my chest. There was no soul. No heart. No guts. I was cavernous. The silence was excruciatingly loud, deafening, and it echoed. I was abandoned. I had no bones or blood or lungs. And how the hell is a man to weep if he is empty? No, there were no tears. There was no argument. There was nothing. Just the pounding drums of death in the quiet. There was only Doctor Clark and his words and my emotionless face.

And why was I blank? The straight unarguable line of it all. The audacity. The shock. It was the clearest evil I had ever witnessed in my life. For I knew that the blackness which took my mother that night had always been there, creeping, waiting and it had finally exposed itself. It had revealed its fangs and had struck. Its deep, insidious nature had finally sprung and the veneer had been shattered forever. No more hiding, no more swimming around in the dusk at sunset. No more ignorance, no more hand holding walks, no more bliss. It was dead. It was all dead. I had seen it. I had witnessed, for the first time, truth, and it was lifeless and foul. And *this,* this was the moment that walls upon walls, all buildings and structures, all the creation inside of me, crumbled to ruin. All the art my mother had shown me, all the shows, all the books. All the loving red seeping kindness had burned and died. I thought about God. And what had been done.

My father said nothing. He only walked away like a ghost while I stayed staring at Doctor Clark. It was as if he had morphed before my very eyes into a revealed mystery, as if he was the savior all along. I knew that I wasn't waiting for grace and warmth anymore. I had no life. No body. No mind. There was just a wave of black.

I don't know how long I stood there but like the saint that he was, Doctor Clark remained stoic and patient. The way I remember it, I stayed there for days, waiting for something to change. And all the others came and went, circling around me, moving in and out of their own tragedies, and paid me no mind. We were the same, in the end. That was one thing, we were never alone. Even in this. We were not unique in our suffering.

All the other doctors ran and scrambled around trying to conserve the very fabric of this here living thing. Even the receptionists, who put on that face of assured calm, received the visiting, healthy, and terrified and did their part. Yes, it was one big moving amoeba of endings, and that was it really. In the hospital you could tell that you were standing on the honest, final frontier. The last battle ground where we sad humans tried to understand the impossible, where we tried to take a stand in the skull-full land of death. And so, surrounded by all the others, I remained firm in that valley. Thinking of God and my mother and waiting for the nightmare to end. But the nightmare would and could not. It was just me and my saint Doctor Clark. And after maybe a month, I sucked some air to my lungs and I spoke before the tears ever came, "can I see her?"

And Doctor Clark did something I knew his type were just not there to do. He let water fill his eyes and his hand rose. He touched my left shoulder. He squeezed it in compassion.

God, you have done this, but why?

I haven't seen my father since that night.

35

I'm running a comb through my hair, the blond likely to fade and go darker as winter approaches. I'm wearing a collared, black, short-sleeved shirt, blue jeans and black leather belt. Cleanly shaved and flossing. Flossing! Rare are moments this clean and committed, but tonight I will be taking Rose out and tonight I must be shining. I'm eyeing my jawline and cheekbones. I've lost a little weight, Leon was right.

"You're skinnier by the day, man, I'm telling ya."

Not enough nourishment. I'll figure it out. I spit the toothpaste out and let the faucet run cold water into my mouth.

I shut the bathroom light off and head into my bedroom. Beige walls, I keep a clean place for the most part, slightly scattered I suppose. An open window lets in the air through a perfect view of my yard. There are some books tossed about. Salinger and Corso and Cheever. Ginsberg and Hesse on the nightstand. Kerouac's *The Town and the City* rests near my pillow. Mr. Michaels, my eighth-grade teacher, and something of a father figure to me, used to assign me all of the greats saying, "You got a shot, Cash. I'm serious."

He believed in me back then, a kid reading Hemingway and Fitzgerald in the back room of the school library for hours. He'd make me write extra essays eventually pushing me through to accelerated English before he bounced out of town to coach football somewhere else. It broke my heart, but on it goes. All those writers are still my favorites. Kerouac and his longing, so sad but hopeful in his rhythmic language and alcoholism, always searching. Hesse and his clear, sensitive genius. They felt like my ancestors in a way, revealing thoughts and feelings that I also carried in my heart and soul. Would they be proud of me now? Tonight, I'd like to think so.

I grab my wallet off the dresser and walk into the living room past the railing that leads up to my childhood room and go straight through to my kitchen. The whole interior of my home is continuous, high ceilinged and wooden. I scoop up my keys, pocket them and head to my fridge to pull out a Budweiser. I crack the seal and think there are few sounds so grounding. The beer goes down calm and golden and helps keep my heart from racing. Every thought of Rose is making me feel damn near boyish. I don't remember the last time I felt this way before a date, but all of my most intense hopes of romance are swelling inside of me. I can't help it. I look out the kitchen window and see a deer sniffing around the salt lick I keep back there. It's a young doe with the mother behind. And the Budweiser goes down easier by the second.

I'm taking Rose out to dinner at a supper place called Tanglewood on the corner of EE and C. They serve things up pretty elegantly there, and it's only a place I'd reserve for special occasions. Other than that, I don't have any elaborate plans. I'm mostly just hoping she'll wanna see me again after dinner. God, if I get even one clean word out tonight that will be a success. The beer finishes as smooth as it started. The deer moves on from the salt lick. I crunch the can down and throw it in the bin beneath the counter. Clearing my throat, I make my way to the door.

There's a subtle autumn chill settling in, and these rainy days have helped the grass grow fast in the face of fall. I have my Saturn parked in the middle of the drive and in anticipation, it waits. *It knows, oh, it knows!*

"Where to, Cash? Where to?"

All polished and fresh and steady. I hop in and turn it on.

Where to, where to, indeed.

This car longs to take me anywhere in vast old America and perhaps one day it will, but for now, it's only a few miles of shadowing country roads filled with changing life on all sides. I can feel the trees and the wind and the sun, all the animals of my land sending their regards. Each reaching, each calling out, aware that I'm moving and breathing deep into the biggest moment of my whole romantic life. I can feel the energy, the scent in the air you only get when you are somewhere locked in the pocket. What a feeling! And my heart beats so rusty and wild you wouldn't believe it. In a matter of moments, I'll be sitting across from all the potential of the world.

I love the faded leather feel of the wheel beneath my hands and the sight of the towering corn in the fields. All throughout sunset those shadows grow bigger, casting long skinny silhouettes of black throughout the countryside. I can sense the river flowing fast and free, though it's a mile or so down from me. It too, knows, and sends its best wishes. I smile because it's a wonderful sensation, knowing you're one with the land. Knowing you're part of the soil, the wilderness, the air. Knowing it's all one destiny, one heartbeat, one astonishing limitless canvas.

I'm playing Johnny Cash and singing as low as I can. I'm getting more hopeful by the second. If Johnny got June, then I can get Rose, and we're all one good straight-step away from a burning passion. I'm imagining Johnny on a stage, drunk and singing desperate songs to the night when he didn't have June. And it's true that he knew her, toured with her, and loved her long before she ever loved him back. I sure did go in for a love story like that. Johnny was committed. He knew what he wanted. And like a coyote on the prairie, he howled up at the moon until that big celestial white lamp came tumbling down to his arms to be held. Imagine! On that stage Johnny dreamt they would share many years, June shining like one thousand stars, and him smiling like a man in Heaven. She loved him. What a feeling, what a life. I'm half a mile from Tanglewood and I think that one of these times I'm going to get it all sorted out nice. I'm gonna hit that first step right on stride.

36

Outside of Tanglewood, Mr. and Mrs. Simmons, the town jewelers, walk hand and hand toward the entrance. In their sixties and wealthy enough, I can only assume they've frequented this place as much as anyone else in town. As I stand there leaning on the back of my car, Mrs. Simmons sees me, stops and lets out a warm, "Heyya, Cash! How are you honey?"

"Good Mrs. Simmons, yeah. You both well?"

"Nothing to complain about!"

"Trying to hang onto summer!" Mr. Simmons chuckles.

"Yeah, aren't we all?"

"You sure look cleaned up!"

She says cheekily, nearly bouncing in glee.

"Ah well. I don't know."

"Be good, son." Mr. Simmons waves.

"So good to see you Cash."

"You too. Enjoy."

"Oh, we will honey."

They walk in and I think how the entire essence of the American Midwest could be summed up in that simple exchange. Those two were still joyful in love after decades of life, striding toward the only supper club they'd ever need, and so full of kindness they could offer me some, free of charge. This place really is something to behold. I scruff my boots against the loose gravel, gray and ashy. The dust rises and floats off with the wind.

God, I could use a cigarette. I'm so nervous I'm actually shaking a bit. Fuck it. I pull one out, and I light it and breathe. That's the stuff. I tip my head to the sun. The Simmons sure are the good ones, the real wholesome backbone of towns just like these. And you could say this about Johnston, most everyone had a kindness in passing. I heard that in some places folks would walk by one another on sidewalks and say nothing. Not even a nod. Well, that's not Johnston.

I search up and over to the other side of the road. There's a house straight ahead, with a rope swing out front, and a singed orange setting sun up above spraying light all throughout the sky as it departs. Complete serenity. No painter or artist could ever recreate it, though they'll keep trying, I hope. The town is down a few miles to my right, and I'm fairly certain it's from there she'll emerge. God. What a beating heart in my chest. I itch the tip of my nose and purse my lips wet. Is there anything quite like this? I tap my foot on the gravel, a slow rhythmic sound. I take one more drag and then snuff the thing out. Right as the clock somewhere clicks seven, I see Rose pulling up in her jeep.

We've all been to the movies, and one thing they get right are those slow-motion moments when the heart stops. It's really like that, ain't it? Rose pulls that green Jeep into the lot and turns it off. She sees me through the glass of her window and smiles. The dust settles off the wheels and the muted music behind her doors fades away. She gets out and hits the lock-horn just once. Like a desert mirage, she starts walking my way, and I know I can't shut up about her walk, but I swear Rose has discovered some sort of equilibrium on the planet floor. Perfectly balanced. It's the first time that I've seen her with her hair down loose. In a multitude of waves, it falls to her shoulders. She wears a fresh white tank that collapses airtight around her body and a light black jean jacket over the top. She's braless and blue-jeaned, wearing brown rugged low blocked heels. She has cleaned herself up, just like me.

Even from the closing distance I see her lipstick glisten and know I'm smiling like wild. From her left the sun sets and she's gilded in it. In the land where it breathes and flourishes, she is magic. Something brought on by God's most patient designs.

"You made it."

"Yes, I made it." She smiles and moves a few strands of hair from her face.

"You look very nice," I say.

"Thanks. Not so bad yourself, all cleaned up."

"Yeah, well, special occasions."

"I'm honored. Shall we?" And I don't know if my tongue will ever catch up to my mind, but I nod and say, "Alright."

I open the door for her and then follow her in, magnetized.

The inside of Tanglewood is a minimally lit space with old red carpets and hanging lamps accented in bronze. Everything is ancient but well kept, in line. There's a tremendous attention to detail about the place. Every napkin aligned, not a chair out of order. Soft jazz plays on speakers and quiet conversations happen everywhere. A retro, 1950s, true supper-club feel. There's a small collection of tables and maroon booths flanking the long salad bar in the middle of the room. Jared, who I never saw anywhere other than here, is the bartender. He's straight faced and efficient, silent and set up in the far back left-hand corner. Rose and I are greeted by Holly Peters, my mother's old friend. She tries to keep it professional but can't help herself.

"Cash, oh God, so good to see you," and she gives me something of a bear hug. "So good to see you. When I saw your name on the list I couldn't believe my eyes. Are you well?"

"All well, all well yeah."

"Sorry, I'm Holly, I'm the host here."

"I'm Rose." They shake hands.

"I've known this one since he was a boy. His mother and I were very close."

"Oh yeah?"

"Alright, alright." I laugh. I know she'll go a lot further down memory lane if prompted. Only in a Johnston supper club does the host hug you in front of your date and introduce herself.

"Ah, okay, I won't embarrass him. Well, so nice to meet you. Follow me." And she grabs a couple menus before guiding us over to the most private booth on the far end of the restaurant. "Arthur will be with you shortly."

"Thanks Holly, great to see you."

"You too, dear. Enjoy."

Rose raises her eyebrows in amusement.

"Something of a celebrity around here, huh?"

"Holly knows everyone."

"Cash, how are you?" Arthur approaches the table, black vested and tall, middle forties. He's worked here as far back as I can remember. His cheeks are hollowed out and rest high on his exceedingly pale face giving him a sort of Victorian elegance.

"Hey Arthur, good man."

"Can I get you started with anything?"

"Uh, yeah. Do you like wine?"

"I do."

"Red?"

"Red is good."

"Can you bring us a bottle of your cabernet?"

"We have a few, Cash."

"Right well, whichever you recommend."

"Will be back in a second."

And he glides off in a seamless turn of a heel.

Rose, again with those eyebrows. "Celebrity."

"It's his job to know my name."

"Whatever."

"Do you like cabernet?"

"Cabernet's fine."

"Yeah. I don't know. I can't taste much difference from one to the next."

"Well, you ordered it with confidence."

"Right. I've ruined that now, haven't I?"

"Completely."

"Ah well, I had a good run."

"It's okay. I don't know the differences either."

"You're not going to twirl it around? Smell it and comment on the legs?"

"Can't imagine doing that seriously."

"There's nothing worse."

She laughs and agrees. "Nothing worse."

In the mood lighting her emeralds shimmer.

"Work today?" I ask. She takes a sip of water and nods, "Yeah, for a second. Saul's been taking a bit more time off, little by little, starting to trust me I guess."

"How've things been?"

"At Jimmy's?"

"Yeah."

"Not bad. It's not exactly a riot, but not bad."

"No, I suppose not."

"But it's work, ya know? I'm happy to have it."

"Right, yeah. You and Saul get on?"

"Well enough, I think."

"He's a tough one."

"Yeah, but he's kind of soft deep down."

"Very."

"He speaks highly of you."

"Really?"

"Well, as high as he'll go."

"Right."

"*He's a good guy.* I think those were his words."

"I'll take it."

"I would too."

"Does he know you're out with me?"

"Nope."

"Nice."

"What would he say?"

"I really don't know. Probably nothing."

"What would he *think*?"

"I'd like to think he'd be happy."

Arthur returns to our table and without a word he sets two wine glasses down. He balances the neck just over the brim, and smoothly pours the red from the bottle. He does this twice and says, "I'll be back in a moment for your order."

Rose grabs her glass by the stem, in between her ringed fingers, and spins the wine in the base of the glass. She leans her lightly freckled nose down to the aroma and breathes in it.

"Ah, just as I expected." With a completely composed face she meets my eyes and tilts her head slightly to the side. It's all I can do to keep it together. "And? Have you recognized its Italian aroma?" I smile.

"Oh yes, of course, the tannins."

"Of course. The tannins." And I follow suit, a quick swirl. I smell what I always smell, a potent, earthy sweet and floral scent of a million unidentifiable flowers or fruits. I smell wine. "And what tannins, exactly?" I ask.

"I have no idea," and she laughs in the middle of the sentence.

"Me either. Cheers."

"Cheers." It tastes fine on the tongue. "So, where's your hideout anyway?"

"Couple blocks off Main, on the corner of Pearl and Factory."

"That red brick place by the water tower?"

"That's right."

"No way?"

"Yeah," her eyebrows raise, "Surprised?"

"A little. I just used to know the kid that grew up there."

"Oh yeah?"

"Yeah, Brock's his name."

"Good kid?"

"Troubled."

"How troubled are we talkin?"

"Ah. A few arrests."

"He didn't like, commit homicide in my house, did he?"

"No, he did not commit homicide in your house."

I laugh.

"Good. I like the place."

"Yeah, that's a good spot. Good as any."

"Yeah."

"You'll stick around for a bit, then?"

"Looks like it, not really sure where else to go."

"Do you miss home?"

"Doesn't feel like home there anymore."

"Right."

"So."

"I think you'll really like it here. Eventually. Place grows on you."

"Yeah, I think you're right."

And Arthur comes back around. Though we haven't even looked at the menus. We pick them up and find ourselves relaying our orders. I'm settling in a bit now. I know she's given me something of a hard time over the past few weeks, but why shouldn't she? I like that. I'm thankful just to sit across from her. To hear whatever it is that she wants to offer. I close my menu and set it back on the table. Rose tells Arthur what she'd like. She's kind and respectful. All the world is behind her green eyes. The desire to move mountains for her rises in me, the longing to make her smile and laugh. She makes you earn it and that's just fine with me. Arthur nods and moves away swiftly.

"And what about you?" She asks.

"What about me?"

"You've always been in Johnston?"

"All my life."

"How's someone come to live their whole life in Johnston?"

"Easy as any other place, I imagine."

"Never wanted to get up and go?" From the corner of my eye, I notice Mr. and Mrs. Schultz shuffling out the front door, elderly and slow. I believe they too have spent all their lives here in Johnston. My heart grows fond for their long journey. "I wouldn't say that. I've thought about leaving. Here and there."

"Just never happened?"

"Nah, never did."

"Why's that?"

"Ah I don't know. Guess I always thought that one day I would. Day just hasn't come yet."

"Right."

"Maybe looking for a reason. A real one anyway."

"Hm."

"And Johnston has treated me fine."

"Yeah?"

"Yeah. I love it. I really do. The people, ya know. It's a family, in a way."

"Your parents still in town?"

"Nah. They're not."

"They move on out?"

"Something like that."

"Right. See them much?"

"Not really."

"That's tough."

"Can be. You been alright with all that?"

"My mom?"

"Yeah."

"I don't know. Not really. Good days, bad. That's a cliché but, yeah. You know it wasn't a shock or anything so, ya know, it was such a slow fade kind of thing. She was fighting for years, so, by the time it came, she had just been coming to terms long enough."

"Does that help?"

"What's that?"

"Having it happen slowly."

"You mean instead of a tragedy or something?"

"Yeah."

"I think so. I don't know. I'd imagine so anyway."

"I'd imagine too, yeah."

"But that's why havin Saul nearby is nice. He's all the family I got now."

"I can tell he's happy you're around."

"Yeah, well, it's something. It ain't all that much some days, but he is my brother."

"Yeah, I hear you."

"After my mom died it made me think more about family. What it means."

"Mhm."

"Not that I didn't think of it before, but it feels different now."

"Yeah. I agree."

"I do feel a little alone sometimes though."

"Me too."

"But everyone loves you."

"Everyone *knows* me."

"Yeah, yeah whatever." Her lips on the glass hypnotize me.

"They must miss you in Ryland?"

"Maybe. But I had to go."

"Won't ever move back?"

"I don't know. I don't think so."

"Johnston it is then."

"Johnston it is."

And she takes another sip. I do too. It's a rich sort of wine that I've already forgotten the name of. It couldn't matter to me less. I have a fervent warm feeling in my chest just hearing Rose talk about anything at all. Like me, I can sense she has sky-high walls built like gates to her heart. To summit them will take work and resilience. Each bit of reflection she offers is a gift that somehow climbs its way over those walls and reaches me. And what gifts they are. I begin to lament my decision to not tell her the truth about my parents, since she has spoken so honestly about hers. Well, another night. I just haven't talked about them for a while.

She sets her glass down and says, "so, what is it you do, Cash?"

"What do I do."

"How do you survive?"

"It ain't easy."

"Never is."

"Ahhh I don't know, little of this, little of that."

"What's this and that?"

"Well, I paint houses, mostly."

"Oh yeah?"

"Yeah, been doing that for some years now."

"How'd you get into that?"

"Ahhh I guess I grew up painting, mostly with my mom. She was always real artistic, ya know? So, always loved that kind of stuff. Music, art, all of it. So, I'd paint with her every now and then. It ain't so hard painting plain walls and stuff, so, yeah, I do it from time to time."

"What else?"

"What else? Um, I used to do construction. I help people move sometimes."

"Like their houses?"

"Yeah."

"Coulda used you a few months back."

"I'da done it no problem."

"Really?"

"Free of charge."

"Damn."

"Anyway, yeah. I do some of that. I also help out on some farms doing odd jobs. I'm kind of all over, like I say, little of this, little of that."

"And what else?"

"Well, that's it, pretty much. I write sometimes."

"Ohhh, you're a writer?"

"Why do you say it like that?" I laugh.

"I'm not saying it like anything. I really like that."

"Yeah, well, I don't know if I'd say I'm a writer."

"No?"

"Used to say I was, when I was younger. Used to write all the time."

"But not anymore?"

"Not nearly as much. Sometimes. Haven't finished anything in years."

"That's okay."

"Yeah I'll pick it up again."

"Someday."

"Yeah."

"I'll find you on a bookshelf somewhere."

"Wouldn't that be somethin?"

"And for fun?"

"What do I do for fun?"

"Yeah."

"Well, all the rest of it's fun."

"Hm. I love that."

"What about you? What do you do for fun?"

"I like to play guitar."

"Really?"

"Mhm."

"You're a musician?"

"In the same way you're a writer, I think," she smiles, a little bashful for the first time.

"How long have you been doing that?"

"Taught myself as a kid. On and off since."

"I'd like to hear you play."

"I don't know about that."

"Someday then."

"Someday, maybe."

"See you up on a stage."

"Don't get carried away."

"Can't help it."

And after a few more minutes Arthur is back and he sets down our plates. We've both ordered the steak. "There's nothing in the world like a tender-loin," my father used to say. Well, he was right about that. Can't tell ya the last time I went out and ordered myself a good steak. I know the evening is gonna cost me a decent sum, but I don't mind in the slightest. I don't remember the last time I took a woman out and wanted to spend everything I had on her. The flame charred meat still sizzling on the iron plate reminds me of my father. It smells, how he put it, like nothing else in the world.

"This looks incredible," she says.

"Best in town."

"I believe it. It's been a while since I've been to a place like this."

"Me too."

And something about this similarity is special to us. A flicker of the lamp off a clean fork and knife. A shared smile and a gratitude for life. The steak is hot and medium rare, it nearly melts in my mouth, and in between bites, Rose and I further explore the little intricacies we both seem to like most about life.

"It used to be my parents'. I like fixing it up, keeping it in order."

"You love living out there huh?"

"Yeah, I do, the freedom of the country. There's nothing like it, all that land and God, it's the best right now."

"The trees changing colors."

"Exactly."

"It's my favorite time of year."

"I love driving through it all. Some nights I'll hop in around sunset and just go."

"I do that too."

"Just drive for hours playing music all night."

"The best. Windows down, cigarette."

"You smoke?"

"Sometimes. On drives like that I do."

"Yeah."

"Or when I'm drinking."

"Always when I'm drinking."

"You love drinkin, huh?"

"How'd you guess?"

"Ah, I can tell."

"Well yeah, I do."

"What do you love so much about it?"

"I don't know. Everything."

"Hm."

"The taste. The freedom, nostalgia."

"All the above."

"The romance."

"Romance. You think so?"

"I do."

"That's nice."

"To a point. Too much of anything, not always good."

"Yeah. Not always."

"What about you? You agree at all?"

"I do."

"I knew it."

"You knew I'm an alcoholic?"

"I didn't say that."

"What'd you know?"

"That you saw it same as me."

"You think I do?"

"Do you?"

"Maybe."

God, her smile lights me on fire.

"My dad used to say it ain't gonna drink itself," I say.

"I'm sure my dad loved that one."

"It all started with my father, yeah."

"He's a big drinker?"

"You could say that."

"Maybe we aren't so different, you and me."

"No, maybe not."

"We share that, anyway."

"Suppose so. How's the steak?"

"Unbelievable."

"Right?"

"So good."

"It might sound crazy but sometimes I feel closer to God when I drink."

"What do you mean?"

"All the noises turn off, you know? They go quiet. It's just that hum. And sometimes, I just feel like I can really listen, or I can really see. And I get inspired or I tap into the real feeling. Sometimes I'll write for hours, sometimes days. Sometimes I just stare at the sky and listen to music. It's crazy but it could be anything."

"I don't think that's crazy."

"No?"

"Not at all. I'm the same."

"Really?"

"Really, yeah. Always been. I remember I would sneak some outta my mom's cupboards during school years and I'd hide away in my room or run off outside somewhere and do it. I was so curious about it. Like a science experiment or something at first. I just wanted to know."

"Same."

"Some nights I'd stay up playin my guitar softly in my room or out by the field. Drinking, dreaming. I thought that maybe I was strange. A bit of an alien."

"Not at all."

"I don't know, I loved it though."

"I'd really like to hear you play."

"Okay."

"Okay?"

"Okay. Someday. Not tonight."

"Alright."

"I don't play for just anyone, ya know."

"That doesn't surprise me."

And it's almost unbelievable, I'm tellin ya, but Rose is looking at me differently now. She's more happy and free, starting to trust me. "You're different than most of the guys I've met around here."

"Different how?"

"Just different."

"Well, you aren't the only one who feels like an alien sometimes."

"Yeah?"

"I never really fit in, not fully—"

"Me either." The words land and we feel it, that moment you see your reflection in another. I knew it from the second I first saw her, but I'm more sure of it now. We drink our wine and enjoy the taste, whatever mysterious tannins are inside it.

Before long, we finish our plates and Arthur takes them away. Rose's chest is rising and falling, her cheeks are a little red, as are mine. I'm sure they're warm to the touch, soft. I know we both have much more to share. Her forest green eyes. I know they see right through me. I'm exposed. I know it, she knows. So it goes. So it goes. She taps her fingers on the table.

Radiating, she asks, "So, what now?"

And I have no chance to hide the wide smile that plays obvious across my face.

"You wanna keep seein me?"

She smirks so fine and silly and says, "Yeah dummy, I do."

37

We pull into the small parking lot of Johnston Park and there's something faintly romantic about the crooked skinny streetlamps along the dark edges of the grounds under starlight. The air is full of promise. I can't help but grin. Who would have imagined it? All these years have passed, and the place still carries the allure that drew me to it as a kid. I hadn't thought I'd ever bring someone out here again, not like this. Rose closes the door of her Jeep behind her and says, "What are you all giggling about?"

"Nothing, nothing."

I'm walking up a tiny hill that rises to the playground with Rose matching stride. "Under that pavilion over there we must have had a hundred picnics, this town. People still get together there all the time." A hundred times, a hundred years and onward. We wander over to the purple swing set which is rusting over the metal and look out over the baseball diamond below. All the games of my youth flash before me in one ancient cloud of dust. I can still feel those sunburnt summer days. I can still hear my mother in the crowd cheering loudly as I crack the bat against that ball and it sails out of sight.

Rose sits down on a swing.

"When's the last time you actually used one of these things?" she asks.

"I couldn't tell ya."

"I used to love these things, man. I'd go for hours."

And she starts swinging. Her legs begin slowly pushing and pumping through the air to gain speed and for a moment, I just watch her. What an image of momentum. I finally sit down on the cracked black rubber seat to her left and follow suit. It's funny what comes back to us, like all the innocent, limitless times I just enjoyed an afternoon on a swing. Doing it now, at twenty-nine, guides me back. Back to a time where I was rid of all burdens, any fears or worries that could sit heavy on my shoulders. Suddenly, all my anchors are gone. I let them fall and they are lost in the wood chips below. I feel magnificent now. Rose is laughing.

"I told you!" she says. "It's the *best*. Tell me it doesn't feel like you're flying, Cash if you close your eyes."

And my God, it does. Seeing her on the swing next to me, soaring and weightless, makes me recognize the children in us both.

"Close them, Cash. Are you closing them?"

"I am."

"You'll be flying in no time, do you feel it?"

"I do."

"I used to do this all the time when I was a girl. We had a park about a mile from my mom's. Whenever I was upset, I used to wander out to the swing set and just close my eyes. I would rock there and fly."

So, we're flying. We are all born into this big mess with a purity, with a goodness. No hate, no anger. It's only over time, with the pain that comes through the course of life that we get strapped with all the unfortunate things that happen to us. What a shame. We grow older and more careful, hardened and quieter. But every once in a while, you'll catch a glimpse of yourself in another and maybe you'll feel like you're flying. You'll find a good swing and be reminded that when we strip ourselves down, away from all those things we carry, we are free. We are free as we were at the start. As I watch Rose fly beside me, I think this is about as close as we come to that feeling. Where we are infinite on the Earth, light and soaring. We are born to move through the sky with our wings, laughing and swinging beneath stars.

The baseball diamond in front of us was the host of young dreams. It was the arena of so many battles, the remains of which lie hardened in dirt, immortalized. I think back to my sun-soaked days baking to a crisp out there looking up to the bleachers at all the people of Johnston. Family, friends, and the like, younger siblings playing in the park and caring nothing about the game. My mother in the stands, watching intently and me wanting nothing more in the world than to make her proud. I'd wonder where my dad was, and if he'd ever see me take a nice cut with the bat. I'd pull the brim of my hat back further down my brow and look out to the field and swear all sorts of prophetic things to myself. That I'd hit a home run one day and be lifted to Heaven like a king. I would be a hero right there on the Johnston diamond.

"I must have played a thousand baseball games down there. My ma would sit right on the far end of those bleachers."

And we swing, back and forth, back and forth.

"Alright," she says. "You have to jump off. Deal?"

"Deal."

"Count of three. Ready?"

"Ready."

"One... two... three."

And we jump through the air, nearly stumbling down. We catch each other's arms after our feet hit the grass and we're laughing like wild, like kids.

"God, I haven't done that in forever."

"Come on, let me show you something," I say.

We walk along the fence of the diamond, and I let my fingers drag across the sharp metal. Rose picks up a small rock and studies it in her hand before tossing it into the grass.

"I had a boyfriend, way back, who was convinced he was gonna make it all the way up to the majors." She laughs.

"How'd that work out for him?"

"He didn't quite make it."

"I think many of us guys in these little towns spend a decent amount of time believing we could end up in the majors."

"Yeah, there's something really American about the sport, and that dream. Don't you think?"

"That's exactly what I think."

"I remember my grandpa was obsessed with the Cubs. Every afternoon he'd watch. Never miss a game."

"Oh yeah, mine were the same, but they loved the Twins. My dad said my grandpa would sit in his living room, same old rocking chair, and sip a pack of Pabst every day while my grandma was off somewhere helping in political causes or teaching at the middle school."

My Grandpa Darrell had this big old beer belly in his later years and was a heavy smoker. He would eventually die from cancer in a hospital waiting room, his least favorite place, where there was never any baseball being played. Whenever I thought about the sport, like Rose, I often thought of my grandfather and how he loved America and the game of baseball more than most things. She found his story sort of sad, but I just shrugged my shoulders and didn't let it sit for too long.

At last, we begin our descent into the valley beneath Johnston Hill. The grass under our feet has taken on the dropping temperatures of the burgeoning evening, thick as ever on the brink of fall. The valley lawn is lush with well-watered grass from the hill's many runoffs. Rose takes her heels off.

"I want to feel it."

It's like she read my mind, and I do the same. Boots in hand, the valley envelops our feet as we begin to make our way up the hillside. It's the kind of grass you should sleep on at least once in your life.

At the top of Johnston Hill, I stood by her side. We are ambassadors for those before us and those coming soon.

"Beautiful," she says, and I couldn't agree more. The blanket of night gets heavier above, the black is speckled only by the tumbling planets way out in the universe. There's a long never-ending corn field to our left and the valley below. From this hilltop it's always so clear, the air swirls and the tiny homes of the city go to bed, one by one. It's the best view of Johnston by a mile.

And I think of all the times I stood on this very ground as a young man and saw the same things, just differently. That says a lot about life, don't you think? The whole circle of growing up and changing perspectives. I take a deep breath of the cleanest air in the world and can't help but dance back in memory. All the promising nights on this hill, looking as far out as I could, pretending it was my kingdom. I had no conception of things to come.

Rose stares out over my hometown, covered in nightfall. She looks peaceful and pleased. This will all be hers now. Johnston will fall to its knees if she lets it. We take a seat and lie down on the bed of the Earth. We don't speak for what feels like an hour. On our backs looking up to space we are one with the immeasurable moment. The sun now hidden in the evening and the moon in its place. And what is that noise that I hear in the wind? What is this moon song? It floats down in a gentle amble, born from these constellations and stories, the patterns we trace with our fingers. And when we look into each other's eyes after staring at planets, it's only one moment we need. I see the same design in Rose's freckles, the same orchestration I saw when she first walked through the door to the bar. Her eyes mirror my own. There's a feeling in them that I recognize. A feeling I couldn't miss if I tried. Rose, you will come to love Johnston just fine. You have it, you know it, the blues.

It's more subtle than crying. It's a quiet longing etched deep in the soul. It's a permanent thing, non-lethal. I've always believed that the blues is a sort of power. I believe it's a gift. A sensitivity. An attachment to a faraway dream worth holding. A feeling that you were living on the other side of the veil, just enough, so you understood something mysterious, this truth manifesting in your life. An ongoing, just-off sadness that arrives with a feeling of knowledge, through pain, through struggle and loss. It's the real heartbeat in the caverns of living.

I've never seen the blues in the eyes of a child because I don't believe we are born of it. The blues is a feeling so deep and so settled that you could forget it was there, but it is an essential element in your blood. It's a recognition that things are fleeting and fragile and changing, and they'll never stop being that way. People will come and go and the highs are never long stretching roads but more often peaks off the valleys. It's an admission that God hasn't made the walk easy or kind all the time, and life is a journey, full of harsh nights, cold mornings and scattered stretches of yellow sun. To have the blues is to know that it's all more worth it that way, together, it is. There's no fighting, no swimming against the current. It is a friend with ocean eyes and arms as wide and engulfing as the very space above our heads. The blues fills you up and hugs you tightly. It's a forever feeling.

I can't tell you how many people in Johnston have the blues, but most of us do, and it makes all the sense in the world to me that Rose has it too. *Maybe we aren't so different, you and me.* Her voice floats through my mind in a whisper. No, I don't think we are. In the surety of the moment, of this very realization, I decide to tell her my secret. A truth that I keep hidden most days, best I can.

"My mother died too." I say quietly. "And my father hasn't been here in years." And I confess the whole heartbreak. Her eyes water. She nods, calmly. In her silence I can see she understands. She has the blues in her soul, after all. I don't have to explain.

"Think they're up there now, looking down?" she asks me, softly.

"I do."

"Me too."

And I think about all the people we've seen come and go. The names of the folks who would fade into history with the same recognition as a daisy on the side of the road unless someone kept them alive somehow. And I think Johnston is so complete, so thoroughly made up by the lives of such people. People you'd never hear about. People that didn't line the tops of your newspapers in Chicago, or New York, or Los Angeles. Just people who loved their families, planted their feet in the soil, and nourished it with their sweat, with their loyalty, with their families, with their faith in God, in one another and in beautiful things to come.

These people, I love. These people are pieces of myself, fragments of my past that I now recognize as my lifeblood. Johnston is a mirror. Johnston, is a long line of edge walkers. Quiet, simple talkers who get up early hours and do their jobs. They get their hands filthy and calloused and make just enough money. They take care of their homes, try their best and get little rest. The clock, hung on the wall by a rusted nail, ticks on and on, and yet up they go again, as they always will. These are the people of God's Earth that won't detail your history books. They won't make all that much noise.

What a shame it would be if nobody knew their stories, if nobody remembered their names. Saul and Prince and Leon and Deangelo and Tommy and Rose. So, on evenings like this, looking out to the universe and searching for answers, I always write their names in the sky. I write the names of my parents, of every person I've ever loved. Every person I've ever longed to know, or understand. Every single beating heart in the streets of my hometown. There is no way to go through the world and not have our name in the Heavens, written by someone who knew us. I tell Rose this and she says, "If you write mine, then I'll write yours."

"Okay."

She points her finger about an inch from the moon and traces my name near its light. She whispers to herself as she does it

"Cash."

And I've never been so moved in my life. With her hand silhouetted by thousands of stars, I join her in that painting, and I write her name as she did mine.

"Rose," I say softly.

She touches my finger with hers, for only a moment, and smiles.

"Now, we live forever."

And she's right.

We are just like those tales of old. We are ants of Johnston making a run of it in the middle of nowhere America. Getting up day after day and still going, in the face of our cosmic smallness, chasing all that's infinite. I feel close to it now, on this hill with my hand next to hers and can see we are as big as the epics and bigger. For there is nothing greater, there is nothing on Earth that is Heaven but love. And lying on the grass, saying nothing, seeing Rose and the blues in her eyes with God's midnight canvas above, I feel like one of those heroes I heard about in stories all my life.

I take Rose's hand. And the light wind that dances around us fills up my chest. I believe I will one day fly from this feeling alone. All past erased, all future possible. The electricity pulses through me, flashing lights, emanating from my eyes. My pulse hammers softly through my wrist and moves through the bones of my hand. We search one another as her fingers curl around mine, and I could die, here and now. Right here on the hill I could die. For this is the feeling of God. The feeling of angels and harmony. There are echelons and this is the golden pyramid.

Her hand is soft. Her thumb makes the slowest, most gentle circles in my palm and it's true that the hand is the soul. And we are all of ourselves, from the heart through the blood, from the feeling to thought. To know that Rose made her thumb move and so she was her touch, do you see?

Rose's sandy blonde hair is woven into the ground, and the moonlight paints her face around my shadow. The way that she softens, her hand drifting to my cheek, I can't help but believe. I believe that we're one burning flame then we're gone. I believe that we're put on this planet for this, to be lost in the world with one another. I know I don't know much. I will know more in time. But tonight, we are endless. We are spirits in Johnston and on the road right to Heaven. We are the story. I lean myself down. My hand, hers. A green kaleidoscope, the entire universe in the sea of her eyes. And that smile. It will be with me forever. Hearts in rhythm, her fingers brushing the line of my jaw. I have her, and she has me. We breathe together, warm and magnetic. Hovering for a moment, the scent captures my life. I fall all the way down. We kiss. Soft, and then passionate, like we've waited a thousand years. Together on the hill, on a blanket of grass. We kiss. We kiss. We are stars in the sky, like far away lamps, in a blues dipped, infinite world.

Part Two

38

THINGS DON'T WISH TO LAST. My father told me that.

Pat is playing acoustic guitar in the pavilion off Main Street and I'm sitting at one of the far-off wooden picnic tables with the paint peeling off, all alone. With fading curly hair and a thick beard, Pat does what he was born to do. His rings shine on his fingers as they strum, and tattoos cover his neck and arms. Though born in Johnston, he sings with a bit of a southern drawl. He has a full round stomach and the saddest, most gentle eyes you've ever seen. He's playing through a set of folk tracks that settle like heartbreak into the fifteen or so of us here to listen.

"Mamma don't worry, mamma don't cry, I'm heading home now mamma, I've got the song to make the drive. Mamma don't worry, mamma we're fine, we'll ride along the road, we'll wind along this road of time."

And I swear Pat's eyes glisten with water as the evening falls around us. It's rare that Johnson houses anyone quite as talented as Pat, but when wanderers like him come through I almost never miss them. Around here, if you see a man with a guitar, then you oughta stop to hear the music just in case.

I've just finished working a long day painting the back rooms of Mick's Grocery and feel exhausted. On the way back to my place I saw Pat walking by the pavilion, and I immediately turned over to the side of the road and parked. He's cradling his guitar and beginning another ballad.

"Darlin I'm beat down, the sun's gone off and set now, so I'm draggin myself back down through the door." Pat seems beat down, just like me. He's only thirty, but seems much older. Some of these folk heroes, the good ones, sing with the soul of a thousand years if they get it right and find their voice.

Pat has it alright. Off to my left the sun sets earlier than yesterday and the day before that. It also seems a bit sad in its early descent, but maybe that's just me. We see the world as we paint it. Van Goghs, the lot of us.

God. Am I going to think about Rose every time I see an acoustic guitar for the rest of my life? I never even got to hear her play. I only hope she hasn't ruined me forever. It's been two weeks since she left town. She disappeared just a couple days after our night on Johnston Hill. Word had it she went to go check on things in Ryland and do some sorting out. I don't know what the hell that means really but that's what Saul told me so, that's all I know. He so casually mumbled the news to me I couldn't believe it. He told me as if it didn't feel like the end of the world. It plummeted my heart to my stomach. There was no voicemail on my answering machine, no letter at my door, just a graceful, quiet exit. Senseless. Things had gone so beautifully, too.

I could fucking pound my head on this chipped paint table. I'm nothing but a child, in the end. An angry ruined sad mess and tantrum prone. To think I only kissed her once, only held her once. I imagine she'll be back, but I can't be sure. She was gone in the morning like a ghost fit for dawn, so I've told myself it's over forever. Maybe I was wrong about everything after all. Two weeks of radio silence, staring down the barrel of confusion, I admit my mistake. What a thorough disaster I've made. I really opened myself to it this time. To think I was fine before she showed up. What a fucking drag. I rap my knuckles on the table but it's not to the music.

Pat, the bearded wanderer, is on that pavilion stage tonight and it feels like he's traveled here for me. When he sings about stitching up his eyes not to cry, I feel we are one. Isn't it funny how we're all the same, together but alone? The Peterson family is close to the stage, and they've brought their boy. The kid must be three or so and is impressively well adjusted and thrilled. The mother and the father and the kid. The chosen few. They each hold one of his hands and sway to the music. The American brave and content, I think that kid's got a chance. It's true that there is nothing more fortunate than a good family. A father being around, and a mother all filled up with love. I gotta say, I'm a little envious of that Peterson boy. He crouches down and falls to the grass in a soft little heap. He picks at the blades and has no damn clue how swell he has it. He'll find out one day. He'll know what I know—that family is everything.

I haven't seen much of anyone lately. No Leon or Prince or anybody. I've dropped off the map, in a way. I'm prone to these sorts of stretches sometimes. Even as a kid I would try to run away and disappear after a fight with my father or a bad day at school. I'd never make it in the forest through nightfall and Ma would throw a real fit, but I couldn't help it. I can get pretty isolationist sometimes. I've gone through entire seasons of life feeling dramatically alone. And I knew that all it would take would be a phone call, or a knock on the door, but for weeks I could pretend as if the world had abandoned me, and it would continue to do so from there on out. I'd become convinced that all my friends had left and that they had never understood me in the first place, it's the blues at its worst. None of those lies were true, but I would find that tune anyway. Pat sings about it now, today and most days.

Maybe I'm finished. Maybe I won't reach out anymore. Maybe I'll hit the road and finally disappear into the wide American frontier like my ancestors. I'll figure it out one sweaty, dirty day at a time and make a real life. Wander to exhaustion, sleep on the floor of subway stations, climb mountains and on. And in my later years, I will then sit and rock and look back and be proud of the adventure. No memory to drag me down. Only the future - the future! Maybe I oughta hop in my Saturn and be a prisoner to nothing and no one. Find a fine river and stand in the water, be swept up in the current. Where to? Where is my purpose hidden? Fuck's sake, I feel restless. All at the hands of a woman. Maybe I'm better alone, standing still amongst all the scramblers and desperate people for love. Not me! I am an island.

Pat plays on as the day finally relents and the air starts to carry just a little more bite. It fills my lungs.

Come down and stay a while, come down and stay.

I close my eyes and try to breathe a few memories away. Things will get better. Keep your head up, Cash. One black night at a time, try and face it. I have to be back at the store at six a.m. tomorrow to complete my job, but Pat will be finishing up any second now and I know that he'll need a cold beer.

A half hour later Pat and I are sitting on the pavilion stage sipping a few Budweisers I snagged from the Shell. He is leaning back against one of the pillars and scratching at his beard.

"Came in yesterday. Fuckin, haven't slept man. I don't know what it is, I come home sometimes from the road and can't sleep a wink."

Pat will go months at a time in Nashville, but has spent the past five years or so mostly on the road doing small gigs, just barely getting on. Pat's family wasn't around Johnston anymore, but he still stopped by to pay his regards.

"It'll always be home Cash, you know that."

The only thing tugging at his heart was the woman he left behind in Tennessee.

"She's a good woman, you know, she's tired too, I think. It ain't easy waitin around for me comin back, I know that. Shit, Cash, it's just a circle, ain't it? The comin and goin. I love her, though. I do. It's been a dead week. Had to make it home."

"Are all those songs about her?"

"Lot of 'em." He nods, scratching that beard again and taking a long pull of Bud. Of course they are.

"You ever find what you're lookin for out there?" I ask.

"Travelin?"

"Yeah man, out on the road."

"I don't know."

"Are you lookin?"

"Think we're all looking for something, ain't we?"

Pat was prone to talking about life in these giant philosophical ways sometimes. He knew they could mean anything. That's how he deflected.

"Where'd you stop along the way?"

"Shit, Cincinnati. Cincinnati for a couple. One outside of St. Louis. Stopped over through Bettendorf for a few. I don't know. Everywhere Cash, any place that'll have me." His guitar lies loyal by his side, the pick guard completely shredded by decades of strumming. It has a real soul, a worn and rugged history to it that all the best guitars have. Pat never really did anything else outside of playing that guitar.

"Life of an artist," I say.

"Shit. I don't know, Cash. Feels more like work some days, I gotta tell ya."

"Really?"

"Sometimes. Sometimes when I'm really burnt and strugglin, yeah. Broke as hell."

"A craftsman then."

"A craftsman, yeah." He laughs a low pleased chuckle. "I like that. Yeah."

"We're all craftsmen around here, Pat. That's what we are."

"You got that right."

Pat here has been living out of his truck for five years and he's still making the rounds. Sure, he may be broke, and he may be tired. He may miss the woman he loves, but he is right in the heart of it. He's a moving piece of the grand expanse of America and going after it. He is free. No matter how ragged he looks before me now, I admire him.

"Will you be sticking around Johnston for a beat?"

"Nah. Leaving in the morning for Sun Prairie."

"On it goes."

"On it goes."

To think the man had played to no more than fifteen people tonight, got paid only a few bucks, and still, he would pick up that guitar and try again in a new town.

"What's in Sun Prairie?"

"Hell if I know, Cash, hell if I know." He cracks open another beer and searches the night. "I know you think it's rad on the road man, but what you got here, you got it right."

"Greener on the other side."

"Maybe. But you're part of something, ya know? Community is important. Out there it's lonesome as hell."

"You're part of everything all at once though."

"I don't know what's comin one day to the next man."

"Ah none of us do."

"Well, I envy ya. How're the boys?"

"Good man. All good."

"Leon still at Sureland?"

"Yeah. Like clockwork."

"Prince still Prince?"

"Always."

"Miss those guys man. Been ages."

"They're around. They'd love to see ya."

"Yeah well. I don't know, man. Honestly. Sometimes I get to thinkin maybe I oughta just come home."

"Here?"

"Yeah man, of course here."

"What about the music?"

"I can play anywhere. Could get a real job. Ask Janey to come north. I don't know."

"You're alright man. Something's coming."

"I don't know."

"You've got a gift, Pat. I ain't lyin."

"Thanks Cash."

"I'm serious man."

"I know you are. Thanks pal."

"Just keep on rolling. It's gonna work out. It's gotta."

"Yeah."

He takes a pack of Camel Reds from his flannel pocket and offers them to me. I pull one out and he hands me his lighter. There's few things as settling to me as that quick roll of the lighter, that soft snap and the flame. I breathe in the smoke, and I toss it back. He does the same. All quiet on the Johnston front. I hadn't ever seen Pat so lost before. Never did I think I'd hear him say he may move back to Johnston. All I can do is encourage him. He was living the life on the road, and though he may be a little down on his luck, I knew what he was after, even if he'd forgotten. I remembered that promise, that sovereignty over his nights and his mornings, that embedded adventure at the root of everything that was so moving about his music. I have to believe that everything is waiting for him, just around the next bend of a midwestern freeway.

"When are you back to Nashville?" He takes another nice long gulp of his beer, lets out some breath into the Johnston air, scrunches his face and thinks. He looks out, far out to the frontier, down every road he's ever trudged along.

"Maybe a month."

I take a drink, then a smoke and I think about the whole countryside of America being heartbroken and looking back on their past with the same eyes Pat has, deep and affected, sad and longing for something unknown. I want to tell him that he'll get it right again someday, that he'll catch the wave and be okay. He'll be alright, somewhere, sometime.

"There's so much of America left."

"That there is." He takes a drag. "Cash, tell me somethin."

"Alright."

"I gotta know. Why have you stuck around here all these years? You say all this to me, and ya always have. Ain't nobody pullin for me more. Making me promise I'll keep wanderin around."

"I don't know man."

"Aint ya thought about it?"

"Course I've thought about it. I'm always fuckin thinking about it."

"Well?"

"I don't know. Feel like I'm waiting for something."

"A woman?"

"Nah."

"Your pops?"

"Maybe."

"Shit. I hear ya."

"Yeah."

"Ain't anybody that loves this place like you, man."

"I don't know about that."

"Promise me, Cash. That you'll leave someday."

"I will."

"At least for a good while."

"I will man."

"Shake on it." He reaches his hand over, and even though I shake it, my destiny has never seemed more elusive.

"You know," he scoffs, "I'm too tired to make it all the way to Tennessee, even if I wanted to."

And there you have it. If someone left for long enough, traveled far enough on foot or by dusted wheel, they could be lost to it forever, full of rags and unable to begin again where the story had started long ago. Even though he's beat down and full of doubt, Pat is roped to something moving. A wild horse or freight train. And maybe that's how it should be.

Pat and I finish the last of our beer and stand to our feet. Wearing his smoke-stained flannel, my friend wraps me in one of his bearhugs and says, "Love you, buddy."

"Love you too, Pat."

"On it goes, yeah?"

"On it goes. Proud of you man."

"Proud of you too."

He squeezes my shoulder and picks up his guitar. Off he goes with nothing more than a salute.

"See you soon, brother."

"Godspeed."

He lumbers a bit as he walks, that best friend guitar of his swaying by his side, a trusted companion in the long journeys through the night. His form slowly disappears into the shadows of the dark sidewalk. On it goes. The leaving. And still, I can't keep her out of my mind. I suppose Rose is like Pat, in a way, a vagabond, wandering place to place, looking for a home. What shadows are you walking through now, Rose? I hit my fist on the pavilion pillar, just hard enough to hurt. What the fuck is the *meaning* of it all? God, I can't even blame her when I try to. Whatever it is she's looking for I just hope she finds it.

Way off, I see the lights of Pat's truck shine as he revs the thing up and then drives away. I know he'll be lost again for a while, singing his broken ballads to anyone that'll listen. Well, we're all lost Pat, at least you're looking. And that severe longing stabs at my heart in my chest. *Promise me Cash,* that's what he said. Maybe it's finally time I get around to my wandering. Until then, I'll be searching these same city streets, waiting for a ghost to emerge from the dark. The half-moon above looks like a smile. I can almost hear it say to me, "You know Cash, if you can't find what you're looking for in Johnston then maybe you won't find it anywhere." I laugh. God, to think that might be true.

39

When I was eight years old, my Mom took me to a waterpark a couple hours from Johnston. A few times a year she and I would go on these tiny vacations and be the best of friends. She'd pack my favorite lunches, we'd wake up before the sun, and we'd climb into the car and make our way.

At the waterpark, we'd run through the wet sidewalks and smile so big it would hurt. We'd climb the tallest slides and head down in tandem, loving the thrill. Her hair would be saturated and dark brown and the sun would pour out of her laughter. We'd open the trunk of the car and we'd sit on the bumper, eating peanut butter and jelly sandwiches and she'd giggle with me about all the silly things that were on my little imaginative mind. I would tell her all my eight year-old secrets. I would lean my head against her freckled warm arms and daydream. She'd always ask, "Are you happy, Cash?"

And I'd scoff or roll my eyes. "Yes, Ma."

On one of those trips as a kid I got to the park and felt a bit out of sorts, lightheaded and weak. I made a try of it, anyway and a couple hours later I was standing on the brink, overlooking an ocean-sized wave pool. My vision started pulsing in and out as I tried to keep balance. From many yards back, my mother saw me wobble and came running, splashing to my side. Before I lost consciousness, her arms were around me. Delirious, sweating with fever, my mother helped me all the way to the car. Through my haze I remember my mother whispering to me from the other side. She was promising me that everything was going to be okay, that I was strong, and I was safe. We drove home as she held my hand and I slept. In and out.

That particular bout of the flu kept me bedridden for three days. My mother made countless trips to my room, offering me water and cold towels, soup, and love. I don't remember much other than I thought I was dead and that she was my only hope. Even now, on my worst days, I close my eyes and remember my mother catching me in that wave pool with the water rushing around our heads and bodies. Saint-like and more, she looked after her son as he fought off all the assailants, weaknesses, and doubts.

Mom. I close my eyes and I see you now.

And in my dreams, you are there.

And you ask me again, soft and caring, "Are you happy, Cash?"

Ma. Where are you now? Why has this year got me so turned around? You've been on my mind more and more and I don't understand a damn thing. When I lean my head down in the evening, it's on the arm of the lifeless old couch and you're gone. Ma. I'm sorry. I'm sorry I left you alone. All crashed in the ditch. Bleeding and broken and cold. I should have saved you somehow.

I should have been there to carry you home.

40

The cold has come. September mornings. Gone are the days of birds on the ground, sifting through dew for their worms. I walk out to my Saturn with a packed bag in my right hand. Breath leaves my lips and hovers like mist before departing for good. There's something invigorating about these dim mornings before the sun in early fall. My father used to say things about that, way back.

"Cash, you have to beat the sun up, do you understand? Be there to see it rise. Make you a man."

He wasn't wrong. I open the car door, toss my faded black duffle inside, and get in. I turn the key over and wait, looking at my home. It seems mournful in departure. The air grows warmer from the vents. I close my eyes and pull it all together, mind wide and growing wider. It's time. I put my hands on the wheel and drive.

I'm spinning it fast out to Cambridge, Minnesota and I haven't told anybody my plans other than a scribbled note I left with Mo for Prince and Leon. *Heading out for a bit. No worries. See you soon.*

Mo gave me a long hug and didn't ask me any questions. My grandpa and grandma used to live in a small log home out in the Minnesota wilderness. They never sold it, and nobody has taken any care of it for years, but it was still standing out there, waiting for someone to come back. I would greet it with love no matter what state it was in. I know a few folks in the town from spending summer months there as a kid, and I figure I can find some kind of work and get busy. Maybe I'll fix the place up a bit and see if there is any life to be had out there for the winter months. Who knows. Maybe I'll figure it all out and stay for good. All I'm sure of is I need to go. So I am. And I haven't told a soul where or why.

I feel a bit bad about Prince and Leon and leaving them behind. I wonder what they'll think or if they'll have any inclination to come find me. It's been weeks anyway, the longest period of time we've gone without hanging out in years. None of us moved against it, but why? Why had we all taken this agreed upon hiatus? I wonder what they've been scheming and moving toward, or if they were going through it like me, head rattled and heart searching for something hidden. We are all in the midst of our own winding path, I know that. A month or two on our own would be good for us in the end. Still, I miss my brothers, even though I'm trailing away from them both and saying nothing. Nothing! On it goes. I imagine briefly how one late fall morning Prince would drop by and see my place still abandoned and think *enough is enough*. He'd call up Leon who'd say he still hadn't heard from me and that he didn't have a damn clue where I was. Only the note I left with Mo, and one brief conversation with Saul. I told him I was heading out, that's all, that I was alright and if anyone came looking then he should tell them only that I was going. I'd be back for a beer and my bar before long, though I didn't know that for sure. I know nothing for sure. I'm keeping Leon and Prince in the dark a bit, but I figure it's best this way. Did we or did we not need one another as we thought? Time will tell. First, a little mystery and breath of adventure and change. So long, Johnston. You house of all past, good and bad. We will see. I am no longer attached. I am tethered to absolutely nothing on God's whole blue and green Earth. The old house will be there, waiting for me in Cambridge, dusty and lonely from abandonment. I will greet it with open arms, truly ready and alone, free at last to travel and drive and take root somewhere new.

*

Four fucking weeks since Rose ditched town. The thought alone makes me race down the freeway. Not a call, not a word to her brother, nothing.

"Saul, man, c'mon. Where'd she go?"

"I dunno, Cash."

"I know you do."

"I dunno, really."

"What, she just fucking left?"

"Seems so."

"Didn't say a word to you?"

"She said she was going, yeah."

"That's all?"

"That's all."

"What the fuck does that mean?"

"Cash, I told ya I dunno."

I nearly pulled my hair from the scalp. I dragged my knuckles against the wood of the pool table and somehow didn't strike it. I stormed out of the place and slammed the door behind me. It didn't make any sense. I picked up the nearest rock in the gravel and hurled it towards the lamppost. I missed and the stone bounced down the road straight out of town. Not a soul in sight. I got in my car and tried to breathe, frustrated anger and confusion welling up like a torrent inside of me.

"What, the *fuck*, man!" I yelled.

My chest heaved. I closed my eyes. I couldn't stop shaking my head. Ten, twenty minutes. That's that. I put the key into the ignition and left.

One week later.

I'm not saying I'm driving all the way out to Cambridge because of lovely, green-eyed Rose, but her departing like that, disappearing from the town like a phantom, set me off on a wild set of thoughts about leaving. She cracked something in me I didn't know could be cracked. God, why had I opened myself up like that? Left in the fucking dust, man, like all of it never happened. At least my grandparent's house will know something about that.

All of the thoughts tumble down. All the near misses and losses. Rose and Saul. Not getting Jimmy's Place. Prince nowhere to be seen. Leon busy. Tommy. All the thoughts about Mom and Dad that wouldn't leave me the hell alone. The wandering. Kassy and almost crying. God and moving. Pat and the road, and the painting the painting the painting, every damn thing, every damn day. I'm not in the pocket anymore, that much is clear. Goodbye Johnston.

Rather Cambridge. Rather a colder Midwest and the grounds of my mother's parents, where she always cherished going to sit out in the yard to talk about life with her gatekeepers. I remember long walks through the woods, finding stones and forgotten forts. I remember her there, happy and alive, and my heart rate settles. I'm reminded, this is why I'm going. I left something in those woods. Perhaps my mother is there, in Cambridge, patiently waiting for me. Ma, I'm on my way. I know there are centuries of bones in the backyard, stories written on the bark that need reading, secrets and truths being carried on the wings of the wind. All my ancestors and their souls, cold, lonely, and waiting for my journey to conclude. Waiting for me to line up the sight for a second or two and see it all clearly.

The sun is starting to float over the horizon, and I place a cigarette on my lips. I light it. The leaves on trees are beginning to die in their wondrous display of color. Ready to bid me farewell. And to the horses released from their stables I share solitudes. For another day, and another. The gray calming smoke lets itself out through the window. It too, whispers goodbye. And all my endearing and eternal thoughts about Johnston disappear. Cambridge! Here I come. Let the ghosts run up through the roots and take form. Wait for me, out there. Wait for me in the woods. We'll reminisce in the Minnesota sun. We'll talk it out at last. When I get there, when I stay.

41

My Grandma Ruby and Grandpa Bill lived in a tiny home buried away in the Minnesota woods for years. With fading blue paneling and a black roof, and all sorts of leaves stashed away in the gutters, it is sheltered year after year beneath an assortment of towering maple trees. It has a narrow wooden porch and a walkway built into the side of the home which extends out into the shortest driveway you've ever seen. A canopy Grandpa Bill built covers the parking spot from the downpouring rain and heavy snow throughout winter, but does nothing to protect from the below zero temperatures. Not that either of them minded much about that.

When I pull into the driveway, there are piles of dirt and scattered debris in the corners. Leaves, nests, rodents and more. Years of neighborhood matter collected and settled. I close the car door behind me. I get my bag and head up the walkway to the front door.

Every third or so step is unsteady as some of the wood boards have become rotten and soft. All around is silent and anticipatory. There are a couple squirrels battling it out on a branch overhead. One black, one brown, chirping at one another, scrapping, what a life. I get the key out of my pocket and push the metal into the crusted lock, the same after all this time. It feels miraculous as it turns over.

In a sense, it's just as I remembered. I open the blinds to let the sunlight break through and illuminate the particles in the air. The furniture has remained steadfast and willing, the dining table is stable and nearly ashen with dust and the kitchen is planted where it always has been. It's all one connected interior, the kitchen is one with the dining room and the dining room is one with the living room. A small space. Standing in the entrance, I drop my bag down to the floor. The kitchen is to my right, scattered and lifeless. Long gone are the days where Grandma Ruby shuffled along and cooked cinnamon rolls that would melt the hardest of hearts. I can almost see her silhouette there behind the counter, bouncing and humming to herself. Some drawers are cracked open and are likely housing mice. I spot their droppings strewn around the counters and feel nauseous, but this was what I expected. I guess someone deserved a run of the place while all the people moved on. Grandpa Bill's rocking chair and Grandma's pale burgundy couch are off to the left, lining the living room walls. The 1950s television sits also in ash, most likely dead, and I walk forward a few steps to stare down the darkened hallway which leads to the bedroom back there. The walls are hung with pho-tographs—pictures of me, my mom, and my dad—and that same eerie feeling I got as a kid creeps along the back of my neck. What waited for me down that endless hallway of black? And out of the corner of my eye, I am already seeing ghosts. There Grandma is again, aproned and smiling, dark graying curly hair all frizzled and precious as she spins and she dances and delivers good news. Grandpa, meanwhile, in his rocking chair, a loose skinned, strong war vet, smiling and thankful for a heartbeat and a chance at any day at all, sings a tune by Johnny Cash. I rub at my eyes and handle it all, best I can.

The dust is thick and tastes of neglect. The once white carpet needs a wash, and mice scramble around, peeping through cracks, thinking *who the fuck is this*? Well, their guess is as good as mine. They've probably had one hell of a circus of things in my absence. I can only imagine the free living and seance, but playtime is over. This place has stood firm after all these years, never giving up hope for resurrection, and it's time I fulfilled the prophecy. I reach for a cigarette as the spirit of the place gives me chills. Years of memory, ricochet in my body. I head out to the yard, where the leaves continue to fall. I light my cigarette and kneel down. One leaf in my hand, I spin it by the stem. What a day in Minnesota. Here I am.

42

I am convinced that my days are paying homage to my mother and her par-ents. Every night, after working diligently, I wander through the woods and find a place to watch the dusk settle in, to have a wonderful stare down with

God as the sun dies. Though I do not know what I'm looking for, I am finally looking. And up in the darkening sky, or in the familiar forest, I will find my answers.

During the days, I purge the house. Strip it down to its bones. Repaint everything, every inch. Light blue for the kitchen and white for the living room. Coat after coat, for all the days to follow. Let it shine and beat on for the rest of my life, and longer. Let the walls breathe again. The power of the brush is in my hands. Even the first of us painted the walls of dark caves long ago.

On hands and knees, I scrub and dig into the very roots of the place. My dirty nails clean the cracks, and though I am focused, the hours pass in a blur; before I know it days pass. There's no clock to be found except the one above the stove that has long since given up. Those wooden hands of time grew tired. In determination, I scrape out the cupboards and reset the walkway with fresh boards. I flush the carpet completely, vacuuming and fanning the water. Every second is a rebirth. Every morning, I wake up with a purpose, with a clear and decisive aim to commit myself to the *work*, to be set right again, believing if I can make the house new, then new will be my soul. So, I scratch and I clean.

And finally, in the quiet evenings, I sit in Grandpa's chair and have a few beers. I stare off, far off into the oblivion walls and try to have conversations. I think back on all the holidays that we celebrated in this very room. We came here every Easter. I remember Grandpa's big old grin and his hand wringing as he watched me in my pajamas scooting all over the house in search of colorful eggs. I remember that effortless joy. I remember the day in the woods where he led me along a path and taught me how to shoot a bow. I remember the day we built a fort and afterwards he sat me down and we had lunch meat sandwiches while he talked about the war and then let me have a sip of his beer. Grandpa was well through his eighties and still a tough, competitive man. He had plenty of wisdom to pass on. I always looked up to my elders with adoration, but Grandpa Bill and Grandma Ruby were special. They could have told me anything and I would have believed them, and told me they did.

Oh Grandma, if I could see you now.

If we could talk about it all. Her feet had these big old bunions on the side of them that swelled up to near tennis balls, and I always found it miraculous that she stayed walking at all. She was, along with my mother, the kindest woman to ever walk the Earth. Grandpa would put baseball on the television and Grandma would squeeze me tight to her body. She always wore delightful sweaters and was so warm. Plenty of fat on her bones, and so undeniably, overflowing with love. *Grandma Ruby, what would we talk about now? What would you tell me?*

There are things I think you should know. Would you hold me as you once did? I miss your smile in the harsh days of winter. You had old, weathered teeth, but I didn't care. You never smoked and you never drank. You were the best cook in the world, and God, were you holy.

I remember one walk most of all. My mother and grandma were moving slowly, meandering on for what seemed like the length of the continent as I mindlessly played with a football, throwing it high into the sky to myself. I remember them talking about my father, who rarely came on the visits. I can't remember what they said exactly, but it was about him. I remember Grandma was sad, and I wondered why. They stopped on the path and they hugged there, the woods framing them in a divine sort of picture. I've never forgotten that image. Years later, I can only imagine sweet Grandma Ruby was imploring my mother to remain steadfast. To channel the grace of God and choose love. Grandma, I know you were the same, and yes, you died a saint, while the rest of the creatures ran on. I've never seen the light of the world quite the way you did, and to this day I wish I could. You either believe it or you don't. In the October evening I rock back and forth in my grandfather's chair and realize I am almost in tears thinking of it all.

*

I carry on like this for over two weeks. Day in, day out. Two weeks, and the house is nearly finished. All around me it is awake and thriving once more. As for me, I'm in my grandfather's chair again, my nighttime ritual. I am surrounded by the visions of my mother and her parents, reaching out and whispering. I look over to my grandma's old maroon lace pillow on the couch, feeling lonesome. It hasn't quite done the trick, all this. The place is alive and clean, but I remain something of a mess. I lie down on the carpet, close my eyes and I dream. When I was only a child, Mom would say, "Breathe Cash, just breathe."

43

A week later, I meet Nancy.

In her eighties and remembering me from my days in Cambridge way back when, she is thrilled to offer me a job fixing up her old place.

"Oh, believe me, you chatted all ways this and that, you were the nicest little boy."

Imagine that. She has wonderful memories of me from a time I can hardly remember. A time where I was bounding around, pure and happy, and a chatterbox. I only wish I could recall her as she did me.

"Oh, you were too young, must have been five, six years old! Sure do miss Ruby and Bill, sure do. They were sweet. Good folks. Sure is *something*. To see you all grown!"

She lets out so many ohhhs of excitement and has that indelible kind nature, like she knew some heavenly secret.

A few mornings ago, I was chatting up this mustached fellow named Jeff at the local Casey's gas station. The place was deserted, and Jeff seemed a rugged enough, hardworking man, so we hit up a conversation. Turned out Jeff had moved to the area some years back to help out his parents with the station and just hadn't left. I laughed about that. I'd heard that story before, a thousand times. For many, once they got down and attached to a responsibility, they didn't look up till they were nearly sixty and done. It's only then that they reflected back on their lives, bewildered. Well, Jeff was doing well enough regardless.

We were splitting a pair of cigarettes and trading stories. Jeff hadn't had the opportunity to meet Bill or Ruby when they were still around, but he

said, "they sound like one hell of a pair. I only hear good things about 'em."
It warmed my heart to know it. "How long you stickin around?" he asked.

"Your guess is good as mine. Just lookin for a bit of work."

"No shit? What can you do?"

"Anything man. Anything with my hands anyway."

"Good with a hammer?"

"The best."

"Can ya paint?"

"I can."

"Well damn, ya know, there's the nicest old lady, just in town. She's got
this spot off Acres, big place, real nice, just off the corner there. Sweetest thing
she is. But she needs help on her place. She's loaded too."

"No kidding?"

"Let me get you her number."

A few puffs later I was off to my ways, thinking how nice a guy Jeff was and
if I ever needed a solid, no strings attached chat, I'd be back his way. I wished
him the best and that was that.

Jeff wasn't lying. Nancy's place was the nicest, most epic home in the
neighborhood. It didn't even seem to need that much work. Nancy was
married to an insurance guy who ran a pretty successful joint in town for like
forty years. Forty! They weren't exactly hurting for cash and turns out the old
guy, rest his soul, had taken great care of lovely Nancy here before he went off
adventuring to the other side.

Nancy is a retired schoolteacher. She has short clipped white hair and is
frail, but still all there. She uses these endearing terms when talking to me,
making me feel as if she had helped raise me through the years. She emanates
a specific warmth that I've found only in elderly women, the warmth of a
hundred generations. It seems to me that once you made it all the way to your
eighties, women like Nancy somehow meshed their soul with the all-knowing
and carried extraordinary, yet simple, wisdom and love. Nobody under thirty
could ever dream to be so patient and calm and kind.

Well, Nancy adopts me on sight. I show up in my grandfather's leather
jacket, smiling, offering my help for dirt cheap. She makes lunches, lemonade,

sandwiches, cookies, and such, daily. She interrupts my work so frequently to talk that it's immediately obvious to me why she really needed me around in the first place. I decide to work much slower and talk as often as I can. Standing from the top of my ladder, removing gunk from her gutters, she walks slowly below, throwing questions my way, always checking if I'm hungry or tired or anything at all.

"Nah, Nancy I'm fine, I'm fine. Thank you."

And she'll begrudgingly shuffle away for a half hour at most. One day while painting her ceiling, she stands beneath me for fifteen minutes just looking up.

"Who taught you how to do this anyway?"

Brush in hand, smoothly gliding it along, I smile.

"My mother."

And so I help her paint everything anew. I replace some boards in her deck and clean the floors and cupboards. Overall, it's nothing too serious. It's the company she needs, and that's fine with me. I need it too.

Over midday sandwiches and chips, Nancy tells me stories about her late husband and her incredible life stretching as far back as her high school days. She had this crazy romantic story about prom.

"John took another girl, Susie was her name. John took Susie to the dance. Silly. I never knew why he did that. Said he was too nervous to ask me. Bless him. He was making eyes at me all night! And you'll never guess, but he drove me home that night. He drove me home. Suppose I got him in the end."

She chuckles, and my God, is it beautiful. Is there anything more wonderful than a woman, eighty-eight, still living all strong and alone and ignited, retelling the stories of her life and being happy about them? She is the highest sort of genuine light I've seen in ages.

"Nancy," I tell her, "all the novels, they're written about you."

And she blushes!

"Oh shush, stop that, stop that. That's sweet."

Well, it's true and I believe it. I am positively convinced that women like Nancy are the undeniable lifeblood of the world. In the back roads of the smallest towns in all of America they were everywhere, having done more than their fair share of good work and living out their days in holy spirit and angel-like energy which seeped straight to the soil of the Earth and spread itself to everyone, everywhere. It's healing being with her, though I become sad whenever the days come to an end and I have to depart, reminded that she lived in that big house all alone.

"Nancy, if I could, I would stay with you forever," and she blushes some more.

"That'd be nice," she whispers, and she's right. She takes a sip of her coffee, sitting across from me at her dining table covered with elaborately embroidered silk placemats. "Cash, you've never really told me why you're here."

"Jeff gave me your number, remember?"

"No, no, Cambridge."

"Ah right, well you know, my grandparents."

"Yes, of course."

"Yeah."

"But why?" She asks softly, gentle. And she sees right through me. It's that wisdom in action. The coffee warms my hands through the white ceramic, and I stare down into it. I nearly confess everything to her.

"I don't know."

"Young man like you. Must have a home."

"I do, I do."

"Friends, family."

"I do."

"Where's your father these days?"

"Couldn't tell ya."

"Is that right?"

"That's right. He left after Ma's accident."

"God help him."

"Think it broke him. Yeah. I don't know. I don't know where he is."

"Are you okay?" And her deep blue, divinity eyes nearly shatter me. They stare at me with such compassion. I swear that simple question posed in such a genuine, empathetic way could make the hardest of men weep.

I nod and say quietly, "Yeah. yeah I'm okay. Anyway, I think I came back here for her. My Ma. And to get away for a second. Needed a change. Find what I'm looking for."

"Have you?"

"I think I'm starting to."

"You will. Keep your heart open and listen. Give God a little space to work."

"Yeah."

"You're welcome here any time."

"Thank you, Nancy."

"They never really leave us, you know."

"No?"

"Can't you feel them?"

"Sometimes."

"You just have to listen."

And so we do. We sip our coffee in the cold afternoon, and we listen. I've spent about a week with Nancy doing anything imaginable to help her, but we've finally gotten to the point where there's nothing more to be done.

"I'll stick around for a while yet. You're not rid of me," I say.

"Okay good, good."

"I don't know when I'll head out, but I'll tell ya. Don't worry."

"Good. That's kind of you."

She nods, and a little sorrow colors her voice. She's downright depressed to see me go, and it breaks my own heart in two.

"If what you say is true, John, Ruby, and Bill are here looking over you in the meantime."

"They are. They definitely are. Your mom too."

"My mom too."

"It's true, Cash, it's true."

"I believe you Nancy, I do."

44

In the days following my mother's death, our house became the eye of a hurricane. She was so adored in the community that everyone felt the need to come through and pay their respects and check in, days before the official wake and funeral. Emotionless, essentially—gone and alone—I dealt with it. My father was nowhere to be found. Nobody could wrap their mind around that.

"What do you mean he's not here?"

"Cash, I'm so sorry, my God."

"He didn't say *anything*? Are you sure?"

"Honey, I'm sure he'll be back any second."

Blankly, I nodded and felt nothing. I didn't care if he came back or not.

The night after I left my mother in the hospital, I went driving. I left town in search of the place where it happened. Sure enough, the few remnants of the crash were still there, fresh streaks through ice and snow. The truck had been towed out of the ditch so there were only bits and pieces of fragmented metal scattered around. I got out of my car, coatless, and walked down into the ditch. I hadn't slept in two days. The wind ravaged my skin, but I didn't care. I wanted to feel what she felt. I was possessed by numbing anguish. Slow and steady I walked down into the ditch, the snow swallowing my legs. I went forward until I was at the bottom. I buried myself in the snow with all intention of staying there. I started shaking, hyperventilating, and going mad, and finally started to seize when a car came by. I heard screaming from the road above. Some woman I would never see again came and helped pull me out of the snow, which I knew was more than willing to keep me. Later, in the hammering heat of my car, the woman sat by my side. I tried to explain myself, but it was pointless. All I mustered was that my mother had died. She said she was sorry, and we sat. Patches of frostbite burned red on my arms. She didn't leave me until I was roasting in the car for another hour. Looking back, I'm sure the whole nightmarish scene had really freaked her out. Crazy, but I don't even remember her name. I still think about that woman and where she was now. Has she saved anyone else? Without her, I would have been dead. After she left, I don't know what stopped me from heading back to the ditch, but I didn't. It was pitch black when I made my way home. I didn't sleep that night and wouldn't sleep again really for a year.

If not for my brothers, I would have endured the whole mess all alone. My mother was an only child and her parents had passed the year prior. Both of my father's parents were long gone too. Leon and Prince never left my side for weeks. I think they were afraid to have me on my own for too long. The day after I waded out to the ditch, the three of us sat in my living room, morbid and delirious, staring down Priest Charles as he spoke to me about God's love and the relationship he had with my mother, how special and singular he found her to be.

Charles had this red curly hair and donned the biggest square glasses you'd ever seen in your life. He wore the priest garb and was calm and extremely well spoken. Even in despair, I admit, he was full of the holy spirit. I gave credit to the religious folk when they deserved it. My mother had always been fond of him.

Charles sat straight backed, delicate and sad as all hell as he spoke to me about my mother. I could only manage to half listen as he eventually started going over the particulars of the funeral arrangements.

"Cash this is one of the many unfortunate parts of it all. I know it's the last thing you want to think about."

"It's okay."

"We'll make it as easy as possible."

"Okay."

And he went on and on, talking about St. Mark's off Main, the only substantial church in town, and how they orchestrated things. Caskets and all else. He was right. It was the last thing I wanted to talk about, or I thought it was anyway, but then he asked, "Do you know where your father is?"

And there was a flicker of rage, somewhere buried deep in my chest, but I paid it little mind.

"No. I do not." And I knew Charles had more questions about that, but something must have been threatening on my face. From then on, he assumed my father wouldn't be around and he was right to assume that.

I was so thoroughly smothered in blinding shock that I couldn't even process my father missing. Gone. He had left me alone and had bailed on everything at last. I fancied him dead and rotting but I left those thoughts way back in the cracks, hanging crooked on the nails in my skull. I pretended it was all one stupid story someone had told me long ago and convinced myself I never had a father in the first place. My mother had raised me by herself and that's the way I would tell it from now on.

It's bizarre, death and shock, priests in living rooms. And it's even more bizarre housing, in rotation, hundreds of people and their flowers and crying faces while unable to reciprocate their displays of heartbreak. They said sweet things, they really did, though I remember so few of them. All I really remember is they were deeply grieved, sobbing and red faced. I understood and I believed them to be sincere. Still, their mercies fell on me meaningless and deaf. During those days I was a ghost. Stoic and strong in the face of it all. I accepted reality as a dark, mute poison.

Well, that's all it was. The people of Johnston stopped by and offered their support and occasional questions which I answered, robotic and lifeless. I was hanging on by a thread. I was devoid, completely drained, and broken. I was, quite frankly, barely alive. I had half the mind to drown myself in the bathtub or go back out to the snowbank to suffer freezing in the snow like she had or starve myself to death. I contemplated everything. And I couldn't tell you why I didn't. I really couldn't. Even when I think about it now, it seemed obvious that I could pull the trigger, but people stick around and keep beating, don't they? Through all hellacious life. In the face of unimaginable loss. We collect our scars and move forward. Life.

And where was my father? Where the fuck was my dad?

"We could find the fucking guy," Prince said, sitting on my couch, leaning over his knees, wringing out his hands in anger. I shrugged.

"I'm serious Cash, how hard could it be?"

"I don't know, man."

"We fucking—I don't know—we ask around at least."

"We have."

"We can ask the other towns."

"Jimmy might know," Leon suggested.

"Jimmy won't know shit."

I ground my teeth. All of a sudden, Prince sprung from the couch and slammed the side of his fist into the wall.

"I'll kill him. I swear to God, Cash."

"I don't know what to tell you."

"I know man. I'm sorry. I'm just fucking, I don't know. I'm gonna get some air."

And head down, jaw clenched, he left the room. Leon took a long beat. Then we met eyes. Decades of life, decades of trouble and joy, tragedy and brotherhood. Every high and every low. We didn't have to say a word, it was all there. We traced it all back and what was there to say in a time like this? Finally, he sighed and looked down at his hands.

"He'll come back."

"I don't think he will, man."

"Do you want to look for him?"

"No."

*

It wasn't until the funeral that I became truly furious, standing stoically in my black suit. Something about the multitudes of crying people, searching for answers, searching for comfort, drove me an inch away from madness. The grief had pierced my flesh, and I was bleeding on the inside with rage. My father was still nowhere to be seen, and at the wake I stood by my mother's side, close casketed, knowing she was in there but also convinced she was not. And the longest line of sorrow stretched out the building doors and down the street. All of Johnston was there, the whole entire suffering town.

Much later, I would think back on that and cry. I'd kiss the feet of Johnston for the rest of my life in gratitude. For on that day, they had shown me true grace and warmth. Everyone was there. For my mother, and for me.

But in the moment, I couldn't process a thing. I was out of my mind, running down some harrowed country road of pain and trying to find somewhere to hide. I was growing vengeful with God and my father. I wanted to burn the building down, myself along with it. I wished to disintegrate, to be reduced to ash and be swept up by wind. There was nothing but the hate for my father beating loudly in my chest. And with each person that shuffled slowly and despondent through the doors to either hug me or shake my hand, I looked up, like a five year-old boy, hoping for my dad to come home. But he never did. He never showed. And at the foot of my mother's grave, I knew the heart-break of life, the truth of its brutality.

I wouldn't really cry until almost half a year later. And it happened in the strangest of ways. All I did was bite into a strawberry. My mother used to dip them in sugar.

During those months, I would walk out to my front porch and wait for my father. I believed in my gut he would come back one night, spinning drunk, and I'd fight him. Month after month, every evening, I would go out to the porch, and I'd wait. The moon tracking its path in the sky, shining above as it always had. I thought of my father driving, never stopping, somewhere lost in America, trying to use that moon as a compass. I asked myself the same questions over and over again. *Where are you now? What have you done?*

God, I needed to see his face, and I needed to know. I had to see it in his eyes before he went all the way. And what would the punishment be, for me killing my father? These questions haunted me as I reached out to God. Did he feel guilt or fear? What it must be like to be gone, in a bar in some back town trading nothings with the keep and swilling it down till he pruned. He wouldn't be sober a second, I knew that. And I feared that the smoke and the booze and the regret would put an end to him before I ever got the chance, and yet, the child, the child, the child in my heart still clung to a rope. Still clutched to the dream of *the father,* was still seeped in the hope of the American leader who was strong and courageous and loving. And so on the cold porch I sat, night after night, thinking that on one drunken black evening he'd return. Shoes worn and vest tattered, flannel faded, he'd step out from his truck and he'd reckon at last with his son. I sat there and waited for months, but he never showed. He would never come home.

And so *that* was my plot still in Johnston, if you asked. My mother, that house, and waiting for my father.

In the years after, I had made it my own. The place on Woodland Drive was mine, and I kept it alive for my mother. I knew it had saved me in the years that followed her departure, and for better or worse, I still felt her there. Maybe that's why I could never leave, not for nothing.

*

I think about all of this as I rock in my grandfather's chair. It's been a month since I arrived in Cambridge. I'm figuring it out, one slow day after day in the house I have made whole again. Nancy told me the spirits are here. She's not wrong. I've known that all along. And still, something's not done. I can't run the clock out quite yet. I am moving along on this grand perfect web that is spun.

45

I've found myself in an early morning Casey's conversation with Jeff. I have a nice hot cup of coffee in my hand and he's going on and on about his past job and whole life he had down in Indiana.

"Car mechanic, yup, car mechanic ten years."

Man can he spin a tale. He almost has me rolling.

"This big old jackass came in, ordinary afternoon, his arms all full of grease, like, all full. He's pissed up talking shit 'bout how he can't fix his damn engine. This poor fucker's ass cheeks were squeezing themselves up his jeans man, up and over, and he's rambling, man is he rambling. He's telling me all about this morning he was having, his wife. Guy's a lunatic I'm thinkin, for sure. Looked like he hadn't slept or bathed in a month. No lying. Anyway, he's getting worked up and I haven't said a word. He's just turning red in the face man I've never seen anything like it, this guy. Anyway, this poor bastard starts havin a heart attack! Right there in the shop! Not lying! Oh Jesus he kept sayin, *here we go again*. He kept saying that. *Here we go again*. 'Parently, this happens to him all the time. I'm panicking calling 911 ah God the whole thing. He was alright though, don't worry, don't worry. He ended up bein just fine."

Jeff has some pretty zany yellow teeth, but my God does he have an honest smile. The way he's bulleting on and on into this six a.m. story makes me start laughing, and I damn near can't stop. He's bringing tears to my eyes. The coffee is setting in and I'm buzzing. To think I had zero intention of saying a word to Jeff this morning.

"Anyway, what the hell is it you really do, Cash?"

"What do you mean?"

"You know, when you're not painting and shit."

"Good question. I like to write."

"No kiddin?"

"Yeah man."

"Man, that's crazy, that's crazy because I used to be a writer. I used to! My pops had this real old fuckin typewriter stored away in my basement, ya know? And I used to sneak on down and get that thing spinnin, I tell ya, I swear to that! I coulda been Bukowski!"

And now I'm really enjoying myself because I loved Bukowski, but Jeff really *meant* what he said. He really believed he coulda been Bukowski if he'd only kept at it. I found that endearing as hell, and hysterical too. I knew that any kid in the world could pound away on a typewriter, and that being *Bukowski* came down to an altogether different thing, an altogether different life. I don't know how to explain that to Jeff and also, I don't want to dampen his hard earned high. The world needed more of honest Jeff's enthusiasm, that's for sure. How the hell would I know if Jeff had the juice? I couldn't tell ya. He certainly filled the air with phenomenal tales, so eccentric and everything. Maybe he coulda been Bukowski after all.

Whenever Jeff paused for two seconds to ask me something about myself, I couldn't bear to tell him the whole truth. I didn't want to go too deep because pretty soon he'd be back rambling about his life, which I found much more interesting.

"Ah damn Cash, I like ya man. You know I imagined I'd be just about anywhere but here. Figured I'd be doing some other work by this point, not here. Maybe I seriously oughta sit down and see if I can make the typewriter dance."

"Make it dance!?"

"Make it dance baby."

And I fucking lose it again laughing. What's up with this maniac? Everything about him I'm finding earnest and hilarious. He said it with such a straight face, I swear. Make it dance. I liked that.

"Listen man, I believe you can do anything in the whole wide world, but if you're gonna do it, you better get round to doing it, ya know? You're not getting any younger."

"God do I really look that old?"

"You know what I mean."

Crazy Jeff. My coffee is damn near gone and I kid you not, there hasn't been a single other customer that has come through the place since I arrived.

"God Jeff you sure get swamped mornings, huh?" And he really snorts at that and cackles.

"That's a good one," he says, pumping some tobacco into his lower lip.

"Fuck's sake man, ain't it a bit early?"

He shakes his head and says, "just depends how you're keepin time."

I'm enjoying Jeff more and more by the second. He's his own man. He could chat about damn near anything, but all at once, he gets sort of quiet and serious. He leans in a tad.

"You know, man," he goes, "I would never propose, or go 'round tellin nobody bout nothin like this usually, but I like ya and well I might as well get to it, there's a guy outside of town that's been gettin his hands on this Alice man, solid for years, and I see him from time to time."

I squint at him.

"Alice? What the fuck are you talkin about?"

And he gets this stupid grin on his face and goes even lower with it, barely a whisper.

"Come on. man, shrooms man, mushrooms. Alice in Wonderland."

Ah, of course. Are they really calling it that now?

"Anyway man, I'm tellin ya, just cuz you been sayin how you're hunkered down and all and kinda bored sometimes and what not, and I see you're kinda on this odyssey right? Least that's how it seems, I don't wanna assume nothin, but ya know I have something for that, more than usual from a recent trip out and if you want a bit, it's yours, man. All yours."

And what an absurd comedy Jeff and I have found ourselves in this morning. All jazzed on coffee and riding a positive jam. It shouldn't surprise me that he offered me drugs, but somehow it caught me off guard. Wild Jeff was hitting Alice on his off nights and mornings, and that extra glint in his eye made a little more sense to me now.

"Well?"

And I laugh a little, shake my head and say, "Yeah man, why not?"

46

I'm not one of those big psychedelic adventurer types. While that whole scene fascinated me, and I always listened intently to the stories, I've never been the guy who chased those particular highs. Most of my knowledge of drugs came from my conversations with Prince and a small group of guys we grew up with that fell into a pattern of experimentation shortly after high school. Prince was the first of my friends who had done acid and reported back to us just a little differently than we had known him the day before. Honest, not one person in my life was the same after a real acid trip, that was a fact.

I'll never forget the day Prince showed up on my doorstep, hair messed and greasy and shirt drenched in sweat. He sat me down and said he hadn't slept. He went on to tell me the long traumatic story of what might have been one of the worst trips anyone had ever had. He looked frightened, like a kid.

"Two straight hours. At least. Maybe three. Just, fucking, staring in the mirror, Cash. I couldn't stop. And I tried."

He shook his hair from his face as he stared down at the floor, pausing for a second, gathering himself. In a flurry he slicked the mane back.

"I watched my fucking face morph. It morphed man. It morphed into my fears. Every single one of them."

"Whoa."

"No. Worse than *whoa,* man. You don't understand, Cash, I could fucking see them. All my worst parts. They— they *manifested* into my face. And I got super old and then young again and all hallowed out and shit man, it was the scariest fucking thing I've ever seen. And my eyes got pure black and large. I looked like a *fish*. And I was drenched in sweat. And then I looked like my father, but worse. Like bloodied and dead like when I saw him after he fell. And then I was fat, Cash, fat as fuck and my cheeks looked like they were going to explode and then I was a skeleton and dying with AIDS or whatever the fuck and I *hated* myself man. That was the worst part. I hated myself. I was disgusted by myself."

He went on and on and on, still sweating like crazy in my living room, twenty and alone and utterly panicked. And all I could do was talk him through it. That was only the first three hours of his trip which he claimed lasted like ten hours in total.

"Then I was looking at a painting on the wall—you know the one—of the field and that one tree under the moon. And even that turned into my father. God man the whole thing, the whole place was him. He was communicating with me. But it was dark. It was *alive*, man. You don't understand."

Man, man. Prince really lost it that morning, and I did what I could to keep him sane. Later, when I finally got him to calm down, he slept for almost an entire day in my guestroom with the windows pulled to black.

All to say, I only tried my luck with acid once, though Prince almost scared me off the stuff completely that day. I didn't need any hallucinatory hauntings, but I knew that at some point I'd have to try it. I'd have to know just what it was. In the years to come, I heard from plenty of buddies who had much better experiences than Prince did. In fact, many came back with glorious stories of beautiful colors and images, ideas, and feelings of love.

So, a year after my mother died, I finally gave it a go. The following night I showed up to Prince's for a bonfire with a few buddies, but I was running on no sleep and was still pretty scattered. I didn't even sit down before I started talking.

"I painted for ten hours guys. Ten. There I was, and Prince, man, I know I said I'd wait to take it together, but I cracked a beer last night in the kitchen and all of a sudden, I *knew* it was time."

"Fuck yeah." Prince smiled, clapping his hands together.

"So, I took it and didn't do a thing at first. Just put my mom's *Rumours* record on and sat down on the couch. I was rocking a bit, just listening to Fleetwood Mac, and out of nowhere it hit me man, it hit me that I was supposed to be fucking painting, that I was *always* supposed to be painting. God, it was so real. So, I went into my cabinets, and you know I have a hundred old pails I never use, and brushes too. It felt like this ancient blue one was fucking placed there by God man, I'm tellin ya, it was calling out to me. So, I took this old brush and pail of blue paint and went downstairs to the basement. You know that huge white wall I've never done anything with. God, I swapped Stevie out for Zeppelin man and let *Physical Graffiti* start rolling. It's the only thing I listened to the whole trip, and I just started fucking painting man. All. Night. Long. Anyway, this morning I stopped and just walked upstairs. I didn't even sit there to look at it. I don't know why. I can't explain it. I haven't gone back down all day. You guys wanna see it?"

My buddy CJ busted out laughing and Seth, my childhood friend, said, "You're out of your mind Cash, you know that?" He joined CJ in laughter, but Prince wasn't laughing.

"Fuck yeah I wanna see it, man. We're going right now," he said.

"You guys coming?" I asked.

"Yeah, yeah, of course, Picasso, why not?"

CJ and Seth stood up.

"What a change of events," Prince said.

They followed me to my car, and we left.

I walked us down to my basement, not really knowing what to expect. I know that sounds insane, that I had painted the entire night but I really had no conception of what I'd created or what I'd think of the piece now that I was sober. Something told me when I was finished to just let it be and only return when I was ready. Well, I waited all day. As my feet moved down the stairs, I began to grow a little nervous because I had invited my buddies to come with. Ah, fuck it. How bad could it be? I took a breath and swallowed what I could of my anticipation. I reached the carpeted floor, flicked the lights on and rounded the corner. There it was, my illuminated canvas.

I'm not kidding, I lost my breath. I don't know what sort of acid I had taken but whatever it was had transformed me into a modern-day Pollock.

"Jesus Christ," Prince whispered in awe.

"Holy shit," CJ murmured. I couldn't believe my eyes. I had painted a magnificent mural of abstract cuts and swoops, splashed and chaotic but somehow specific, right on the money. The wall looked like it was crying, like it was hemorrhaging blue. I had covered the entire wall of my basement in blue graffiti.

"Are you fucking kidding me, Cash?" Prince asked. "You painted this last night?"

I didn't know what to say.

"Yeah, man."

He walked up real close and ran his hands along the design, tracing some of the movements and then stepped back. "This is the greatest fucking painting I've ever seen in my life."

After the boys left my house, I went back downstairs and I stared at that painting for hours. *How had I done it?* Sure, I could paint, but I had never done anything like that. I could feel the blue slashes of pain, the torment, the chaos, all together with the serene, calm areas of relief. There was ecstasy in the assortments of lines, the tiny collections of dots, leaving tails of paint behind them like comets. It was my life. That's the only way I could describe it. It was all of our lives. The curves and the explosions and the gashes and the smooth waves, all blue. I stayed up again, well into the evening, tracing each stroke, recalling my inspiration as it had come to me the night before.

I thought about Johnston, about everything and everyone. I thought about our lives, and the graffiti of our town. We each left our mark. We are cracks in sidewalks, bent street signs, rusted gutters, and train tracks. We are nails in wooden boards, handprints in cement. We are creaks in the doors of diners, stains from cigarettes. We are streaks of graffiti, blue as the sky.

Well, it was the last time I did acid, and it was the last time I ever painted like that. I could never recreate it even if I tried. To this day, I have no idea how I did it, and the wall in my basement is still adorned with blue paint.

There were a hundred different stories about drugs and what they did to us, each different from the next. My buddy Mark stayed up on molly for like a week straight once before he almost killed himself.

In Jimmy's one night he laughed and said, "The shit you do when you're young."

We were still in our twenties. Would we all pay the piper in the end? My friends and I had our own scattered past of ecstasy and acid and shrooms and the whole mess of them, no doubt, but the truth is I probably had the most love for drugs out of anyone on Earth who didn't really do them that often. I mostly was there for my friends in the aftermath, listening to all of their crazy tales while drinking my fair share and smoking cigarettes. *Alice*, Jeff had called it. I sorta liked the name now.

I haven't done shrooms since last fall when Prince and I went west to La Crosse and rented out a place off-grid. We went exploring, and ate them high in the bluffs and saw wondrous things. We spent the day hiking and communicating with the deer and eagles and the other wild beasts that were roaming the land with us. We spoke platitudes to the trees, and the clouds formed mystic images. It was a fine day in my memory, but it was long ago. When Jeff smirked, asked, and offered, I figured, well, what the hell. It had been long enough. I *was* on an odyssey after all. He was right to assume that.

So, here I sit in the afternoon haze with a small bag of Alice in my grandparents' revitalized home. The smell of the shrooms isn't all-consuming, but they're quite dark and carry a specific musk. Jeff told me a few things about the guy that he got them from to comfort me, but it didn't matter. I trusted Jeff and that was enough. It was an instinct, at least. I take the shrooms out and

I put them in the palm of my hand. What mysteries will they hold? There's only one way to find out. I put the whole stock in at once and chew them, scowling at the taste. I hate how they stick to your teeth, I forgot about that. They really are foul in flavor. Even cooked mushrooms, prepared and sauteed, were liable to give me chills from time to time.

They make their way down. I know I have maybe forty-five minutes or an hour before they start setting in. Maybe sooner, I'm not sure. I haven't eaten breakfast or lunch. I get up from the rocking chair, put my grandfather's blue and black flannel coat on, and first go to brush my teeth. I have to get the foul taste out of my mouth.

In the rusted mirror all the way back near the bedroom, I run my fingers through my beard and remark upon my age. I haven't cut my hair in months. It's been almost half a year. I haven't shaved for weeks. I am becoming one with the vagabond life. I chuckle. I spit the toothpaste out and gargle some water doused in iron. It makes me think about my buddy Cameron from grade school. In middle school he had to go to the hospital every week because of a severe iron deficiency. He could have just drank this shit. He was so skinny, you could easily miss him in the crowds of youth. Cameron ended up being one hell of a friend, and I wondered where he was in the world. He moved out of Johnston almost ten years ago now to somewhere in Iowa. His blond and brown hair used to fall out and leave him like it had some other place it had to be. He must be bald these days, but I hope he had the iron thing figured out. Resilient Cameron. I wipe the water from my beard and walk my way to the front door almost forgetting about the hallucinogens in my stomach.

I'm deep in the woods when the ominous clouds begin to roll in, the type that bring the night. It's early afternoon but it's starting to feel like evening already and I'm a couple miles out from home, too far out to turn back this early. No abnormal feeling has set in, I'm still sane of mind. The wind is picking up and I think, if lucky, I'll be part of one hell of a storm. I have this thing about the rain. When I was young, I would run out into our yard during rainstorms in my underwear and go crazy. I'd sit beneath drainpipes and let the water crash and cascade all its omnipotence into my young skull.

Even in the lightning I would play; and the fiercer the wind, the better. And Ma would call out from the doorway and plead for me to come back inside, but I was gone, wholly convinced that I belonged in the downpour, soaked, and getting more so all the time. I was wild and alive. As I grew older, I still couldn't help it. I would wander down to the Fox and watch the water fall. All the minor drumbeats would play out, thousands and thousands each making their indents on the surface of the speeding current, and if you listened close enough you could hear their spirit. I could feel it against my skin. I adopted the rain as my communion with Heaven and was swept up in its magic. I let no rainfall pass me by without at least reaching a hand out to feel it.

I look up to the darkening clouds. In a matter of minutes, it will begin to come down and cover me completely. Sooner or later, I'll be tripping, lost in the woods and the rain. I smile like a cinematic protagonist. The wind picks up and begins whispering secrets. I envision the ground rising up around me, flowing in water and earth like the flood that lifted Noah to the sky. Today I am him, convinced I can ride the wave right up and swim to salvation. I have total clairvoyance.

I'm trying to find the fort that Grandpa and I made all those years back when we ate sandwiches, and he told me about the Second World War. Imagine it now? The fall leaves crunch beneath my feet and I think, yes, fall, make the most of your music. Let your orchestra play before the water turns you to mush, soundless. You deserve your final symphony, and I, yes, I, will listen and remember your last dying song on the planet. And it happens.

Somewhere in that thought, things start to shift. The sound of the forest begins to grow more crisp and intricate as I begin to trip. For all I know, my footsteps are echoing all the way back to my land out in Johnston. It wouldn't surprise me to learn that there are endless reverberations to everything, traveling further than we could ever imagine. In one smooth effort they traversed the whole globe in an illustrious call to arms. Each indentation I make sounds so varied and purposeful that it becomes clear, this communication. I smile. I know this is just the beginning.

I'm sheltered by the shadows of the woods. All around me is an ocean of dead leaves, brown and getting darker. Soon they will be snowed upon and buried down to the generation before them, and the one before that, making way for the younger, more beautiful crowd. And it's true that it is the same with us all. What's left of us, anyway, running around. God, what a wide ocean of brown. Even the bark on the trees is a gorgeous thick brown and black. Sometimes chipped and faded, sometimes wet and saturated. Some have the sap and some have been burrowed by woodpeckers, but they're all of one body. One towering bunch of guardians with life in their branches, filtering the air and taking care of us daily. How would we ever repay them?

Far off, I hear my first bit of thunder but still the rain has not started to fall. I'm beginning what I imagine will be a long journey into chaos. A thin layer of sweat coats my neck but when the rain hits, I'll be chilled to the bone. This is what I need. All around me I can feel the woods breathing, matching my tempo. It's really something to see the bark shiver and swell. To see the few squirrels taking cover, and in the distance, all the deer, bounding to safety in the woods they called home. White spots dance on their sleek and athletic spines.

I lean down and pick up a particularly thick branch. This will be my staff. And didn't Noah have a great giant staff? He must have. And the mist begins to settle all over my body. I can taste it now. There are few more inspiring moments than the ones before the swell, before the monsoon from the skies. As the wind picks up the fading dry leaves and sweeps them away to another place, I close my eyes and let my arms stretch all the way to the coasts. My left hand grasps at the hot coal sand in California and the right cleans the glass of the Empire. It's true we are limitless. All the atoms stretch far from my nails and grip the ocean weathered borders of my continent. I begin laughing with a joy purer than I've ever remembered.

I feel it all. I feel God and the unbounded beauty of everything. Swimming and dancing and playing around. To be in the middle of everything! And this is possible for anyone! Yes! I am sure of it. A raindrop hits my eye, right beneath the lashes and it's here. At last! And the thing about a good storm is that it doesn't come all at once, not always. The best ones start slow.

I open my eyes and through the bare branches above I watch each individual orb fall blue and clean from the sky. Slowly at first, then faster, and faster, and faster until I am surrounded by rain. I hold my arms up and spread them apart, still holding the country together as the water begins to wash my face. What richness it offers, what rebirth. And it all makes sense to me now, how in the Bible they talk about that. Those stories all at once are clear, that big flood and all that came with it. Every evil thing will succumb, will be purged, and then perish. It's all a cleansing. The dark will always, eventually, run its cruel course before it returns to the layers of Earth where we walked, where we buried and built up once again. This is the flood, and these are the times of revival.

I am all at once astoundingly gone, spun everywhere at last. My mind has fully morphed as I continue forward through the woods. The wind swirls even stronger around me as the leaves grow dense with water. I can see all of their tiny veins absorbing the wet, bemoaning the fact that in a way, it is too late for them.

Where have you been? says the leaves to the rain, and also, to me.

So, I step forward and the forest floor attaches its body to my boots. We are one moving entity now. Onward I go, my hair plastered to my forehead and falling over my eyes. I push it away and run my hands through my beard. I am back, back, back to the past. I am my great great great grandfather gathering steam and gaining honest intellectual thought one hard earned day at a time, in the middle of nowhere.

Convinced that the rain will keep falling, and that I will be carried away in its wake, I at last come upon the lost fort. There, hanging before me, disembodied, are the remains. There are some boards scattered about, a few of them hanging off the tree at an angle, clinging desperately to rusted nails. Strands of rope still hang from the branches, waving about in the wind. The only part that stood the test of time is the floor, which now looks like a small diving platform stretching out from the stomach of the tree. It catches the rain, sheltering a patch of dry ground beneath. It has been a lifetime since I first made this fort with my grandfather.

I think about all those who came across this place since. What did they think about the creators? Did they know who this was for and why we had left it? In the downpour I walk to the bones, and I kneel. I scoop up some sideboards. There's a long holy panel of wood that I believe was once a door. I stand it up on its side and think, if it floods, we will glide on the water together, forever to the new world.

My clothes are drenched and heavy now as I stand beneath the platform for a second to watch it all fall down, crashing in sheets around me. What a storm. The strongest I've seen in years. What a song. Surrounding me are the cacophonies of the water and bark, animal, and branch; ringing out in intelligent, spontaneous creation that personifies genius, coherency. It is elevated and above my imagination, but I gather something transcendent. Like Beethoven or Bach or the rest. The savants, the powerful, the divine.

It is the Mother's turn, above and sending sheets of herself down around me, telling a story so ancient it surpasses words. And it is dark, but it is blue. Blue sheets of rain are falling in patterns, epic all around me. Another hour of this, and everything will flood. I kiss the tree where my grandfather once rested his tired spine; and decide to make the trek back.

It's becoming colder and a shiver shakes through me. In the blink of an eye, the forest is nearly black and for the first time, I begin to have doubts I can make it back. The wind is thrashing now, blowing phenomenal gusts that could rip the smaller trees from their roots and it too, has a color. Mirrored in the lightning through the vapor, it shines. I swear it is silver and moves vicious and violently beautiful through the maze in the woods. Like a moth to a flame, I feel the temptation to be close to it. I almost beg it to lift me from the Earth. As I walk on, I cling to the trunks of the trees. I will make it, I think, or I simply will not.

I am only climbing higher. I am only further lost in my hallucinogen expanse, and the storm is raging, gaining momentum. Lightning and thunder begin to shred the sky around me and I have no concept of time. All I can be sure of is that it is freezing, and the evening is setting in quickly. My heart pounds in my chest. I can hear it. I am breathing heavy and shaking. I am muddied and desperate, searching for the paths I have walked all the days prior.

The problem is, of course, the water. It is now rushing along the crevices and the small, wood hidden ditches. It is washing away any trace of the life that passed before it. There is no path to follow, there is no certain way forward. I am lost and seeing visions, embodied by darkness. I begin to think of things most negative and feel close to my capture. To death.

"C'mon, Cash, c'mon," I repeat to myself as I force my way forward, one step at a time.

This is no rain, no more. This is something entirely cosmic. This is nature's whole reckoning with the world. I know it. She is having it out, at last, with me and the rest of us. She will have her answers and revenge for her sorrows. It is clear she intends to take me. The skyward black walls are closing in. I am drowning. When I look at my hands, they are ancient. They are swollen with water and wrinkled, and my boots are like roots, unmovable now. They are cratered with mud, water, and woods.

Still, one step at a time, I fight onward, looking out for a light or an angel or hope. Big heavy breaths fill my lungs until finally, I collapse. I go down to a knee. Am I having a heart attack? All around me images dance like nightmares. The lightning strikes violently everywhere. The thunder is shaking the Earth.

I begin to see cats on branches. Hundreds and hundreds of cats. And in the corners of my vision there are red eyes from wolves and witches. I hear sounds ricocheting off the pounding water. I hear all sorts of demons. High pitched laughing and screeching. I crouch down, close my eyes, and try to focus. It isn't real and I know that, or is it? I keep shaking the rain from my eyes just to see clearly again but I'm hopeless. I am engulfed by storm. It has gotten me at last. I sink deeper into the Earth. Beneath my knees it feels warm, welcoming me to the mud. What a nice long sleep could do for the lonely and broken.

I open my eyes one more time and standing before me are the ghosts of my whole washed up life. All lined up and staring me down. My mother. My father. Grandpa Bill. Grandma Ruby. Tommy. Jimmy. Prince's father. So. this is it then? Dead and beaten, delusional and freezing, wet. In the worst storm of the Midwest, in the woods, I will be consumed. I am staring at the gates which wait like Hell, just for me.

I claw at my beard and my face, and I shake my head, but the images remain. If I am to go, then I'll go, but before that, we must have it out. I begin crawling through the mud and I'm yelling questions into the abyss. I'm spitting out water from my mouth. I'm throwing fistfuls of earth at the ghosts. But nothing calls back. There are no answers here.

Finally, I stand. I stumble forward now, mad. Foaming over my teeth and sick. Dying in the rain where I am failing to breathe. And I remember as a kid thinking I was the storm, and the storm was me.

I am as naked as ever, though cloaked in my grandfather's coat. And my mother is standing so close. Her eyes unblinking, morose. And I'm losing the strength in my bones. I keep shaking my head, the image must go, but it won't. It stays, and at last, the group gathers. The line comes closer, together.

What is it you want?

What have you learned that I haven't? And Grandpa, don't you know that I found our great fort? Grandma, your house! Have you seen it? It's back! It's finished!

I slap at my face and whip it frantically back and forth as they take step after slow moving step closer, if they reach me, I know it is over.

Ma. Say something, Ma. Say it, and then I can go. Please.

I fall to my knees, and my hands follow. They strike the ground and sink deep through the mud. The water is running like madness around me. I yell at the top of my lungs. The ghosts suddenly stop. I look up to my mother so near. Her brown hair is soaked wet in the torrent. She is smiling.

Ma, you're smiling! Ma! I never thought.

I try to stand, but am useless. She kneels down, and slowly draws a warm cross on my forehead. Like she would every night before bed. She has blessed me, again. She stands, and I'm spinning so fast. She walks back through the woods where she came.

Ma. Ma. Ma!

I close my eyes and try to steady my breath.

I open them, and they're gone. *But to where?*

I am dead.

The heat of eleven suns gathers, it presses its light to my flesh.

I'm kneeling at the gates before God and the rain never stops.

The woods are gone.

It is white. It is white. It is white.

47

The next morning, I hit the road.

I awoke in the late hours of night, sopping, freezing and trembling, still coming down from the trip. Turns out I had made it about a quarter mile from the house and in the earliest a.m. hours, I stumbled the rest of the way back. It felt like a miracle I was alive. I was shaking so severely from the cold I thought I'd permanently damaged myself. When I dragged my legs the last steps home, I threw the front door open, stripped off my clothes, and collapsed on the couch with a few thick blankets wrapped tightly around me.

A few hours later, I came to life in a daze and forced myself to the shower. As the warmth gently fell against my skin, I recounted all the things I had seen and vowed to never take Alice again. God, I thought I had died out there in my grandparents' woods. Clearly, I had taken too much. I would be sorting my way through those visions for months to come. My body was all scraped up and bruised from my struggles, and I still couldn't breathe calmly.

After the shower, I gathered my few belongings and said my final goodbyes. I blessed the place, promising my grandparents that I'd be back. I was still fogged from the shrooms, but one thing was clear—it was time to go home.

The damage from the storm moves outside my car windows. As God would have it, the only homes that seemed to be spared were my own and Nancy's. I stopped by on my way out of town to say goodbye. "It's a miracle, Cash, I can't believe the whole house didn't fall." We shared one more hug and I couldn't help but feel she knew something inside me had shifted. "Bless you, Cash. Bless you."

"Bless you too, Nancy. I hope I see you soon."

On it goes. There are broken trees in the yards of almost every house I pass. Big oaks are split and fractured. There are power lines down and leaves scattered everywhere. Broken recycling and garbage bins have been tossed through the streets. The people of Cambridge will be cleaning this up for weeks. And so, the storm really was that bad. It was a warning of some kind.

A cleansing. I am reminded, more than ever, that mother nature will always show the people where things stood. There is no denying the everlasting power she possesses. She is the one that shakes the planet and takes the structures down if she pleases. It is a privilege to walk on her surface, and perhaps the reminders are necessary. I rub my eyes and try to focus on the road as the events of the prior evening play out in my mind like the remnants of a dream.

An hour later, I'm driving my Saturn with a strange calmness. A serenity settles inside me. Whatever the truth was, I had learned a small piece of it. In the midst of what I would later find out to be the worst storm of Cambridge's past fifty years, I had found a few answers. I had seen my mother and father, and all the rest. They had passed along some surety to me. Some blessing. I had been broken, gathered up, and released again. I know that whatever is waiting for me in Johnston, it is finally mine and mine alone. I will start anew. I am no longer shackled. Maybe I'll return home forever, or maybe I'll leave again someday soon. I don't know. I'm not attached either way, but the dawn is coming.

In the dimming haze of the mushrooms, I have a proverbial peacefulness. It's been over a month since I left Johnston. What had happened in my absence? The midwestern countryside begins to open up as I hop on the highway and drive straight as an arrow can fly. All around me it feels as if the day is in lazy mourning. It is recovering, regrouping. You and I both. I roll the windows down and feel the cold fall wind on my body, swirling like always.

Something has changed.

48

When I opened the door to my mother's hospital room, I had no trace of a pulse. With the doctor behind me and a nurse in the corner, I stayed in the doorway for what could have been an eternity. There she was. Her face was bruised, cut, bandaged, mangled. I waited to make sure she wasn't going to move. I almost expected her body to rise up out of the bed and go skyward, out of sight. And it's true that no son should see his mother like this. The world had taken the single most beautiful thing it had ever created and destroyed it. All the rest of us were allowed to beat on. How could this be? How could everything keep moving as if nothing had happened? How could this be the plan? If I hadn't seen it with my own eyes, I never would have believed it to be true. My mother was gone. The angel song had finished. *Ma, seeing you in that hospital bed was the worst thing I've ever done.*

I walked toward her and stood, quiet. It was the first truth I knew that she didn't. For the first time in my life, I had the irrefutable secret knowledge that she was never privy to. But I was too late. I could no longer share it. I couldn't save her. If only I could have called her that night and said, "Ma, there's a conspiracy against you."

The blood was gone from her face. It made me ill, beyond repair. *Was this in the stars, written?* Why had God taken her? I hated the red streaks, the indents across her nose and cheeks. How dare anything maim her in this way? And to think she didn't even die with the impact.

Ma, what were your last thoughts? Who were you whispering to when it mattered most? Ma, how much pain? Did you think of me? Did you wish I was there?

I reached down and I took her lifeless hand, devoid of strength but still hers. None of her fingers were broken, somehow her whole hand was intact. If I blinked my eyes closed and prayed hard enough, would she come back? With faith like a mustard seed. Ma, how has this happened? You were your savior's favorite, were you not? It didn't make sense. Can we ever go back? Ma, I'd trade my life to reverse the whole order. I don't need much, I'll give it all up, if we could be in the waterparks together again. If we could share a lunch and I could see you laugh.

Forever.

The word was rattling around in my head like a bomb. There would be no more crosses. No more dinners and praying hands. I would have no more late-night phone calls where you checked on me softly, without Dad knowing. It's true we were the best of friends. The best. And I loved you like I would love no other. So, forever? How could it be? Would you not be around? Where then? Where would you stay? How can I leave you, motionless in dirt?

I leaned down and I kissed her cold forehead. I drew a cross there too. There was nothing I could do, in the end, in the end. It happened. Things were dead and done.

I forgot the doctors were there. I had the idea of taking her body and running out of the hospital. I would go out to the country and bury us together. We could have that, at least. I didn't need to move on. What was there, in that vast, empty country? Was there anything, if not your voice and spirit? *Ma, where will I go?* Where can I run? Even in foreign nations I'd imagine myself rallying against the all-knowing finality of your death.

I want to climb in the bed and become small. I want to curl into a ball and nestle in your arms. Hidden and crying and clutching. Bury me with my mother. The blankets she wore did nothing for her now but shield the air from her body, now turned off for all time. What a crime. What a devastated life it is, Ma.

I love you.

I take another couple steps back and am finished in a way I never knew was possible. It felt as if my ribs had ripped through my chest. I knew I could never rebuild. I could never retry. There were things that happened in life that stopped the clock. Once you lost it, there was no getting it back. It was immediate, mechanical, final.

There was nothing spinning in my heart. My soul was sinking to an oceanic rock that nobody frequented. Nobody even knew it was there. I was finally alone. It's true that the human soul knows no bottom, not really. There is always further to go. There is, out there, a never-ending dive. I was riding that loss all the way. I felt the anguish twist in my stomach and I viciously wretched on the hospital floor, all over my shoes and the tile. In my memory, it was red. It was the love in my chest. Crashing to the ground in despair, a suicidal effort. And I think the doctor rushed the nurse to get the mop and put his arms around me but I'm not sure. I don't remember.

I'm sorry, Ma. I failed.

I took one last look, her brown hair still shining in the white hospital light, and I hated myself, I hated all life.

"I love you Ma. I'm so sorry."

Agonized, I tumbled out of that chamber. I gagged in the hallway. It was over. I would kill myself in the snow. Brutal and cold and slow. It's the land of the dead, don't you know?

49

Hard to believe, but I've found my way back to my booth in Jimmy's Place.

Prince and Leon sit across from me and we're pulling down pitchers of Budweiser. I called them up as soon as I was back in town.

"Well, I'm glad Mo told you, anyway."

"Dramatic as hell." Prince smirks.

"I think I kinda snapped when she left."

I spent almost the whole first hour telling them about my date with Rose. How promising I thought it all went and how she disappeared anyway without a word. "But you know I've been planning to head out there for years regardless."

"That's where I thought you went," Leon says.

"Yeah?"

"Yeah, didn't I tell you Prince? Cambridge. I said it. You were always talkin about how you oughta fix that place up. I bet you went there. We knew. Didn't I say that?"

"He did. He said that a few days after Mo told us you left."

"Another week, and we woulda driven on out there to be sure though," Leon shrugs.

"Appreciate that."

"Better now?" Prince asks.

"Much. I was thinkin a lot about Ma and all. My pops. I don't know. I needed a month."

"Yeah, yeah." They nod.

"I didn't wanna explain. I just wanted to go. I wanted to feel like I could."

"Course you can. It's good. Need that." Leon says.

"Anyway, the place is good as new. You two gotta see it. Whole thing is redone. But the craziest shit happened."

And then I get around to telling them about the forest mushroom trip. Best I could, I relayed every detail from start to finish. The guys grew damn near giddy hearing it all.

"Good for you, man," Prince laughs, "Fuckin good for you, Cash. That's the stuff. Hell, sometimes all a man needs is a solid trip."

Leon smirks, amused and drinking his beer down easy. He did his fair share of psychedelic experimenting, but was way calmer and more collected and professional about it all. Before we know it, we're laughing and reminiscing on everything like I never left in the first place. And God bless them for it. They understood it all. At the end of the day, they thought I was a bit crazy for leaving without much of a sound, but they were just glad that I did what I had to do, and that I had the adventure and returned in one piece. You know how it is with best friends, family. It was just like yesterday, so the saying goes.

After the first pitcher and my stories, we start talking about what I'd missed in Johnston.

Leon, minimal, gruffs out, "Not a whole lot's changed. Honest."

"Gotta be something man. How's Mo?"

"Mo's good. She's always good."

"Work?"

"Ah well, we're commissioning this new project over at the high school. Renovating the entire field house, actually."

"The whole field house?"

"You bet."

"That's a big fucking deal, man."

"It's good, yeah. It's work, ya know."

"Yeah, but it's great work. *Nothing's changed*, he says."

"All good."

And he shrugs as I laugh. Most humble guy you'd ever meet in your life. Everything to Leon is always, simply, all good. That's Leon's adjective for just about everything, good. *Good man, good.* You had to really pry with Leon sometimes if he wasn't buzzed up and willing to ramble on his own accord.

"And how about you? I know you've got something for me."

Prince gets that sly look of news on his face and says, "Oh I've got something."

"Talk to me, ace."

"Shit. About a week or so after you left, I had a call with a buddy out West. He's the one running that weed empire I told you about."

"Yeah, yeah."

"The guy basically has this greenhouse now, hidden away in the back of his storage garage. Anyway, he's really, really pulling in the paper."

"How much we talkin?"

"Well, I don't actually know just how much he's really pullin in exactly but he was telling me 'bout all the opportunity out there, ya know? Just for business in general, man. And he said the women are all class. He says a guy just stumbles headfirst into shit out there without even trying. And get this, he offered us a job. A gig. He says it's basically legal out there and nobody comes running around none. He said if we wanted, we could help him expand it. Not saying we should, but it's interesting man. Fucking interesting."

And the whole time he was talking, I drank and thought that I saw an altogether new glint in his eye. He's at it again. This is Prince at his best, in the concocting of elaborate plans. He's always having these slick business ideas which almost never materialized. This one has him buzzing, though, there's no doubt about it. I'll just say he looks different. Maybe it's the beer, or us being back together again after far too long, but our voices are imbued with a real possibility. I have the thought that Prince may be heading out West after all.

For now, though, we're rolling in the bar we know best. "I fuckin missed you guys, man."

"Same, pal," they say.

And I believe them.

I missed this bar too. Saul behind the counter, towel over shoulder, scowling at nothing in particular. Springsteen on the juke. It's good to be home.

After a few more beats or so, Leon goes, "Ya know, Cash, I really thought about not sayin this, but I saw Rose here like a week or so back."

"What do you mean you saw her?"

He shrugs.

"I mean exactly what I said man, I came through here for a quick one after work with Mo, what was it, last Monday? Yeah, well sure as shit she wandered through here for a second. She was chattin with Saul, helped serve for a minute, and left."

"And what else?"

"I don't know what else."

"What else man? That's it?"

"That's it. Yeah. I wasn't starin or nothin, Cash. My back was to her and what, I didn't even know any of this other shit till you told me just now."

"Right."

"Whatcha thinkin?"

"Nothing. I just figured she was gone for good is all."

"Well, I don't know. Maybe she is. It was just the once."

But just the once was just enough to get my mind out reaching her way through the universe all over again. I don't know how to feel, honestly. The news takes me by surprise. God. Alright. It's fine. I finish my glass, and I let it out of my head. For all I knew, Leon had things all messed around in his mind and was confusing the dates, or maybe it was a different girl that looked just like her, I don't know. I tell myself I don't care and choose to ride the good wave with my friends.

I stand and take the pitcher to the bar for another round. Saul shakes his head.

"Really thought I was rid of you."

"Not yet, pal. How the hell are ya?"

"Good. You?"

"Never better."

I suppose he looks about the same, more or less, so I take him for his word. *Good*. I have the impulse to ask about his sister, but I resist and am proud of myself for it. The woman had left me and hadn't even called. But I was a new man, was I not? I had seen some shit, as they say. Saul fills the pitcher.

"Thanks, man."

I head back to the table. I'm officially in the perfect ride up for the buzz. You know the feeling? When the feet start dancing and the body gets lighter and swift? What a sensation. I return to the booth.

"Tell me more about this motherfucker out West."

A couple hours later we've plunged our way through four or five pitchers. A massive return to action. We're right back at it. We're young and reckless once again. I know it was only a month or so, but my time away made us reenergized. My brothers. I'll paint them heroic in my stories, all my life. I'll write about them for ages, and they may never understand how immortalized they'll be. Well, in their own way, I think they'd do the same. I'm sure they'll tell their kids about me one day and I'll be the hero in those tales.

"Fellas. I was gonna wait to tell you but, fuck it. Mo and I are trying."

"No fuckin way?"

Prince's eyebrows raise.

"Yeah, man."

"My God," I say and I reach out my hand. He shakes it in pride.

Honestly, I'm convinced now more than ever that Leon would be in Johnston till he died. I couldn't be more proud of the guy. There's no doubt in my mind he'll be a sensational father. And that daughter of his, or that son, would grow up happy and strong and fulfilled. They'd be one of the real building blocks of the nation when things threatened to grow more complicated. Have no fear, Leon will be raising a bright piece of the American future, and that makes me feel better about everything.

Mo and I are trying, he'd said. And the responsibility expanded his chest. He's hopeful and capable. One of the good ones, the best. Before I know it, the doorbell will ring, and it will be a little Leon at the door. Looking up and smiling wide at me. I can't wait.

We're growing up. Always. A celebratory night in the promise of more life.

"Cheers to that," I say.

We clink our glasses together, an ageless pact.

Home. Good old Johnston. Jimmy's Place. We're back.

"Cheers to that, Leon man, cheers to that."

50

I'm falling asleep on my living room couch listening to Joni Mitchell. I find her voice to be the most soothing sound in the world and I'm exhausted. She's lonely, living in paint boxes, and scared of the devil. She believes love is touching souls, and her lover pours out in her words, from time to time. The night has left me drunk and delirious. I'm dreaming of wide open cornfields in the midst of a light falling rain. I'm running and running, I'm looking for something, but what? The running pauses. I hear a quiet knock. The sound grows louder and louder until it brings me to life. Waking up, dazed, I realize that it's coming from my front door. I look at the time. Just past midnight. I've been out for less than a half hour.

I squint my eyes and shake off the slumber. The knocking continues. *Who in the fuck at this hour?* The sleep is fading from my eyes and I'm more alert as the confusion sets in. I make my way to the front door as the knocking continues. I take a breath, turn the lock, and I open it up. The blood drains from my body. There, standing before me, like the ghost in my nightmares, is my father.

He's wearing a tan, heavily stained work jacket over a flannel. He's bearded and silent, staring at me in the night. Sometimes in life there are moments of such dream-like quality they appear illusionary. There are seconds that pass in which time is a construct, the moment is either too stunning or perverse to comprehend. Am I still asleep? My stomach sinks straight through my feet. I feel that and then nothing, only a shocking numbness spreading under my skin. For how long did we stand? As if waiting for confirmation, we are silent, with no wish to shatter the mirage. I cannot fathom this. I have not seen my father for five years. Five full, continuous years. I'd banished him from my mind best I could. He was dead. He was gone. And yet, standing and hunched, eerily quiet, he is here on the doorstep.

He's lost some thirty pounds, at least, and is more gray than I remembered. His beard is thicker, and his blue eyes are even further away. His face has grown shaded with a faint maroon pigment. He looks ancient and worn. He only breaks my eyes when he starts to cough a bit. He tries to hide the noise behind his mouth, but it still sounds thick with phlegm. I recognize that cough. It's the same cough his father had before him.

And we stand there for longer, saying nothing. I am empty, have zero. Everything and nothing at once, no speech. There is no electricity between my mind and my tongue.

What is there in his eyes? Sorror, remorse? Is there a gentle, meek flicker in the dark? I hardly recognize him.

"Hey son," he finally goes. "I ehm, tried to get here earlier. Bit later than I ehm, than I imagined. I called. I did call. Came up through Illinois. Figured I'd catch ya up and about still. Maybe. Saturday and all."

It is true that a father carries an enduring power over his son. I feel something else, something unexpected and tender. *What the hell has happened?* The way he spoke was soft and defeated. There was a pleading in the way that he enunciated. This man is not my father. There is no ice in his voice, no distance. This man is stripped, battered.

I stand dumb in the doorway. I search for the gag. Perhaps this imposter will peel off a mask. Perhaps he'll float up to the sky. Perhaps he'll get into that truck in the driveway and drive. But none of this happens. Just a man, looking at his son. What is madness, truly, in the end?

"I know this, uh, well I know this, uh, is probably somethin of a surprise after all," he continues. Me bein here now. There's, uh, well there's some things I oughta say. And, uh, look I'm sorry it's late."

And it's somewhere in that wandering sentence that I finally begin to come down. The current is back, and it starts to course through me. All of a sudden, I'm nearing a blackout avalanche of emotion.

"I think you should leave," I say.

Quiet. And there's that heartbreaking softness again in his reaction. The lines on his face grow just a little bit deeper. My words hurt him. They surprised him somehow. What was this? Never in any of my memories had a word pierced his flesh, not from me, not once. But here he is, damaged. His eyes look all watered and I cannot believe that, so I don't.

"Son—"

"Go on."

"If I could just have a—"

"If you don't leave—" My pulse bangs against the borders. "It ain't good. You being here. You shouldn't be here. I don't feel right. You need to get the fuck out of here."

And I'm starting to shake. And I'm scared. I feel a dangerous bent grasping for my spine. It's the reckoning, the sadness of all planets and the rage that comes with it. I have the honest impulse to take my gun from the kitchen drawer, but I keep it all down and try to breathe. My hands are trembling, I'm on the edge of completely convulsing. He knows it. He can see me. As do I, him. Shattered and half a man. A stranger. If he doesn't leave, I fear I will hurt him.

He senses this and says soft and down low, hardly a whisper, "I'll be back, at, ehm, a better time."

And he takes one last long look at his son. The color of his eyes is faded in the light.

What have you seen? What have you done? He takes a few steps away and slowly limps his crooked body back to the truck. He gets in. He sits there for a moment, then ignites it. The engine turns over and he pulls away into the night. I'm starting to violently shake. I close the door and my eyes fall to the wooden floor beneath me. My body plummets down and down and down. I disappear into the center of the Earth. How long did I stand there transfixed? I don't know. An hour maybe. Maybe an hour or maybe much longer.

My soul is detached. It's reaching out desperate, searching for solid ground. It's possible it won't ever come back. It's possible I'm hollowed out for good. I imagined that single moment in my mind countless nights. It never played out like that, but it had. An irregular heartbeat. A tectonic slide. I've known in my gut the whole time. My father is alive. I knew it all along, deep down, I knew. I just didn't think he'd come back. But he had, he had. I saw him again with my very own eyes. I shudder. Can't cry. Back. Whoever that was, that corpse at my door, I know I do not know that man.

51

I'm on my tenth beer or so and am the only soul still at Jimmy's. Two a.m. I haven't checked the clock for hours. Poor Saul is behind the bar and going drink-for-drink with me because, I imagine, he didn't have it in his heart to send me home. The neon is spilling strong behind my shoulders as the hungry shadows grow more encompassing, but I don't mind at all. There is no other universe than this. I haven't been so roaring drunk in a year. I'm red eyed, philosophizing and asking, "Did you know, Saul?"

"No, I didn't know."

"You ain't even know what I'm talkin about—"

"C'mon, Cash. I know. You been bouncin 'round it all night."

"Yeah, well"—I squint him up and down and swallow the last of my Bud—"admit it."

"Cash, I ain't seen him. Nobody 'round here's seen him. Only one who's seen him is you, and I promise you that."

"It doesn't make sense."

"I couldn't tell ya. I don't get it none either."

"Five fucking years, Saul. Five."

And Saul slides me the next round without judgement. He pours another for himself. Bubbling and ice cold and healing. Springsteen's "The River" is playing on the jukebox. He's going on about the valley and following our fathers. One of the best.

"Saul, this is one of my favorites."

"Yeah. You put it on, pal."

"I know. But I'm just sayin."

And I stand up and sing along about everything vanishing into the air.

I'm looking around the bar like a newborn with wide eyes. Everything radiates, undiscovered and mysterious. Everything has changed except the green felt on the pool table always like a sprawled-out field of Wisconsin summer grass, and the lamp above with the perfect amount of dying yellow light. The off-black tiled floor looks brand new, covered with discarded peanut shells.

"What a fuckin place," I say to myself. "Yeah, what a place."

Saul replies, his voice seems a million miles away. And I'm closing my eyes and spinning more. I have a pool stick in my hands that I don't remember grabbing.

"Take it easy, man, take it easy, why don't you come have a seat?" I hear Saul murmur, but I don't pay him any mind. I sit on the pool table edge. I point the stick at Saul's head like a gun. Like a long wooden rifle, skinny and bruised.

"How you think we woulda fared in 'Nam, Saul?"

"Not well."

"Speak for yourself." I set the weapon down. "Fuckin Saul. Fuckin good poor Saul. What are you still doin here, man?"

"Could ask you the same."

"No, no no no no. I got reasons. So many reasons, Saul, so many—"

"You and me both, pal."

"We are pals, aren't we, Saul?"

"I guess so."

"You could be anywhere man, don't you understand? Anywhere Saul! How about the Rockies? Or California? Or Arizona? Or Texas man. Texas! You should hear the stories about the land out *there* Saul, I swear."

"Yeah, suppose it's nice."

"It's wide open Saul. Wide. Open."

And I'm weaving my hand through the air like a painter of visions on an imaginary canvas, like I'm conducting an orchestra. I want him so desperately to understand.

"How often do you think about *your* dad?"

And he doesn't answer at first. He takes a drink and wipes his face slowly in perhaps his greatest contemplation to date, like it's his own drama unfolding.

"Sometimes, yeah. I do sometimes."

"Yeah. I know."

"Not like you do, though."

"What's that supposed to mean?"

"I mean you're romantic about it somehow."

"Romantic?"

"Romantic, yeah."

"I'm not fuckin *romantic* about nothin, Saul. Especially that."

"Bullshit."

"Bullshit?"

"Always bringin it up, always talkin 'bout it like it was this great thing in our past. Like it has purpose or whatever. You know, it ain't always that."

"It ain't always that."

"No. It ain't always."

"You're talkin romantic yourself, Saul. You see—"

"What I'm tellin ya, Cash, is that it was all around bad. Nothin romantic 'bout bad."

"Mmmmm."

"It's fuckin true, man. And I don't hold onto it like you do."

"Oh yes you do, yes you do. You just don't know it."

"No, I know it, I don't do it."

"You do. You do, man. How don't you see that?"

"I don't talk about it none, Cash. Never. That's the difference. I don't need to, that's it. That's that."

"Don't you get it, poor Saul?"

"Stop callin me that—"

"Saul, they fucked it all up. They fucked it all up. They were drunks—"

"So are we—"

"No, Saul. I'm sayin. Saul, we didn't have fathers. Not like we shoulda. No fathers."

"We did."

"We did not—"

"We did. They just weren't any good at what they did, Cash, that's all. And neither were their fathers. And that's, that's where that ends. It's as simple as that. And ya have to leave it there—"

"But it doesn't *end* there, Saul—"

"If you let it, it does—"

"Saul, fuckin look where you are!"

"I'm in the same place as you pal—"

"I KNOW, SAUL, I KNOW, THAT'S THE POINT."

I'm all worked up and I lean a bit too far forward off the table and fall. The bar's floor is much colder than the air and a bit wet.

"Fuck."

"You alright?"

"Yeah, yeah." I pull my body up slowly, walk to the bar, and sit back down again. All torn up and dirty and done.

Saul looks at me now with an empathy so real it hurts. And maybe he's the blood brother I never had. Castaways, truly, the both of us. And I'm about to say something like that, all poetic as hell, but from behind me the door to the bar swings wide open, and in through the gates walks Rose.

She glides in and out of my vision, all the way up to us and I'm convinced I've officially died and moved on. I must have hit my fucking head so hard on the tile that I died. Surely not now, in the pit of drunkenness, has Rose wandered into Jimmy's so unabashedly unfazed. So beautiful and deadly like a snake. I close my eyes and take a breath, but when I open them, she's still there, standing to my right, looking at me with this sorry expression, as in, she feels sorry for me. The audacity.

"Cash," she says.

Just my name. And she says it, just like that. Like that's the full sentence. I'm staring right back, and I kid you not, I laugh. I let out a genuine, pent up laugh worth about two months. I look at Saul as if to confirm I'm alive, to confirm what I'm seeing is real. He shrugs his shoulders and I know now, it is. Everything's real, unfortunately.

"You called her?"

He nods.

"Sorry."

And I laugh a bit more. "Oh Saul, what the fuck? You idiot. You fuckin moron, Saul."

I'm shaking my head and looking down at the wood, unwilling to meet her eyes. I'm trying to find some sort of ground to stop moving. To the perpetually unpolished bar I utter, "What are you doing here?"

"Thought maybe I would take you home," she says.

And with that, Saul sets his towel down and leaves us. He walks right out from the bar and says, "I'll be in my office."

And I know that he's had a conference with Rose behind my back. *When did he call her?*

I have no recollection of it, but somehow they've hatched a plan while my mind was off in the distance or wherever the fuck I was. Things settle down just long enough for me to hold her gaze.

"Are you kidding?"

"No."

"No?"

"No."

"Take me home?"

"Yes, I want to take you home."

"What the hell are you talking about?"

"I want to help you get home, Cash."

All I can do is sit there and drunkenly blink at her, utterly convinced that at any second the truth will be revealed, or the show will conclude. Nothing comes. Nothing but all the memories and thoughts of the past two months. They become fumes in my body. I stand up and shove myself from the bar. I stumble a couple steps before regaining composure. I'm growing disgusted by the fact that she's found me in this stupor. I head straight for the exit, demented and determined to go. I am at odds with my life all over again. I am unbelieved. I am faithless. I shove the door open and am released into the freezing cold evening.

Up top, the stars shake their heads and mutter things amongst themselves like, *dear boy, he has done it again.*

"Are you really going to drive?"

"Fuck this," I mutter.

Yes, I'm going to drive. I need to leave. I have to go as far away as possible. My car is one of three, all the way down near the edge of the gravel. The world spins in inebriation. I walk straight for it, furious. I can't believe it. She shows herself here. Now. Here and now. God, I'm nauseous. I should just fucking walk home. I should just keep walking until I can't anymore.

Behind me I hear, "Cash!"

So, I turn.

There she is, stranding near the entrance.

"You don't even have your keys, man."

Huh? I check my flannel coat pockets and my pants, she's right. I do not. Fuck. FUCK it all. FUCK. I must have left them on the bartop. I massage the brim of my nose near my eyes. *When are you gonna get it together?* That's what she said to me all those days ago. Now, I can hardly see straight. My mind is muddled with alcohol and the return of my father.

When am I gonna get it together? Not tonight. Rose showing up has ruined it all. Absolutely exasperated, pissed, and helpless, I look up to the black heavens.

Rose walks toward me like a slow-moving arrow. I can no longer look at her. This woman who burnt me, who I had wanted so badly. Who had touched me then left me to rot. Like everything else. She's ten feet from me now and I can't help but say, "What the hell do you want, Rose?"

"I told you. I want to take you home."

"Why?"

"Because you're drunk."

"So?"

"I don't want you to drive."

"I'll walk."

"C'mon."

"I've done it before."

"I'm worried about you."

"Oh, give me a fuckin break."

"I am, Cash."

"Worried about me?"

"Yeah."

"You haven't seen me in months. You—you—" and I'm nearly laughing again, what the hell?

Her voice, the way she said it. *Worried about you*. Like every other sentence that had floated from her lips since I'd known her, it was honest. She meant what she said, but it doesn't make any sense. I'm barely standing straight, on the last rope of any hope for clarity.

"I don't understand."

"What don't you understand?"

"You left."

"I know."

"You just left."

"I know."

"You didn't call. You didn't leave a fuckin, I don't know, a note. Nothin."

"I'm sorry, Cash."

"I thought it meant something."

"It did."

"I thought, you know, I just. I thought I'd see you again."

"I had to go, Cash. I tried to call."

"C'mon."

"It's true, ya know. And I did call."

"When?"

"A few weeks ago, I should have sooner."

"Right."

"I had to go."

"And now you show up, out of nowhere. Tonight. I'm drunk and—"

"It's okay."

"You don't know."

"What don't I know?"

"Where did you go?"

"I went home."

"Why?"

"I don't know, Cash, I had to, you know. I was all turned around. I was fucking confused. We had that night, and that was—I don't know. I don't have nights like that."

"Neither do I."

"I had to go, okay? I didn't think I was ready."

"Ready?"

"For Johnston, for everything. I just settled. I don't know. So, I went. I left. It's what I do. I've done it a million times. But I called, I did. But you weren't there. And Saul didn't know where you were, nobody did, and so that was that. I even checked your place."

"I don't get it."

"Where did you go?" She asks.

"Doesn't matter."

"I thought you left for good too, ya know."

"Yeah, well."

"So. Where?"

"Cambridge."

"Okay. Cambridge."

"My grandparents' have a spot there. I always said I'd fix it up."

"Oh, I see—"

"Why are you back?"

"I'm just back. I'm sorry, Cash."

"Right."

"I heard about your dad. Saul mentioned it."

"Yeah, I fuckin bet he did."

Without another word, Rose walks the remaining ten feet between us and wraps her arms around my body. The gesture shocks me, but I don't ask any questions. I don't care for questions anymore. I don't know why she's here, or if she'll leave me again. I don't care. I only reach out and hold her as close as I can.

She's my last bit of light in the dark.

52

There's a bassline in my skull. The sun just starts to creep its pretension through the blinds and my ceiling fan spins quickly above. I'm in my boxers, sheets thrown about the floor. I've been kicking and thrashing all night. I sit up in the worst kind of state, sweaty and gut turning over like a colony of ants are inside of me feasting. I somehow grunge my way out of bed and put on my oldest pair of shorts. I open the bedroom door and step face first into the morning.

Rose sits patiently in the dawn. Somehow, I feel like an intruder in my own home. The night flashes through my mind, jagged and painful. I close my eyes as the headache stabs. I could wretch my entire self away if prompted. All of it comes back to me. Rose. Jimmy's. Outside. Drive. Talk. Sleep. And now, she's here. She's stayed. She looks breathtaking while I embody the worst regrettable drunkenness. I'm rather pathetic, standing dumb in my dumbest shorts. I look like pure hell and Rose drinks a coffee in the burgeoning sunlight, sitting at my kitchen table. God, of all the ways I'd wished to awake one day to Rose, this isn't one of them.

"Good morning."

She smiles. I push my hair from my forehead and say, "I'll be back. Don't, just don't leave. Please."

She looks out to my yard, then back.

"I won't."

"Thank you."

I turn the shower on and tap my forehead on the wall. What a fucking disgrace I've become. I get my toothbrush and toothpaste and fall into the scalding water. I don't care enough to adjust it. I deserve to be uncomfortably hot. I let it hit my face in penance. My back leans into the tub floor as the water almost burns me. I scrub the scum from my mouth with toothpaste. After a solid spin of the brush, I spit the stuff out and wash my body with vigor. Whenever I greet the day with a crippling hangover, I always feel so damn shameful and stupid. The only thing to do is to wash. To try and start again. The shower helps as much as anything can, but how much can a shower do for the soul? I'm killing what I can of the prior evening with soap, and the rest would have to slowly fade.

I turn off the faucet and dry myself. Even my softest towel feels abrasive. In between thoughts of self-hatred, there is Rose. I have half the mind to believe that when I exit my room she'll have gone. I'll be alone and things will make sense.

*

Coffee helps too. Outside there's one of the finest late fall mornings you've ever seen. Turns out we're right in the sweet spot.

"Look at that, you see 'em?"

"I do."

She's pointing off to a little Bambi and her mother taking turns at the salt lick.

"So cute."

We're at the kitchen table taking sips and admiring the morning. Rose watches Bambi and I watch her. She purses her lips without knowing, scrunches her nose as thoughts play across her freckled face and I wonder what she's thinking. After the deer leave us for another pasture she asks, "so, what are you going to do?"

"'Bout what?"

"Your father."

"Oh."

"Too early?"

"No. Good question. I don't know."

"Where is he staying?"

"No idea."

"Hm."

"He said he drove straight into town from, God, I don't even know, Illinois? He didn't say where he'd be staying."

"Right."

"I doubt he'll be back."

"Something tells me he will be."

"We'll see, I guess. He just left, ya know."

"Yeah."

"Just fucking, disappeared."

"Yeah."

"Maybe I imagined the whole thing."

For all I know, it could have been a creation of my subconscious. Maybe I was sleep deprived and neurotic enough to conjure something.

"How was home?"

"It was okay."

"Just went back to your place?"

"Yeah, right back to the heart of it. I don't know. I didn't have anything waiting for me. Some friends. Not sure what I was looking for. Went looking anyway."

"I get that."

"I think I didn't want to admit I was settling somewhere."

"And now? Do you want to be here?"

"I do, yeah. I do." She nods.

"I've always wondered what it's like for people moving to Johnston. You don't have all the earlier years to grow fond of it."

"Yeah, but you can feel it."

"Yeah?"

"Yeah of course. It's special. Really is."

"I agree."

"Isn't everywhere?"

"Probably."

Rose sure moves through her turmoil gracefully. Her existential crises don't result in her spinning out of control. Her eyes stay steady and locked. When she speaks it's soft but definitive. Her gentle fingers spin the coffee cup in small circles on the table.

"I didn't know when I was gonna see you again," she says.

"Same."

"I should have said something to ya."

"I don't know."

"I should have."

"You did what you thought you had to."

"Yeah."

"It's not like I expected you to stick around this place just for me, you know."

"I know."

"I was just down about it, is all. End of the day I know we only had the one night, really, so, yeah."

"We've had a few."

"We have, haven't we?"

"Who's counting?"

And that one sentence fills me with an assurance that life rarely seems to offer. Had she counted the nights, like me? Did she hold close even those brief moments of passing?

"You know I remember them all. All of the times," I say.

"Yeah?"

"Every single time I've seen you. Talked to you. Yeah. Of course I remember."

"Me too," she admits softly.

"What are you going to do, Rose?"

"I think I'm doing it."

My heart swells. I look back out to the yard, shake my head and smile. If only it could stay fall forever. All the boys and girls of America are in the prime of it now. This is the time.

"Whatcha smiling at?" she asks.

"I have a very hard time believing you're here."

The potential of all beautiful humanity lights up her face as she blushes. Red cheeked, humble, graceful.

"Me too, a little bit."

"I'm sorry you saw me like that last night."

"It's okay. You weren't that bad."

"My head is a fuckin war zone."

"Do you want to tell me about it?"

And for the first time in years, I feel willing. Her kindness, her honesty. Her vulnerability. Here she is, in my home, with enough courage to come back. To see. For the first time in years, I want to tell someone everything.

"I've just been all over the place this year."

"Same."

"Just insane. Restless. Confused. So many thoughts of my mom. About this place. What I'm doing. Now my fuckin dad shows up at the doorstep."

"Yeah."

"And you."

"What about me?"

"I don't know. I've been in this town all my life. I've never seen anyone like you in Jimmy's that night. Not in Johnston, not my whole life. I wasn't lookin for anything, ya know. I swear I wasn't. Or I didn't think I was. But that night was the spark of something. Everything's changed since. It's crazy. It's like you set everything into motion. I'm trying to keep up with my own life."

"I saw you that night too."

"You did?"

"It's not that big of a place, Cash."

"Suppose not."

"You were with Prince and Leon."

"Yeah, yeah I was."

"I just got into town a couple days before that. I didn't know what the hell I was gonna do. Everything's changed for me too, since then. Wild how that works."

"You must have known how I felt right away."

"I didn't know anything about you."

"I just wanted to be next to you."

"All I knew was that you were one of Saul's friends from way back."

"Yeah."

"He didn't say anything about Prince and Leon. But he told me you were a good guy."

"Effusive, ain't he?"

"For him? Good's a hell of a lot."

"True."

"Anyway, I asked him about you one day."

"Really?"

"After you guys pitched your idea."

"Ah."

"I was curious too. I think. Why he didn't sell. Then he got to talking. I couldn't help it."

"Couldn't help what?"

"Asking about you."

"What'd he say?"

"You'll never believe it."

"God."

"He told me a story about you two."

"You're kidding."

"Swear. Saul told a whole story."

"Which one?"

"You're really not gonna believe it."

"Go on. I can take it."

"Okay. Well. He told me a story of when you two were in eighth grade. I don't know if you'll remember this but maybe you will. Anyway, it was this really nice story about how one day he had to go to school even though he had a couple bruises from my father. Jimmy was drunk the night before and Saul forgot to take the trash out, I think. So, he got a little physical with him and Saul had to go to school the next day with some bruises on his neck and cheek or something like that. Anyway, some of the kids in class saw the bruises and were making fun of him for it. Calling them hickeys and shit, I don't know, just making fun of him. And, the way he tells it, instead of going out to break that day, he went to the bathroom and locked himself in the stall. He told me he couldn't stop crying no matter what he did. Said he was in there the whole period just crying over everything. But before the hour ended, he told me that you came into the bathroom. And apparently, he tried like hell to stop crying

246

but he still couldn't. He was in really bad shape, ya know? Well, he says that you could tell it was him right away and you wouldn't leave him in there. You wouldn't leave the bathroom because you had to make sure he was alright. He said you told him everything was going to be okay, that you were pals and what not, and that he could talk to you if he needed to. He said you told him *every-one needs someone to talk to, Saul.* And of course he didn't really talk to you that day, but you still didn't leave until you thought he was at least a little better and had stopped crying. He said he made you swear not to tell anyone about it and that you never did, and that you never brought it up again. He also said that you almost fought those kids in class later that day when they tried saying something to him about his bruises again. He said there were three of them but you woulda fought them anyway and wouldn't have cared if you lost. Yeah, so. He told that story about you. He said, *that's all you need to know about Cash.*"

"I remember that," I say softly. I can't believe Saul still thought about that, or that it meant enough to him to tell Rose about it on my behalf. God. The whole thing nearly makes my eyes water.

Of course I remember, Saul.

"Well. It's because of that story that I said I'd go with you to dinner."

"No kidding."

"That and your smile. I love your smile. And your eyes. Okay. That's enough."

"You can keep going."

"No, I can't give everything away."

"I love your smile too. And your eyes."

"Thank you."

"I'm happy you got dinner with me."

"Me too. Tell me more."

"What do you want to know?"

"Everything."

So, I tell her about Cambridge and my days out there. What I'd done, not done, and all about my existential experience, all the ghosts and the whole messy plot of it. How I had thought, at the time, that it was a brush at near death. How when I made it back after that exodus, I felt more whole somehow, and when I finally returned to Johnston, Leon mentioned he'd seen her, and how that spun me out again a bit. Then I get to the guts.

"My father was always a huskier, hardened sort, ya know. He fought in the war. He was stoic, mean sometimes. I think only my mom saw the side of him that was soft enough to really know or love. He always had this sharpness to his gaze, ya know, but he was quiet, always. He was harsh and dismissive, but mostly, hard. Closed and stubborn and tough. No affection. Not that I could find, anyway."

How the hell is she doing it? She's just listening and the details are spilling from me. I have the impulse to tell her anything I can think of. Any secret I've buried, any lie I've told.

"I didn't know my father very well. But I might describe him like that, just like that. I know they were the best of friends," she says.

"They were. And you're right, Jimmy was similar. They were as good a pals as men like that can be."

"Crazy."

"But the thing is, when he was out there the other night, just standing there looking at me. All of those things were gone. Maybe I imagined it, but I swear it wasn't even him. His form had shrunk. He was skinny. His eyes were deeper and heavier set, but they were sad, ya know? Fragile almost, but sad. Yeah. He was sad."

"What'd you say to him?"

"Just told him to leave. I was shaking. I thought I might hurt him, honestly. I don't know. I've seen sadness in his eyes before, but it was always buried. It was like concrete in his stomach or something. If you blinked you might miss it, but this was different. He seemed hollowed out. Scared."

"And he left?"

"Yeah."

"Then how'd you feel?"

"Sick. Angry."

"Right. I used to feel that way about my dad too. Every time I'd see him that's how I felt. I could hardly have a conversation with him. I kind of regret that now. I sort of wish he'd show up on my doorstep."

"What would you say?"

"I don't know. I'd forgive him, I think."

"After everything?"

"I think so. Set us both free, ya know?"

"Yeah."

"I think your dad will visit again, Cash."

"I'm not so sure."

"And if he does?"

"I don't know."

"Can you forgive him?"

"I don't know." I shrug. I watch a fox run through the yard. What a question. That's something my mother would have asked me. *Could I forgive him?*

"Freeze."

Rose smiles.

"Freeze?"

"It's what mom used to say when she'd catch me daydreaming. She'd say that, and I'd have to tell her exactly what I was thinking."

"I see."

"So?"

"I think what you just said is beautiful. About forgiveness."

"Forgiveness is beautiful."

"I think you're beautiful, Rose." I reach over and take her hand in mine. "Thank you for coming back here."

"Right back at ya."

I stand up and walk around the table. I sit next to her. Whatever it is we're looking for, we've found some of it here. We reflect one another.

"Your eyes are like sapphires," she whispers.

And I kiss her in the sunlight. Life, we both know, in its entirety, is more and more fleeting by the second. Nothing exists but this moment. She slowly moves and sits on my lap, her arms crossed behind my neck. She brushes the hair off my forehead and softly kisses me there, her lips warm and gentle. Her hands border my jaw and her mouth hovers near mine. She is intoxicating.

We sit there, eyes closed, her breath, mine, the small crashing winds of life. There is nothing I'd rather feel, there is nothing I'd rather taste, smell, nothing. Only her.

I wrap my arms around her waist and pull her closer. We are intertwined. I want to kiss each and every one of her freckles. I slowly press my lips to her cheek, then the other, then her chest. She hugs me tightly, her hands moving through the hair on the back of my head. She wears the cross around her neck. I kiss that too. And all that is love is then holy.

"I want you, I want you, Cash," she whispers.

"I want you too."

"Take me to your room."

I gather her in my arms and lift us from the chair. We stand there, lips meeting, slow dancing for a second on the wooden floor. I carry her from the kitchen and push open the door to my room. We lay our bodies down.

My hands move through her hair. Our breath is like the warm summer in which we initially met. She pulls up on my T-shirt and I take it off. I lean her back down to the mattress and my necklace falls on hers, they lie together on her breasts, the metals shining in the afternoon sun, still tempered by blinds. She stares into me, endless forests reflected in rivers.

"You are so beautiful," I say quietly, and I know I'll say it a thousand more times if she'll let me. She runs her finger down the bridge of my nose and then traces my bottom lip. My hands drift to her stomach which rises and falls with her accelerating breath. Her ribs are strong on each side and I slide her tank up to her shoulders and off. No bra beneath, her breasts are sculpted by light. Her nipples are round and light brown. With my hands sliding down her back, we sit up, our bodies pressed together. Chest to chest, heartbeat to heartbeat. Our shapes fit perfectly. She moves her fingers through my hair again and we kiss. The passion builds in slow careful movements. My lips brush her collar bone, her skin is soft and flushed.

I kiss her breasts with an ignited fire. My tongue traces circles, and she sighs. Could we live forever in this moment, if we tried? My hands cradle her back, fingers curl through the loops in her jeans. She grips the sides of my face. My jaw then my neck. A smile of desire spreads across her face, her nostrils flare as she breathes. We release. Burning now, building. Our tongues move in rhythm, in and out. She tastes like a dream I once had of love. I kiss her nose, then she kisses mine. I kiss the lids of her eyes, then she kisses mine. We play this call and response, and she giggles. I love our mouths connected. I have never in my life wanted to be so completely another. I want to be one. Our bodies aligned, her hands move to my shoulders and turn it all over.

I'm on my back and she is straddled above. Her sandy blond hair is thrown about her freckled face. She bites her lip, and she smiles. Fireworks erupt in my chest. She leans down and kisses me there, right above the heart. She puts her hands to the waistband of my shorts. She takes my briefs as well and pulls them down off my feet, somewhere they'll wait on the floor. I'm erect and alive. There is nothing between us anymore. I've never been so consumed by desire. Our souls are our bodies. Everything is connected, and I understand it all now. The heavenly purpose of love. How this is the top of the mountain. There is nothing more sacred.

Rose leans further, kisses my abdomen and then down. I pulse with need for her. Her lips press soft to the top of the head. She moves her tongue from the base and then up. She kisses me all around. I can hardly sit still. I reach down for her and bring her back up to me. I need to be with her now, here, and always. Our lips come together again. I turn her over. Her chest rises her breasts, then descends, it moves heavy with want. There are more freckles by her collarbone and a small birthmark by her neck. She wraps my necklace in her hand. Pulse racing, we're enveloped by the nerves of the first time. She sends a lifetime of feeling through her eyes. Trust. I take her hand and kiss it and hold it there by my lips. I return the feeling completely. I have you. You have me. I bring her hand just above her head, fingers still locked, and we kiss. I kiss her breasts. I lay my ear on her chest and can hear her beating heart. I move my lips along her rib cage and then her pierced navel. I take the bronze button of her jeans and push it in through the slitted fabric. The zipper goes down in a slow-moving line. My hands glide over the edges of her pants and bring them down over her hips. A sensual dream, the jeans fall off her legs and careen to the floor.

"Kiss me," she whispers.

I move my lips and bite around the top of her white panties before I move up to her lips once again. Rose. There is nothing else. Her hands on my face. Her wet lips and mine. This is the one true limitless feeling of life. She's breathing more heavily, a flame. I go back down. I love the silver ring which is pierced through her belly button. I bite at the edges again.

"I'm so wet," she says. And I feel it. I love it. I kiss her there above the fabric. The damp warmth nearly overtakes me. I pull her underwear away from her body and off. We are naked, together. Both vulnerable and on fire. More alive than ever. I will never forget this first image. Her hand just beneath her left breast. Her hair pushed back and thrown. Her lips flushed in waiting. Her right knee bent over her body, covering.

I kiss her with all of my being. I will love you, Rose.

"Rose." Her name effortlessly floats from my lips. Now and forever. I know. I place my right hand on her knee and spread it to the side. We are completely exposed. I kiss her again.

"I want to taste you."

And I spread her other knee to the bed. I kiss slowly down her thighs, strong and tan and soft. My tongue licks their distance then down and around, I lightly meet her lips. My tongue outlines her folds. I'm in love with the taste.

"Cash," she says, biting her finger then running that hand through her hair, "oh my God."

I've never wanted to be inside a woman so badly in my life. My lips kiss the top, my tongue goes in and out. Her sighs of ecstasy are divine, they consume me in desire. My passion rises. I almost black out. I'm kissing her, I want to love her. I want to make her feel incredible. My tongue moves in rhythm as her hips rise and fall against my face. I bring my fingers to her opening, massage and then enter. Her hand comes down to my hair. She grabs tightly in pleasure.

We're in a stunning new high. I could kiss her like this till I die. Her moans are tender, alluring, erotic. To take her further and further is to live all throughout time.

"Cash, Cash. I'm going to come."

"Come for me, Rose."

"Cash." Her nails dig into my shoulders, they grasp at my hair, my fingers move in and out faster, I feel her walls closing in. Her thighs clench. She cries out. Her chest rises and falls. Her eyes slightly watered, she looks down.

"Come here," she says, panting. And our lips meet again. She tastes herself on my mouth and I'm more aroused than I ever thought possible. She takes me in her hand and moves up and down while we kiss.

"I want you inside of me," she says. I kiss her again and shift my torso to hers. Still in her hand, she guides me inside. Tight and warm and wet, we shudder with desire.

"You feel so good," I say.

And all I can see are her eyes. I know Rose, only Rose, will matter in the end. Even in the darkest corners of my life, this will always exist. This will carry me through. My hand goes behind her head and as we start to move together, our foreheads are pressed together. Our tongues and our lips, we are something of ancient design. I move slowly, in and out. We are one body. There is nothing so pure in my life. Her hips move into me and away, her legs curling around mine. Her arms wrap me tightly. Her breath fills my ears. Her sighs of pleasure and beauty are the symphony. We accelerate. Rose, I knew it from the beginning. I will love you.

And in tandem we move together like the ocean, figuring it out one heartbeat, one rising tide at a time. And there's sweat on our skin now. We are warmer and warmer.

"Cash."

"Rose."

"I'm going to come."

"Me too."

"Come with me."

I can feel her muscles tense. Our eyes lock and it's transcendent. We turn completely to fire. I want to stay inside her as long as I live. We are closer and closer and closer. Nearing climax she kisses and holds onto me. We need this. It's her and it's coming and as I pull out, she takes me. My hand takes her too. We move each other and fall into our rapture. The sensation takes us, shakes us. We are wet. We kiss, our moans mesh and are the same. We kiss and we are eternal. The entirety of life and the future. Her eyes, mine. The purpose of everything, life. All the love we've waited for. All the lonesome nights, poems, and broken guitar strings. We're breathing heavy, together, pulsing and melded in our arms. We hold on.

And it could be the rest of the story, right here. We kiss lightly, our hearts calming. But we will never come down, not fully. Her eyes fill with tears and all that I once feared is myth. Fear doesn't exist. It does not. It does not. There is nothing but this.

Rose, I will love you. I run my hand down her back. Rose you can have me—you, you alone.

"Freeze," she whispers.

From the center of her heart, my great something.

In my bed, in the afternoon, here she is.

I do not want to leave. We are here.

We kiss.

"You."

"You."

We fall asleep in the arms of the day.

53

"Did I ever tell you about the last conversation I had with my dad, Cash?"

Prince and I are sitting in his living room sharing a good old-fashioned smoke. He's been hitting spliffs as well and is floating much higher than I am. There are shreds of tobacco strewn about the table that look like little insects at first glance. I have a couple beers in me and we're enjoying the night conversation. Prince and I can keep the ball rolling forever these nights. And the wheel turns.

"No, I don't think you have."

"Didn't think so."

He takes his black lighter and raises it to the edge of his tightly rolled spliff. What a movie star Prince is. He ignites one end and the embers spread quickly around the borders. He breathes in the air with practiced ease and lets the hot gray smoke gather in the lining of his lungs. By the time he sets it free, it is a thin fog, streaming straight down to the carpet.

"He had been goin on for months about the way this branch was hangin out all long and ugly in the yard. It was blocking his view of the land from the deck. For almost a year he had been talkin about that branch. Well one morning"—and he takes another long drag— "we were standing on the back porch having a coffee and he starts tellin me this story about how when his father got back from the war, as a kid, he had developed a terrible limp. Joshua was my grandpa's name. And dad tells me how Grandpa Joshua had a horrible time of it coming back home at first getting adjusted and all. He was so fucked up, you know. Thought he was Quasimodo or something. But he goes on to tell me how his dad never once complained, never once. He said his dad was damn proud of what he'd done. That he had helped save the world at twenty-one and the rest would fit in how it would. He got over the limp. He said that he lost friends. Family. He said he was lucky, he got to go home to his mother after all, you know? Who was he to complain about a limp?" And Prince takes the last hit of his spliff. He thinks for a moment, "He said all that and then walked out to the shed, got the ladder and put it straight up to that fuckin branch. And I followed him. I was supposed to keep it steady. And I tried. That was that. You know Cash, I'd take on more than a limp for the rest of my life if I could chop it up with my dad one more time."

"I bet."

"And I mean, just, one, more time Cash. Just one."

"Yeah."

He pushes his black hair back and out of his face and stares up at the ceiling. He's soaring higher than ever, flying over the past and all the lessons that were left for us there, "I ain't defendin your dad none, Cash. You know I ain't."

"I know."

"I'm just sayin, I wish like hell I could talk it out with mine."

54

The truth? Even if I wanted to see my father again, he hadn't been back to the house for two weeks. I assume he's run off on some dusty highway again to take up a life in South Dakota or Montana or somewhere even further off. I don't know. Johnston may have been a pit stop on his own endless exodus, and only in one transient moment of spirit and bravery had he decided to stop by and see his only son. It's possible he took one look at me and remembered what it was that made him leave in the first place. He lost his constitution all over again. I try to let it slip from my mind.

It's all made easier by everything Rose. I've found myself completely taken in by her gravitational pull. All day I find little things, normally mundane, made sensational in her honor. And by cleaning this dish, I will make myself good. I will take care of the world around me, as I will take care of her. As I stand, brush in hand, painting the Cornells's living room, I find myself steeped in a higher attention to detail, inspired. Each shade more nuanced, each glide of the brush more meaningful. It's all new creation, it has depth, it is significant. All because my heart is on fire.

Never have I been so motivated to instill every second of my life with purpose, renewed by the belief that if there is meaning to something, there is meaning to everything, and so on. I am not only the holder of the burgundy paint brush coated and primed, I am Vincent van Gogh. I see her face in every shadow, her eyes in every color. Her laugh behind overheard jokes, her thoughts on stories. Her fingerprints on any guitar and her hands on any glass of beer. With her so alive in these details, they all become vital. Every small, hidden design. There is magic everywhere. I am riding a wave of phenomenal promise.

All day, Rose.

When will I see you next?

What is your first thought that comes new to you each dawn?

I want to know the whole history, thought and feeling.

When I sit at Jimmy's and she serves drinks to the customers, it takes only one shared look to engulf me in flame. I am burning inside. And in the evenings when she is lying in my arms, I feel closer to the real meaning of life than ever before. As she hums quietly, gently shifting, kissing me softly before she slowly falls to sleep, I feel a peace I never imagined. Each time is the first time with millions to follow. Over and over into the unstoppable future. Oblivion. There is life, then there is this. Well, I will never stand in the way of it. I have given myself over to its mechanisms. I stand prepared to be ground shaken and rearranged. I fear no pain. I believe that it is all worth it. I will double down, and keep digging further, and there, I believe, lies our cosmic gift. With each part of myself, with each memory or truth or secret offered, I am given one in return, and this is the heavenly exchange of love. So, as the nights inevitably settle in, we wrap tightly around one another and dream. What a feeling.

In the post-midnight hours, we lie together in darkness and Rose tells me secrets.

"My mother came home crying one night after work. Late. I was like thirteen, supposed to be asleep. I could hear her through my bedroom door, and she couldn't stop. Eventually, I wandered out in my pajamas to try and help her. I knocked on her door and went into her room. She was just sitting there in her bed, so I joined her. I gave her a long hug, but she never did tell me what was wrong. I stayed there with her for an hour and then I went to bed, but I couldn't fall asleep. I had it worked up in my mind somehow that she was crying over my father. I don't know why. And before I really even stopped to think about it, I went to the kitchen, grabbed her keys, got in her car and I drove all the way to Johnston. The whole way. It was crazy. I drove all the way to my father's house, and I didn't get there until like four or five in the morning. And when I made it, I stepped out of the car and stood there looking through the front windows from the street. I swear to God. I'll never forget it. The side door of the garage opened, and Saul came out with his bicycle, and a big bag hanging from his shoulder."

"Oh my God. Yeah, he did the route every morning. He delivered the paper."

"That was it. I didn't put it together at the time. I was so shocked. I couldn't move from the street, and we just sat there staring at one another for a long,

long time. He was short, stocky. Had nice eyes but seemed scared of me. We hadn't seen each other in years. I don't know if he even knew who I was. I wanted to say something to him, but I couldn't. Eventually I just got back in the car, and I left. He was just frozen in the driveway the whole time. Never said a word. That memory always comes back to me at the strangest times."

"I bet he remembers that too."

"You think?"

"For sure."

And one night she told me about her mother.

"She was 5'6" and scrappy. A real hustler, ya know? She secretaried at an accounting firm and ran the place through and through. Sometimes when I was younger, she would work shifts at the gas station too and be out most of the night, just to provide for us. I used to sit across from her at breakfast and cry about the bags under her eyes. I thought she might be dying. *Just tired, honey*, she'd tell me. When I got old enough, I took over the gas station shifts and finally mom could rest here and there."

Rose looked up to the ceiling and smiled. Her mother was her hero, and you could tell. The admiration was beautiful in her voice. When she spoke of her passing it was always with a deep, quiet pain. This was one of many things we shared. One night we traded stories of our mothers all night. And then we laughed, and we tangled, and fell quickly to sleep just to dream.

Remember sleepovers as a kid? You'd stay up all night in a black room chatting and giggling before falling asleep? Sometimes it'd go on for hours. God, how simple it was then. There was no dark future. There was nothing but chatter and joy in speaking secrets with a best friend before rest, and you'd lull yourself to it in time. In the morning you'd wake all the better. Well, this is my life with Rose, every night, and I think I love these moments best, right after the last person whispers and we drift off together. Serenity. Talk talk talk until finally no one continues. Together you take a sweet glide into peace.

We wake before the morning sun. Rose off to Jimmy's for one thing or another. She's started keeping the books, serving and restocking and cleaning and such. And I'd maybe have something lined up. A paint job or whatever it was. It's a renewed hunger in me. I've never wanted to work like this before.

I'm after something entirely reimagined. There are mysteries to be discovered, meaning to be seen in the walls which I color. The truth is, everything is just a bit more magnetic with Rose on my mind.

And yet, the thought of my father still wandered in and out like a serpent. One minute around, one minute not, moving silently with danger. It is true that a son is a son for all time. The presence of the father never leaves. Even those that linger in the sky. Even those that you hear tales of from centuries past. They are like planets, always above, looking down, looking down.

I've spent the last five years wrestling with the truth of my father. Anguishing over him throughout countless sleepless nights, cursing whichever path he was walking. A son abandoned by his father is a vulnerable stone. And how many of us there are. America is scattered with our harbored pain and anger.

Still, swimming through my blood are the remnants of love. How can this be? What is it inside that calls out to my father like a lost child? Perpetually craving some sort of adoration, respect, or appreciation. Just love. After everything, I still have thoughts of making him proud and living up to a standard of honor. I have ambitions of becoming a man he can applaud, or wink at or hug. This is a man who never seemed to love me in my life, not really. I can hardly remember him saying the words. I don't remember many smiles, or kind gestures. He provided a roof above my head and put food on the table. I suppose that was more than some in the end, but he was so angry with me, all the time, as if he regretted something in me. I frustrated him somehow, continually. In me he saw an enemy, but why? I rallied against that feeling my whole life. Even as a child it was true. When I looked up to my father like a Greek God or hero, he looked down at me, ant-like, small. I never understood. Into my teens I pushed my way forward, burrowing always into something or another aimed at earning his grace. It took ages for that longing to die in my chest.

It wasn't until late high school that I began to resent him, to hold him accountable. It was only then that I slowly started treating him like the failure I feared him to be. I wanted to punish him for his constant despondence and lack of faith in me, his only son. By the time I got to my early twenties, there were moments I hated his guts. And what does that do to a young man? To hate his father? It was an enormous cloud spreading larger over my life all the time. Every visit to my parents' house. Every conversation with my mother. Once, amidst my heartbreak, I told her to leave him. Imagine that. I hadn't considered the pain that would cause her, and I lament that now. I was lost. The truth is, by the time of Ma's accident, I had felt finished with my father for years.

At that point, he wasn't even actively against me, he was still just shuffling to work, forever bent to it. Saying nothing to anyone. He was still getting geared up at Jimmy's. Still putting food on the table, paying bills, showing up to dinners. What did I know as to why? It was simply as if he had forgotten who I was. As if he had forgotten he had a son in the first place. It was always the distance that bothered me most and broke my heart. Even in my younger years, when he had struck me for disobedience, it was better than other nights of silence, the nights where he ignored my existence. Those were the worst—when he was apathetic and departed.

When he finally pulled the trigger and left, he was just rounding out the metaphor, playing his part. He went off to the horizon in real time and I wasn't surprised. I just wasn't. I told myself it made little difference to me. He had always felt many state lines away. I told myself it didn't matter a thousand times until I began to believe it, but of course, deep and buried, it did. It mattered to the child in my heart, the part of me that spent hours obsessing over the moment before he turned the ignition and left me, alone. How had he decided at last? What went through his mind as he sat there with the key in hand? Was it always his plan? Was it the snap of stretched cord? A culmination of many years dealing with the dying soul that he carried? All I knew was my mother had left, and the tethers were gone. He had served his sentence and was free. I don't know. And that's the truth about me, I don't know a fuck damn thing about anything.

*

I spent almost ten hours today coating layers in the Cornells's basement and bedrooms, ruminating on the state of my life. I listened to Dylan all day.

I don't care what Prince says about you, Bob. You're one of the best fucking writers to ever live. Rose has a late night scheduled out at Jimmy's, so I won't be seeing her this evening. It's eight and I've just gotten home. I'm putting together a plain lunch meat sandwich for dinner. God. How many times have I taken wet slices of ham and turkey and turned them over on bread? A million simple habits make a man. I take a bite and breathe deeply through my nose as I chew, releasing all of the knots in my mind. They unravel, one at a time, and I lay them at my feet in circles. The phone rings and ruins the image. I take a step toward it and swallow the meat to my gullet. With my tongue making rounds through my gums, clearing the way, I say dryly, "Yeah?"

"Hello, son?" A recognizable gravel. "Hello?"

The thing is, it could be the easiest motion of my life. You never saw such a close distance between my ear and the button on the phone stand below. I am still and silent for a moment, then relent.

"Yeah?"

"It's your father."

"I know."

"I uh, I was just callin—ehm"—and he lets out the most vicious cough you've ever heard as he stalls for more time. He takes a second or so to find the words in his convoluted mind—"I wanted to see, well, how are ya?

I don't know what to say, so I don't say anything.

He continues after the phone line stays silent. "You gettin on?"

"Yeah.

"Good, ehm"—again with the hacking—"look, I uh, I'm sorry it's been some days. I wanted to give you a second since I saw ya"—and he pauses again as I wait, stout mute—"Uh, I know showin up like that was, well, not the best planned."

"Yeah."

"I just, well I wanted to see ya, and so I showed."

"Yeah."

"Yeah, but, uh look, son." He trails off once again, sadly unpracticed in speaking his mind. "I want to see ya again, is what I want to say now."

It's wild, but my heart in my chest is pounding. Nervous spasms threaten to run all across my spine, and I feel short of breath. It's as if I'm gearing up for an attack and getting ready to defend myself. I feel primitive. So much memory lies dormant in my body. Still, I'm silent.

"Cash. You there?"

"Yeah."

"Would you have a coffee with your old man?"

Before I can answer, I hear the voices of my mother and Rose echo in my mind. *Forgiveness is the face of God.* Ma spoke about it at length, giving platitudes and virtues to me daily on its behalf. And I hear her now. Unprompted, unsolicited, she ascends from inside me, she rises to my heart for the reminder. Perhaps it is her voice that floats from me now.

"Okay."

"Okay?"

"Yeah, okay. Tomorrow morning."

"Tomorrow morning?"

"Yeah."

"Okay, uh, yes, yes tomorrow morning. That works."

"Alright. Eight should be alright."

"Eight. Alright. Okay. Eight it is."

I hang up the phone.

I've ventured so far into the ocean that I no longer see land, not a ship, not a bird, not a thing. In the deep blue unknown there I swim, treading water and searching for life. I am delirious, salt soaked, no longer tied to solid ground.

It's true that in life, everything's changing. From one day to the next, it's a new story. Sometimes the change happens rapidly, all at once, like a long, black-and-white domino line falling. The narrative re-routes completely. This is my life as I know it. In the middle of my kitchen, near a half-eaten lunch meat sandwich, I am blank. My only audience is God. He's sitting on his throne and nodding. What a great understanding He possesses, and how little of it He shares with the rest of us.

55

I can't sleep. I keep falling in and out of dreams, wandering one massive factory of frantic thought and feeling. My eyes close and I'm in the middle of a vast desert, explosive with light. All colors of the sun paint the expanse from blood red to orange, purple, yellow and on. I am lost and running through mountains of sand. The dunes rise before me, but I must continue on. Scaling these dunes, I move forward, all the while the setting sun is dying. If I don't make it to the horizon before darkness comes, I'll be done. Vultures circle ahead. They cry out to one another in a language nearly decipherable but too distant to know for sure. There are scores of bright green and red lizards sprinting through the sand all around me, followed closely by hordes of snakes and desert rodents. Mongoose and rats and the like. I push on at breakneck speed, exhausted and hyperventilating in the scorched air, beginning to panic. My legs fight beneath me about to rupture but I am possessed to keep moving. This never-ending race continues until, at last, the sun has set. There is only the red fading horizon, too far away to light my path. From the top of the highest dune, I fall to my knees and tumble forward, spinning down and down and down.

I awake. Breath rushes to my lungs. I rub my eyes. My heart races. Nightmares. Never-ending nightmares.

*

Coffee in hand, the clock approaches eight, I've barely slept, and feel as if I've been strung out for ages. I gather up my cup and pour another for my father. I go to wait out on the front porch like I did every night five years ago. I am drained of emotion, even my anticipation is numb this morning. Perhaps I have passed through the trauma and have run straight into a prairie more serene. When you're twenty-nine and you've seen many things. I light a cigarette. It soothes me further. What a brisk, frigid morning and I've found myself in. It's almost December, the snow will fall in a matter of weeks. The smoke sails into me smoothly, through the throat and the lungs and the mind, satiating the frenzied synapses which cause me unrest. I breathe the last of it down and press it to the ground. Down, down to the Earth. The hour is passing. Maybe he won't show after all. I look to the sky, resigning myself to the possibility when the classic red Ford comes rolling from the road to the drive. Behind the steering wheel and blinking, there he is. My father.

The shape of the defeated. A burly man in my memory, beer-gutted, and strong, now steps rigidly from the truck, withered and frail and sick. He looks as if he's been starved for years in jail or somewhere dark. He was sometimes prone to slouching, but now he is fully bent to the ground. Slow step after slow step. He wears that same beaten and beige work jacket with suspenders and a gray shirt beneath. He dons weathered jeans with rips and tears that cling to his hips a bit loosely, leading all the way down to the oldest work boots you've ever seen. He is bearded and wears one of those old flat brimmed Minnesota Vikings hats with the logo stitched to the front. His hair has long since forsaken him, but little tufts stick out the side. The way he heads toward me seems ancient, a humble beggar. Each stride is a decision, deliberate and focused. He barely lifts his feet as he walks, every movement costs him.

I've imagined my father in the worst of conditions over the years. Often, I would turn a TV on or read a newspaper in anticipation of coming across some sad brief story about a forgotten old man without a family who was found crumpled and rotting in a sewer somewhere. I've imagined him decrepit, hopeless, dying. I've imagined him broken and ravaged by guilt. I've imagined him hurting in all ways, but I somehow never imagined this. The way he grinds toward me is the sorriest thing I've ever seen. *How can I hate the weak and broken?* By the time he makes the short distance to the bench where I sit, he has a husk to his breath. He looks at me once, and then stares out to the yard and his truck, to the road that winds up and beyond.

Where have you been, old man? He leans to his right and picks up the cup of black coffee.

"This for me?" he asks quietly.

I nod. He raises it to his nose and smells it. I can't tell you how many times I saw my father drink his coffee over the morning paper in our kitchen growing up. Never once had I ever seen him smell it. He closes his droopy eyes and takes a careful, thankful sip. What a sight.

I can't watch his every movement, so I gaze back to the yard and notice a hawk circling high above the elm across the road. Its black body shimmers as it hunts for mice. They'll be tough to find now, friend. Winter is coming, don't you know?

I look back to my father and he observes the heat in his veiny dry hands. If I had a brush, I could paint that just right. The hands of a tired, shattered, solemn father, gripping his coffee in the morning as he stares into the brew for illusive, nondescript answers. Well, we are all staring lost into something, I suppose. Finally, he gathers up a run of conviction and begins.

"I saw that farm out on UU on my way in."

"Yeah?"

"The big one out a couple miles west."

"Yeah the Hamards's."

"That right? He's grown it."

"Oh yeah. He's got his sons workin it now, too. Doing well."

"Seems like it."

"Yeah."

"So many farms."

"Yeah."

"You remember when your mother and I took you to that pumpkin patch as a boy? On that farm up north near the bay?"

"I remember."

"Was thinkin 'bout that this mornin."

"Yeah?"

"I was. I was thinkin back to that first time. You were young. Very young. There were all these other kids there. It was a petting zoo, right, at the same time. Llamas and other things around. Some donkeys. Horses. Dogs. And we thought you'd want to play with them kids. But you didn't go and make friends. You were off by yourself. I remember you were climbing the fence by the horses and just starin at 'em, like. Nobody else around. And you didn't care much about the pumpkins, but you helped pick one out at the end. But you remember the big thing from back then?"

"Jasmine?"

"You do remember."

"Of course—"

And something of a small grin spreads across his face. So bizarre. Jasmine was a dog that I had, a chocolate lab, for no more than a year as a kid. I found her because she was part of this litter at the farm my father was speaking of. I hadn't thought of her in forever. My parents sold her to some construction guy because she wasn't training well, and Dad thought she was disobedient. He continues on with gravity, with phenomenal slowness.

"Well, you had it in your heart right when you saw the little thing that you loved her. And we stayed there an hour more just so you could play with her. I wanted to leave but your mother insisted we stay because you were so happy. Before I knew it you had convinced her to keep the thing."

"Yeah."

"I didn't want it."

"Right."

"But you and your mother did. So."

"I remember that."

"Well. I was drivin past that farm today and I thought of that."

"Ah."

"I hadn't thought of that dog in twenty years."

"Yeah. It's been a while."

"Got me thinkin 'bout the day when we told you we were sellin her. You remember that?"

"Not really."

"Well, we sat you down in the kitchen and we tried to tell you 'bout the plan. And you didn't understand. You kept saying *but I love her*. I thought that was silly. The way you kept sayin that. And you started to cry. And were beggin us, trying to change our minds. And your mother left the kitchen and it was just me and you."

"Yeah."

"You were lookin up to me, little, sitting in the chair. With your big blue eyes and you asked me, I ain't lyin, *how could you?* You were five. And it was like I had done some grave injustice against you, and you knew it. I didn't really care too much at the time. The dog was pissing on everything, and didn't listen. And so I sold her. That was that."

"Mhm."

I don't know if I've ever heard my father tell a story this long before.

"When Chuck came through to get her, and Chuck was a solid man, mind you. You came 'round the corner and you were huggin the dog for dear life. You were sayin all this crazy shit to the guy, and beggin your mother not to let him take her. Really freaked Chuck out. I remember that. I had to talk to him outside and remind him you were a kid and all. Well, somehow your mother got you to let the dog go and so she brought her outside and Chuck took her. And inside I could hear you wailing in there. Really screaming about the dog."

"I remember."

Everything he said was true, and though I hadn't thought about this particular moment of my childhood in many years, I remember the details vividly as they are described to me now.

"And the whole night you locked yourself up in your room and you were cryin. All night. The whole rest of the evenin and later, long after you went to bed. And your mother would go up there to you and she'd try and calm you down some. And she would return to the room and look at me all serious and say you need to go talk to your son. But I had no interest. I told you'd be over it in the morning. That you could cry yourself silly but at some point you'd stop. Thought you had to. Nobody can go on forever—"

"Yeah."

"You know that night, middle of the night, your mother woke up and you were still cryin and makin noise? She shook me awake and I heard you too. I remember bein so damn mad that I stormed up the steps to your room. You were pounding your little fists into your bed. Face all swollen and hysteric, honest to God. I never saw nobody cry like that in my whole life. After I swung the door open, I yelled you shitless. Yelled so loud the neighbors half a mile down probably heard. Said that enough was enough, all that. You remember that part?"

"I do."

"Your mother didn't talk to me for a week. Maybe more. After that."

"Yeah," I say, and he's still staring into his coffee, speaking slowly and delicately.

"Well, I thought about that, after I saw the farm on my way over." And herein lies, to date, the most shocking moment of my life. The most stunning, most impossible to believe. Reality dives off the clifftop.

He finishes the story about Jasmine and begins to cry. Water comes brimming to his eyes and it silently falls to the ground. It rolls ethereal down his nose and then drops. I haven't seen my father cry since his own father died on that rainy night long ago. In a moment I am transformed into a son all again.

I know something has deeply and fundamentally changed. Something is wrong. I don't recognize the man who just told that story. I cannot fathom the delicate nature of his speech, nor the softness of his manner. His physical prowess is gone. This man, who I've hated, is bleeding from a foreign nature of grace and sorrow. And is it covered in shame? Regret? Everything about him is steeped in a sadness so palpable it's almost too painful to look at or hear.

What's happened to him? He is small, crushed. He is clinging to the edge of an intangible darkness, I sense it.

Through tears he says, "I'm sorry I did that."

He wipes at his nose, but the crying doesn't stop, and I say nothing. I am frozen in the most unsuspected compassion and confusion. I sit like a statue as he cries quiet in the morning.

Of all the stories. Of all the moments. Of all the many, many days and harsh clashes between father and son. The beltings. The apathetic stretches. The ghost-like existence. The drunken, hopeless late evenings of which there were thousands, millions. A whole lifetime of seconds. The night he left me in the coldest Wisconsin winter, alone with my dead mother, where he had been witness. Complicit in her passing. He could have spoken about anything, but he talked about that. He talked about Jasmine.

As the tears roll down his wrinkled face and into his beard, I understand that it is an apology for everything. How had he done it? Before me is a man completely riddled by debt. He is the owner of an anguished soul utterly wrecked with havoc and regret. Here he sits, weeping quiet into his coffee and his hands. And what is it really in a son that loves his father like a God?

As I sit and watch, my blood runs with compassion and indescribable loss. I am filled with a yearning to help and to love. This man. This man above all others. I have no clear reconciliation. I have all grievances. And still, as I watch him cry, none of that matters to me anymore. All this time. What happened?

After some minutes, the tears subside and we sit together silently, still. He wipes his face off with his hands, takes his jacket to his beard, and lets out a gust of old, congested breath, clearing his throat. He hasn't brought himself to look at me much. It's okay.

At last, when the hawk has long since flown away, he says, near inaudible, to himself and to me, "Cash, I'm dying. Don't imagine I'll make it past winter."

And the words hang in the mid-morning air. They take root in the sky there to stay.

56

After my father left, I went down to the river.

I'm under a gray and dull sky. Sometimes you can see the clouds moving, heading out, with places to be, but today, they are stagnant. I am sitting, despondent, on the stump of a dead tree. The morning rings about with the finality of a church bell at midnight. Somewhere along the way, the old man developed lung cancer. The pink tissue beneath his ribs had been slowly eroding for years, blackened, dead, and now it was almost completely useless. You could sense it in the way he breathed, feel it in the way he coughed, but it was the words he uttered that were terminal.

"I've felt sick for years," he said. "I put it off and put it off."

He still never told me a damn thing about where he'd been all this time or what he'd done. He spoke very little about any of that, and I hadn't asked. There'd be time for it.

"I saw a doctor a month back and he gave me the news. My body is full of it. I'm finished." Thousands and thousands of packs down the pipe, ignited and inhaled. They had done their damage.

Cancer of the lungs and it has caught my father, just as it did his father before him. He worked hard for it since a kid and had earned it, but it wasn't just that. The truth is my father had been slowly dying for ages. The drink and the smoke and the guilt and all else. And the guilt is the worst of them all. There is nothing more green and vile and desperate to devour a spirit. Guilt can rob the soul from a man's chest. The gray clouds above begin to make the strangest shapes.

There was little else to say after he explained his diagnosis. My mind was blank. I was an infant, lost. I was under a spell of numbness.

"I've been staying at the Motel 8, just waiting things out. Haven't even driven through town yet. Can't bring myself to it."

"Not much has changed." Which, of course, isn't true.

"Haven't slept much in years but the last few months have been the worst. There's no escape anymore. My mind. I drove to the house three times without stopping, son. Took me three times to knock on the door. You have every right to hate me. I know that."

And still, I wasn't able to say a thing. All I could do was listen. The whole damn time I muttered only a small handful of words. I had never heard him speak so much. It was something to behold. I wanted to preserve it.

After all these years, it'll be cancer that does it.

"It's hell. But it's not the end of the world."

Isn't it, though? What's left of his hair is turning gray. What to say? I feel remorseful for his life. I have so many questions. In time.

"A few months I'd say. The energy's going. It's a feeling. It's a feeling."

A letting go. A passing. And so again I must grapple with death. All across my Johnston life, it is lurking. The worst friend I have, but a friend nonetheless. Death, at least, is loyal. It makes eyes with me around every corner. I can find it anywhere if I look close enough. It is in the eyes and the bodies of everyone and everything. Why did it seem to come to roost in Johnston most of all? Death. Why reaper, do you choose to shack up here? Don't you have the whole wide expanse of America to travel and torment? To think that some grow up without its constant reminder, its presence. They are feinting the feist, but that isn't me. That isn't us. The people of Johnston have been looking down the barrel all their lives. Are we better off? How many of us had lost our parents, friends, sons and daughters? Was it like this everywhere and for everyone or have we been chosen? I don't know. And what do any of us have to offer in the face of death? The fish in the river are quiet, nowhere to be seen.

A wake for my father. I can't comprehend. I can't statue myself aside a casket again, especially not his. I won't bear the long line of empathetic, inescapable eyes. Though who would even show? There is no healing to be found at a funeral. But if not there, where?

What a dark day it is, and what dark depressing thoughts consume me. I have half the mind to start from scratch, but it's true that at times the sadness feels better, and the losses stitch us all together somehow. Like one impenetrable strand of DNA. All one. No name, no face, no future. We are more continuous and flowing this way. And I remember when Leon told me how all the ancients were so much better with transition. That dying was celebrated and a beautiful part of life they all cherished. Well, if there was any place out there today, anywhere that was close to this everlasting understanding, it'd be the simple town of Johnston. It'd be us. I throw a stick in the river and watch it float away in the current.

Sometimes I find my wonderings barren. I become tired of myself. Looking up to the changing sky, I admit I still know nothing. I have a buddy who has the smiliest little brother. He once said to me, "it's because he's stupid, Cash, and I mean that as a compliment." I thought about that often. Maybe he was right. Maybe the kid caught wind of the secret after all, the one that eludes the rest of us so easily. *To believe like a child*, as Ma would say. She was usually right, that's the thing. In all my memories.

Shock. What kind of delusions had I carried before today? Had I honestly thought I wouldn't see my father again? Or that I would, and that we'd build something together, anew? In the distance an eagle explodes off the bank of the water. It swoops down and picks a fish from the river.

I think deep down I have always known that he'd show up on the doorstep. But to be so weak and dying and sorry? Where has all my rage gone? My hate? Looking at his slumping body I could not find it anymore. It died in the desert like my dreams. It was washed away by my loving blood and adoration for the almighty father. And that was something, wasn't it? To be forever a kid at his father's side, looking up. We rally and rally trying to become better men, to be proud and able and strong, to have our fathers reach down from their tower and ruffle our hair in the wind. I'm uncontrollable in mercy. My mother had forgiving hands, and I am infused with her wonder for God whether I like it or not.

Why had He brought my father back from the dead? Why had He dropped him at my feet like a mouse? I could have made peace with one thousand demises, each more gruesome and fit for punishment. But even now, there is something else working. I don't want my father to die. I don't want him to leave. There was a grace in his weeping admission. He knows now. He understands. But it's too late.

I hate a farce. It could have been a fine morning in my youth in which he had seen God's white light, but it wasn't. Rather, it was months before the grave in which he finally came stumbling home. What depravity. What confession. And still, I am sorry. So infinitely sorry for my father and for myself. For my mother, dead and gone, and all the souls of Johnston who just didn't catch their break in time.

Everything changes. Things aren't built to last. When I stroll the streets next summer, all will be different. I will again see the people walking with badges of survival on their chests, proud and happy. Sweet Johnston, maybe you are nirvana in the end. With your tough souls and courage and perspective. You are the heart of the country and more.

Well, what will it be? God, when will you take him from me again?

I'm lost deep into the river. It moves quickly. It's hurrying off to another pair of eyes also trying to make sense of the world. And it's true that we will never put it all together. Not a single one of us. There is no intellectual or artist out there. Not Marcus Aurelius or Aristotle. No King. No Nietzsche or Dostoevsky. No Plato. No Rembrandt. No Kahlo. No Ginsberg. No Kerouac. No Austen. Nobody. No Mozart. No Pollack. No O'Keefe. No Socrates. No Shakespeare. No. No one. The truth is, we all make a mess of it, every one of us. We aren't sure of much.

Are we owed some divine response? Some answer? Maybe. It's possible. I do not believe we are meant to be forgotten. Abandoned. Abused. We deserve words, love. We are to be delivered, no matter how long we spend our time lost, wandering our deserts, thirsty and longing.

We have each other, there is that. I believe we are to take care of one another, to see our fellow man's reflection in ourselves. This is about all I know. And to abuse an opportunity for love, to forsake your fellow man, that is a sin most severe. And I understand this is why I have harbored such harm in my heart, for so many long desperate years, for my father. But now, there is only one voice I hear, and it's my mother's. It is her song of forgiveness that plays in my ears. It rings out like a chorus of angels. It is all okay. It is all okay. I surrender to the truth.

I will miss my father even so.

57

After Leon and Prince are through having a real stunner of a time putting the pieces of my story together. We sit around a fire in Leon's backyard having a few beers. I think they're more shook up about the whole thing than I am. They love me, man, they really do. God. You shoulda seen their faces when I first told 'em the details. They practically rallied for justice. My brothers. They flew through all the questions, but when it came down to it, I didn't have all that much to share. There are the facts of the story, but who the hell knows anything about the rest?

"I'll know a lot more when I see him tomorrow."

He'll be coming over again in the evening. I have all the intentions in the world of getting dug in deep with him and hashing out everything. No stone unturned. There are five years on the table.

"With him dying, what else is there to do? Might as well burn the ground and air it out."

So, I'll grill my father a burger outside the house he had long ago built and abandoned. We have a landscape to traverse, and we will see.

"Proud of you, man," Prince says and Leon echoes, as if I had done something honorable. I don't see it that way. There is simply a deathbed, and he is saddled beside it. I don't know when he'll climb in, so while I have him, we might as well scrap it out. *Does he have any fight left?*

We share a few more beers, and it dawns on me more than ever that we three amigos are on the cusp of the biggest season of change we've ever had. And what a miracle it is that we are still around in the first place. One way or another, we've made it here. We have survived, and surviving is something in itself. Don't let them tell you otherwise. We have strung all these days and months and years together somehow. Together. What a thought. Not everyone is so lucky and blessed. That's the truth. I pat them both on their shoulders and leave them by the fire. I take my dreams to the night. I get in my car just to drive.

I am picking up speed. The wind rushes like ice across my face. How ephemeral are the black shadows of the towering trees flying by, streaked with moonlight. And always the fields, reminding me that anything is possible, that at any second we can run it all the way. We are limitless. I look down at the clock and see it's almost eleven. Rose will be off in five minutes. For her, I'll steer the car home.

*

On the edge of the bed, she wraps her arm around me. I bury my face in her hair, and I kiss her.

"He's sick."

"I'm sorry."

"You should see him. He's smaller now."

"Maybe you're bigger."

"I don't think so."

I smile.

"My mom lost weight too. Never ate."

"Things never happen how we think, huh?"

"You want to make God laugh, tell him your plans."

"I thought I'd be so angry."

"Yeah."

"I thought I'd hate him."

"It's hard to hate our parents."

"I don't hate him."

"No, you don't."

"I've thought a lot about what you said to me about forgiveness."

"Yeah?"

"You're right."

"Can you say that again?"

"You're right. You're always right, Rose."

"Thank you. I try."

"I want to hear it all. Where he's been, why he left, I need to know."

"Of course."

"And then I'll tell him."

"What will you say?"

"We don't have much time. And I forgive him."

"Yeah?"

"We can be free of it. For what it's worth. For however long we have."

"You won't regret it."

"No, I know."

I bring her closer. Tomorrow will bring what it will. With Rose here, I manage some peace.

*

Hours later, I can't sleep.

In the murky dawn I lay exposed to the frigid air and watch Rose as she rests. It can't be much past 4am. The freckles on her face, forever a map of stars in the dim light communicating with me. I dream about figuring out the secrets of our broad, malleable universe in the details of those freckles. And here's to Galileo and all the others who believed such things were possible. Maybe God detailed his most intricate plans in the tiny birthmarks on Rose's face.

Tonight, my mind is heavy. My pillow feels inadequate, and my skull is full with iron and lead. There is no sleep to be had. So, I look to Rose. *Whisper to me your dreams.*

She has the most even, easy breath. Calm. God, what it must be like to do everything with such effortlessness. She lies on top of her left arm and shoulder, hugging a small pillow to her chest. And to think this woman possesses the most spirit in the world, and she sleeps. Even the most indistinguishable lights must be dimmed from time to time. What a shame some went out for good. *Rose, how have you come here, resting so soundly beside me in this house?* I thank God. There is no other way. I kiss her forehead and bring myself up and out to the world. It is waiting.

58

I've beaten the sun up. Might as well go for a drive.

With a coffee in hand, I find my keys and leave Rose a quick note.

Good morning, baby. Out for a drive. See you at Jimmy's.

There's somewhere to be, though I'm not sure where. It doesn't matter. The thing is to go.

I decide to drive into town and check up on everything. The ambient feel of Johnston before sunrise is always potent and wonderful. There are flavors of post-apocalyptic fate about it and one can imagine it completely abandoned. There is nothing new or overtly clean. The buildings are small and unmodern. The lawns along Main Street are mostly left askew and mismanaged during this time of year. And most of all, there is not a single soul in sight, just the few muted lamp lights from some of the earliest risers, all of whom I imagine are in their 80s, reading.

I almost stop by one of these lit homes and ask for company. When the elderly caught me at the right moment, I could get so damn emotional. I could all of a sudden be overtaken with an extraordinary feeling of compassion. I could sense their tangible nostalgia. All around, the people they saw were unconsciously waving flags and singing them farewell. What was it like at the end of such a long rope? I can't help but fear some may look back on an unfulfilled life. Have they missed anything? Why are they sleepless? Are they by themselves? How many phone calls from grandchildren did they get these days? Who was it, out there in the void of the last leg of their journey that they clung to? Perhaps God, and God alone.

They have my admiration and respect. I only hope they know they're invaluable reminders, testaments to life-lived and true possibility. Perhaps they are fragile today, but they were strong long before the now fading image. I think about Nancy in Cambridge. I wonder if she's missed me at all. I miss her. Sometimes, I miss everyone all at once. Nancy. What must it be like to see oneself in the mirror grown older? Once, she was young. She had blood flowing freely. She had a fit body and drove all the boys crazy. How did it feel to let go? We don't know 'till we know. I love them all. Those I've met and those I haven't. Those that have gone and those still to go. I thank you for paving the way.

I drive past Sal's Auto and on. It seems like Frank and Charlene have made the most of their storefront. Maybe they're flourishing. I make a note to stop by. The Shell station and Mario's. It seems like forever ago I passed out on that pavement. A lifetime had come and gone in months. The high school, the mill, the insurance agency, the grocery store, and the salon. These are the usual landmarks, and I enjoy them, eternal as they are. They're sleeping and I sing to them softly. Dream Johnston, please. Dream yourself so strong that you will live on and on, forever in obscurity. Promise me you'll never die. Promise that the truckers down the highway will always have a place to hang their weary heads and get well.

I think about Mo, she's probably already at the joint. I contemplate visiting, but right now I can't stop. I'm memorizing all the details again. I'm driving through the tiny neighborhoods and remarking upon the homes like it's the first time I've seen them. There are always little changes, not to be missed. There's the chipped paint and eroding wood. Clean lawns and toys left from children. There are half flown flags and curtained windows. There are sidewalks run crazy with grass, weeds sprouting up from the cracks. There are potholes in the middle of streets, those that had long since lost their painted lines and I know that these roads will survive longer than us all. There are iron rusted gutters where only the most desperate of animals wander and hide, and all the trees in the yards have gone bare, preparing themselves for the merciless winter. The railroad that runs straight through Main Street hasn't housed the roar of a train for a decade and so and it too, is rusted, a relic of days gone by. Johnston. What will be your fate as the rest of the planet moves on? Will these train tracks lie here for centuries?

Still, the sun has not risen. Perhaps it has grown tired at last. I keep driving through, winding and winding around the street blocks looking back on the immense past. Will it always repeat? On our knees we pay homage to ancestors, but do we hold on too tight? We do it well around here. Perhaps the best. To think as a kid I rode my bike down these streets, and still I remain. Do we outgrow anything? Do we ever leave ourselves behind? Is that my reflection in the gray dawn sky?

I decide to make the drive back out to the country. I'm going to the Motel 8 to have a word with my father. There's no use in waiting till tonight. If we're to have it out, there's no better time than the morning. The whole landscape is clear, the world illuminates before me.

59

The Motel 8 is the shittiest place you could ever drum up. With a decaying roof, and stained gray paneling lining orange brick, it looks grotesque. Truly rundown with no business, the place is essentially deserted. Imagine the folks that wind up here when just ten miles up and off the highway there are far better spots. The owner of this motel is an old crank named Mel who I've never had a meaningful conversation with. He comes through Jimmy's Place every blue moon, dirty and snaggled out mean for the most part. Still, like all these hardened jackals, I have a suspicion there's a human somewhere underneath. Could anyone take the time to find out? Maybe one day. As the wheels of my Saturn turn over the gravel, I find my father outside the motel. He's leaning up against his truck having a cigarette. Marlboro Red. I didn't need a closer look to know that. I park and walk towards him. He has a small smirk playing across his face, happy to see me.

"What's the point in stopping now, eh?" I say.

"My thoughts exactly."

"How you doin?"

"Worst mornin on record."

"That bad?

"That bad." He lets out a breath of smoke and shakes his weary head. He rubs his eyes. He's wearing the same set of clothes as the day before.

"You sleep any?" I ask.

"Nah. What are you doing here so early, son?"

"Couldn't sleep."

"You like the spot?"

"Place is cut from hell."

"That it is." He laughs. "That it is. We get what we deserve."

"Wanna take a drive?"

"I could use a drive."

"Alright, then." I nod for him to follow.

The man would benefit from the aid of a cane, though he'd never be caught dead with one. Neither foot makes much height as he limps. A few steps in, he leans over to grasp the bed of his truck for balance. He lets out a violent phlegm cough to extricate the black from his lungs. His heavy life has eaten him inside out. There isn't even tar to be spit. Eventually, the attack relents, and he attempts to continue. Before I know what I'm doing, I walk to him and offer my help. In one look there are a thousand words, and his painful blue eyes say it all. His exhaustion helps him surrender and he grabs onto me. His calloused, purple, spotted veiny hand takes root in my shoulder and we walk slowly together in silence. It's probably the nicest moment of my whole life. A slow journey. We reach my car. and he says, "You still have her, huh."

"Oh, yeah."

We get ourselves into the silver bullet. We drive. His jacket smells like my memories, drenched in cigarette smoke. All the car rides of my youth were accented with ash in the air. It calms me now. I wonder when he last bought some new clothes. I can't help but notice how dim the light in his eyes has become. With every cough I fear he loses just a little more ground.

"I missed these fields," he says softly as he stares longingly out to the late fall Johnston landscape, once so familiar to him.

"They're the best. Even this time of year," I say.

"Yes, they are."

So many questions fly through my mind that I become non-committal to each. Why did the silence feel more healing? And it is true that the answers are here, in this very car. They are written all over our faces and hang on our breath.

"Still haven't been around town yet, yeah?" I ask.

"Haven't made it there, no, not yet."

"You want to?"

"Sure."

"Nothing's changed."

"Oh, I doubt that."

He knows as well as I that a great deal has changed, little by little. Still, I couldn't help but try to make him feel better about not missing out on all of it. He looks downright awful enough without me adding to it any. He's fidgeting while he sits, in a nagging discomfort.

"Cash. Tell me somethin 'bout your life."

I can just about see Johnston out in the mile ahead and I find it most poetic, the timing.

As we begin to approach his old stomping grounds, I can see his chest rise and fall with a heavy sadness. He smiles at some of the sights, and I tell him what I can. I tell him about Rose, and the guys, and the odd jobs and such, my painting, my trip to Cambridge.

"Is that right?" He keeps saying, "Is that right?"

Yeah, Dad. "That's right."

When I speak about Rose, he is the lightest.

"You can meet her. If you want."

His blue eyes turn themselves toward me, and the little red rivers which run through them seem to dissipate, just a bit. He is nothing more than a tired, sick man.

"I'd like that."

Truth is, I can't access any of the resentment I've harbored for so long. I simply cannot bring myself to that doorstep. Dad looks at the grocery store and at Sal's. As we pass he says, "that's one place I oughta stop by."

"Yeah, he still brings you up, every time."

He laughs. "Is that right?"

Yeah, Dad. "That's right."

I've given him the simple run through of all I had going on in my life. I figure we can get down into the finer details in further conversations. For now, I'm giving him plenty of time to smell the old scent of Johnston and grow fond again. I know he loved the place more than the rest of us, deep down.

As we pass by Mario's, he has another vicious coughing attack set on by nothing in particular.

"You okay," I ask, and feel sort of helpless saying it.

"I'm okay." His lungs must be so thick with darkness. "I'm alright, I'm alright. Don't look at me like that. I don't deserve it."

Whatever spirit came down and filled my father's chest has taught him something about gentleness. He continues his paused train of thought after wiping his lips with his sleeve.

"I don't deserve much of anything."

And those words hang in the air, slowly sinking. Everything that comes from him flows with finality.

So, I say nothing and drive. I drive through the blocks of the town and let him remember the paths.

"What do you think?" I ask. He grunts a small laugh and says, "The whole thing's the same."

And that makes me smile quite wide.

He starts up again, serious and says, "Son. It's unforgivable what I did. Unforgivable. And I ain't gone a day, not one, without thinkin of you and your mother"—he hacks himself into his arm and continues—"I know that ain't really worth nothin much. Or nothin at all. But it's true. And I want you to know that."

I feel water trying to rush to the surface of my eyes and find myself biting the inside of my left cheek.

"We don't gotta get into all that now."

"I just want you to believe that."

"Okay."

"It's true."

"Alright, Dad."

"You believe me?"

He's staring into me now. Soft, desperate eyes of regret. An entire life of sorrow and love in a look.

"I believe you."

That's the last we say for a minute. I never imagined I'd hear him confess something like that. I keep the car rolling and he smiles as he figures out where we're heading. I take a left off Main and turn into the gravel parking lot with my father in the passenger seat. I feel we've ascended into another story. Jimmy's Place, in all its glory.

"There she is," he says, and I pull into the same spot that I've kept safe and sound for him for years. After all this time, even now.

"Wanna go in?"

"Someone's around?"

"You bet. That's Rose's Jeep right there. She does some of the books early."

"Is that so. Well, what the hell."

I laugh. I just love the look on his face. There's something boyish about it. And I can't tell you how good it feels to be in this place with my father, to have momentarily forgotten all the nightmares, to release their hold on my heart. I get out of the car and walk around to help him move. The sun has come up, but it's completely swallowed by the clouds. It's a dark, dark morning and windy again. He uses most of his strength to lift himself up and out of the car seat and grabs my shoulder once more. He has a little smirk while he does it.

"Thank you, son."

It's simple but true, in this moment I have only one thought.

My Dad loves me.

We walk around the front of the car, and I'm reminded again that poor Saul oughta pave this damn parking lot. There are so many stones in the dust. Dad has to stop and put a hand on the front of the Saturn. He's coughing violently into his left shoulder, and like the other fits, we wait it out. It's long but it eventually stops.

"God," he says, and he chuckles in admission of sorts.

We take a few more steps and he's breathing ragged and terrible. He breathes in some air, and it catches again. His right hand grips my shoulder tightly as he convulses through the tar. Another extended session. It's fucking painful seeing your father in such a decaying state. Maybe I can get him a beer inside, and it'll help some. He catches his breath again, but he's wheezing now. It doesn't sound quite right.

We're about to move but I ask, "You sure you're okay, Dad?"

"Yeah, I'm alright. Thank you, son." He takes one more step but then stops again. He's staring at the gravel trying to find his air. He looks up to me. The son, taller than the father. His blue eyes are iced out and in unfathomable torment. And in this moment those eyes move straight through my own and into my wavering soul, etching themselves there forever. I feel my father is far closer to me than ever before. It shocks me, the feeling. It's the most intimate moment of my life.

He gets ready to speak. He says, "Cash," and then takes a breath to finish. But the breath catches in his lungs, and I hear it again. This is different. One quick cough releases into the next and a momentum starts to build. His fingers are sinking deep into my shoulder as he grows weaker by the second. He's moving to fall but I reach around and grab him by the waist. He's thinner than I thought. I hold him amid the acceleration. He's coughing deeper and more frantic this time.

"I got you, I got you, Dad, I got you," I say, and he's barely standing, convulsing horribly into my chest and his other hand. He grabs onto my shirt and jacket. His jacket. But the coughing doesn't stop. His legs give out and all his weight crumples into my arms.

To the gravel he falls with me aiding the descent. He is seizing and hacking for air. His face is beat red and purple with pressure. I feel a warm sensation spreading across the front of my body. I look down at myself and it all becomes clear. My father's blood is coated across my chest. A deep searing red.

"Dad," I gasp, and I hold him as he shakes on the gravel, desperate and viciously coughing. Blood is spewing from his mouth. Gone is any kind of thought. I stand and sprint through the entrance of the bar. The dark atmosphere makes it nearly impossible to see. I find myself screaming. Shouting to call 911. And I see Rose behind the bar in a shocked panic. She rushes to the phone, and she dials. I run back out to the world and my father is lying in the fetal position like a baby, still coughing. The blood is coming out in bursts and it's mixing with the dust.

I kneel down to his side and pull him up, thinking maybe if he sits, it will help him, someway. I lean him back against the Saturn and he's curling in on himself. He has this terrifying panic in his eyes, and he reaches out to my body. One bloody hand grabs ahold of my shirt and the other the side of my face. I have nothing. He's looking at me and he knows it. I can tell that he knows it. He has run it red to the bone. He looks at me but can't speak. His throat and lungs are drowning, collapsing, giving in. The panic leaves his eyes and relents. And for the briefest of moments there's peace. In the blue there is peace.

"No. Dad." The words leave my mouth without thought. And his life, like a settling wave, comes to rest in his eyes. "Dad."

And I've left my own body. I hear myself saying the word. Dad. Over and over and over. I repeat only that word. I can say nothing else. I know nothing else. I'm crying out to something unknown. To God and the void as he goes. The world becomes black as I bury my head in the blood on his neck. I try to crawl into his arms. I wrap myself around his chest. I feel Rose behind me, but it's all gone now. It's all finished. The blood is hot on my face. It's wetting my hair. And still I'm saying that word. *Dad Dad Dad Dad Dad Dad Dad.* Something in me is shattered. I am the malfunctioning clock, stuck in one place. Rose is crying I think, screaming. Her hands reach to pull me from death. But I understand now. The way forward is clear. I will be buried with my father. I will follow him wherever he's gone.

60

Pitch black night fills my veins and I'm flying down a road consumed by darkness. There are no lines on the pavement, but I cut straight as an arrow through the apocalyptic reservoir. The void. Faster and faster, I accelerate. Light begins to explode around me. Exceptional bolts of lightning crash on all sides of my vision. Miles ahead, I see a colossal beast, foaming at the mouth. Eyes red and menacing, they lure me in like a pair of dueling burning suns amidst a cloudy shifting body. Volcanic, it is swallowing the world. This is the devil incarnate, breeding and growing in its existential form. I fly straight towards its chomping, starving mouth while the lightning strikes in battle. The luminosity flashes from all angles of the sky, bursting from the outskirts and fighting for ground. One second alive, and gone just as fast. I stride forward with more urgency, but the road is but a path now, and beneath me is a horse.

A white stallion with a long flowing mane is bucking and galloping against the current of the wind. It lets out deep howls of courage. I wind my hands and arms up in its enchanted hair. Faster and faster we ride. The lightning engulfs most everything, all but the beast which roars, pitted against the boundless noir expanse.

Closer we speed, gaining ground. Fearless, set against it. The stallion roars beneath me, a revolutionary noise. The beast ahead is growing more vicious, magma pouring from its teeth. I sense its ancient power. It lets out a scream so vile it makes me flinch. Carnal venom moves the air. Onward we push.

Guttural sounds of war emanate from me. My ancestors fill my lungs with bravery, every soul that's faced the devil before me. I am the last of us. We are thunderous in attack. We are scrapping for ground against the shrieking devil. Phenomenal wind batters our bodies. The muscles of the white stallion are tremendous, undaunted, meshing with my flesh. We are one. We are the same. We are the only hope. The devil's open mouth grows wider, gaping and drooling lust and at last, no distance between us remains. We have crossed the grand frontier and the ground shakes. As the lightning battles on we ride into the mouth of the beast. To the beast. To the beast. To the beast.

The walls of the stomach drip with hate and death. The slime reeks of hell, and here in this belly is my father. He is lying on his side in a heap. Barely breathing, lifeless and weak. Renewed with desperation and strength, I charge on into the land which he passes. I jump down off my stallion and run to him. All around me is the air of decay, mangled dreams. The rotting souls of millions waters my eyes. I am in the untamed graveyard of demons. The wind runs hot like breath and encircles me. I kneel by my father. His eyes are closed, lifeless on the wet dark ground. I pull his frail body into my arms. I carry him on my shoulders. I mount the stallion once more.

Together we ride back the same way we came, while the rotting breath around us grows more thick and vile. It rumbles and hisses. Back back back we rage through the path while the lips of the monster are closing. My father, dying on my back, is light enough to carry but becoming heavier. The stallion rallies. It fights every stride while poignant piercing light flashes on my skin. The devil's mouth is closing around us. In moments we'll be swallowed.

We charge on. Every forward stride renews us with faith. Enormous, out beyond the grave, the light starts beckoning. On and on and on. We exit the mouth of the beast just in time, just before it closes we escape. It's some miracle of love and bravery. The power fills me with light. There is nothing that cannot be conquered by light. The stallion flies through the air with my arms completely entangled in its mane. With the lightning and the beast behind, I begin to speak to my father.

Dad. I have you now. Do you know what you've done? Do you see what you left behind? Dad, don't you know that I love you alone? At the base of your feet, I am loyal, bound to your every step. For your heart I have toiled my life! Where have you gone? What have I done? Dad, do you hear me? In the void, searching, screaming, desperate, was I always to rescue you? Have I failed? Where have you hidden the truth? This is darkness, this is the bottom of the pit. I cannot leave you here wailing. We will not leave our hearts here to die. I do not sleep. I will not stop. There is nothing. I will travel to hell for you, don't you know? You could have been anything, if you loved me.

Was your back turned from the start? Dad, do you hear me? I am your son. You are broken. You are small. But I have you. Dad! Back back back into the void I have traveled, for my life I have wandered for you. And you never knew. I found nothing in broken cathedrals. There were no spirits in the ruins which I waited, wishing and wanting for you to return. And now you are dying. You will be taken from this land to the next. In your closing eyes just whisper you're sorry. I know that you are. Dad, I am scared. I am a boy all again. What awaits you in the void? What will God do with you? It scares me. Dad. You did not make the leap, but I am here. I am here and I'll save you. I'll carry you from the mouth of the devil. Even after this life, I will find you. I will throw myself from this high mountain in pursuit.

You are safe now. Forgiven. You will not take the journey alone. In this world and the next, I'm your son.

I love you, do you see?

61

I was seven and sitting in church.

My mother gave me a lecture that morning about affection. She was trying to teach me how kind it was to give someone a hug when they needed it, or to hold their hand. She was always saying things like, "Everyone and everything that God created needs love." Well, I told her I understood and buttoned up my collared shirt. Off to church.

I was sandwiched between my mother and father and the pastor was rambling his sermon. Pastor Carl was a taller, skinny, old bald fellow. He had glasses and was by all accounts funny, though at the age of seven I was always laughing and nodding a split second after everyone else, and only then so I could maybe fit in. Before the service started my mother had taken me off to the side in a hallway. She knelt down a bit and looked me straight in the eyes, her curly brown hair falling clean and shiny down to her shoulders.

"Cash, I want you to hold your father's hand today."

"Huh?"

"You heard me."

"Hold his hand?"

"Yes."

"Why?"

"I think you know why—"

I gulped. I couldn't remember ever holding my father's hand once in my life. I always believed that he didn't like that sort of thing. I hardly ever saw him holding hands with my mom, let alone me. Well, each service lasted about an hour and so that was the time I was allotted. There were twenty or so minutes of singing at the start, which I always prayed to God would go longer because, for my money, the songs were by far the best part. Truth was, when the pastor got to speaking, I always found time to be torturously slow moving.

I was sitting in a metal fold up chair and shaking. My heart was racing in my chest simply at the thought of reaching my little hand over six inches and grabbing my father's. What would he do? And what would happen to me? Terrified. I thought about nothing during the entirety of the hour service but hands. One big and one small. I stole a couple glances at Ma and she gave me no reminder, though I knew she was watching, waiting. Why did it mean so much to her? I made about a thousand glances at the clock. It was creeping its way towards noon and that'd be the final bell. If I didn't do it before then...

Tick, tick, tick. The second hand was on a mission. I tell you my heart was in my throat. I feared I would start sweating at any moment. I felt in my bones that the pastor was coming to his final point so, at last, I held my breath and went for it. I reached over soft handed and grabbed the inside of my father's left hand. His working hardened mitt. In my fear and youth, I couldn't even look him in the eye when I did it. I stole one single glance. He kept his gaze on the pastor who roamed the stage and gave us those valuable lessons on life.

There I hung, like a suspended tiny monkey on a branch, heart pounding and vulnerable to everything. What on Earth would happen next? After a few seconds, he squeezed my hand back, and like I mentioned, that was the signal. When he released me, I couldn't help but look his way again. Up and to his quieted, strangled soul. He was looking down at me in one moment of softness and love. It was brief, just a blink and he was back to the pastor again. I followed his lead.

I remember my mother winking at me then, smiling wide. I was very proud that morning.

I thought often about that look Dad gave me over the following years. It's indelible. That look. It's woven itself into the fabric of my story even though I think I only saw it twice in my life. I saw it in the church as a boy, when I held his hand, and I saw it as we sat in the gravel outside Jimmy's, when we were covered in his blood, and he left me there for good.

62

When an ambulance comes through Johnston the whole town hears the sound. My father was dead long before the thing ever arrived. They rushed him away regardless, though there was nothing to be done. I remember thinking it didn't seem necessary, or even right, but the details are blurry in my brain. There are giant gaps in the specifics of the whole experience, but it did trigger some existential behavior and thinking on my end. All I knew for sure was that my father was dead, and he had died in my arms. I went home to shower his blood off my body and Rose was with me. That's all there was. I don't remember a single word being said.

In the water that afternoon I wept like a baby. I was there for hours, long after the hot water ran through, convinced that I would never be able to clean myself off. Not a thousand more showers would clean the blood from my skin. I sat on the bathtub tile and let the faucet run itself dry while I felt five years old all again. What a pitiful sight I must have been, curled and shaking. I blacked out in remorse. I think I fell asleep in that tub before Rose came and found me.

Thus began a horrid series of days. Unlike the week following my mother's passing, I didn't let a soul inside the house. There wasn't even a third of the broken-hearted crowd that came around for my mother but still, most everyone in the town had known my father, and they all knew me. When they came by the house, I didn't care about their intentions, I didn't know what they were seeking. I stayed hidden away in bedrooms or in the kitchen while Rose either answered the door or they left their flowers on the porch. Blue, orange, yellow and red reflections of life scattered and piled outside. There was something nice about that, but for the most part everything was black and white.

One night Leon and Mo and Prince came through. Rose put this wonderful spread together and they were all filled with compassion and love, but it was almost worse to see them in a strange way. The sadness in their faces, I couldn't bear it. They were the ones that were crying. Mo was beside herself when she saw me.

"I'm so so so sorry, Cash."

She kept saying sorry, over and over, as if it were her fault. Mo was such a beautiful person I really hated to see her cry. I had no way to make her feel better. What could any of us say? There was nothing to pronounce, nothing to cover. Everyone in the room knew the whole long story and I think, in a way, how it ended made sense. It fit somehow. I don't know. It just made sense, in a way, it made sense.

So, we shared a couple drinks and talked about funny stories of our childhood, or they did, mostly. Rose's fingers mindlessly rubbed the back of my neck as she laughed at Prince and Leon reminiscing. They did their best to keep their sorrow hidden deep saying, *"Remember that one night, Cash..."* And there were so many stories. So many moments with my father that we only now found humorous. The way he ruled with an iron fist and grew crazy about countless things I did or didn't do. Some of the memories actually made me smile. We all lived through some fucked up circumstances, there's no doubt about that.

"He would have actually liked you, Rose, you would have been one of the only ones he liked."

It sure did feel natural having Rose around the group. She fit in so seamlessly it was almost as if she had grown up with us too. We all shared a history in more ways than one and we understood each other. They were already growing to love her and that didn't surprise me at all. In the end, it did help seeing them together, laughing and enjoying themselves thoroughly. God, that's how I wished it all to be. They stayed for some time, but after a while I think they knew there was only so far we could take the thing. They all hugged me and said their goodbyes. Mo cried again and they left. We watched them disappear into the night. Rose grabbed my hand.

"That was nice."

I could be finished, I don't know. I felt so numb, so incompetent. I couldn't really carry on a conversation with Rose, or with anyone. I couldn't think of a single damn thing to say. I had half the mind to believe that I'd been permanently stunted. I spent so much time staring lost into space I would forget where I was. Time passed but I didn't notice. Lights were on but nobody was home. I knew my mind was out to sea again, wandering somewhere far away, perhaps never to return.

*

I thought it'd be a small funeral for my father but the thing about Johnston is, when someone dies, crook or saint, the whole town comes out in droves to pay their respects. So, as the sun arrives bright in the day, so do they.

"They really love you, Cash." Rose says, eyes wide at the ocean of compassion.

There are hundreds. All the usual suspects are showing up, Leon, Mo, Prince, the Millers, Mario, Sal, Saul, Deangelo and Lyla, Frank and Charlene, but there are many more, some that I haven't seen in ages, or ever. There's this white-haired woman named Chris who tells me, "One time, you know, and you'll like to hear this, your father helped me with a bum tire. Right off of

Main Street. He sure was kind. Fixed it up real well. Didn't rush."

She's right, I did like to hear that. I thank her for passing it along and marvel a bit at everyone dressed up so fine.

It's a brisk sunny day and I stand by the casket in my best suit with nobody around me, not a soul. That's that. I have no family. Not one. How many at twenty-nine could say it? Stoic, I do my best to hold my ground with the entire weight of the universe pressing down on my neck. I shake their hands and I nod. I give a hug and I listen to their stories, condolences, and well wishes. Soft voices. Gentle, kind, warm voices filled with empathy. All the while my mind is still out to the water, sailing further and further away.

When the time comes for me to say a few words about my father, I'm afraid I'll come up pathetically short. Are there a million people packed into this church? Each face stares up at me with a unique history, with a unique relationship either to me or to my dad. Hundreds and hundreds of years are gathered in the pews. There's enough heartbreak in the room to kill a man and enough love to keep him living. I clear my throat and tug at the collar of my black shirt and suit. I find Rose in the audience. In a black dress, she sits straight and is a beacon of strength. She nods the slightest of nods. She believes. I clear my throat again.

"My father was... My father was a hard man to know. And I tried like hell most of my life to know him. Suppose sometimes I knew him most through how he was with some of you. Listening to him at Jimmy's. Watching him talk shop at Sal's. Being with him and my mother, picking pumpkins, or sitting in church or at dinners. Working in the yard. My father was a worker. He never once complained about work. Not once. He provided for us and ran it to the bone. He loved a beer and a cigarette. God, he loved a cigarette. And a bonfire and a well mowed lawn. And a good truck. And his friends. And this town. I do believe he loved this place more than most men love a town. He always had such a damn quiet way of showing it, though. Didn't he? My father could stare into your soul. That's how he said what he needed to say. He was tough. He knew war. He was a fighter. He loved one woman his whole life and when she left, so did he. My father had his faults. Like we all do. Still, if I'm honest, I always wanted someone to come up to me one day and say, *you're your father's son*. I think I wasted too much of my life thinking he didn't love me. I don't think that anymore. I don't believe that's the truth. I believe he loved me but didn't know how. And he did the best he could. When he left, I didn't try to find him. I just let him look. Dad was always looking for something. I knew that long before I knew what that really meant. In his tough love and tougher hands, I grew up. He was troubled. He had an anger and sadness in him that kept him at arm's length. But he was unwavering. He had his values. He was loyal. I didn't think he'd ever come back here but he did. I thank God he did. In the end he came back, and I think that's all that matters to me now. I love you, Dad. I'll miss you. I will. I'll really miss you, Dad. I think I always have."

*

It's been a week since the funeral.

In a T-shirt and shorts, I sit outside, alone. The middle of the night moon watches over me. It's the coldest night of the approaching winter and from the sky the white starts to fall. It floats down, elegant, graceful. Quiet and charming, magnificent. And it's true that Heaven is mirrored in snow. It's the most gorgeous white you'll ever see, the first snowfall. I am shaking uncontrollably but stay rooted in my chair on the porch. I stare up at the sky and watch it all come down. Soon the ground will be bright, shining like diamonds. The clock will keep counting. I think about all the animals and the plants that have to fight to survive. Most will die in these winter months, but the next generation waits in the wings, patient to begin anew. The snowflakes will blanket us all. They will cover the town. I give it an hour before the first white canvas is settled and finished. Above, the stars are where they always are. Funny how no matter what goes on down here, they remain. Forever calling us home. I remember Ma saying, *we are all made of stars*.

We are stardust, Ma. I think you were right about that.

My skin is turning blue and my teeth bang against one another in tremors. The back door opens behind me.

"Cash. What the fuck are you doing?"

"Just watching the snow."

63

It's funny how it happens. One morning at a time you feel just a little bit better than the one before. It's cliché as hell but it's true, time heals all wounds.

Here's the thing, the wheel keeps turning. Before you know it, you're eating full meals and you're going to work, and you've got yourself distracted again. You're filling your time with beer and conversation and you're letting laughter win again and again. Your best friends are rallied, all encouraging the healing, and it happens.

But for me, most of all, every morning when I open my eyes, Rose is the first thing I see. Peaceful and dreaming. There is nothing more healing than waking to the world in the arms of someone that has your heart. She alone helped me greet many gray dark days. I'd softly kiss her good morning and we'd whisper gentle nonsense to one another. Other times we'd laugh quietly, stretching and slowly moving our bodies awake. Sometimes we'd make love. Her breath and mine, her life and mine. I crave her touch. It heals me day after day. It makes sense to me, in the end, that as long as you are together, moving forward with someone you adore, one tiny inch at a time, everything will be okay. There is still so much and so many to love, and that, in itself, is worth it. Night could have taken any of us, but it hadn't yet. On we go. One day turns into another, then another and another until you wake up one morning and there's a couple feet of snow on the ground and you're believing in all sorts of ways forward.

Somewhere in these mornings, these long days of thinking, dreaming, and healing, I've somehow got it in my mind again that I need to go. I'm not sure where, but it's in me, stronger than before. There are spirits in my house. Maybe they need the roost for a while.

But where to? Rose is finally all settled in at Jimmy's and really loving her time there. Saul has given her more and more control and she's making all sorts of friends at the bar. I don't think I have to explain how everyone at that place goes wild over a girl like her. Some nights of her random choosing, she'd break out her guitar in the late a.m. hours and play for whichever lonely hearts were left there to hear it. To see her in the bar light, strumming and singing like Joni herself, changes me. Her soulful voice fills holes in my heart. I couldn't be more on fire. I could watch her for hours and hours. Rose is so beautiful, it makes you more spiritual. She's grounded but somehow, free. Tough but gentle; funny but straight. Her dualities inspire me. She's the biggest damn hit Johnston has ever seen in its life. God, how I adore her. I'm falling in love with her, and she knows it. She must know it. She is a piece of Johnston now. She is happy. So, I stow away my thoughts of departure. I'm in no kind of rush.

*

I buried my father out in Johnston Cemetery next to my mother, a few miles from my house.

I stand with my father's jacket cloaked around me looking down at both my parents, trying to convince myself it will all be okay. I leave flowers on their graves. I run my fingers in a cross on their tombstones.

I never want to stay for too long...

*

I'm driving home with Rose in the passenger seat. I'm holding her hand. Even in the winter we keep the windows cracked. The fresh December air is like nothing else. She scratches some white paint off my right thumb nail which is still coated on there from work I'd done this morning. Dave Matthews is playing on CD. She sings along and I can't help but follow her lead. We sing about playing time, dancing through troubles, and finding our way out.

Later, Rose gets out her guitar. I make a fire and the smoke curls up through the chimney, the heat fills the whole wooden house. In her blue socks and sweatshirt, she strums fine as ever. God. When Rose sings it, I care about nothing else, no other voice or sound will do.

She shares her soul, taking the feeling from centuries past and bringing the future with too, the way all special musicians do. Countless decades layer her voice. She plays it so raw, calmly and true. She plays for an hour, and I don't want her to stop.

"One more Rose, one more..."

She smiles bashfully and continues. Sitting by the fire in the freezing winter evening, I think about asking her to marry me here and now. It's the first time I've ever had that thought in my life. I can't help it.

"What are you smiling at?" she asks.

"Nothin," I say.

And I crawl up to her legs where she sits.

I hug them tightly to my chest and try to freeze time.

64

There are a few bikers back in Jimmy's Place having a funny argument about the placement of their cue ball while a family of four some ten feet away enjoys peanuts. Ed Simpson has made an appearance and sits crooked at the bar. Ed is one of the janitors up at the high school, a well-meaning old cat. He's joined by Jen Linsey and her husband Tom who both also work at the school, teaching freshman English and History respectively. Rose is working and chatting with them all, seamlessly making them feel important. They all enjoy a laugh and I notice the tiniest of flickers in the neon Budweiser sign on the wall near the entrance. It needs a new bulb. Prince sits across from me and says, "Buddy. Remember that guy I mentioned out West?"

"Weed guy?"

"Yeah," he laughs. "I mean there's more to him than that, but yeah that guy."

"Yeah, I remember."

"Well, he's expanding man. It's happening."

"What's that mean?"

"You should hear some of the numbers he's pullin man, thousands and thousands. Not that it's really even 'bout the money man but he needs someone who knows some ins and outs."

"You know some ins and outs?"

"I know a few."

"Doin what?"

"He can't handle that kind of cash. He wants to invest, expand man, make it legitimate and shit. That's the side we'll be on, nothing illegal obviously."

"Right."

"It's good man, it's real good."

"I believe you."

"Doesn't matter, even if it's a bust, it will be an experience."

"Yeah."

"You wanna come with?"

"To Arizona?"

"Yeah man."

"What about Rose?"

"Rose comes too."

"Man, she ain't gonna wanna go to Arizona."

"How do you know?"

"She's just got this thing rollin."

"Have you asked?"

"No I haven't asked, why would I have asked?"

"Exactly."

"What the hell am I gonna do out in Arizona?"

"Anything man."

"Shut the fuck up—"

"Nah really man, whatever. Same shit you do here, if you want. There's a fuckin thousand things you could do out there."

"Won't be cheap."

"Oh, fuck the money, look, if you come with me, I'll cover it—"

"You ain't paying for shit—"

"I'm serious, man. Not only that, first couple weeks I'll give ya half of what I make—"

"Prince—"

"I'm serious, man. Like I said, it ain't about the money, you know it isn't. I just wanna do it. I wanna go. And I want my best friend with me, who also just so happens to wanna go."

"How do you know I wanna go?"

"Cash. C'mon"

"Arizona."

"What's the worst that could happen?"

"I don't know."

"We go out there a couple months and come back? Your place is paid off, so is mine. They aren't goin anywhere. We don't gotta go forever. We can always come back, and knowing us, we will. But Arizona, man. Arizona."

"Arizona."

I watch Rose behind the bar. She serves Ed another cold one. Her eyes glance at mine for a moment and she smiles.

"Well, it wouldn't hurt to ask her," I admit.

Prince takes his glass, and he clanks it against mine. He downs the last of his beer.

"Hell yeah. That's the spirit. No man, it would not. It definitely would not. I'm getting another round."

*

After the place has cleared out for the night and Prince leaves me to it, Rose joins me at the booth. Behind her silhouette, the Budweiser sign flickers, and she leans on her right hand, looking up at me, blinking slowly.

"You look tired, baby," I say.

"I am tired, baby."

Saul shuffles his way towards the back door and gruffs, "Night y'all."

"Goodnight pal."

And he's gone.

"He looks more like your father by the day."

"Doesn't he?"

"Crazy."

Saul sure said some solid and kind things to me in the days following my father's funeral.

"There's something biblical about it, Cash. Him coming back and seeing ya. Dying outside the bar." It was the most romantic shit, I'd ever heard him say. After Saul slumps out that same back door like he had thousands of times before, Rose and I are alone.

"Freeze," she whispers.

Every second of the past year flies through my mind like a firework memoir. I know that anything she wishes, I will follow.

"How would you feel about heading west for a while?"

She closes her eyes, and she smiles.

65

I thought about everyone all over. I thought about the bikers and the junkies in hidden apartments. I thought about the movie theater dwellers and the homewreckers. I thought about Tommy. I thought about the sky divers and construction workers. I thought about Jermaine and Sosa and Matchbox. I thought about architects and prophets. I thought about Trevor and his cows. I thought about the teachers and the clowns, the tightrope walkers. I thought about Cole and Mario and his pizza shop. I thought about Saul and the bartenders. I thought about Sal and his two sons and the hunters. I thought about the hardware shop owners and the grocery clerks. I thought about Frank and Charlene. I thought about the writers and the artists. I thought about the businessmen and plumbers. I thought about the drug dealers and the office janitors. I thought about Kassy. I thought about the carpenters and Jesus. I thought about Jesus. I thought about how God was in every one of us and how we were all a transforming body. I thought about love. Grandma Ruby and Grandpa Bill. I thought about God and his creation. I thought about us. I thought about Jenna Ollie at the park. I thought about every last one of us, trying. I thought about Johnston and the families. I thought about Scotty. All the generations of Midwest America. I thought about the farmers and the crop. I thought about Ben and the military. I thought about Cameron. I thought about fathers and their sons. I thought about Nancy. I thought about Jeff and the gas station workers. I thought about all the acid and mushroom trippers. Pat the guitar player. I thought about men and women. Deangelo and Lyla. Casey and Dalton. I thought about the lumberman and the miner. The clocksmith and the shoeshiner. The chef and the waiter. I thought about Jesus the carpenter. I thought about Jesus. I thought about Priest Charles and Doctor Clark. I thought about how God was in every one of us. I thought about my father. My father. My father. I thought about the belly of the beast. I thought about that kid Connor. I thought about Rose and true love. I thought about everyone. The saints and the gamblers. Amy and John Miller. The painters and the laundromat owners. The soldiers and the skaters. The alley dwellers. The surfers. I thought about Prince and his father. I thought of Leon and Mo. I thought of Rose and her mother. I thought of Ma. My mother. I thought of revelation. I thought of red lights blinking on tall buildings. I thought of humans as ants beneath the vast empire. I thought of California and the coast. Arizona and the desert. Soft and hard beds. I thought of one hundred million windows. I thought of garbage men and strippers. I thought of chiropractors and insurance workers. I thought of Jesus the carpenter. I thought of God. I thought of Johnston, and how the whole entire universe is in a penny. So why not in the heart of small-town people? Johnston, your streets are pulsing. Bleeding from the cracks. Beneath, your heart is pounding. You are always coming back. Johnston. I love you. Yes, I feel you even now. Your homes are filled with the real people of the Earth, they are walking, one by one. Two of their kind. Hand in hand.

66

Leon and I stare out and over his property saying nothing at all. Our breath is crystalizing into a fog and disappearing after a couple moments of glory. Finally, after a cold long swig of beer he says, "You suppose things go on forever sometimes." I wait a moment and think about that, "What do you mean?" He takes another drink, "I mean I think we take things for granted while we got 'em sometimes."

"Yeah."

"I don't imagine we'll ever know much about when or how things are going to end. They just do."

"We'll be back man. Who knows how long we'll last."

"Yeah, I'm just sayin though. You know, I'm just sayin. It's true."

"Yeah man, I suppose it is."

"You're a good friend, Cash. A damn good fuckin friend. My best friend in the world. Don't know how this place will get on without ya."

He brings the can to his lips and just kind of nods to himself, having solidified this great big truth in his mind. Big old Leon looks over to me then. He has blue tears in his eyes. "I love you brother."

"I love you too."

He sits there and nods a couple more times. He had said all he could say, and it was more than enough. He looks up to the black night and the stars are scattered, particularly spectacular in the sky.

67

It's a mysterious time. There are no definitive answers to anything. We are uprooting our flag for a while. Prince is in the back of the Saturn lighting a joint and looking out the cracked window through his black sunglasses as I'm speeding west and gaining momentum, donning one of my father's old flannels, shaved and clean. There's a light behind my eyes that I can feel. My heartbeat has worked its way up to my mind, the whole instrument is aligned.

Springsteen is playing and Rose is sitting to my right, humming along. In the rearview mirror I can see our various bags stacked on top of one another, Rose's guitar among them. She has this black cloth-coat wrapped around her shoulders and her right knee is bouncing up and down electrically. I reach over and move my fingers through her freshly washed hair. The feel of endless silk. I briefly massaged the back of her head. There is no part of life I have loved, no part I have wanted more than her. I am convinced that I can lose all else but if she remains, I can walk it on forward and continue.

All three of us are peaceful. We're an hour or so in and we have settled calmly into the journey. As is with all road trips the initial buzz always calms into serenity. My imagination, as well as theirs, is traveling too. I am filled with the future, the potential of an open road. Before leaving, in my driveway, we hugged Leon and Mo and said our goodbyes as Mo cried. Leon, my brother, I will see you again. Woodland Drive sent me straight out of Johnston.

All vast America is turning under my fingertips. The unknown awaits us out there in the desert. Will we last a week or a year? What will we find? I think of all the promises I've heard about the exciting life out there in the wide open, the biggest skies in the world.

Of course, I think most about Johnson and pray it'll flourish in my absence. I want to return to it blooming and renewed. I have faith that I will, whenever that may be. It isn't so hard to believe.

Whenever I'm on the brink of a big change in my life, I can't help but be a little melancholy. I am filled with a thick, heavy, nostalgia. That's the thing about me, I am always trying to preserve things. If I ever stumbled my way into something pure, good, and precious, I would shake at the thought of leaving it behind, or it leaving me. I was in constant effort to grab it up in my careful hands and run away with it into the wilderness forever where we could live safe and happy together for the rest of our days. To set free what we love, what an art. If I could only bottle it all up and freeze it. If only we were eternal. I suppose, in a way, that's what I really want.

We take everything with us. We all do it unconsciously or consciously, and sometimes we can hang on too tight. There exists such a thing. I cannot wring out all the beauty of life. It will stay with me willingly if I let it, if I trust its faithful nature, and that's the truth about everything. It is in the air around us as we pass through the country.

It is in the wind, in the trees, in the rain. There are spirits all around. Everyone who has gone before and is still going strong, they're guiding the way. And it becomes clear to me that when something imprints upon you, it is there for all-time. We carry things on. We are gathering up and continuing.

So we feel every ancestor. And it's impossible to hold anything still. They will all come and go, these blessings. They will all be replaced and renewed. Like the fields of corn falling dead to the snow. Like a loyal lover, they too, will come back. Different and more beautiful still.

Well, that's the thing, this rebirth. The unbelievable chance at new beginnings. Each more impassioned than the ones before. We are growing taller all the time. We are becoming limitless. We are accepting the things we deserve. The universe is conspiring for us all and it is a practice to accept it, to love every waking second. I know now more than ever that no feeling is bad, no memory so defined. It is all just the sensation of living.

Well, it's something like that anyway.

All to say I will embrace this beginning again, holding fast to my faith in the bright future. No matter how wonderful or terrible the past, what is ahead will be special. It will be the way. This is the thing. This is hope.

*

I am leaning up against the Saturn at a gas station in Waterloo. There's slush gathered next to the concrete slab which holds the pump up from the ground. I move it around with my foot. Prince is fast asleep in the back seat and Rose is inside the station. There isn't a single car around.

The winter has settled itself solid into the blood of the entire Midwest now. It has a stronger bite by the day. I don't mind. I can feel my face growing warmer and harsh against the wind, revitalized. And the numbers on the dial move higher.

I hear the gas station bell ring quiet but sharp in the distance and Rose strides through the ancient metal doors. I notice how she has her Ninja Turtles shirt on beneath her sweater and jacket. She wears this wonderful smile on her face as the wind swirls all around her like a cinematic star. She walks towards me with that transcendent alignment. That cosmic balance, always. "Freeze." She says as she comes closer.

"You know you were wearing that Ninja Turtle shirt the first night I saw you?"

She looks down and tugs a bit at its collar. "This old thing?"

"Yeah, that old thing."

"That's funny," she says as she walks around to the passenger door. She gets fake serious for a second and whispers, "It's a sign Cash, a beautiful sign." She giggles and takes shelter in the car.

I look up to the sky and try to see if any sunlight will be breaking through today. It doesn't seem so. Just another cloudy winter afternoon in the middle of nowhere America. If I didn't know any better I'd tell you God is speaking in the wind. I'd tell you He is speaking all the time, in everything. He's been sailing the ship all along, in no hurry.

How are you fairing up there, Holy Father? Is there anything pressing that you'd like to share? I wait, looking around as I always have, for an obvious sign. Well, there is none to be seen. That's just fine with me. The numbers on the dial click to a stop. I pull the nozzle out and hang it up. I lock the tank.

I grab the ice-cold Saturn handle and move on.

Acknowledgements

I want to thank my family.

To my mother and my father, who have always believed in me. Your love and tremendous example of goodness, honor, humble kindness and tenacious willpower have inspired me my entire life. You've always showed up. You never missed a second. You put your children first in every way. Being your son is, and always will be, my most cherished blessing. Thank you for everything.

To my brother, the first person I shared this book with and the first person I share most anything with. You've read it all, seen it all, listened to it all, been there for it all. There is nobody in this world I'd rather have in my corner. Your patience, profound intelligence and gentle heart move mountains. Thank you for being with me.

To everyone at Unnamed Press, Allison, Brandon, Chris, Jaya, and Cassidy, for believing in a first time author and this story. This wouldn't have been possible without you and you have the complete depth of my gratitude. Thank you for your thoughts, your art, your guidance and your support.

To Matt, David, and Jim, for sticking with me and seeing this vision from the start. For loving this book, for your dedication, for teaching me the ins and outs and sharing a passion for the real stories hidden in the heart of the country.

To Emily, Jodi, Kelly and Eric for your generosity.

To Chelsea, Angel, Tyler, Jake and John, your words early on meant the world to me.

To the girl with the harmonicas, for wanting to hear the words out loud. I'll never forget those nights.

To the place that raised me. To all the people living in the middle of nowhere America.

To my grandparents.

To my best friends.

To Sean.

To Jack.

And to you.

With all my heart,

Thank you.

I love you.